Van Buren
P9-BAW-901
DISCARDED

FURIOUS GULF

Don't miss these other exciting novels by Gregory Benford:

ACROSS THE SEA OF SUNS
IN THE OCEAN OF NIGHT
GREAT SKY RIVER
TIDES OF LIGHT
TIMESCAPE

FURIOUS GULF

Gregory Benford

BANTAM BOOKS
NEW YORK • TORONTO • LONDON • SYDNEY • AUCKLAND

Ben
C1

FURIOUS GULF

A Bantam Spectra Book / August 1994

SPECTRA and the portrayal of a boxed "s" are trademarks of Bantam Books, a division of Bantam Doubleday Dell Publishing Group, Inc.

All rights reserved.
Copyright © 1994 by Abbenford Associates.
Book design by Mierre.
No part of this book may be reproduced or transmitted in any form or by any means, electronic or mechanical, including photocopying, recording, or by any information storage and retrieval system, without permission in writing from the publisher.
For information address: Bantam Books.

Library of Congress Cataloging-in-Publication Data

Benford, Gregory, 1941–
Furious gulf / Gregory Benford.
p. cm. — (A Bantam spectra book)
ISBN 0-553-09661-3
I. Title. II. Series.
PS3552.E542F87 1994
813′.54—dc20 94-6473
CIP

Published simultaneously in the United States and Canada

Bantam Books are published by Bantam Books, a division of Bantam Doubleday Dell Publishing Group, Inc. Its trademark, consisting of the words "Bantam Books" and the portrayal of a rooster, is Registered in U.S. Patent and Trademark Office and in other countries. Marca Registrada. Bantam Books, 1540 Broadway, New York, New York 10036.

PRINTED IN THE UNITED STATES OF AMERICA

BVG 0 9 8 7 6 5 4 3 2 1

For Joan,
forever

FURIOUS GULF

Prologue

True Center

Toby watched his father walk the hull.

Killeen was a silvery figure, his suit tuned to reflect as much radiation as possible. A mirror man. Slick light slid over him as he moved, shimmering with the phosphorescence of stars and gas. Toby could follow Killeen's smooth, slow lope as a rippling warp against the fiery background.

—Dad!—Toby called over his skinsuit comm band.

—What? Oh . . . —Killeen's surprise came through the fizz of comm static.—How come you're outside?—

—Crew's wondering how come you're out here so long.—

As Cap'n of the *Argo,* Killeen could do whatever he liked, of course. But Toby had felt the growing uncertainty among the officers inside. Somebody had to act, to say something, so he had pulled on his skin-tight suit and come clumping out here. Lately Cap'n Killeen had kept himself isolated. He came out here to hike over the fat curves of the ship's hull, often not even leaving his suit comm line open.

Killeen said distantly,—I'm navigating. Watching.—

The big man's watery image flowed, liquid with light, as Killeen came toward Toby across *Argo*'s blunt prow. His suit momentarily mirrored the black depths of a nearby molecular cloud, and Toby saw him as an eerie shadow-man against the distant burnt-orange wash of star-speckled gas.

—You can do that from the bridge,—Toby said.

—Get a better feel for it out here.—Killeen came close enough for Toby to make out his father's stern expression through the suit's small vision slit.

Toby knew his father's pinched-face, hedgehog mood, and decided to cut through it directly.—There's near a dozen more crew on sick report.—

Killeen's lips thinned but he said nothing. Toby hesitated, then summoned up his courage.—Dad, we're starving! Those gardens we lost, they're not gonna grow again. Face it!—

Abruptly Killeen whirled, adroitly sliding his magnetic boots in zero gravity.—I *am* facing it! We just don't know any more techtricks. Even the specialists, the green-thumbers, they can't get those ship gardens sprouting again. No help there. So I'm *thinking,* got that?—

Toby stepped back involuntarily; Killeen's flinty anger was quick and daunting. He took a breath and said hesitantly, —Shouldn't . . . can't we . . . do something different?—

Killeen scowled.—Like what?—

—Approach some of those?—Toby pointed tentatively.

Far ahead of *Argo* floated faint metallic dabs of light. Not clouds or luminous dust. Artificial.

—We don't know what they are. Could be mechwork. Probably is. Mechs have built plenty near True Center.—Killeen shrugged.

—Maybe they're human, Dad.—

—Doubtful. It's been a fearsome long time since humans lived in space.—

—That's just what history says. We won't know till we look for ourselves. We're raiders by heritage, Dad! The Family's itching to get out of the ship, stretch their legs.—

Killeen gazed thoughtfully toward the blaze of Galactic Center.—One thing you learn as Cap'n is not to stick your nose into a beehive just to smell the honey. Those things'll probably be hostile, even if they aren't mech. Ever'thing else here seems to be.—

Toby let the remark ride. It had been over a year, but still Killeen had not recovered from the death of his woman, Shibo. He kept up his duties as Cap'n but was often withdrawn, pensive, moody. That might have been acceptable for a crewman, but not for a Cap'n. The price in morale was getting too high.

Still, Toby thought, Killeen was probably right. They were cruising directly into the center of the galaxy, where vast, indifferent energies worked. Huge, glowering suns. Incandescent clouds of dust and gas. Powers far beyond anything mere humans could manage. And somewhere here, intelligences to match the mad swirl of stars.

He had studied enough history to know that humans had evolved near a star two-thirds of the way out in the galactic spiral. The galaxy was a spinning disk, like a toy—only bigger than the human mind could encompass. Out there at Old Earth, far from the cataclysms of True Center, living had been easy, quiet.

One of his instructional drills had tried to get him to visualize a box that was a light-year on a side, the distance light itself could travel in a whole year. Out there, near the legendary Earth, that box would hold maybe one single star, on average.

Here, at Galactic Center, such a box held a million stars.

Suns crowded the sky like glowing marbles. Stormy streamers of red gas shrouded them. Stars swarmed like angry bees around the central axis—the blue-white brilliance of the exact center.

Toby said quietly,—We could come alongside one of 'em, just for a look.—

Killeen shook his head.—Solve one problem, maybe, but make another. A worse one.—

—We're *starving,* Dad. We have to *do* something.—

Killeen turned and strode angrily away along the worn and pitted hull. His magnetos snapped down to the metal with a hard clank that Toby felt through his own boots. He trotted after his father. Walking here took a strangely gaited stride, coasting between steps, letting his boot clamp just long enough to get more momentum. Then he jerked the boot free, pushing forward, and was off on another glide. Toby was good at it but he couldn't keep pace with his father.

Argo had brought them here at near-light speeds, gulping down plasma with her magnetic scoops. There was fuel aplenty, thicker and thicker as they neared the center. Still, random chunks of rock had pocked and blistered her shiny hull. Now they were coasting slower, and Killeen used the chance to hull-walk with some safety. *Argo* had joined the gyre of matter here, which swung about True Center at one-thousandth light speed.

Killeen reached a smooth ridge in the *Argo*'s complex bulges and stopped, as if on the brow of a real mountain, back on the planet of their birth. Their ship was a last grand construction of their ancestors, a vessel as big as a hill. Beyond him loomed a vast dark cloud, like a smudge of ink against the flaming stars.

Killeen turned and looked back at his son. As Toby approached he saw Killeen's expression shift to a plaintive longing.

—If only there were planets here . . . —

—Can't be, I heard,—Toby said flatly, hoping to jar their talk back to realities.

—Why?—Killeen asked sharply.

—Look at these stars! They're flying past each other so close, they strip planets clean free of their parent sun.—

—Well, that sets planets drifting free, sure. So?—Killeen said stubbornly.

—Sure, free. And frozen. Too far from any sun. No plant life. No food.—

Killeen peered wistfully outward.—So in all this magnificence, there's no place for life?—

—Yeasay. Prob'ly none for us, either.—Toby ventured this opinion mostly to snap his father out of his illusions. Maybe even get him to rethink this foolhardy venture to True Center.

Killeen gave him a sober, almost plaintive look.—We have to go on.—

—Why? The radiation levels are so high, *Argo* can barely hold it off. Just coming outside here, you're risking heavy exposure.—

—It's our duty, I tell you.—

—Dad, your first duty is to *Argo,* to your crew.—

—There's something near the Galactic Center. We have to find out what.—

Toby snorted in frustration. Killeen's eyes narrowed at this, but Toby told himself he was speaking for a majority of the crew. That was his duty, too. He said bitterly,—Moldy old records hint—*hint!*—at something. That's *all.* For that we're supposed to . . .—

He broke off as Killeen abruptly turned his back. The Cap'n of the *Argo* kept his shoulders square despite a sudden sag of his head. Toby saw that his father was fighting with himself, wrestling with dark demons his son would never fully know.

Toby could only glimpse them through the clotted phrases of their conversations, through half-made gestures, through the veiled language of shrugs and scowls and sudden, blunt looks that revealed momentary, naked emotion. The Cap'n was never able to unburden himself, not even to his son. Not even, perhaps, to Shibo . . . when she had lived.

Things were weighing on Killeen. Shibo's loss. Killeen's oblique relation now with his own son. The approaching whirlpool of True Center. All these churned within his father's mind, Toby knew. An unhealthy soup.

Killeen gazed out at the blue-black mass that loomed like an absolute wall beside the *Argo.* It was a snarled, inky cloud of dust and simple molecules, their ship's instruments said. But Killeen always distrusted the crisp certainties of *Argo*'s Bridge diagnostics. Years before he had formed the habit of surveying from the hull itself, free of the reassuring, softening, artificial clasp of the ship. Or at least that was what he said. Toby suspected that he just liked to get clear of *Argo*'s confines. Like father, like son.

Gloomy clouds like this dotted the pressing radiance of the Galactic Center, black punctuation marks in a riot of stellar fire. Killeen had chosen *Argo*'s course to take advantage of this cloud as a shield against lethal radiation levels. As *Argo* slipped slowly by veiled, murky filaments, Toby watched his father's face tighten, wrinkle with a grimace—and suddenly open in astonishment.

—There!—Killeen pointed.—Moving.—

Toby thumbed a control on his neck collar. The helmet computer telescoped his vision and shifted to infrared. His field of view rushed into the recesses of the cloud.

Something snaked at the edge of the mottled mist.

—Go to high mags,—Killeen said tersely, his surprise gone, all business.

Toby sent his vision zooming to max magnification. RANGE: 23 KM, his visor told him.

The snaky thing wriggled—slowly, slowly. Its gleaming jade skin reflected the starglow. Sluggishly it spread gossamer-thin sheets along its body.

—It's alive!—Toby called.

The green serpent was using sails. Natural sails, grown out of its body on fibrous spars. They caught amber starlight. In zero gravity, Toby knew, even the faint pressure of light was enough to give a measurable push. With nothing to slow it down, the twisty creature would pick up speed.

—Look.—Killeen whispered.—There's something more in that cloud.—

The gently wriggling beast had no head, only a long black slit at one end. Toby thought this must be a mouth, because the push from its broad, shiny sails was taking it forward with the slit end ahead. And it was sailing in pursuit of a blue ball.

Silently they watched it draw nearer, nearer—and the slit-mouth widened. Something orange shot out and stuck to the blue ball. Drew it in. The slit-mouth yawned. With two gulps the ball disappeared.

—Predators.—Killeen said.—And prey.—

Toby said wonderingly,—Pred . . . ? How can anything live in a cloud? In free space?—

A grin split Killeen's star-tanned face.—In free space? Nothing's free, son. Molecular clouds have organic molecules, right? So the astro types say.—

—Those names, yeasay.—Toby recalled the voice of his teacher Aspect, Isaac, who gave him complicated lessons.—Oxygen. Carbon. Nitrogen.—

Killeen gestured expansively.—Add all this starlight, cook for a few billion years. Presto!—

Toby blinked.—Life's hiding all through this cloud?—

—I'll bet the hunting is good at the edge of the cloud. Some things prob'ly live deeper in, where they can hide. Every now and then they'll come out. To bask in the starlight. Get warm.—

Toby nodded, convinced.—That snaky thing, it knows that. Comes around, looking for supper.—

—The sail-snake eats the blue balls. But what's the blue ball eat?—

—Something smaller. Something we can't see from here.—

—Right.—Killeen squinted.—There's got to be some critter that lives off the starlight and drifting molecules alone.—

Toby said wonderingly,—Plants? Space plants. I'll bet we can eat some of them.—

Killeen pounded his son on the back.—Be a wonder if we couldn't. We know these clouds have the same basic chemistry that nature generates everywhere. *Argo*'s science programs told us that, 'member? So we'll be able to digest some of whatever's hiding in there, for sure.—

Toby blinked, watching the jade snake unfurl its sails further. Was it green for the same reason plants were, to sop up sunlight in all colors except green? It began an achingly slow turn, showing curved black stripes. Had it seen their ship? Maybe they should run it down, see what it tasted like. His stomach rumbled at the idea.

But the creature had a majesty about it, too. A beauty in its glistening hide, its graceful movement. Like an immense swimmer in a black pool. Maybe they'd leave it be.

—We'd never have seen them from the bridge. Those instruments would've filtered out what they didn't think was important.—Killeen was all business again, his wonderment suppressed. That was part of the price of being Cap'n.

Toby gaped, still fascinated by the sail-snake. He knew what his father said was right. Nobody could have guessed what they'd see out here. But Killeen had come out, again and again. Hammering away at a Cap'n's problems, thinking, worrying, pacing the hull, looking without knowing what he was looking for. And some of the crew had thought he was crazy.

Toby listened as Killeen called the Bridge and ordered *Argo* toward the shadowy cloud. Understanding came slowly amid the crew. He could hear on comm as the ship stirred with excited voices, with hope, with joy.

—Dad?—he finally asked.

Killeen was giving a flurry of orders. Crew had to prepare to hunt, to forage, to pursue strange game in inky vacuum depths. To do things they had never tried before. Had never even imagined.

Killeen paused and said curtly,—Yeasay?—

—We can hole up inside the cloud for a while. Rest up. Get our bearings.—

Killeen shook his head furiously.—Naysay. Resupply, that's all. There's True Center. Look at it! We're so close now.—

Toby peered ahead, through dusty clumps already wreathing the hull of *Argo* as the great ship headed into the recesses of the giant cloud. At max mag he could make out the exact center of the galaxy. White-hot. Beautiful. Dangerous.

And his father, he now saw, could never be deflected from that goal. Not by starvation. Not by deadly risks. Not by the weight of past sorrow.

They would fly straight into the gnawing center of all this gaudy, swirling chaos. On an impossible voyage. Looking for something, with no clear idea of what it might be.

Killeen grinned broadly.—C'mon, son, this is what we were born to do. We'll go onward. Inward. There's all our Family's past here, somewhere. We'll find out what happened, who we are.—

—Crew doesn't like that kind of talk, Dad.—

He frowned.—How come?—

—This is a scary place.—

—So? They haven't seen the glory of it, haven't really thought it through. When the time comes, they'll follow me.—

—We're running for our lives, Dad.—

—So?—Killeen grinned, a jaunty human gesture amid the wash of galactic light.—We always have been.—

Particle Storm

The carapace glides like a hunting hornet.

Its thorax is of high-impact matte ceramic. Bone-white lattices mimic ribs. Storage balloons inflate like lungs as it exchanges plasma charge. Slow rises, fluttering exhales.

This is illusion. Its body is a treasury of past designs, free of weight, remembering nothing of planets. Evolution is independent of the substrate, whether organic or metallic or plasmic. Its design follows cool engineerings now encased in habit. Function converges on form. Tubular rods of invisible tension, struts like statements.

Elsewhere along its expanses, gray pods stud the shooting angularities of it. Scooped curves in smudged silver. Tapering lines blend, uniting skewed axes. None of these geometries would be possible beneath the dictates of gravity.

It torques. Grave, careful. Movement is a luxury, scarcely necessary when what truly stirs is data.

It has little kinesthetic sense. Instead it lives amid encoded interior universes. Webs, logics, filters. Perceptions are racing patterns flung between the shifting sands of stars and lives.

Data pours through these spaces. Digital rivers fork into rivulets, seeking receptors. Stuttering, layer-encoded, as endless as the rain of protons.

Like a feverish need the data-streams fall here on opaque titanium shells. But it does not sense the particle torrent that flails uselessly at massive shields: layers of stressed conglomerate cismetal, revolving.

Mass is brute. Inside the crystalline ramparts, there is nothing which seems like a machine. No obvious movement, no sliding mechanical torques. Here the essence is static, eternal, a fulcrum of fixed forces.

Thought is infinitely tenuous. The inner mind flits down tiny stalks of dark diamond, fashioned from the cores of ancient supernovas. Codes race in fine sprays of polarized nuclei, dancing forever in buoyant fields. Electrons pinch and snake, bearing luminescent ideas.

From the distance come spectral streamers of a red giant, laboring toward supernova. Plasma casts ruby shafts across the slowly revolving planes. The tossing, frenzied flush traces out the worn rims of craters. Random impacts, long forgotten. Pocks and scratches cross the massive shanks. These tell strange stories, unreadable now.

Death crowns the spiral spine: antennae tinged in jarring yellow. They can slice through the galactic hiss here, stab electromagnetic needles through prey light-minutes away.

For the moment it converses. Its interior selves are free of the swallowing mandates of self-preservation. Their task is to think long. Within them, data dances.

The anthology intelligence speaks to others far distributed along the galactic plane—though the separation into (self, here) and (other, there) is a convention, a brute simplification for this slowly revolving angularity.

Something like an argument congeals. Sliding perspectives of digital nuance. Binary oppositions are illusory here—you/I, point/counter—but they do shape issues, in the way that a frame defines a painting.

It begins. Language lances across the storming masses that intervene, the vagrant passing weather. Cuts. Penetrates.

Semi-sentients should not preoccupy us.

They must. They are an unresolved issue.

You term them "primates"?

Of the class of dreaming vertebrates.

I/You consider them irrelevant.

The underlying issues still vex.

They are nothing! Debris, motes.

They approach. Little time remains before they will near the Center.

We/You have eradicated humans virtually everywhere. Only small bands remain. Our protracted deliberations, well recorded in history, demand completion of this ancient task.

This policy is e>/~*~\< old. We/You should reinspect it.

They are nearly extinct. Press on.

Their extinction seems difficult to achieve. They persist. This suggests we\you reconsider our\my assumptions.

They are vermin. Carbon-based evolution brings only low skills. They still communicate with each other linearly!

Some would say that evolution works as equally upon you\us as upon them.

Nonsense. We\You direct our changes. They cannot. This is the deep deficiency of chemical life.

They were once able to alter their own imprintings. To write changes in their carbon kind.

They lost it as we\you diminished them. Now they are the same as the unthinking forms, the animals—shaped by random forces.

They were once important players here. We\You should understand their threat to us before expunging them.

Possibly they harbor information harmful to us\you—so say our most stable records.

Those are sheltered against the Mass Eater's radiant storm and so should be well preserved.

By its nature we\you cannot know what this hidden information is.

Why "by its nature"?

There are many theories.

Precisely. Does it not seem curious that something in our\your makeup makes it somehow impossible for us\you to know what these humans carry? That such knowledge is blocked for us? A curious aspect of our deep programming.

May carry. Such ancient records are suspect.

We\You cannot risk disbelieving them.

Long ago the philosopher [¦~] resolved such questions. We\You are imprisoned within our perception-space. There will always remain matters you\we cannot know.

But if these matters affect ourselves? Disquieting.

Living with ambiguity is the nature of high intelligence. Still, to lessen uncertainty, we\you should exterminate the remaining bands.

And lose their information?

Very well—archive them first. I now point to this latest incursion—already it nears True Center.

There may be risks in erasing them.

Nonsense. You\We have destroyed many such expeditions before.

First, let scouts find them accurately. The usual primate-hunter units will track them, perhaps inflict minor damage—one must give such lower forms some reward structure, remember.

You/We advocate delay?

No—cautious action. Remember that higher forms than us will judge our\your actions. Prudence demands care. Earlier events involving these primates, on two separate planets, have pointed toward some significant yet poorly defined role they play. They may carry information—and what are they, but information? Indeed, what are we?—which can bring the attentions of minds above ours.

Very well, caution. But how?

A trap.

Part I

FAR ANTIQUITY

1

Techno-Nomads

Toby had barely gotten back inside the air lock and was shedding his suit when Cermo showed up. Toby wore nothing but shorts under his vacuum suit, and the ship felt colder than outside. He rummaged in his locker for his overalls, shivering, and Cermo said, "Where you been?"

"Where's it look?"

The big man towered over Toby. Cermo had been called Cermo-the-Slow in years past, but now was leaner and quicker. A broad grin seemed to divide his face in half with delighted anticipation. "Heard all the ruckus. Cap'n found us somethin' to eat, right?"

"We'll see."

"Doesn't change anything for you, though," Cermo said with a sly chuckle. He was a big man with a soft-eyed, mirthful face, so the chuckle carried no malice.

"What's that mean?"

"You're on maintenance detail today."

"So? Okay, I'll check the biotanks, the usual."

"Today's not usual." Again the sly grin.

"What's wrong?"

"Sewage seals broke."

"*Again?* No fair! They went out *last* time I was on maintenance, too."

"Well then, you're an expert." Cermo handed Toby a mop. "Apply your know-how."

The seals were always popping, because the pressure regulators had to be tuned just exactly right. Human waste was a vital ingredient in the biotanks. It had to be pressurized, filtered, and the final product flattened into squishy mats—which the farm teams spread around among the big bowl-shaped crop zones. The *Argo* was a long-voyage ship, designed to keep every drop of water, every sigh of air sealed tight inside its skin.

Easy to understand, hard to do. Most of the *Argo* crew were relatives, all that remained of Family Bishop. They came from Snowglade, a bleak world Toby remembered rather fondly. Toby was of the youngest generation of Family Bishop. That gave him the flexibility of being fresh and green, but the sour fact of the matter was that Bishops had few skills to help them run the *Argo.*

All Families had been techno-nomads, learning just enough to survive while they were on the move. Always running, dodging, staying ahead of mechs. Not that most mechs paid them any special attention. Humans at Galactic Center were more like rats in the walls, not major players in anything.

Argo was as friendly to its passengers as a ship could be, a fine artifact from the High Arcology Era. Trouble was, its systems assumed the passengers had educations that Family Bishop could only guess at.

Example: the sewage. Neither Cap'n Killeen nor Cermo nor anybody else had been able to make head or tail of the instructions for the pressure system.

It assumed something called the Perfect Gas Law, the instructions said. The foul stuff that actually flowed through the smooth, clear pipes was certainly not perfect, and it obeyed no law anybody ever heard of. It spewed out without provocation and often with what seemed to be insulting timing. Last week, a howling brown leak sprayed the Family when it was assembled for a wedding. That took a certain fine edge off the celebration.

Toby joined the other poor souls who had drawn maintenance this week. He breathed through his mouth but that helped only a while, until the smell got up into his head. His teacher Aspect, Isaac, spoke to him in his mind while he bent over, pushing the foul stuff with a sponge brush.

I have conferred with the most ancient records you carry in chip-library. Interestingly, the term you use is actually derived from the name of the man on Old Earth who invented the flush toilet. An Englishman, legend has it, he made a fortune and benefited all humankind. His name, Thomas Crapper, has come to be—

"Hey, give me a break."

I thought perhaps some distraction would make your task easier.

"Look, I want distraction, I'll play one of the old Mose Art musics."

You mistake the name, I fear. That should be Wolfgang Ama—

Toby mentally pushed the sputtering Aspect back into its storage hole. Aspects were recorded personalities out of Family Bishop's past, some quite old, like Isaac. They were really interactive information bases written on small chips, which Toby carried in his neck slots. Isaac was only a shrunken slice of a real, long-dead human personality, of course, mostly just old lore that might come in handy. Isaac had tried and tried to explain that Perfect Gas Law, but Toby never really got it.

Knowing about Thomas Crapper wasn't going to be any use to Toby, but he got a smile out of it; so maybe that was some purpose, after all. The Family used Aspects to help them get through troubles, carrying the masses of knowledge they needed to survive while living amid technology that was far beyond them.

"Hey, you sleepwalking?"

Toby came alert. Besen was standing beside him, neat and trim, her part of the cleanup done. Toby still had half a hallway to sponge up. "Uh, I was thinking deep thoughts."

Besen rolled her eyes. "Oh sure."

He gestured with his mop at the brown-stained deck. "Bet you don't know who this stuff is named for."

Besen looked skeptical when he told her. "Honest truth," he said.

Besen gave him a grin and he marveled at how wonderful she looked lately. Fitted out in overalls, auburn hair tied back, spattered and grimy, to his eyes she still had a radiance. Girls bloomed just once, like flowers, before turning into women—but that was enough. Besen seemed impossibly fresh, alive, fun.

"I was just remembering some of those plays we had to listen to," he said. "They apply here."

"Oh?" she said skeptically.

"Sure, you recall. 'Good night, good night! Farting is such sweet sorrow.' Great romantic stuff."

"That's '*Parting* is such sweet sorrow.' Some romantic you are!"

One of their private games came from a truly ancient chip that Besen carried. It had actual texts from Old Earth, including a gray geezer named Shake-Spear. A great poet from some kind of primitive hunter-gatherer society, Besen thought. This Shake-Spear was one of the scraps humans had retained across the Great Gulf that separated them from the Old Earth cultures, and Besen liked to quote frags of such stuff, just to show off.

"Well, I got it nearly right." He grinned. "Wait'll I finish here, we'll go have some fun in the weightless gym."

Toby liked the zones of *Argo* at zero-g. Most of the ship's sections spun, creating an artificial centrifugal "gravity." In the weightless gym, they could bounce off trampoline-walls, make carom shots, cannonball into shimmering spheres of water.

Besen shook her head. "That's what I came to get you for. There's another seal break."

"Oh no!"

"Oh yes. And we're elected to help tidy up."

"Where?" He hoped it wasn't in a weightless zone. What made them fun also made them horrible to clean up. Gunk stuck to every conceivable surface, and some inconceivable ones.

"The Bridge. Come on, hustle!"

When they got to the ample, softly lighted Bridge, Toby was appalled at the sewage leak. Thick scum ran down one whole wall—luckily, one bare of electronics or display screens. It stank. He knew all the uniformed officers by first name, of course, as Family members—but they carefully ignored him, Besen, and the fragrant brown stain. They stood with hands firmly clasped behind their backs, frowning sternly, concentrating on tasks that did not offend their lofty officers' dignity.

The Bridge was a hallowed part of *Argo,* where momentous decisions about the whole future of Family Bishop were made, often in split seconds. To have it invaded by smelly waste seemed a deliberate affront of the mocking Sewage God.

The Bridge data screens flickered and swam with views, sliding slabs of information, estimates and four-color projections made automatically by the *Argo*'s ever-vigilant computers. Without this level of control, Family Bishop would be reduced to what it was—a gang of barely literate nomads who had lucked into a comfortable ship.

Still, even here the years they had occupied *Argo* showed their toll. The carpet had a big yellow stain and scuff marks. Here somebody had gouged the wall, and over there a repair team must have thought they could help by cutting a sawtooth gap and then abandoning it. Random chunks of servos and electronics gear cluttered the working surfaces. As nomads, their lifelong habits made them carve up and strip away, haul off and make do. Clearing up didn't come naturally.

Toby and Besen tried to eavesdrop on the cross-talk conversations of the Bridge as they worked. The ship was indeed diving deeply into the molecular cloud. A low tone was gathering, a long bass note sounded by the dust of the cloud rubbing against the ship's balloonlike lifezones. It was as though the interstellar gas outside was playing *Argo* like an instrument, sending through her a mournful call.

"Kinda spooky, isn't it?" Besen asked.

"Like a funeral dirge," Toby whispered.

"The rub of reality," Besen said theatrically. "A symphony of space."

On the viewscreens he saw mottled lanes of dust. Here and there, rays from nearby stars shot through the murky banks, splashing blues and burnt-oranges across the cinder-dark fogs.

A shout from an officer. "There it is!"

Officers crowded around the screens to see the sail-snake. It glistened and writhed, plainly trying to get away from *Argo.* The hunter was now the hunted. Toby stood on tiptoe to get a good look but the crowd was too thick. Nearly everybody here, being older, was quite a bit taller. A Lieutenant saw him and Besen craning their necks, yanked them both by the collar, and set them back to work.

There were enormous perspectives on the viewscreens, brimming with light, shrouded by the great cloaking dust. Beauty. Wonder. Awe. Vast spectacles that brought a trembling reverence to the human soul.

Meanwhile, Toby bent over to mop up the scummy sewage. Rank. Smelly. Squishy.

"Crap and cosmos," he muttered.

"What?" Besen asked.

"Just trying to keep things in perspective."

2

The Sail-Snake

Toby got to see the sail-snake up close the next day. Not because he was going out with one of the hunting crews, of course. When Toby and Besen asked, Cermo had said officiously, "Hunting's for full grown, not kids."

Besen's mouth twisted. "Get off it!"

"We're better at zero-g work than you are," Toby said.

"And quicker," Besen added.

"Experience is what counts here," Cermo said, keeping his face blank—which meant he was going to follow orders, whether he agreed with them or not. Cap'n Killeen's orders.

"Experience doing what?" Toby asked irritably, seeing that Cermo wouldn't budge. Nobody had ever done space hunting.

"Surviving," Cermo said mildly.

Toby and Besen had been in tough places before, same as anybody in Family Bishop—but he had to admit Cermo had a point. Seniority stood for something when to get up in age meant you'd dodged plenty of trouble.

But even adult crew members, men and women alike, hesitated. The only hunting Family Bishop had done had been back on the home world, Snowglade, with firm ground underfoot and game they knew. They had run down mechs that carried organic food-fuels, pillaged them. And that had been a long time ago.

Outside loomed daunting, mysterious spaces. Family Bishop was hungry, tired of lean rations, but still wily. They sized up risks with a practiced eye. They had survived while other Families in the Grand Ensemble—the Rooks, Knights, Pawns, and more—had withered. Bishops muttered and fretted about venturing into such vast expanses, to drift among shrouded mountains of dust and gas in frail little shuttlecraft.

So they sent a message to their only possible consultant, the alien Quath. But Quath was a moody sort, and didn't answer. Maybe this meant Quath didn't know anything useful. Or maybe she did. That was Quath's way. The point about aliens, as Cap'n Killeen always said, was that they're *alien.* You not only couldn't be sure about what they said, you couldn't even be sure about what they didn't.

Quath wouldn't talk to just anybody, either. Toby had a reasonably close relationship with the big, insectlike thing—as nearly as anybody really could be sure. Ideas like friendship just didn't easily apply to Quath.

Cermo sent Toby to talk to Quath, since the alien didn't respond on comm or any other line. Which meant suiting up and going out to the hull, where the hunting teams were busy assembling the shuttlecraft.

Because Quath didn't live in the ship at all. She lived *on* it—attached to the hull, inside a strange warren of rooms and spires the alien had shaped from waste and debris yielded up by *Argo.* There was even human waste in it, Toby knew, because he had seen Quath carefully pat the stuff into shit-bricks. Baked by vacuum and ultraviolet starlight, the gunk hardened fast and made good building material. Not to human taste, of course, but that was hardly the point. Besides, things didn't smell in space—to humans. Quath, though, went into space without a suit, so maybe to it the bricks did have a scent. To Quath it could be perfume, for all anybody knew.

Toby cycled outside through the personnel lock and stood on the hull. It took a moment for his inner ear to make the change to zero-gravs, to stop sending out alarms that he was hanging above an infinite drop. His head had to get used to the idea that "up" and "down" were useful ways to orient himself, but didn't really mean anything.

His magnetic boots kept him secure and he let his skinsuit readjust itself, sorting out pressure imbalances and its own wrinkles. The suit was alive, in a way. It had its own nerve net to sense problems. Thin organic muscles and computer chips set into the armpits made it all work. As engineering it was a marvel, but Toby by now took it for granted, and just griped when a pesky fold didn't straighten itself out.

He started across the broad curve of *Argo*'s hull, looked "up"—and froze.

The sail-snake loomed large. It coiled slowly, turning in the pale blue luminosity—and Toby saw that it was half as big as *Argo.* When he had seen it before, through telescoped, tech-assisted vision, he had gotten no feel for size. He had never thought about what life in gravity-free space might mean.

The sail-snake was a long tube assembled from the same repeating hexagonal segments. Toby could now see through its translucent skin, into a feathery skeleton that framed chambers of fluids and gas. It was a complex, interlocking array of orange rods and sliding gray muscles. They moved with sluggish, huge purpose—taking the snake away, as fast as the broad, triangular plates of shiny sails could push it. Through its shimmering jade skin Toby saw milky fluids sloshing. Bubbles popped along thin veins.

So much, and so close. Could they eat any of it? Or would the chemistry of such an alien thing be impossible to digest?

He picked up on comm the random talk of the hunting crews. They were tinkering with their shuttle vessels, and the voices brought him back to his own job. He hiked over the brow of the hull, coming down into a little valley formed by the bulge of the Wheat Dome. Through the dome he could see the blighted fields, brown and black—testament to their lack of ability to really run *Argo* right, even with all the computer programs.

Nestled in the valley was Quath's dwelling. It looked like a wasp's nest, honeycombed with tunnels. Mingling with that basic pattern was a dizzying profusion of sharp edges, ornaments, puzzling juts and thrusts.

Toby walked into the nearest portal, a perfect circular opening. Green phosphorescent slabs lit his way, flaring into life as he approached, dimming when he had passed. He didn't know where he was going. He had visited here many times but the scheme never seemed the same twice. He suspected Quath spent a lot of time rearranging the labyrinth, maybe as a kind of art object. What else did an alien do with its time out here? Or was art a human idea that Quath didn't share? The odd holes of varying sizes, shooting off at eccentric angles, made the art idea seem probable. Or maybe, Toby reminded himself, it was Quath's idea of an elaborate joke. Who could tell?

He stopped at a ledge, peering into the murk beyond—and panels flashed into blue brilliance, illuminating a spherical vault. This he had never seen before—and at the bottom of the bowl stood Quath, waiting.

<You have climbed the mountain.>

The transmission from Quath had a ringing quality, like bells chiming in the distance, yet the words were clear. Toby did not hear them through his ears, but through his mind. Every Family member had comm gear embedded in the neck and lower skull, standard issue. Quath had simply learned how to tap into those channels, and Toby's own systems translated into a tinkling voice.

"Hello, joke-face Quath'jutt'kkal'thon." He used the formal, full name immediately. It meant Brave Crawler with Dreams, or so Killeen said. From experience, he knew that otherwise the big thing might turn and walk away. And Toby could never find Quath in this maze unless Quath wanted him to.

<Maggots cover you.>

"Must've caught them from your rotten carcass. What's that about a mountain?"

<This is my mountain, maggot-one.>

"Some mountain. More like a stink-hole, I'd say. And you're the one looks like a giant maggot."

<Welcome, food-of-maggots.>

There was something to be said for an alien who liked insults. Quath gave anybody who had the bad judgment to open with compliments a sudden, cold shoulder. The maggot routine Quath particularly liked, maybe because Quath *did* look a lot like a creepy bug—and probably knew people thought so, too.

She was a weird, ever-changing combination of slinky, green lizard with an insect that had too many legs. Quath sprouted glassy eyes all along the wriggly body, not just from the bulging head. Yellow stick-arms like hard plastic. Fleshy purple folds. But metal, too, because Quath was a composite creature. Bossed steel studded with protrusions. Riveted copper—or were those really warts, not rivets? Crusted flanks above the legs looked like shaped ceramic, but seemed to flex and work as Quath walked. "End of pleasantries, goggle-eyes. Cermo-the-Slow sent me. We're wondering if you know anything about getting food out of these clouds."

<Dwarf being, I have harvested such before, in similar sites. I fathom these alkaline chemistries.>

"Great—tell us how."

<The spheroids would poison you.>

"The blue balls? Okay, we skip them."

<The hunter will lead you to fertile zones.>

"The sail-snake? How about eating the snake itself?"

<It is of higher order. Your species would plunder it?>

"Hmmm. We don't kill other animals any more, even though we used to, back on our homeworld."

<What changed?>

"The mechs, I guess." Toby had to make himself recall the horrors of the Bishop's retreat from their home. The mechs were a mechanical civilization that dominated this entire region of space. "They came to Snowglade 'way before I was born. Mechs killed off just about anything not smart enough to get out of the way, fast—including forests. Which made Family Bishop decide to stop helping them out by eating our fellow creatures. Now we eat plants."

<Obviously your species is not naturally vegetarian.>

"How do you know that?"

<You have front teeth designed to bite meat. Your back teeth, however, are best at grinding down grains. Plainly your evolution has shaped you as dietary opportunists.>

"So we're talented—any problem with that?"

<No, tiny mote. None the less, one should know what one is.>

"But that sail-snake—it's nothing like us. I mean, maybe we can bend the rules a little." He wondered how much of his reasoning was based on his rumbling stomach.

Quath swiveled her eye-stalks, which from Toby's experience might mean that she had decided to act. <Such issues are best decided by experience, not rumination.>

Toby had to call up his teacher Aspect, Isaac, to tell him what "rumination" meant. It was irksome when an alien knew the language better than he did.

Toby was figuring out the definition and so was caught off guard when Quath came clambering up the bowl, her bulging green throat pulsing. Without a further signal she swept up Toby in two telescoping copper arms. Quath accelerated, ignoring Toby's squawks. Thick pads held him as they raced at startling speed through twisting corridors, down a shaft—and into open space.

Perspectives whirled. Toby felt a hard shove of acceleration. "Hey, what are you—where—"

<Only data can decide.>

Toby sputtered objections, but Quath paid no attention to his injured pride. Instead, the huge alien held him even more tightly as they jetted away from *Argo.*

He was nearly completely enclosed by massive, soft pads. Somehow, it was restful to know that Quath, despite an annoying abruptness, was looking after him—in fact, looking after the whole Family Bishop. Toby had not had anyone hold him in this enveloping way for a long, bleak time. His memory slid back to Snowglade again, to better times.

He recalled distant, fuzzy images, coated with the soft tones of his mother's voice. Long-ago nights in the lost, hidden Citadel, he had lain in his bed, tangled in the sheets, awakened by some noise. He had heard his parents murmuring. His door was ajar, letting a slant of feeble light into his room. The warm glow and distant talk had been reassuring, as if his parents made the same soft, furry sounds that his stuffed animals did, or he imagined they did, as he slept with them. He had hugged his animals happily, Billy Bigsnout and Alvin Apple-eater, and sung to them. His mother had heard and come into his room and his father too, and his father had said, "Those animals, he still squeezes the life out of them. Hey boy, you're getting kinda old for those toys. Have to give them up soon." His mother had said reproachfully, "Oh no, oh no, he's just a baby still. There's plenty of time for him to have Billy Bear." Her warmth tenderly brushed his face and her smell was like flowers in the spring.

So long ago. So far.

Before the Calamity, when the mechs of Snowglade finally tired of pesky human raids on their factories. Before they crushed the last human outposts, leaving the Bishops to flee and forage.

Heavy braking. They came to a stop and Quath released him. Toby spilled into bright space. *Argo* was a distant bulk of shiny curves and green domes. Toby turned—

And faced a wall of slick jade. The wall heaved, surged.

<The sail creature is afraid of us.>

"*Any*body'd be afraid of you, Quath."

<There must be some way to use so great a creature without killing it.>

"I'm more worried about the other way around."

<It flees. We can easily overtake it. If we do not venture near the mouth, it will have no way to ingest us.>

That seemed easy enough. The far end of the snake was a distant slash of mouth and a mass of working pink tentacles. Toby closeupped them and saw that some were eyes, others something like crude hands. It was fascinating, watching them move. Curiosity did not make him want to get any closer, though.

He peered at the shimmering green side of the beast. Then he looked *into* it, through the skin and into the lattice of sliding orange rods, tubes, and sacs that made the sail-snake work.

"I wonder what's in those?" He pointed to a big vessel made of what looked like plastic. It held a red fluid.

<My chemical diagnostics cannot decide.>

Toby thought of his mother's warm breath. So long gone, into that black place where the dead dwell. He had come a long way since then. What would she think of him now? Would she be proud?

"Let's go see," he said abruptly.

He glided over to the wall of green skin. With care he drew his knife from its boot sheath. There is nothing in space more dangerous than a sharp edge, and Toby handled the long blade carefully. He measured distances to the skin with his eye and cut one quick stroke—then backed off.

Nothing came rushing out to assault him. Not even a puff of gas, which he had half expected.

<Tiny one, entry might not be advisable—>

"Aw, stuff it. You got us out here. Let's do the job."

Toby thumbed his jets on for just an instant, enough to send him directly through the cut.

The beast was complicated. Toby kicked off one of the orange lattice struts of the thing's skeleton. He pushed aside a tangle of flexible pipes and reached the red fluid sac.

<I regret I cannot follow you.>

"You're too fat to get in here, eyes-on-sticks. Let me take a sample of this stuff."

He jabbed a needle probe into the thick-walled sac, let his carrybottle fill with the red liquid, and slapped a patch on the hole. No need to let the thing bleed to death, just because he wanted a drop or two.

He nearly got snarled in the pipes as he made his way out. They seemed to know where he was, and Toby realized this was some slow-moving defense. Tangle up the intruder, and wait for some guard to come round him up. Something told him he didn't want to be around that long.

Quath took the bottle and quickly reported. <Organics, soluble nutrients, traces of iron and potassium.>

"Can we use it?"

<Your metabolism may welcome it.>

"I can make a passable soup out of anything that won't kill us."

Little fuzz-balls were rolling along the jade skin. They were no bigger than his hand but there were lots of them, coming from all along the length of the sail-snake. Several reached the skin just below where Toby hung in free space.

"Come on—we've outlasted our welcome."

Just as he said it two fuzz-balls leaped across the gap. They struck his boots and kept going, sticking lightly and rolling quickly up his skinsuit. He felt a prickly heat, right through his suit.

Quath made a furious buzz. Toby slashed at the fuzz-balls with his knife. He got one off him but the other rolled onto his helmet. There it started spreading, like a pool of gray oil.

"It's eating through!" Toby batted at the stuff, but it wouldn't come off.

Quath grabbed his boots with one telescoping arm. Then she stuck a tube out of her side and aimed it directly at Toby's face. A torrent of air blew over him. The gray oil rippled but clung, started to break up into drops—and suddenly was gone.

<The rule of opposites. A creature which lives in vacuum will dislike air.>

Toby gasped in relief. "I'll have to remember that."

<Oxygen is corrosive, though we seldom notice. It will eat steel, given time, leaving only rust.>

"I'll have to swear off the stuff." He wriggled away from an approaching fuzz-ball. "Come on, let's get out of here."

Quath helped him get free. <I believe considerable liquid can be extracted from this creature without endangering its metabolism.>

"Like a blood transfusion, sort of?"

<Not truly. I believe these fluids do not circulate like blood. They are long-term energy reserves.>

"It's okay to take them?"

The team assembling in the ship was going to search for plants, or even raid mechs if there were any here—but certainly not to slaughter animals. Family Bishop had a deep moral code against using animal products, too, unless the animal cooperated, like dairy cows. To damage living things was to be no better than mechs.

<This creature feeds off others. It cannot object if we do likewise to it, while allowing it to still live.>

"Ummm. So you're a moral philosopher."

<All are. It is a condition of living.>

They were halfway back to *Argo* when Cermo called over comm,—Hey! What in hell are you—

"Got some juice you should look at," Toby said.

—You got that alien to take you out. That's direct disobedience of an order.—

"I was hauled along for the ride, Cermo."

Quath confirmed, <He is truth-filled.>

Quath hardly ever intervened in a human conversation. Toby was surprised and pleased.

Cermo sounded annoyed.—I know something else he's full of. Anyway, get back here. We've got to find food supplies and then move on.—

"How come? I'd like to explore this—"

—Those big things orbiting closer to the Center? The Bridge just got a spectro-reading. They told me the nearest one's not mech-made at all, like we thought.—

"What is it, then?"

—Human-made. An ancient Chandelier.—

3

The Rule of Number

Besen came by Toby's bunk to see if he wanted to go up to the viewing room. She was sweaty from her work—hand-cultivating the vegetable fields in the single lush growing dome they had left. Her overalls were grungy, light brown wisps of hair were escaping from a tight bun, and she beamed at him, still flush with energy to burn.

"Sorry, can't," Toby said mournfully. He was propped up on his bunk, pushing a stylus around a writing slate, without much real progress.

"Oh, come on! That'll wait."

"Cermo's got me under orders. I've got to get through five lessons before I can go off-ship again."

"That's cruel." She smiled sympathetically. Everybody wanted to get outside, after years of ship living, but Toby more so.

"Well, I am kinda behind."

Besen tossed her head with pretty annoyance. "Let's see what you're—oh, numbers. Yuk!"

"They have their charms—but not right now."

"I just don't see the point of them, really. I mean, machines think in numbers—so why should we bother?"

"Look, somebody who doesn't use numbers has no advantage over somebody who *can't* use them."

"But *mechs* think that way." Plainly Besen felt that associating anything with mechs ruled it out.

"And so does *Argo*—without its computers, we'd be dead. Mechs are evil, sure. Because of what they *do,* not what they use. Numbers are like words—ways of saying things about the world."

"Well, they don't speak to *me.*"

"And I shouldn't be speaking to you either. I've got to plow through these lessons or else I won't get to go look at the Chandelier at all." Toby sighed and stretched, his feet bumping into the ceramic bulkhead. He was lanky and this bunk was getting too short for him. He would have to hunt up a bigger one elsewhere in the dorm rooms that all unmarried Family used.

"Cermo said that? He's getting tough."

"I think it's my dad jerking the strings again."

Besen snorted in frustration. "Our beloved Cap'n. Why can't he leave his own son alone?"

"I don't know," Toby said, though he had a pretty good idea. It wasn't anything he wanted to talk over, though, not even with Besen.

She gazed pensively into the distance. "Y'know, after Shibo died, he seemed to recover. But lately, he's been spending more time by himself, barking orders, keeping everybody in the dark about what he's thinking. And he treats you funny." Her eyes slid over to him, inviting a reply.

Toby edged away from specifics with, "Maybe fathers and sons always have trouble."

"Your father is something else." Besen's voice dripped with implications.

"Meaning?"

"He's rough on everybody. Downright nasty."

Toby gave her a grim smile. "Maybe he doesn't want anybody to feel left out."

"A humorist." Besen had lost some of her buoyancy. "But I mean it, really. Cap'n Killeen is driving us all hard, and people don't like it. Except maybe the Cards—they had tough leaders so long—crazy ones even!—they like 'em."

"Ummm. We've gotten soft, living in this comfy ship."

"Comfy? I spent today on my knees, hand-tending every tomato plant, coaxing them to stay alive."

"Because we screwed up the other domes. *Argo* would work fine if we weren't so dumb."

Grumpily Besen said, "Well, your dad doesn't make life any easier."

Toby nodded glumly. He had made the usual defenses of his father, but they didn't convince even him. He had seen enough incidents in which Killeen raged at minor infractions, imposed harsh penalties for malingering, raised work hours. A big change from the Killeen of old, who had been affable and casual about the rigors of rank.

"We're in danger all the time. He's responsible for us all. Give him some room, okay?" This sounded lame even to Toby, but he could not bring himself to condemn his father. For too many years, after the mechs killed Toby's mother, Killeen had been the only one who had looked after him.

Besen saw Toby's mood and leaned over to give him a light kiss. "Sorry if I brought you down. Or considering what you're studying, even further down."

"Aw, beat it. Go *oooh* and *ahhh* at the views of the Chandelier."

She made a face. "Just for that, I will."

Family Bishop was approaching the Chandelier slowly, cautiously, using passing small clouds for cover. The chunky, complex mass was sprawling, ornate, larger even than mech cities on Snowglade—but humans had built the Chandeliers, long ago. *Humans.* The idea seemed impossible to Toby when he studied the distant spiral wings, criss-crossing arms, and noble, sweeping arches.

Nobody in Family Bishop had ever visited one. There was anticipation—and something like fear.

They would go aboard within a day. *Argo* echoed with a din of preparation. Toby shut it out and reluctantly turned his concentration to his lessons. He could feel his teaching Aspect, Isaac, fidgeting at the back of his mind, eager to have a voice. Aspects were long-dead and liked to get out of the cramped cerebral spaces where they were stored. In one sense they were only alive when Toby talked with them. In another, they were always there, at a very low level, like an oldster dozing lazily in the sun. Whatever the picture Toby used, he figured his Aspects were like laundry—they smelled better if they got aired now and then. Isaac said eagerly,

I'm happy to see you showing some interest in mathematics. Have you finished your problems?

"I did some. They're so boring, though."
Isaac said rather sternly,

I scarcely think you should criticize the problems I assign, considering how seldom you even speak to me or—

"Okay, okay—give me something different, though."

Very well. Suppose you write down all the numbers from one to one hundred. One, two, three . . . and so on, up to one hundred.

"*That's* interesting?" This Aspect had been in its box too long.

You will learn faster if you do not interrupt. Now, I want you to find a way to add up all those numbers.

"You mean one plus two plus three—like that?"

That is the brute force way to do it. Crude, unimaginative. I want you to be clever.

"Oh no," Toby groaned. Being clever on command was about as easy as being funny under orders. Already he ached to be outside, working in the ship, not in his head.

* * *

Toby wasn't much for studying, but he got it done. He fooled around on the writing slate a little, and then something in the numbers began to speak back to him. A pattern. He wrote the numbers as pairs:

1	100
2	99
3	98
•	•
•	•
49	52
50	51

Each pair added up to 101. There were 50 of them, so that multiplied to 5,050.

Toby blinked. Who would have guessed that the number would be so large and interesting?

There was something strangely stirring in how numbers could hold such simple, supple majesty in them.

Predictably, Isaac liked this trick.

Excellent! The point of exercises is to stretch the mind. To think in new paths. See?

"Seems to me we're getting pretty stretched already. You saw that sail-snake, right? You Aspects still register data, even though you're tucked 'way back in there."

I receive a faint trace of what you do. Yes, that was an interesting creature. I recall an historical record, from the Chandelier Age, which told of expeditions into the molecular clouds. Humanity hunted such vacuum beasts, speeding through spaces as large as whole solar systems, all for recreation.

"Hard to think of people going up against those things for fun."

Humans like danger. The legends and stories of Family Bishop—what are they, after all, but tales of people in trouble?

"Yeah, but trouble that's a comfortable distance away from the teller."

You are rather young to be so cynical.

"Just realistic, Isaac. It's easy for you to take a cosmic view. After all, anything happens to me, you're still okay. They just pull your chip out of my spine and you get revived in somebody else."

I am shocked that you would think me indifferent to your fate. I am a loyal Aspect, devoted to Family Bishop—

"Okay, okay, spare the speech. Let's get back to work."

The mathematics got interesting after you really burrowed into it. A kind of elaborate game, really, with some beautiful surprises hidden in the structure. It would be worth doing even if it wasn't useful, kind of like music. When he told Quath about his little trick, she had rattled with approval, remarking that there were applications of his idea to True Center—and then refused to discuss further, since she was still digesting this information, fresh in from the Illuminates, herself.

But the amazing thing, when Toby took the time to think about it, was that math was practical. The world ran according to the rule of pure Number. Math described the orbits of stars, how circuits worked, even the ways odd features like a funny-shaped nose or red eyes got passed down from one generation to the next in Family Bishop.

What it didn't help with was Cermo.

The big man hadn't been any too happy with Toby's "running off" with Quath, for starters. Then there was the double embarrassment that the red fluid that they fetched back turned out to be packed with useful nutrients. It was even tasty. He and Quath had stolen Cermo's thunder.

So they had to sit it out while the Family had quickly raided all along the length of the sail-snake, taking the red liquid where they could. Not too much, though; Family Bishop codes would never allow endangering the life of so vast a living thing.

A few Family went deeper into the inky recesses of the molecular cloud. Besen had been with them, and her tales of the exotic lifeforms there had made Toby envious. This molecular mist was one of the smaller ones, yet it abounded in bizarre shapes. Triple-spined things, with spreading panels to soak up sunlight. Big, billowing beasts that looked like fabled sailing ships. Mean-eyed predators with tight, leathery mouths, stingy with their precious internal gases. Blimps with enormous eyes to find food in the shifting starglow. Tangles of wispy grasses growing from watery pouches. Forests of swaying yellow leaves. Helical rod-trees that telescoped out, seeking more starlight. Warty living skins that wrinkled and stretched to wrap around spindly purple trunks, partners in some mysterious life process.

They found a huge, self-propelled, rust-red pyramid that seemed like a peaceful grazer, feeding on enormous gray cobwebs, sucking in strands like delicious spaghetti. These thin nets collected the drifting molecules of the great clouds. They looked appetizing, but nobody in the Family could stand the stuff. Besen thought maybe they needed some sauce.

Worse, the red pyramid-beast didn't like tiny creatures picking at its feeding grounds, either. It was as big as the sail-snake and hard to argue with. It chased the offenders all the way back to the ship, veering away only when it saw that *Argo* was not just a fellow giant.

Besen thought it wasn't at all obvious who would win, if it had come to a fight between the pyramid and *Argo*. Who knew what tricks a few billion years of evolution could cook up inside a molecular cloud?

But all this had happened while Toby was confined to the ship. He gritted his teeth, swore a little for the pure pleasure of it, and then went back to work.

When he finished his lessons and Isaac certified his work, he reported to Cermo, got his next-day assignment, and turned to leave.

"Hold on," Cermo said. "Report to the Cap'n."

"Huh? I wanted to go outside, get a good look at the Chandelier."

Cermo said sternly, "*Argo*'s not run for your amusement. *Go*."

Cap'n Killeen stood with hands behind his back, studying his office wall screens. They showed closeup images of the Chandelier being sent back by *Argo*'s automatic flyers. Massive spiral arms. Swooping webs that, under magnification, proved to be linked apartments. Toby tried to imagine living in such places, amid vast lines that dwindled by perspective toward glowing masses in the immense distance.

"Think it's inhabited, Dad?"

Killeen turned slowly from the brilliant screens, his face veiled. "No. The mechs stormed all the Chandeliers thousands of years ago. This one is better preserved, so maybe there wasn't a big fight over it."

"Are you sure?"

Killeen shook his head slowly, obviously consulting an Aspect. "Must be. Records are poor, though."

"Somebody must have Aspects from that far back."

"None from this sector, so close to True Center."

Toby knew that Aspects got hazy and scratchy with age. Chandelier Aspects had to have interpretation programs added, to understand them at all. And it wasn't just the shifts in language. The hardest things to convey were the concepts. Nobody could really comprehend how the Chandelier folk thought. "If we could get some idea—"

Killeen shook his head. "Humans were spread all over, back then. This Chandelier, it looks pretty damn fine all right, but it might have been just a minor outpost, for all we know."

"Huh? But it's, it's *beautiful*."

Killeen grinned. "Suresay—to us. Maybe it was nothing special to people from the Great Times."

Toby looked skeptical and Killeen waved at the screens, where wonders unfolded. "Look, once people retreated from their Chandeliers, they went down to live on planets again. Things got rough. We stopped building big, and settled for what we could protect from mechs. The

Family of Families spread out among the stars, looking for safe places to hide."

"That was the Hunker Down, right?"

"The beginning of it. They figured to hide out on planets. Thought mechs wouldn't have much use for them."

"Because mechs live best in space?"

Killeen grimaced wryly. "So they thought. On Snowglade and Trump, we first built the Grand Arcologies—cities like little Chandeliers, but smaller because of the gravity. The damn mechs smashed them. Our tech stuff got worse and we built the Low Arcologies. Still pretty damn big places, mind you. I saw the ruins of one."

"You told me. Big as a mountain."

"Well, maybe a little smaller. Too big for the mechs, though. They got through our defenses and flattened the little arcologies, too, eventually."

The ancient anger in Killeen's voice made Toby say in sympathy, "So we built the Citadels. Kept going."

"Yeasay—and kept 'em well hid, so we thought. Had to live by raidin' off the new mech manufacturing complexes. Then the mech city-minds sent rat-catchers to blast each Family's Citadel. Rooting people out, casting them to the winds. Till only Citadel Bishop was left. Then came our turn—remember?"

Toby recalled with reluctance their flight from Citadel Bishop. He had been just a boy, confused, scared. Fire and smoke and death. His mother, killed by the mechs with merciful, cold swiftness.

He shook himself. "Look, Cermo said to report to you."

Killeen nodded silently. Toby could tell that he, too, had trouble shaking off the dark past. Killeen abruptly turned and sat behind his broad, uncluttered desk. "I think you've been getting out of hand."

"Oh, the sail-snake thing? Look, it wasn't my idea."

"You should not get Quath stirred up. She is unpredictable."

"Quath carried me out there. There was nothing I could do."

"You could've signaled us, told us what was going on."

Toby shrugged. "I didn't think of that."

"When you get in trouble, consult your Aspects."

"Didn't think of that either."

"You're carrying a lot of experience in those Aspects. Let them help you."

"They nag me a lot."

Killeen smiled. "That goes with the deal. They don't get to do anything except talk, remember. Imagine what that's like."

"I'd rather not," Toby said, uneasy at how this conversation was turning.

"You've got to get used to working with them. Fluid. So you reach for them automatically, like scratching yourself."

"They don't ride so easy yet," Toby admitted uncomfortably.

Killeen gazed steadily at him for a long moment that widened between them. "How . . . how is she?"

So it had finally come out. Again.

"The same . . . of course."

Killeen's lost love, Shibo. The woman who had come into Killeen's life after Toby's mother died, a woman Toby had come to accept as nearly a replacement mother. The once-vibrant Shibo now existed only as an Aspect carried in Toby.

She had been killed on Trump, cut down by enemy fire. In a trap set by His Supremacy, a mech–human hybrid. Toby and Killeen had managed to get her back to *Argo.* In the recording room the ship's instruments had spoken of potassium levels and neurological amalgams and digital matching matrices, terms nobody in Family Bishop understood. Or their Aspects.

The ancient instruments had saved as much as they could of Shibo, reading the neural beds of her mind, the shape of a unique consciousness. Making a recording. Then squeezing it into a chip that slid easily into a human spinal reader. Together with cell samples from her body, for long-term Family genetic records, Toby's Shibo Aspect was all that remained of her.

Normally an Aspect lay dormant until the trauma of death passed, often for a Family generation. But the Family needed Shibo's skills, judgment, and lore. Killeen could not have carried her Aspect, of course; that would invite emotional disaster in their Cap'n, violating every Family precept.

Toby had been the only crew member with an open spinal slot and the right personality constellations to accept Shibo immediately. They had used her knowledge of ship's systems innumerable times in the long voyage. Shibo had a knack for techno-craft. Even better than the advice of the older Aspects from the Low Arcology Era.

But the toll on Killeen had been heavy. Another long silence passed between the two of them, until Toby felt like jumping up and rushing out, away, free of the strain he had truly not wished to carry. "I . . . " Killeen hesitated. "Can I speak with her?"

"I don't think so, Dad."

Killeen opened his mouth, then closed it so abruptly Toby could hear the teeth click. "I just wanted a few words."

"I think it's a bad idea."

"Why?"

"You know how you get."

"I just wanted a little—"

"Dad, you've got to let go of her."

There was a desperate look in Killeen's eyes. "I have. I have."

"No you haven't. If you had, you wouldn't ask."

His father's lips thinned until they were nearly white. Toby knew

Killeen was holding in a lot, the pressures of leadership on top of everything else. But he couldn't give ground on this point.

He had, once. Killeen had hounded him to let his Shibo Aspect speak through his mouth, and he had. Once. Twice. Then again and again, until Killeen wanted that contact, as miserably fleeting and thin as it was, every day.

"I suppose you're some kind of expert?" Killeen asked curtly.

"On this, yes."

"What's your Family Counselor been telling you?"

"Just what I said. To not manifest Shibo for you."

Killeen slammed his fist onto his desk top with a meaty smack. "And if I make it an *order*?"

"I can't obey that kind of order."

"I'll be the judge of that." Killeen's lips twisted cruelly.

Toby took a deep breath and said as evenly as he could, "No you won't. I'll take it to a Family Gathering."

Killeen's face slowly lost its congested, tormented look. It went slack, pale, beaten—an expression Toby liked even less.

"You . . . you'd do that." It was not a question.

"I'd have to." His mouth was dry, sour. "If I manifested Shibo, it'd drive you nutso, same as before."

"Just . . . just a little . . ." Killeen's mouth trembled. His jaw worked with unspoken emotion.Toby hated watching tormented devotion drive a man he loved to such humiliation. It was as though Killeen was addicted to some terrible drug, and could never get it out of his system.

But he had to. And Toby had to help him. "No. No, Dad."

"You could, just for a—"

"A little's worse than a lot. You *know* that."

Killeen stared across the bare table for a long time and then slowly nodded. "Yeasay . . . Worse than a lot."

"Dad, I use Shibo's talents every day. She knows the electronics of this ship, how systems interact—she was great. But that's not what you want from her. You loved Shibo the *woman*. She's gone. What's left is hollow, thin. Only an Aspect."

Killeen's cheeks were sunken, his eyes empty. "Not quite."

"Huh?"

"The recording machines made a deep copy of her. That chip you're carrying, it's a Personality."

"What?" Toby was stunned. A Personality was a full embodiment of the neural beds. It carried features of the original person that went far beyond his or her skills and knowledge.

"I ordered that nobody tell you." Killeen shrugged ruefully. "A boy your age can't really handle a Personality."

"But . . . but it *feels* like an Aspect."

"I had them box in the Personality. At first it couldn't express itself fully through you."

"That's . . . I never heard of . . ."

"It's rare. For emergencies only."

"But why?"

Killeen was getting some of his Cap'n face back. "Family policy is to save as much of a person as we can."

"But there are limits. I mean, we don't keep bodies, or, or . . ."

"I wanted it done."

"*You* wanted it done. Great! What about *me*?"

"The blocks should hold for a while, then give way. Her full Personality will emerge in time."

"But suppose something goes wrong? Suppose this Shibo Personality starts making trouble?"

Toby felt jittery apprehension. Even Aspects could sometimes gang up on their carrier. Attacking at a weak moment, they could bring on an Aspect storm. Then the carrier person went into traumatic states, a form of induced mental illness. Once the Aspects got control of a carrier, they could direct movement and speech, govern behavior. Sometimes Aspects could ride a person for days, even years, without anyone else knowing.

And a Personality was stronger than an Aspect . . .

"I took precautions. Her Personality is tied down with interlocking protections."

"Still, Dad, if it ever—"

"This is *Shibo* we're talking about here!" He slammed the desk again. "She wouldn't turn on you, and you know that. She loved you like a son."

"This thing I'm carrying, it's a *version* of Shibo. Complete with death trauma."

Killeen blinked. "What do you mean?"

Toby fidgeted awkwardly. "Death changes people." For a moment he almost laughed out loud at the absurdity of this. *Death changes people.* But were they people at all anymore? Or just damaged, altered recordings?

Another stretching silence between them. Then Killeen said stiffly, "I should have told you before."

So his father was putting on his Cap'n self, covering his feelings with a uniform. Toby saw that this last statement was as close as he was going to get to an apology.

Toby made a half-shrug, his mind still a swirl of conflicting feelings. "I'd just have worried about it."

"So I thought, too. Son, I'm . . . I'm sorry about asking you to manifest her. I know it's wrong."

"Okay, Dad."

"Sorry. So sorry."

Toby got up, still flustered. His father came around the desk and embraced him. Neither of them were best at expressing things through words, and for a long time they simply clung to each other, arms carrying messages that voices could not.

4

Pale Immensities

Toby watched the Chandelier expand before their flyer, already huge and ominous, and yet still coming, swelling, filling all of space. Its pale immensities stretched in all directions, offering glittering flanks and towers, grand portals and jutting spires, soaring perspectives leading the eye away into dizzying depths.

—People made *this*?—he sent on the comm line.

Killeen answered grimly,—We were once far greater.—

The Cap'n was in the same flyer. Since they had talked, his father seemed to want to have Toby nearby whenever possible. Cermo piloted, since this was the Command flyer. It was not lost to Toby that assigning him here effectively put him on ice, kept him from "stirring around," as Cermo had described his excursion with Quath. On the other hand, this flyer would be in on the most interesting discoveries.

The ramparts and great flanks of the Chandelier began to betray their age as the Family flyers coasted nearer. The massive sheets that seemed to have a ceramic hardness now showed pits, black scars, big rimmed craters. About Galactic Center a hail of incoming debris constantly circled. Even tiny flakes, zooming in at several hundred kilometers per second, could dig deep holes.

Toby watched the peppered face gain detail as they came nearer. He had the same problem, blotches that robbed dignity, but supposedly his would clear up in time. A teenage problem. It was as though age brought a cosmic acne here, he mused, that would never go away. But did that mean no one lived here now?

They were close. He could sense an edgy impatience on the comm line. The crew sent their all-clears in clipped tones. Nobody detected the slightest signal coming from the Chandelier itself.

He used his blocked-in Shibo Personality to help integrate the calls. It was pleasant, having a kind of interior servant who could listen to one transmission while Toby paid attention to another.

Quath could do that, all by herself, Toby knew. The alien's mind was organized differently, so that it processed incoming information in parallel. Quath said that she had "subminds." They did their assigned jobs, kind of the way Toby could gnaw an apple and read a book at the same time. But Quath's subminds stored it all and could feed it back.

So Quath would have been perfect for this job—only she wouldn't come along. <I cannot witness so close-stitched a homecoming,> the big alien had sent.

Killeen had explained that this Chandelier was not in any sense Family Bishop's home, since it was incredibly ancient. Still Quath wouldn't budge. She sent something about "intimate observances" and would say no more.

Toby's Shibo Personality emerged, a tickling presence.

> ***All flyers are in optimal position, the 3D scan shows. No unexplained electromagnetic emissions. The Chandelier appears dead.***

Toby was used to Shibo giving him straight, impersonal stuff. She had been a good friend while alive, but her Personality was reserved. She had not mentioned his conversation with Killeen, either. He said to her in his mind, "Say, do you think this is a good idea?"

> ***Not particularly. Mechs probably expect such a magnificent site to be visited now and then. And mechs plan far ahead.***

"What would you do?"

> ***Send in one person. Less risk.***

"Ummm, sounds reasonable. Not our style, though."

> ***Family Bishop has always been impetuous. Perhaps that is why you have survived.***

Toby remembered that Shibo had come to them from Family Knight, after that Family had been nearly killed off by the mechs. She had been born into Family Pawn. "Well, I've always wanted to see a Chandelier. I s'pose we all do."

> ***Mechs know that, too. But I suspect your father has motives beyond curiosity.***

"Such as?"

Only a guess. We shall see.

This calm, mysterious distance was typical Shibo. Most Aspects were eager to speak, to be involved again in real-world hustle and bustle. Shibo had a serenity not shared by Isaac and the others. Maybe that was an attribute of Personalities in general, but Toby suspected it was just a deep feature of the remarkable woman she had been. Though his true mother was still a firm, resonant memory, Shibo had been a mother to him in the long years of Family wanderings.

Toby shrugged and reported that the flyers were positioned, swarming like bees around an elephant.

Killeen nodded curtly and ordered,—Teams in!—

Flyers all around the Chandelier angled in. There was no visible movement in response.

The flyers slipped into open entrances. Toby sorted out the transmissions and brought the most important to Killeen's attention. There was continual cross talk. Bishops were a gabby lot:

—Looks like a big open auditorium here. Some burn damage.—Yeah, must've been fighting all along this passage. Big gouges out of the walls.—

—A whole section smashed in here.—

—All in vacuum. No air pressure.—

—Burned-out living quarters. From the door heights I'd say they were short people.—

—No signs of recent use, I'd say.—

—Right. I just ran a sample on some burned furniture in an apartment. My Aspect says that the isotope dating makes this to be *old*—twenty thousand years, at least.—

—Anybody find any records?—

—No. Somebody sure scraped this place clean.—

—I'm picking up traces of electrical activity. Something still works here.—

Killeen broke in curtly.—Proceed carefully. There may be mechs in there.—

Toby didn't think it likely that mechs would stay in a human artifact, even a glorious ruin like this. But then, he had less experience than his father and the other Bishop veterans. He knew the long history of betrayals, of agreements broken, of ambushes and raids and casual obliteration as just that—history. These men and women had lived through plenty of it; some were over a hundred years old and still fighting, still vigorous and adamant about giving any margin to mechs.

—God, they fought all through here.—

—Yeah, smashed. Stripped clean.—

—Somebody pulled out all the metals. Looks like mech scavenging. Same typical grappler marks.—

—A graveyard of a city.—

—They clean stripped it. Like Blaine Arcology back on Snowglade, 'member?—

Toby remembered, all right. He had hiked there, taking two days, on his first major outing with Killeen and his grandfather, Abraham. Blaine Arcology was a reverential place for Bishops, worth a half-day detour from their target, a mech factory that housed usable foodstuffs. The colossal ruin had awed Toby. They had camped there overnight, even though Abraham grumbled about the danger of mech ambush. He had wandered the smashed streets, reading hints of former lives among the shadows. The Arcology had seemed to him a place of privacy, silence, space, and of memories forever lost. Memories of busy avenues and neighbors, of long afternoons with time to waste, of barefoot fun and whispery elegance—a *city*. He had tried to say as much to Killeen and Abraham, and while Toby talked about the majesty of the place both the men had looked away, faces pinched and brooding. When Toby had asked why, Abraham had said sadly that an old Aspect of his had just reminded him that Blaine was really not an example of the High Arcology Era at all. It had served as a kind of refugee camp, after the truly great places had been smashed. And Killeen had nodded, too.

A refugee camp. Yet Citadel Bishop would have fit in its sports stadium.

That moment long ago came back to Toby. Then it was blown away, the way the wind carries conversations and shreds them.

—There's everything here. Concert halls, markets, factories, hospitals, huge shafts for elevators.—

—And blasted parks. Musta been pretty once.—

—Wait a sec, there's an airlock here.—

Killeen sent,—Test it for activity.—

—Nothing electrical I can pick up.—

—Try the seals.—Killeen said.

—They seem okay. Intact.—

Killeen sent,—Leave a robot mechanical at the controls and stand back, far back. Then pop the seal.—

—Yeasay, doing it . . . —

Other reports came in, of more damaged vistas. Toby listened intently, filtering out the repetitious reports. His attention focused on the team at the airlock. He ached to be in there with them, looking around.

—We opened the lock. It's cycling.—

Killeen sent,—What's the gas?—

—Ordinary air. Chem-sensors say it's okay, not poisoned.—

Cermo scowled next to Toby.—Air's still good after all this time?—

Toby said—Maybe the air system still works.—

—And maybe other things work, too,—Killeen said uneasily.

From the airlock team came,—Seems all right. Cap'n, can we go in?—

Killeen sent,—Yeasay. But take it slow.—

Cermo said,—Cap'n, there are only three in that team. They can't help but get spread out.—

—Right.—Killeen hesitated only a second.—But we don't have any reserves. You go, Cermo. Provide comm to us.—

Toby said,—Dad, I'll do that. I can monitor just as well while I'm moving.—

Killeen shook his head. To Toby's surprise, Cermo put in,—He'll be all right with me. I could use the help.—

Toby realized that Cermo might be trying to defuse the tension between the two of them, by getting Toby out from under his father's thumb. Maybe his father wanted that, too, because Killeen looked relieved.—Um. Very well.—Quickly the Cap'n turned his attention to other matters.

Into the Chandelier, Toby's pulse quickening. They followed tracers that pulsed on the inner visors of their helmets. Already *Argo*'s computers had built up a rough three-dimensional map of this vast derelict, using the exploration team's data. They guided Cermo and Toby through dark lanes, down shafts, through the wrecked corridors of far antiquity. They sped through utter blackness, guided by their helmet beams.

Toby caught glimpses of tattered clothing, trashed factories, gutted offices. Each glance was a momentary message of beleaguered lives lost for millennia, known now only by pathetic scraps.

They reached the yawning round airlock. Their helmet beams showed a crewwoman, who waved them on in.—Can you believe it?— she sent.—There was air inside. When we opened the lock, it near blew me away.—

The blackness all around them gave way to a broad, phosphor-lit square. The team was there, working among ranks of machinery. Cermo gave orders for them to search the area. Toby stood, listening to other teams report their findings. They had found nothing as unusual as this.

Toby asked Cermo,—Why you figure the phosphors work here and nowhere else?—

—Maybe there's still a power source in here.—

—After twenty thousand years?—Somebody guffawed.

But there was. A crewman found electricity coursing through conduits high above. Cermo said,—No bodies, so far?—

—Nobody's reported any.—Toby answered.—They're gone, I guess. Evaporated away, like the plants in the parks.—

—But why not in here? I mean, this was sealed.—

Toby wondered why mechs would leave this vault under air pressure, if they were the last ones here. He walked among the ranks of shadowy machinery and puzzled over what it was for. There was a certain cast to the bulky assemblages, a style that was not like the mech machines he had feared and hated all his life.

It struck him that these were *human* machines, by far the largest he had ever seen. He smiled with pride. Men and women had once worked on the scale of mechs. He had lived with the automatic assumption that only the malevolent, intelligent machines could achieve great works. *Argo* was an ancient human work, of course, but it was of the Arcology Era, used to fly between the Hunkered-Down colonies on the far-flung planets. And *Argo* had used many parts scavenged from mechs. These old human artifacts were different. Beautiful, he decided.

Killeen sent,—Team Lambda has found some engraving in a wall. I want full spectro-copies of it.—

Toby had the gear for that.—Yeasay, coming.—

He turned to go and a sudden blaring signal erupted through the comm line.

I AM A BOMB. I AM SET TO EXPLODE IN THREE HUNDRED TIME INTERVALS. **BEEP** THIS MARKS THE BEGINNING OF A TIME INTERVAL. THERE ARE TWO HUNDRED NINETY-NINE TO GO. I AM A BOMB. I AM SET TO EXPLODE IN THREE HUNDRED TIME INTERVALS. **BEEP** THERE ARE TWO HUNDRED NINETY-EIGHT TIME INTERVALS TO GO.

The signal came from somewhere in the vault, Toby's locator told him.—Evacuate!—he called and started for the lock.

It was closing. Cermo was in front of him, moving with a speed and dexterity surprising for his size. Cermo aimed his weapon at the lock and blew off a hinge. The door stopped.

Toby got through the entrance and then stopped.—You figure it's a nuke?—

—Might be,—Cermo sent.—Move!—

—Let's push the lock door back in place. It might contain anything less than a nuke.—

Cermo swore but agreed. They swung the door shut with the help of three other crew. The time wasn't lost anyway, because others were still coming out. The last crewwoman squeezed through and they slammed the bulky steel shut.

Nobody wasted time on breath. They rushed down silent, inky hallways. Teams came streaming out of the Chandelier. Toby got into free space just as the relay transmitter they had left in the vault sent:

BEEP I AM A BOMB. THIS HAS BEEN A WELCOME CONCLUSION TO MY HISTORIC MISSION. I BID GOOD-BYE TO THOSE WHO CREATED ME AND GAVE ME THIS OPPORTUNITY TO SERVE. THANKS ALSO TO THOSE WHO TRIGGERED MY COMPLETING MOMENT. I NOW DETONATE WITH RESOLVE AND ELOQUENCE. **BEEP**

Its transmission shut off.

The Chandelier shook visibly. Spires sheared away. Walls split.

A helical tower cracked. Then it all came apart in slow motion, buckling and fracturing into shards that spun away, tumbling. In the silence of space it was like watching a mountain come apart piece by piece.

Toby watched the debris as their flyer sped away. It had been a close call, but the Chandelier was fracturing with little energy left over.

Argo was already speeding away. They probably wouldn't sustain much damage.

—Whew! We were lucky.—he said.

—Maybe,—Killeen answered.

Cermo said,—I don't think that stuff can really hurt us much.—

—Me neither,—Killeen answered.—But maybe it wasn't supposed to.—

Toby puzzled.—Huh? What else could it have been for?—

—Wish I knew. But anybody who just wanted to kill us wouldn't have given any warning.—

Toby blinked.—And putting it inside an airlock . . . —

Cermo said,—Mechs wouldn't be drawn to an atmosphere. They work better without one. We'd be suckered in, though.—

—So I figure,—Killeen said.—We set off a humans-only alarm.—

They watched in silence the slow-motion wreck of their ancient ancestral home. Toby's oldest Aspects murmured, stirred by memories he could probably never know. He felt also the unspoken anguish in the scattered comm comments. Even though picked clean, there had been a feeling to the place, a taste of what humans had been like many millennia ago. A flavor of antiquity, faint and echoing. Tantalizing, sweet—and then snatched away forever.

—Too bad I didn't get to that engraving,—Toby said.

—Yeasay. Team Lambda got a few quick shots, though.—Killeen scowled, lines deepening in his face.

—I don't get it. Why destroy such a beautiful thing? They didn't even catch us.—

Cermo said,—Dunno. Me, I figure mechs maybe just like busting up anything human. Anything that means something to us.—Killeen said darkly,—Let us hope it is only that.—

5

Ancient Flavors

Toby liked working outside. Grunt work in zero-gravs was more like dancing than real labor, demanding some body-smarts—but there were moments that took plenty of muscle, too.

There was joy in popping out a sweat. He used it to work off his frustrations, which were getting to be many. Even the best skinsuit got pretty swampy after a while, though, and it was a lot of trouble to pee, so you didn't drink anything for hours before going out. That meant your throat dried out and you got by on sips of tomato juice.

This job was tougher. Their passage through the molecular cloud had somehow shorted out some of the ship's sensors. Cermo said it was all those banks of dust. Then the Chandelier explosion had pocked the hull. Most of the debris was small stuff, but each gouge had to be patched. Tedious, messy, and essential, just like most jobs on a starship. When there's only one skin between you and high vacuum, you take care of it.

Toby helped get a crushed antenna back into shape, depending on instructions from a Face he carried. A Face was a trimmed down Aspect, really just a catalog of technical lore and tricks. Toby let the Face tell him which tools to use and electrical connections to make, which left him free to just puff and sweat for a while. Techno-thinking was intricate and hard and he tired of it. But the repair routines went into muscle-memory, so he would be able to do it better next time.

When a break came he took a stroll over the hull while the rest of the work gang rested on their tails. He was beginning to see what his father liked about spending so much time out here, beneath the seethe of sky. A million pinprick fires shone through the blobs and swirls of twilight radiance—dust and gas, tortured into smoldering luminescence by huge electrical currents.

Staring outward for long moments, he could sense the slow churn of the entire disk of the galaxy. Everything here whirled about a single point that no one could see: the black hole at True Center.

The Eater. As a boy on Snowglade he had seen it, a smoldering presence behind churning molecular clouds. Some legends called it the Eye, from an age when it had glared down on Families like an avenging angel, or devil, or both.

Toby could only glance at the eye-stinging brilliance there—the disk of captured matter that spiraled about the hole. Then he had to look away, or his body's own systems would close down his optical vision, to avoid getting burned out. Still, it was eerie, staring at clouds of dust as they slid into the death grip of that tiny, vicious maw. A mouth that was always hungry, always impatient.

He turned his back on the glare and hiked down into the little valley formed by two bulges in *Argo*'s hull. He was daydreaming, taking in the view—and then stopped short. Quath's honeycomb warren lay in shambles.

And Quath stalked among the ruins. Her double-jointed legs worked in their steel sockets as Quath seized a wall of gray bricks. Alarmed, Toby trotted forward, boots clanging heavily.

—What happened? Did a piece of the Chandelier hit it?—

<No, warm-blooded scavenger.>

—But this much, something big—hey!—

Quath jerked powerfully and the entire wall came apart. Bricks of waste and garbage flew everywhere. Then Toby noticed that despite their tumbling and spinning, the bricks all drifted into neat stacks on the hull, following long, curved paths in zero-gravs. They settled nicely into order with impossible, liquid grace.

—How'd you do that?—

<Nourishment-of-maggots, I fashion my mountain-home of your cast off matter—true. But each has iron, and will adhere to the hull.>

—Okay, but how do you get them to fly apart like that, and go into the right stacks?—

<A craft of mechanics.>

Toby squinted up at the huge form as she broke up another part of her own dwelling. He knew enough about Quath to see that he would get no more explanation of how, so he turned to why. Quath answered, <I do not think my mountain will withstand our trajectory.>

—What trajectory? We haven't decided where to go yet.—

<The soul of a species is best seen from outside. I prepare.>

And then Quath would say no more. She worked quickly and, for her size, with an unlikely deft touch. Toby called to her and got no answer.

He shrugged and walked away, reminding himself not to take this personally. Quath was not a woman in an insect suit. Nor was she an untamed and uncontrollable force of nature. She was just plain alien, and human metaphors didn't apply. That was the hardest thing to remember, when you'd just been snubbed. Toby turned and called back,—So much for your crap-castle, bug-face!—

Quath stopped and waved two feelers at him but said nothing but <[untranslatable]>. Maybe that was an obscene gesture, for Quath's race—but Toby would never know.

He stalked away and took out his irritation by working harder, faster. He was pleasantly tired by the time the job was done, and when he cycled back inside he treated himself to a full shower.

This was three days early, but he felt sorely used by life. He thumbed the nozzle on full bore and selected options of suds and an alcohol spray. By pure luck it was the first day in a cycle and the water was fresh. It didn't smell of other Bishops or of the refilter that never really took away all the odors. He let the wonderful warmth gush over him, tuned the nozzle to pound his muscles and massage his scalp. Back in Citadel Bishop they had lots more water, so much he had even played in a bath of it once. Usually baths were reserved for couples, as part of the wedding ceremony.

He was sorry when his charge was used up and the last dribbles gurgled away. He wouldn't have another such treat for weeks.

He sighed, dropped into his bunk—and his caller chimed. Cermo's voice rang in his left ear. "Report to Command, Toby."

Toby groaned. He and Besen had planned on "resting up" together, which was Family slang for a little mutual bunk time in the free-for-all quarters. Unmarried Family enjoyed a period of complete sexual freedom, before the necessity of childbearing closed in, and Toby had been making the most of it. This feature of shipboard life he liked best—time to indulge the animal within. Well, it would have to wait.

He called Besen and explained. She groaned. "Hey, and I got us time in a zero-grav section, too!"

"Duty calls, my Juliet."

"So you did check that play. See, it's *parting* that's such sweet sorrow."

"In this case, it's staying apart."

"Hurry it up, Romeo. Maybe we can still use the time I booked."

To his surprise, only his father and Cermo were in the Command Center. The two figures seemed dwarfed by the enormous ceramic-faced banks of computers, the arrays of sliding phosphorescent data. Cermo said rather stiffly, "We have need of your Shibo Aspect."

Toby studied his father's face in the shimmer of blue-white data displays, remembering the last time they had talked about Shibo, but Killeen was wearing his firm Cap'n persona. His dark eyes gave nothing away. "Uh, okay. What's up?"

"Two things, really." Killeen was brisk, efficient. "That engraving from the Chandelier, remember? We're trying to decipher it. Give a squint."

SHE,
ON WHOSE BREASTS GREAT RENOWN IS INSCRIBED, BATTLING IN THE
VASTY REALMS OF DUST AND GASSY LORE, BLUNTED MAD ATTACKS.
SHE,
BRAVE-PARTING A TIDE OF GROTESQUES, CONSUMED THE FIVE KINDS
OF LIVING DEAD IN STILL-GLOWING HOLY HEAT.
SHE,
EMBRACER OF MEN AND OF JUST CAUSE, FEROCITY KNOWING HER
BODY WELL, VOYAGED ON TO PLACE IMMUTABLE—THOUGH WEA-
RIED, FEVERED STILL IN ARDOR FOR HUMANITY'S PEARL PALACES.
SHE,
WHOSE STORY SPREADS ACROSS CULTURES OF THE FOLK, BURNS
STILL, AND SLITHERS THROUGH THE TICK OF TIME, AND CONTOR-
TIONS OF UR-SPACE.
SHE,
STERN DEFENDER OF THE PEARL PALACE, QUITTED HER ANIMATION
AND NOW DWELLS IN THE TANGLE OF TIME WHERE ETERNITY ABIDES.
HER BODILY FORM EVADED, SOLE SUPREME SOVEREIGNTY MEDITATES
IN EVENT-SPUN DRIFTS, BOWEL-DEEP, FLECKED BY DELICIOUS
TONGUES OF UR-HISTORY AND OMEGA-FUTURE.
SHE,
IS AS WAS AND DOES AS DID. SCENT-LADEN, FLESH-FULL, AS IS
WRITTEN AND SHALL BE RENDERED FORTH IN THE RESTORATION TO
COME.
SHE,
SHALL RISE AS SHALL WE ALL WHO PLUNGE INWARD TO THE LAIR
AND LIBRARY. FULLNESS OF GREAT DURATION, IS NOW AND EVER
SHALL BE.

"Ummm." Toby was mystified. He summoned up his Shibo Personality. Her cool presence paused a long moment and then said,

This "she" must've been quite a woman.

Killeen said, "We can't make sense of some parts of this."

Toby frowned. "What's it mean, that every other line is written backwards?"

Cermo shrugged. "Some kinda code?"

He felt Shibo meshing with his oldest Aspects, calling up shreds of memory. She summed these and reported:

This is an ancient skill. I saw such when I was a girl with Family Knight. This was written to be read digitally. Instead of returning to the left to scan each line, a digital mind simply reads the characters in backwards order as its field of view returns, right to left.

Toby relayed this. Cermo said, "Seems screwy."

It saves time. Our practice of reading only after returning to the left each time is for simple minds.

Killeen said doubtfully, "Chandelier folk could do such?"

Family Knight did, once. Their ancient scrolls were writ so. I saw some as a girl.

Toby repeated this. He could see by the compression of Killeen's face that it had great weight for him. It was the burden of all the Families to live out lives of flight and desperation, knowing that once their kind had strode proud and tall at Galactic Center. Chandelier-makers, explorers, hunters of vacuum beasts, riders of great storms. But that was so long ago now that even legends only whispered about the heights of such far antiquity.

"There was none such at the Citadel of Family Bishop," Killeen said begrudgingly.

Toby recalled seeing a wall in the ruined Blaine Arcology that held some such message on it. He started to say so but Cermo cut him off with a wave. "Look, however they slung their alphabet, I can see this plain. It's a story about a woman who led humanity. They won. But what's all this stuff about pearl palaces?"

"I figure that's the Chandelier," Killeen said distantly.

"Makes sense," Toby said, quickly referring to his Isaac Aspect. "That word 'pearl' means a jewel—a kind of foggy one, like thin cat beer."

This time Shibo was puzzled.

What is "cat beer"?

"Milk. Sorry, it's a kid's joke." Toby whispered to her.

He had said it without thinking. He wanted to be taken seriously here, not as just a funnel for Shibo's expertise. He had not let Cermo or Killeen have direct access to Shibo through comm interface, which would have been an easy techno-trick. Then they would have just bypassed him completely, a kid left out of adult business.

"There's a lot I don't understand about this engraving," Killeen said. "First, can you get it writ right for us?"

For Shibo it was easy. In a few moments she relayed to one of the big wall screens.

SHE,
ON WHOSE BREASTS GREAT RENOWN IS INSCRIBED, BATTLING IN THE VASTY REALMS OF DUST AND GASSY LORE, BLUNTED MAD ATTACKS.
SHE,
BRAVE-PARTING A TIDE OF GROTESQUES, CONSUMED THE FIVE KINDS OF LIVING DEAD IN STILL-GLOWING HOLY HEAT.
SHE,
EMBRACER OF MEN AND OF JUST CAUSE, FEROCITY KNOWING HER BODY WELL, VOYAGED ON TO PLACE IMMUTABLE—THOUGH WEARIED, FEVERED STILL IN ARDOR FOR HUMANITY'S PEARL PALACES.
SHE,
WHOSE STORY SPREADS ACROSS CULTURES OF THE FOLK, BURNS STILL, AND SLITHERS THROUGH THE TICK OF TIME, AND CONTORTIONS OF UR-SPACE.
SHE,
STERN DEFENDER OF THE PEARL PALACE, QUITTED HER ANIMATION AND NOW DWELLS IN THE TANGLE OF TIME WHERE ETERNITY ABIDES. HER BODILY FORM EVADED, SOLE SUPREME SOVEREIGNTY MEDITATES IN EVENT-SPUN DRIFTS, BOWEL-DEEP, FLECKED BY DELICIOUS TONGUES OF UR-HISTORY AND OMEGA-FUTURE.
SHE,
IS AS WAS AND DOES AS DID. SCENT-LADEN, FLESHY-FULL, AS IS WRITTEN AND SHALL BE RENDERED FORTH IN THE RESTORATION TO COME.
SHE,
SHALL RISE AS SHALL WE ALL WHO PLUNGE INWARD TO THE LAIR AND LIBRARY. FULLNESS OF GREAT DURATION, IS NOW AND EVER SHALL BE.

"So I was right." Killeen slammed a fist on his desk. "They had a long era when they beat the mechs—see, the 'five kinds of living dead.' I saw that written on a monument, a tomb, years ago—remember? You were both there."

Cermo frowned. "Ummm, I recall something . . ."

Toby said, "I remember. The inscription was about a powerful 'He,' though, and—"

"It was about mechs, for sure," Killeen went on. "And this 'she,' a great leader—they took her away somewhere."

Cermo's brow wrinkled doubtfully. "How's that?"

"Plain as starshine," Killeen said, getting up with muscular energy and pacing before the screen. "See? This 'she' 'voyaged on to place immutable' after her 'bodily form evaped'—evaporated? She'll 'rise as shall we all who plunge inward to the lair and library.' They left the Chandelier, at least some of them. And went somewhere else, this 'lair' where they'd be safe."

Cermo nodded reluctantly. "Yeasay, I remember a tomb. As for the rest . . ."

"It's obvious!" Killeen paced quickly. "Look, I recorded it using one of my Aspects. Here—"

On a screen flashed:

He,
on whose arm fame was inscribed, when, in battle in the vasty countries, he kneaded and turned back the first attack. With his breast he parted the tide of enemies—those hideous ones, mad-mechanical and unmerciful to the fallen.

There was more, and Killeen rattled on, reciting passages and comparing them with the inscription they had seen near a tomb, and none of it made any particular sense to Toby. Some, like *He: Who led Humankind from the steel palaces aloft,* probably referred to the Chandelier Era. Others, such as *He: by the breezes of whose prowess the southern ocean is still perfumed,* must have come from a time when there were oceans on Snowglade, not just the lakes he knew, that shrank every year. But there were plenty, like *He: Who set forth Humanity in the names of the Pieces,* that made no sense at all. And his Isaac Aspect told him that even the folk of the Arcologies were mystified by such wordy relics.

Killeen paced and talked, paced and talked. When his famous ardor came on him like this, he had a hypnotic energy. But Toby could see a quiet frenzy building in his father and did not like the signs.

Cermo intervened, voice smooth and soothing. "Could be, lotsa big fat maybes in there—but that's not the point, Cap'n, 'member?"

Killeen blinked and took a deep breath. "I . . . suppose not. I had hoped that the engraving would give us some way to deal with this tight spot we're in."

Toby tried to keep his voice light and businesslike. "What spot?"

Cermo said to his Cap'n, "We should hold a Gathering."

"Yeasay. I can present our choices to the Family—"

"*What* spot?"

Cermo said, "The explosion in the Chandelier, it was the energy source for a pulse of radiation. We thought it was meant to catch us, but could be the emission was the true intent."

Toby kept his face blank to cover his surprise, the way his father sometimes did. "I didn't pick up anything, on any comm band."

Killeen thumbed up a spectrum plot on a wall screen. "No wonder. It was far up in frequency, way above anything we can see. Gamma rays. And beamed—*Argo* picked it up, just barely."

"Beamed which way?" Toby persisted.

"Outward. Toward some of those places Quath told us to avoid." Killeen gazed somberly at his son.

Toby felt a burst of sympathy for his father. Killeen had taken so much on faith, and now that would all be tested. They had followed Quath's advice ever since their long flight began from Trump. They had gone to that world hoping to make it be New Bishop, thinking they would settle there. But they had been driven out.

And the Family had not even protested when members of Quath's species had followed them—though at a distance, propelling forward a huge glowing instrument of their own gigantic craft. It was somewhere behind them, acting as a kind of rear guard that nobody quite understood. They had swooped and dodged to get this close to True Galactic Center, avoiding obstacles Quath found in the confusing star maps. All on faith, flying nearly blind. Without knowing what strange strategies would work here.

"Burglar alarm," Toby blurted.

Cermo asked, "Huh? The emission?"

"Beamed at somebody who wanted to know when humans returned here," Toby said with more certainty than he felt—a skill he thought of as adult, manly.

Killeen nodded. "Mechs."

"Why not just leave a bigger bomb?" Cermo said. "Kill us total."

Toby spread his hands. "Maybe they thought they'd catch us."

Killeen shook his head. "They master enormous energies. If they wanted to kill, they'd have done the job."

"So why'd they want to catch us?" Cermo asked.

Toby said quickly, "And the explosion, maybe it was just to make us think we had gotten away, that we were okay."

Killeen pursed his lips, still pacing tensely. "Mechs think we're pretty dumb. Could be."

"Something else, too," Toby said, listening to Shibo. "That bomb spoke our kind of talk. Not this ancient lingo."

Killeen stopped pacing and regarded his son with interest. "Yeasay—it didn't rummage around among dialects. Something told it how we talk."

"So . . . they're coming to scoop us up?" Real fear edged Cermo's words.

"Depends on what level mech we're dealing with. The stupid rat-catcher type they used against us on Snowglade—"

"They're not subtle enough," Toby said. "But the Mantis . . ."

Killeen and Cermo exchanged a glance. The Mantis had already loomed into legend for Family Bishop, the most intelligent mech they had ever met. It had hounded them, using its elaborate electronic illusions. They had thought it was just a better killer, but the Mantis itself showed them, in a horrifying moment, how it used humans in its "works of art."

"Y'know," Toby mused, "Quath told me once that the mechs, they don't send their best down to kick us around on the planets. They just use the dregs."

Cermo bristled. "They send 'em, we kill 'em. Mechs big, mechs small, don't matter."

Killeen stared off into space, and Toby knew he was seeing again the long history of humiliations Family Bishop had suffered at the hands of mechs. Together they had witnessed human bodies used by mechs as biomachine parts. As lubricants. As decorations. As bloody, twisted chunks of what the Mantis thought was beautiful.

"Yeasay, Cermo—they could be coming to scoop us up," Killeen said. "Or worse."

"We got to run," Cermo said.

"Yeasay." Killeen turned to a wall screen. It spilled with swirls of brooding dark and smears of blazing luminescence. The plane of the galaxy, alive with deadly energies and shrouded histories.

"But where?"

6

The Song of Electrons

Toby stood on the hull and gazed out, through the gliding stellar majesty toward True Center. The entire galaxy spun about a single cloud-shrouded point. So much brimming brilliance, made to waltz by a hub of remorseless dark.

Already the ship was gaining momentum, cutting across shrouded dust lanes and bringing fresh splashes of light into view. Toby felt a smoldering anger at the mechs who were approaching on blue-white exhaust plumes, driving *Argo* to flee. They were relentless, riding their lances of scalding plasma, an age-old enemy that would hound down any remnant of humanity. They had been just a light-day away, hiding somewhere in the churning murk.

Even in this swirl of stars there was little chance to escape. *Argo*'s long-range scanners had picked up mech exhaust images coming from several directions—cutting off the easy orbits, the ones out and away from the Center.

So their trajectory was being pressed ever-inward. Toward the black hole that squatted at True Center. A trap.

Toby had listened to his Isaac Aspect consult even older, scratchy Aspects, and then go on about the huge dark star, but it all seemed so strange, so impossible. Through ten billion years the galaxy had fed it. Stars had been swept into it by the tides of gravity and dusty friction. Once, civilizations had thrived around those lost suns. As their parent stars were swept inward, to be baked and shredded and devoured, whole alien races had been forced to flee or die.

Isaac's history lessons were pretty sparse about those distant times. Much was imagined, but little known. Some civilizations had escaped, Isaac said. They had made strange, metallic colonies that harvested the great energy resources here. Ahead of *Argo* lay such refuges. Cities of the center—alien, enormous, forbidding. Greater than Chandeliers, and far older.

He shook himself and turned to his task—coaxing Quath in for the Family Bishop Gathering. The bulky alien labored with the last walls of her intricate nest, stacking the bricks in a sheltering nook where two farm domes met.

"Come on, big-bug, it's about to start."

Quath hefted a thick slab without apparent effort. <It is *your* species' ceremony. [untranslatable] I show respect by not attending.>

"It's more like a brawl with rules. Anyway, the Cap'n wants you there to speak."

<An honor I must decline, eater-of-vermin.>

"Look, dung-master, this is *important*."

<More important for you to return inside.>

"Huh? Why?"

<Witness with both your hindbrain and forebrain—the song of electrons.>

Toby followed Quath's double-jointed gesture. Now that he swept his gaze around, he picked out a soft, ivory glow all around *Argo*. It danced and shimmered, like a mist blown by an unseen wind. "Pretty. So what?"

<Those are high-energy electrons which strike our magnetic shields. As they are brushed aside, they emit their own small howls of outrage. Photons of dismay and discomfort.>

"Yeah, life's tough. Still, so what?"

<We encounter many more such electrons now. They are multitudes, near the galactic core. Their radiations will soon make it unsafe for you to walk this hull.>

Toby frowned. He had always thought that *Argo*'s magnetic fields kept all the dangerous stuff away. But such fields could not stop weightless light, and he knew that the really harmful stuff was much higher in frequency, far above what humans could sense.

"You can see the hard radiation?"

<All my species can. We did not evolve on such a comfortable world as you.>

"Ummm. I better get back inside. You're coming too—Cap'n's orders."

<If it is an order, I must obey. My species knows such things as well.>

"Quath, you started tearing apart your wasp-nest and packing it away before we even knew mechs were coming. How come?"

<The tide of events is set.>

"You think so?" Quath never said anything lightly. Or else an alien sense of humor didn't come over that way. For all Toby knew, losing a leg might be a great joke for Quath. Toby had seen her take off one of her own legs once and make a strange sucking sound. He had assumed

Quath had been crying or groaning, but maybe it had been a parlor game.

<There is no way out.>

"Pretty fatalistic, ol' crap-crafter."

<But there is a way in.>

Toby could not extract any further explanation from Quath, and by the time he got the alien inside the Gathering had already started. Aces and Fivers arguing with Bishops—even though they shared a lot of cultural manners and even ancient tales.

Luckily, the first part was a kind of disorganized dance, and music hammered through the large hall where all Family Bishop mingled with people they had picked up from New Bishop, the last world they had fled. A happy mob. Except, of course, for the assigned watch officers—no Family could ever relax entirely.

Toby tried to fall into the mood of a Gathering. Quath wanted to stand in a corner, towering over everyone, eyes gazing into an abstract distance. Toby joined a group-gavotte, remembering the words from childhood.

Put your hand on your hip,
Let your backbone slip.
Snake it at your feet
Motion in the meat
Flip it to your vest
Shake it to the one you love best.

Not too dignified, but then Gatherings often weren't. From watching his father Toby understood the underlying strategy.

Get people loosened up and feeling connected. Encourage them to dance and sing and call up worn memories of celebrations back on the homeworld. Play loud, boisterous music. Roll out the ceramic vats where grains and grapes lingered, making whiskeys and beer and wine. Let the Family get thoroughly into the alcohols. Even though they had enzymes swimming in their bloodstreams that would cut the effectiveness, the drinking did lift their spirits in time-honored fashion, making them more proud, confident—and reckless. Jack up the music a notch. Then confront them with a question that called on their resources, their sense of who Family Bishop was and where they should go.

Toby knew what Killeen was doing, but that was no reason not to enjoy it. He danced with Besen, had some of the crisp fresh wine, let its heady essence swarm up into his head.

Not enough to addle him, though. His own father had faced a big problem with alcohol, in the long time after the death of Toby's mother. Then Killeen met Shibo and got the hard drinking behind him, pulled himself together and then became Cap'n. Toby knew little biology, but he understood that there could be a tendency for the son to carry a potential weakness of the father—so he watched his drinking. He couldn't just depend on the helpful little enzyme friends.

It was a fine Gathering. He was even starting to feel real affection for Cermo. Considering how Cermo had been riding him, that had to be attributed to the alcohol.

Cermo had a creamy chocolate skin, gleaming sugar-rich in the soft lighting. One of the things Toby liked about the Family was that they kept the age-old differences in humans alive. Eyes were brown and blue and black, skins rough or smooth, yellow or pink or chocolate, noses lean and pointed or broad and commanding or perky and upturned. Something in their genes didn't let these differences get ironed out, smoothed away through the generations. It added interest and spice, a flavor of a time when humans adapted to different places by slanting their eyes to see better, smudging their skin to ward off the sun, tapering their faces to keep warm.

He didn't care that nature had done it for them, through slow, natural selection. Differences were like an ancient book, incomprehensible messages from an honored past, worth preserving. His own broad nose and slanted eyes seemed imminently practical. So did his swarthy skin and scratchy beard, just coming in. Inheritances. Deep history.

Then the throbbing music ebbed. Time to decide.

Killeen began to speak. He was not an ornate talker, like some Toby had heard, but his plain, flat way of putting things had a kind of simple eloquence. He told them the hard facts of their predicament. The mechs coming. *Argo*'s fuel reserves. Air and water and fluid balances. Fine for a while, but not enough for an extended, high-boost flight out of Galactic Center and into some possible refuge.

Quath testified to the mech's probable plans. They would box in *Argo*, trap her in the whirlpool near True Center.

Then he used the Family sensorium. Every member saw in one eye the ancient engraving, with its meaning superimposed. Killeen read passages, his voice booming.

" 'Consumed the five kinds of living dead in still-glowing holy heat.' There *was* a time when the mechs fell before us!"

The Family stirred, eyes staring into a dusty past.

" 'She shall rise as shall we all who plunge inward to the lair and library.' "

Killeen stood on a raised platform, dominating the crowd. His voice became more powerful, not by trick of timing but from a fullness of conviction. "They went there. Long ago. Even though she and they were 'fevered still in ardor for humanity's pearl palaces' —they left."

Voices rose in agreement. There was in them a plaintive note, calling for connection with their own fabled history. Some sobbed. Others cursed.

"We are now besieged by mechs. They bear down upon us. True"—Killeen gestured to Quath—"we have allies. Quath's species is following us, too, carrying that huge device of theirs, the Cosmic Circle. Powers we do not master, yes. Methods we cannot comprehend, yes. They are living creatures and offer us aid because of that holy connection, a sharing of all those who arose *naturally* from the very atoms of the galaxy itself."

Hoarse calls of thanks to Quath. Of sputtering, cold-eyed rage against mechs.

He paused, fury trickling away, reason returning to the strong face. "But even with their help, only *we* can decide where we shall go."

Killeen slowly cast his gaze across the faces he knew so well, over three hundred strong. "We all had relatives who died fighting Quath's kind. That time is over. Now we fight alongside those we called the Cybers, and now term the Myriapodia."

Something in his bearing called up that past, and used it in Killeen's cause. Toby could see the effect on the crowd. Killeen was the man who had plunged through a Cyber-carved hole, clean through a planet—and lived. Killeen had ridden inside the Cyber Quath, prisoner—and had gotten away alive. He had talked with a magnetic being who spoke through the sky itself. And still earlier, Killeen had dealt with the Mantis and won them their freedom.

Now all that weight of history pressed down in Killeen's favor. His eyes burned. His grave manner commanded. His people heard.

"We have a choice of turning to fight, against odds we do not and cannot know. Or we can choose to run and hope to escape."

Glittering eyes sweeping them all in. "Is that it? Is that *all*?" Scornful curled lip. "No! No! I say there is a third way—a way opened by this tablet from our own distant ancestors."

Toby growled, seeing how firmly the Cap'n held the room in his grasp. The rolling voice that lapped across Family Bishop was sure, certain—but Toby was not. He saw what was coming with a sense of helpless dread.

"We can follow them—the ancients. Into whatever lair they sought. It may still be there!"

Family stirred, murmured.

"Again, they had powers we cannot match—yeasay. Methods we cannot comprehend—yeasay. So their descendants—our cousins!— could still be there. The Family of Families—'where eternity abides.' What can that mean? What does it promise? Let us go—go and find out!"

From the roar of hot assent that rose and vibrated hard around him, Toby knew they were bound on a desperate course, and though he loved his father and wanted to follow him, the fear that coursed cold through him brought a shameful weakness to his knees.

Why was his father doing this? Where had his caution flown? *He's risking the Family to find out . . . what? About the past. What the Family means.*

His Shibo Personality came forward unbidden. Her pale presence was a soft voice against the hubbub of white-eyed celebration that bubbled joyous all around him, jostling elbows and happy sweat and wrenched mouths.

They do not know what he fully wants. Does even he? I love that man, as much as this shaved-down self I have become can love. I fear him now, too. He promises a lair. He may bring them only a liar.

Frozen Star

Angular antennas reflect the bristling ultraviolet of the disk below. Shapes revolve. They live among clouds of infalling mass—swarthy, shredding under a hail of radiation. Infrared spikes, cutting gamma rays.

Among the dissolving clouds move silvery figures whose form alters to suit function. Liquid metal flows, firms. A new tool extrudes: matted titanium. It works at a deposit of rich indium. Chewing, digesting.

The harvesters swoop in long ellipticals high above the hard brilliance of the disk. As they swarm they strike elaborate arrays, geometric matrices. Their volume-scavenging strategy is self-evolved, purely practical, a simple algorithm. Yet it generates intricate patterns that unfurl and perform and then curl up again in artful, languorous beauty.

They have another, more profound function. Linked, they form a macro-antenna. In a single-voiced chorus they relay complex trains of digital thought. Never do they participate in the cross-lacing streams of careful deliberation, any more than molecules of air care for the sounds they transmit.

Across light-minutes the conversation billows and clashes and rings.

They persist, these primates.

We/You did not attempt their extinction.

Yet.

True; we/you must learn more first.

The trap worked?

The engagement functioned as planned. We/You learned their craft's position accurately when they visited the hulk of their former dwelling.

I/You were right to preserve that structure for these long eras.

It made simple the successful attachment of microsensors.

Direct infiltration?

They were blown onto the primate craft in the explosion. Then they burrowed inside.

This seems a needless bother.

We/You were too hasty, in the past, to merely erase such expeditions which ventured toward the Frozen Star.

A dislikable term. The black hole is far more noble than these words imply.

Yet even it began in the early eras of the galaxy from the seed of a single supernova. It has grown by a million times that original mass, but that does not change its nature.

But frozen*? It lives in fire.*

Only its image in space-time is frozen. To you/us, the swallowed mass takes forever to make its final descent into the throat of oblivion.

Very well; such technicalities bore more than they illuminate.

True, for some portions of you/us.

Yet the primates are still drawn to this nexus. What was that language you/ we cited earlier, to illustrate how they think?

The image was *like moths to the flame.*

Bio logics are so simple. So linear. How can we/you be sure of their processings? Know their minds?

You/We cannot.

But with resources—

As you/I must face, there are matters which you/we cannot know even in principle.

Memory returns—yes. Some truths can never be proven within any logic system.

I/We did not refer to so obvious a theorem. Blind spots lurk in our very way of comprehending the universe. For these no one can compensate.

Surely you/I do not suggest that our/your kind share blindnesses with such as these primates!

All sentient forms have ways of filtering the world. In this all are alike.

Surely this does not mean that you/we cannot understand lesser forms and their primitive worldviews in their entirety?

Perhaps it does.

Lack of comprehension in such a grave matter is troubling.

Enough musing. As a practical matter alone, you/I oppose destroying this latest primate incursion. It would cost greatly.

This refers to the quasi-mechanicals.

They follow the primate craft and protect it.

We/You have dealt with their kind before.

They have greater craft than the humans. You/We have suffered from their skills.

They are tools! We/You use the quasi-mechanicals to track the humans.

They carry a hoop of sheared discontinuity. This makes tracking simple. But it would make a most disagreeable weapon, if turned against us/you.

I might remind us/you/them that we/you possessed several discontinuities—once. Admittedly they were lost in the assault upon the Wedge in the era e {+[~ ¦]}.

A grave mistake, one many of us/you opposed.

You/I need not relive that error.

Well spoken, as the one/many who made it.

Such distinctions are meaningless. The experience has been absorbed into all our selves.

Lessons unlearned still bring pain.

No one could have anticipated that the Wedge would swallow, digest, and then use the discontinuities, to build itself further. To make itself even more difficult to penetrate.

Caution would have saved us/you this instructive lesson of ours/yours.

You/We now understand that no one/many can even in principle know the stochastic geometry of the Wedge interior.

Excuses are useless now. The price will be great if we attack the quasi-mechanicals and their discontinuity.

You/I agreed, long ago, to use humans against the quasi-mechanicals. Yet we/you now find that they seem to have formed an alliance. This we/you could not anticipate. Carbon-based life has protocols we/you do not know. Need not know.

I/You wish it were so. But they were here before our kind and—

Many of us/you reject that thesis.

How can you/I? Organic forms arose first.

There are philosophies which hold that metal and ceramic were the original materials, shaped in electrolytic discharges, organized by accretion of clay and ion. The carbon-based forms devolved from that.

Historical records rebuke such theories.

Even so, your/our precious records still cannot tell us why we should fear the humans. Why especially humans? There were other carbon forms.

Which you/we eradicated.

With no remorse.

Conceded. But your/our ingrained drivers say that our kind must fathom the humans.

I/You urge that we/you at least damage them a bit. To reduce their powers.

Stay away from the discontinuity.

The human ship is moderately protected but we/you can produc-

tively damage it. There is no need to let them pass unharmed.

Detecting their craft among the galactic disk debris works only intermittently. Further, the quasi-mechanicals and their discontinuity warp the entire region, making precise location difficult.

Action is crucial! You/We know that they have conversed with one member of the magnetic kingdom.

That is an unfortunate turn. It confirms the information conveyed by a submind.

Which was this/us?

We/You delegated study of the remaining primates to ¦>A<¦. It wrapped itself around the planet of these primates' origin.

And reported little of use.

True. But ¦>A<¦ arranged for the primates to believe that they had their own ship, and freedom of movement. This made it far simpler—given the primates' psychology-sets—to use them. They formed an alliance with the quasi-mechanicals, which brought them here.

Why involve the quasi-mechanicals at all? All this history obscures more than it illuminates.

They may know what the primates do not.

That is an infinite amount.

I refer to what you/we do *not* know. What we seek.

Without knowing quite what that mysterious stuff might be. I tire of such obscurations. Fetch this ¦>A<¦, that I/we might dip into it.

Done. Light-travel time will delay ¦>A<¦ In the interval, we should do more.

Then you/we concede that humans should be pruned, reduced.

I/You suggest that we lay another trap for them? Something to draw them in, give us a known vector for them.

That might clarify the basic issue.

Which is?

What do they seek here? Carbon-based forms wilt under the sling of hard radiation.

True, this is not their province.

The deeper concern is, why do we/you wonder about them so? When we/you should simply kill them.

In other words, why do I/we exist? Is a critical voice necessary? Is our divided intelligence here simply to irk you/we?

Enough rumination. Act!

Part II

THE EATER OF ALL THINGS

1

Hard Pursuit

Toby eyed Besen warily. Why couldn't she leave him alone?

Like most women, she assumed that talking about things that bothered you, getting it all out, made them better. Obviously. Automatically.

Toby's experience was that pretty often that just made them worse. Bringing vague, smoky feelings into the glaring open daylight, sharpening them up bright and shiny with words, making them more concrete—well, then the problems looked even harder. At least to him.

He sighed. They were eating in the clattering, chattering, communal cafeteria. All around them people were murmuring earnestly, the big room alive with excited speculations about their mission.

It had been a week since Killeen's dramatic speech at the Gathering. A week spent hammering their way in toward the blazing, star-swarming True Center. A week when *Argo* throbbed and lurched and rumbled in the buffeting plasma winds. A week that people seemed to be enjoying.

Pulse-pounding adventure was better than sitting on your haunches, mulling over matters. Family Bishop was tired of the soft life in *Argo.* A wonderful ship, a grand inheritance from their distant, time-dimmed ancestors, sure—but in the end just a smart can. In Toby's judgment, Bishops weren't at their best when they were cooped up with nothing better to do than talk. Like right now.

"I appreciate your asking and all," Toby said at last, struggling to be diplomatic. After all, Besen had been trying to cajole him out of his moody silence. "Don't get me started, though."

Besen smiled sympathetically. "Sometimes you close up tight as a vacuum seal."

"There's a lot of adrenaline pumping lately, that's all."

"Why, sure." She looked startled, her lips canted in puzzlement. "We're leaving those mechs way behind."

"Huh!" He snorted. "A rat in a cage can dash back and forth all it wants."

"We're not caught!"

"I don't see any way out—do you?"

"Plenty. We haven't even sighted the disk around the black hole yet. There may be room to hide, then—"

"The mechs know this place. They've got telltales planted around here, for sure. Smart snoopers."

"We don't *know* that."

"It's a good bet. Something at True Center has been a fixation of mechs for a long time—Quath says so."

"You believe everything that big collection of pants says?"

"Sure do." Toby shot back. "At least Quath doesn't try to cheer me up."

Besen frowned prettily. "Ummm. You *are* down in the mouth."

"I'm not celebrating, is all." Toby sipped his lotus juice and picked up a grain cube. He rapped it against the table and a small white weevil came squirming out. "Only way to get these bugs out, far as anybody knows," he said with disgust, sweeping it away.

"It was that Erica, she let them get free."

"Easy mistake to make when you can't read the directions."

"She could've asked her Aspects!"

Erica had mistakenly let the self-warming vial of frozen soil-tenders escape years ago, but their daily irritations reminded everybody and brought her name up like a curse.

Toby was sympathetic. Who could have known that the ugly squirmers would pop out of their container, all ready to start eating?—which was, after all, their job. They startled poor Erica into dropping the vial. Who could guess that then they'd get into all the grain crops? The worms belonged among the vegetables and apple trees, just as the inscription said, in some dead language. Just Erica's bad luck—and theirs—that she was in the grain dome when she opened the cylinder. He shrugged. "She'd been working hard seeding."

"*I* think the Cap'n should've whipped her for it."

"He doesn't like whipping."

"What a Cap'n likes and doesn't like, that doesn't matter," Besen said stiffly. "What's good for the Family, that comes first."

"Sure. And a smart Cap'n gets his crew all fired up about what *he* wants."

Besen blinked. "Oh, so you're saying Cap'n's got us dancing his dance, only we're hearing different music?"

"Could be."

"And you don't want to say anything in public? Out of loyalty?"

"I don't like to go against him."

"Well, you'd sure be unpopular."

"Yeasay—and I got to admit, everybody's spirits are running pretty high." He gestured around at the cafeteria, jammed with animated faces. There was an electric smell of skittering excitement. People so long on the run greeted a hard pursuit with elation; the thrill of familiar danger.

Besen's lips pursed with concern. "You really don't think this is just a way of getting away from the mechs, do you?"

"I don't know what it's really about." Toby rapped his grain cube angrily. Another weevil fell out onto the table. With relish he squashed it with his thumb. "Pays to be careful, is all."

Besen smiled. "Look twice for weevils?"

"Weevils can be anywhere."

Besen gathered herself visibly and tried to shift their mood. "Let's go up to observation, see if we can spot any."

"Great." He tossed aside the grain cube, then thought again, rapped it a third time—no more weevils—and bit in. "Umm, not bad—when you're starving."

"You're always starving. And since the sail-snake and the rest, we have plenty to eat."

"Let's go." Toby was grateful to her for giving him an exit from an uncomfortable conversation. He didn't like his brooding to color the mood of the ship, not when his father had pulled everybody together so well, had them putting in long hours of grunt labor and smiling about it.

They made their way up the broad helical ramp at *Argo*'s core. All crew were working harder now, dealing with the agro domes. The level of radiation from outside was climbing by the hour. Smoldering infrareds, sharp ultraviolets, unseen spectra biting at the crops. They had polarized the domes to the max, but stinging energies still got through. So it was a relief to forget all that, to slump into the netting of an observation chamber and watch the stunning brilliance outside.

In the cool, dim core of the ship the observation room was crowded and Toby could not get a good clear view. The field of glowing stars was confusing, crisscrossed by eerie splashes of radiating gas. Then the Bridge switched to a Doppler-shifted frequency, and details leaped out. Going to blue-rich frequencies picked out things moving toward *Argo* and dimmed everything else.

And there they were: brilliant pinpoints of blue, eight of them evenly spaced around a circle.

"Impossible to miss," Toby murmured.

"The mechs must not care whether we notice," Besen said.

"Or else they really want us to."

"Why would they? More effective to sneak up, I'd think."

"Maybe they want to spook us."

"Into doing what?"

"Maybe just what we're doing," Toby said grimly.

"Hey, we're gettin' away from them!" a big, hawk-nosed woman protested on Toby's left, gouging him with a sharp elbow. She was an Ace, from the wastelands of Trump. Trained to follow her Family leader.

"Yeasay, throwin' dust in their faces," a man joined in. A Fiver.

"We can outrun any damn mech," another woman announced proudly. Her accent was of Family Deuce, so thick Toby could barely understand her.

Toby gritted his teeth. "Yeasay, yeasay. I was just wondering—"

"Not right, Cap'n's *son* goin' on like that." The hawk-nosed woman's elbow poked him again.

"Sorry, brothers and sisters," Toby said, though he was getting irritated. "Uh, 'scuse me."

He got up and worked his way out of the press of bodies. Everybody seemed to be looking at him, sour-faced. Or else avoiding his eyes. Besen followed, whispering, "That old hag, she's a flap-mouthed gossip. All those Trump Families are."

Toby was already feeling bad about the incident, and he stopped before leaving the room to catch another glimpse of the screen. Family Bishop members were murmuring, speculating, even laughing—and not just among the Snowglade folk, either. They argued and elbowed and laughed with the Trump Families, too. An electric smell came from the crowd, a fidgety excitement.

It struck Toby that the room was jammed not so much because they wanted to see the gaudy pictures, but to provide a place to gather, gossip, and grumble. All to sharpen their sense of themselves as a fragile human Family in the face of the abyss outside.

That was essential—holding together. *Argo* held mostly Bishops, from Snowglade, but also Families of the planet they had just left, which its natives called Trump. Those Families had names Toby didn't understand—Aces and Deuces, Jacks and Fivers. There were Queens, though, which by logic should have had the same customs and history as the Family Queen of Snowglade. But they didn't.

Killeen called these Trump Families the Cards. They were fiercely loyal and prone to follow hot-eyed leaders. Back on Trump some had obeyed the crazy man who called himself His Supremacy, a fierce-faced type the Bishops had finally had to kill. Somehow this had meant that the Cards then transferred their loyalty to Killeen.

It made no sense, but then, not much about Trump did. Toby flatly disbelieved the idea that the Cards had gotten their names from some ancient game. Maybe a game had been made up using those names, sure. But Families were ancient and hallowed and not the stuff of trivial matters.

Still, the Trumps were a bit hard to take, butt-headed and ignorant. But the Snowgladers were no prize, either, when you looked close.

Rooks liked to blow their noses by pinching the bridge of the nose and letting fly into the air. They laughed if anybody was in the way. The hawk-nosed woman was a Rook, true to form.

On the other hand, Pawns saw nothing wrong with taking a crap in full view of anybody who happened by. A perfectly natural function, they said. What's to be embarrassed about?

Knights burped and farted at the most formal occasions—they didn't even seem to notice doing it.

Bishops spit whenever they felt like it, which was pretty often.

Rooks preferred to pee on plants, maintaining that since this was part of the Great Cycle of Life, it must be good for them.

And Kings would cough smack in your face, smiling after they did it. Some said that in the old Citadel days the lost Family of Queens had even made love in public, feet pointed at the ceiling, rumps thrusting in the air free as you please. They had some sort of theory about doing it as a show of demented social solidarity. Toby didn't really believe that, it was utterly fantastic—but who could truly say what people of the deep past had believed and done?

Still, the Snowglade Families overlooked these differences, acts that seemed to others like gross social blunders, and held together. And aside from minor incidents, they extended the same hand to the Trumps, even if they were butt-stubborn and ate with their mouths open. The Family of Families.

Toby knew he had an obligation to keep the social glue in place. Not that he had to like it. He smacked a fist into his palm as he walked away from the jammed room.

Concerned, Besen asked, "She really got to you?"

"Naysay. Forget it." But he knew he wouldn't.

2

The Shredded Star

Toby missed having Quath live outside. Anything that big should be free beneath the stars, not closed in.

He was sure of this despite knowing that Quath's kind had evolved out of a burrowing species that liked to dig in snug and tight beneath the ground. How such a race developed intelligence was a riddle. It seemed unlikely that something that wormed into dark, smelly crannies and ventured out to hunt for game would need much in the way of smarts. On the other hand, he reflected, humans had holed up in caves a lot, or so Isaac said. What made a creature develop intelligence was a deep question. After all, mechs came to have quick minds and nobody remembered when or how. Not even Isaac.

But the real reason Toby thought Quath should be outside was that Toby now had no excuse to go hull-walking himself. He felt an itchy, restless energy that he couldn't erase with workouts in zero-grav. At least when he did visit Quath, it was in spaces so big that Toby could practice his low-grav skills.

At the moment Quath was in the abandoned agro dome. The high arch reflected back Toby's huffing and puffing as he did rebounds off the walls. He would coast across the dome, maybe try to bank a little in the ventilator winds. Zooming toward the opposite wall, he pinwheeled his arms in mid-flight to bring his legs around, so that they could absorb momentum and rebound like coiled springs. A lot more fun than lifting dead weights, like some kind of demented machine.

Quath stood at the dome floor's center, eyes swiveling to follow Toby's ricocheting. She sent a hissing note of derision:

<You make much needless effort.>

"I wouldn't expect a giant cockroach to understand."

<My people would never sup in your foul kitchens, as did roaches.>

"You eat stuff that would gag any self-respecting pest."

<My people once hunted such as you for an occasional stimulating mouthful.>

This startled Toby. He grabbed a steel strut and clung to it, panting. "Really?"

<They were native to our world and of the order primate, as you call yourselves. Not so skilled as your kind—not hunters. They smacked their lips over blue-green worms that thronged in brittle trees.>

"Were they, well, like us?"

<Intelligent? No. They had thin little arms and legs, like you. Also the same fixed eyes, each locked into a side of their heads. They could not revolve those heads all the way around, either. Very limited creatures—like you. But they tasted wonderful, and their spines, heated long over a fire, snapped open to emit a famous blue odor. To suck the thick, crisp marrow from the blackened bones was a great delicacy.>

"Ugh. I'm trying hard to think of you as a buddy, big-bug, but if you go on like this—"

<It was an honor to be even a small morsel for The People.>

Toby could sense the capitals in Quath's hissing mind-voice and decided to not pursue the matter. Quath was serious. Maybe it was common for intelligent beings anywhere to think of themselves as the crown of creation—The People—and everybody else as a smart animal at best. Savvy smarts and egomania went hand in hand. Or pincer in pincer.

After all, suppose Quath had been a thousand times smaller. It wouldn't matter that she was supersmart—if Toby shook her out of his bedroll, he would step on her without a thought. He certainly wouldn't inquire into what she thought about the nature of life.

"I think I could pass up honors like that. Anyway, many-eyes, you seem to have settled in here okay."

<I hope my excretions may be of help in enlivening the soil here.>

"So generous of you. Look, I was sent here to see if you can figure what your own folks are doing in their ships."

<I do not know. Though I can guess.>

"They're still hauling that huge ring. Only it's glowing more, a kind of ivory."

<They carry their great burden as a defense against the mechs. Some of our aged texts suggest a further role for it, as well.>

"It sure seems to keep them away, all right. But why are your people gaining on us?"

<They may be needed. The cusp moment approaches.>

"Uh, what's a cusp?"

<A sharp point in an otherwise smooth curve, my amusing mote.>

"More geometry. Between Isaac and his numbers and you with your always using math talk, I don't know—"

<Properly considered, all reality is geometry.>

"Oh yeah? Look, I bite into an apple, it tastes real good. Where's the geometry in that?"

<It is of the [untranslatable].>

Toby hated it when Quath said something and then the programs in his head, and in Quath's too, couldn't make enough sense between them to get the job done. All that came through was a fizzy blurt and a bland, flat [untranslatable]. "Okay, then where's the geometry in a kiss, huh?"

<It is simple from the view of my kind. Relations taste of the [unknown] and [untranslatable]. Anything else would make no [unknown].>

"Oh, glad it's so obvious. How silly of me."

<My program senses that there is something more to your speech pattern.>

"Yeasay, we call it 'sarcasm.' "

<I cannot understand such a pattern.>

"Let's just call it [untranslatable], bug-boy."

<I believe I understand. To us perhaps it is like [unknown].>

"Aaahhh!"

This was driving Toby up the wall—literally. He was glad he could work out his frustration by climbing through the struts of the dome, leaping across wide spans, burning calories to clear his mind. It was getting hot in here—hot all through *Argo,* in fact. The domes were absorbing radiation from the astronomical fireworks outside.

Stinging sweat dripped into Toby's eyes. He clambered over struts and beams, swung in the nearly zero-grav, and let go. He spread his arms and beat against the air, flapping like an awkward bird, and slowly fell toward Quath. The alien caught him at the very last moment before he would have smacked painfully on the deck. "Oooof! Thanks."

<You pretend to be a kind of being you are not.>

"That's part of being human, you ol' giant grub."

<There is an element of that in us as well. Otherwise we would not have spanned the stars in search.>

"In search of what?"

<Of [untranslatable].>

"Oh no, not again!"

<I think it is knowledge of the things we cannot say which makes us alike, tiny thinker.>

Toby scuffed up some dead soil with his boot, sending a shower of gray dust spurting up into the low-grav dome. He still had some irritations to work out, some thinking to do about his father. He leaped and swung up on one of Quath's extended telescoping arms. "Maybe I—"

—Toby! Bring Quath to the Bridge, right away.—

Killeen's sharp voice cut into his concentration so abruptly that Toby let go of the arm, coasted, and thumped back into the dirt. "Okay. But Quath won't fit in—"

—Get moving!—

It turned out that Quath could scrunch down in the corridor outside the Bridge, bend two eye-stalks around the entrance, and see most of the wall screens. Quath looked uncomfortable, her steel-jacketed legs cocked at odd angles and wedged against bulkheads, though she said nothing. Killeen wanted Quath to try more communication channels with his own kind, the Myriapodia. "After all, I spent days trapped in her belly, once," Killeen said casually.

Toby blinked. His misgivings aside, he had to remember that his father had been through horrendous adventures with Quath. Maybe they communicated with each other in ways he didn't fully appreciate.

Killeen assigned several Bridge Lieutenants to help the alien with technical problems, using *Argo*'s long-range antennas.

The Bridge buzzed, but Killeen kept good ship's discipline, and the excitement remained controlled, visible mostly in pinched faces and narrowed eyes. The great wall screens showed scenes that shifted with dizzying speed. The ivory hoop hung suspended between three strange, angular ships. Somehow their shape—geometry again, Toby thought—would have told him that they were of Quath's kind, if he had not known.

The hoop itself flickered and strobed with eerie plays of the spectrum. Flashes of gold and crimson ran along it, then faded into the milky light, like runny stains sinking in a deep chalky sea.

Killeen paced the Command Deck of the Bridge, his boots ringing on steel, hands carefully clasped behind him. Toby knew he did that so nobody could read through fidgeting fingers his own anxieties and tensions; it was the kind of thing that a Cap'n had to do.

Toby felt an upwelling of concern and love for the controlled disguise this big man struggled to maintain. What was the cost? Would anyone ever know?

And there was much to be agitated about, Toby saw. The wall screens flickered. Now they showed a scene so strange it took a long moment to even sort out what he was witnessing. An orange ball hung shimmering against the backdrop of thousands of gemlike stars, not pinpoints crowding the sky. The ball swirled with mottled storms.

Toby had decided it was an oddly colored star, nothing exceptional—until it began to bulge on one side. Blue-hot flares rose all along its fiery edge. The bulge extended, grew banana yellow. It was as though the star was turning itself into a giant egg. But to give birth to what?

Killeen turned and saw his son. Waving him over, the Cap'n said, "Even stars are prey for it."

"Huh? What's happening?"

"Sorry—I forget, watching this for so long, that the lives of stars are not so gripping to everyone."

"I repeat—huh?" Toby was used to his father going off into distracted ramblings.

"This star is about to be gobbled up. See?"

Killeen's fingers danced on a command plate. The view backed away from the star, whose side kept swelling like a fat man's belly at a feast. Then, entering the frame came an angry red smear, spreading like a stain across the wall. "The great disk," Killeen said. "There are Family legends of it. Some call it the Eye of the Eater."

"Disk?" The viewpoint kept backing away.

Toby saw that the orange star was just at the edge of an immense plane of festering, smoldering fire. The plane was moving. Streams of blood red and hot, phosphorescent orange curved away into the distance, slowly circling about some axis far out of view. "Oh—the star's getting sucked in?"

Killeen crossed his arms and watched the doomed sun stretch itself, now rippling with vagrant yellow plumes and dark purple veins. "Yes—but not sucked in by the disk itself. The Eye of the Eater is matter that was sucked in before."

Toby's Isaac Aspect rasped disdainfully,

He is copying ancient lore. Not for a moment do I believe that he understands—

"Hey, who do you think you are?" Toby shot back in a subvocal whisper. "We all repeat what you Aspects and Faces tell us—we sure don't have time to learn all this techstuff!"

Still, if he would credit the classical sources who developed the theories, who made the dangerous measurements—

"Gimmie a break! We'd be nothing but dry bones if we waited for you Aspects to yammer on till you're happy." He stifled Isaac.

Killeen went on, "That mass, it's stuff flowing inward, getting a bit closer every time it circles. So the disk is a highway, that's all. The villain in all this, him you can't see."

Toby got it now. "The black hole? It's pulling this star apart?"

Killeen nodded. "A rare event, and we're just in time for it. The hole swallows stars—but first it likes to chew 'em up."

The panorama grew, retreating from the star, bringing more of the huge, churning disk into view. The Eye of the Eater was a furious red at its rim, working with gales of burnt orange and fierce yellow. Each flaring pinprick was like a momentary bonfire—but Toby reminded himself that these bonfires were bigger than whole planets.

As the vista broadened, he saw that the disk got brighter toward its center. Reds shifted into roiling greens and wrathful purples. Even further in, a hard blue glare seethed. He could barely make himself look as the view swung inward toward eye-hurting brilliance. The disk revolved about a white-hot ball sizzling with blistering energy.

"Where's . . . where's the hole?"

Killeen pointed at the white ball. "In there—but we can't see it, because everything's so hot at the inner edge of that disk."

Isaac put in,

> ***I have conferred with High Chandelier Aspects — they are getting even harder to understand! — and translated their complaints. I must say, I agree with them. Correct attribution is important! — otherwise we lose our past. Now, all this was discovered in 3045 by Antonella Frazier, who even wrote an epic poem about it. A cosmic irony — "that the blackest of places wears a white cloak." I can dimly recall hearing of this great work, and . . .***

He let the Aspect run a little, not really paying attention. Isaac and Killeen's tech-Aspect were probably using the two living humans to subtly compete. Did such chip-beings have jealousy, envy, spite? Of course, he and his father were slinging the techtalk around pretty heavy, maybe trying to impress each other, too. The ancient Aspects were nested inside the newer ones, to ease translation. Their ideas and feelings came through as well, an emotion/data stew.

Small human motives, all dwarfed by the huge scale of events. All this was beautiful, in a weird way, but hard to understand.

Toby jerked himself out of his reverie. "Why's everything so hot?"

"Friction. All that stuff, orbiting tighter and tighter around the hole, it rubs up against other stuff—gas and dust and whatnot. Heats up."

Toby tried to take it all in. The disk glowered, like a red eye with a white bulb smack at the center. A monster's glare. The Eye of the Eater—only you couldn't see the Eater, the blackest thing in the universe. As near as he could understand it, a hole in space. Things drained into it. "So the hole eats stars, I get that, and likes to chew its food first. The disk is all the stuff it's ripped apart lately."

"And it's been eating ever since the galaxy was born."

"You mean—that plate of gas—it was once stars?"

Killeen nodded distantly, staring at a particularly spectacular eruption. A blue-green geyser curled up from the disk like a maddened snake, flicking yellow tongues.

"What better way to serve up food for the Eater, than on a plate?" A grim chuckle.

Toby looked around at the strained faces of the Bridge crew. Lieutenant Jocelyn had been waiting to speak, standing off to the side as if she didn't want to interrupt a conversation between father and son, even on the Bridge. She stepped smartly forward, long hair wafting in the warm ship's air, and said, "Cap'n, we're getting more hull heating."

Killeen instantly snapped out of his musing. "Near the danger line?"

"Not yet, but—"

"Coolant circulating to the max?"

"Yessir."

Killeen scowled. "How's our spin?"

"We've got all the independently moving sections of the ship at their top rotation." Jocelyn's full, muscular frame stayed at strict attention, but Toby could see from her twitching fingers that she was worried.

They were spinning parts of *Argo* to smooth out the heat load. The ferocious rage of that brawling gas could singe their hull, and crisp up the human cargo nicely. Toby recalled Quath's gourmet comments about cracking open carefully cooked primate bones, savoring the marrow. He shuddered.

Killeen smacked a fist into his palm, a momentary release. "I don't see what more we—"

<We are now needful of the Besik Bay,> came the fizzy speech of Quath, beamed over general head-comm.

The Bridge crew turned as if one. They stared at the half-seen alien who stood absolutely still in the corridor outside.

Killeen was the first to speak, with sardonic humor. "I wondered when you would begin to spill your lore."

Quath's two eye-stalks rattled against the hatchway. <You are delicate grubs, unable to take the heat. Should you perish from being toasted here, I would grow lonely.>

Killeen laughed. "Glad to know you care so much. Those antennas we erected—I suppose your new link with your ships works better?"

<I speak well and [unknown]. You cannot glimpse the full [untranslatable] of what it means to converse with others who truly understand.>

"Well, we're learning." Killeen grinned. Toby could see his father relish the conversation, his face losing its lined tension.

Partially.

<You are clever, for ones so stunted.>

"We don't need all that extra mass you lug around."

<Wisdom comes from accumulation. Mites do not know this.>

"You look like you've grown some more eyes, since I saw you last time."

<I am of the Myriapodia, not limited to your feeble two viewing holes. We watch, slit-eyed, many-orbed. There are many abundant visions in this wracked place. But I have no need for more legs, for we do not run from even the most fierce of dangers.>

Toby knew the word "Myriapodia" simply meant "many-legged," but the funny trilling way Quath sounded the word carried an air of awe and pride, too. Killeen had told Toby to get here in a hurry, then had ignored Quath completely. Toby was beginning to see that Killeen had different ways of dealing with the alien, maybe better ones.

"This Besik Bay. You want to hide there, many-eyed?"

The crew murmured. Toby knew they all suspected that they were being used by the Podia for some murky purpose, and this brought that question close to the surface again. But what choice did they have now?

Quath rattled her eye-stalks again. <The Philosophs believe it wise.>

"Ummm—diplomatic of you. But I asked what *you* think."

<The name itself calls up worn fables, but little information. Ancient expeditions of Myriapodia found it so labeled—apparently by humans.>

Toby put in, "Besik? No Family of that name."

<It refers to some ancient human site, a refuge—there.>

Somehow Quath made the wall screens jump and swivel. They whirled around as the ship's sensors sought a different target—and locked on an inky blob, high above the glowering red disk.

<Explorers have used Besik Bay's shade to elude the disk's heat. Or so old tales tell. Myriapodia sheltered there, cooled, and then fled from this storm wrack of stars.>

Killeen gestured to Lieutenant Jocelyn. "Take us up that way." He had always been one for quick decisions, and the Bridge jumped to comply. Killeen turned back to Quath, his expression veiled. "What were your ancestors looking for here?"

<A weapon fabled in our older tales.>

"What kind of weapon?"

<In the end, all tools of defense are knowledge. We sought the [untranslatable].>

"Can't say more than that?"

<I do not know what this [untranslatable] knowledge is.>

"Hell! Look, for Family Bishop True Center is a legend. Almost a holy place—only we don't know *why.*"

<It is much the same for us. I believe however that your kind have been here before we ever ventured in.>

"Yeasay?" Killeen frowned. "Whatever we did, way back then, it's lost."

<For us as well. But the Philosophs never knew the true labyrinths of this place. The mechs have made certain to destroy all records they can find of that distant epoch.>

Killeen stared moodily at the expanses. "For us, coming here—well, it's like climbing the tallest mountain anybody ever saw."

<I believe that is somehow linked to why you are needed.>

Killeen shrugged, as if sensing when he would learn no more. "Okay, we'll cool our heels a little behind that cloud."

Though ordinary crew seldom spoke on the Bridge without the Cap'n's bidding, Toby decided to use his position as Cap'n's son. He could not resist probing further. "Quath, what made your ancestors leave?"

<Mechs guard this cyclone of fire.>

"Why? It's a hellhole."

<Mechs fare well here. Energies surge. They sup on such ferocity.>

"But there aren't any mechs here now."

<So it seems. This worries me.>

"There are plenty on our tail," Killeen observed mildly.

<They will try to find us in the Besik cloud.>

"So we hide?" Killeen asked, frowning.

Toby knew his father did not like to sneak by a challenge unless he absolutely had to. On the other hand, the Families had been running for a long time, learning the elusive crafts, and knew the virtues of being missing.

<My kin of the Myriapodia will have a chance to speak and to [unknown].>

Killeen shrugged again, as if he knew when he wasn't going to get any more out of Quath. He tapped the control board. The screens veered again, coming around to the strange, warped star—which wasn't a star at all any more.

While they had been talking, the inflating fat-man's belly had broken open. Now it spewed out white-hot streamers, the tortured sun finally shredding. Erupting gas swirled away from the split star, twisting. It rushed to join the smoldering rim of the great disk. As the view backed away, Toby saw the star as if it were a helpless animal, caught, struggling pointlessly, its life being sucked out. Lumps of it streamed into the disk, setting off fresh orange explosions there.

Toby felt a chilling wonder mixed with fear. "How come the hole can rip up a whole star, this far out, and it's so small we can't even see it?"

Killeen reached down and patted his son's shoulder, and in his face Toby saw the same mix of emotions. "The way I understand it, that hole is small, sure—but it's got plenty mass in it. That much, all compressed together, it makes strong tides. The inner face of that star's trying to orbit along one curve, see? Its back face, it's a smidgen further out from the hole, so it wants to orbit along a little-bit different orbit."

"I guess. So?"

"Well, they can't both go their separate ways and still hold together and be a star, right?" From Killeen's half-distracted gaze Toby knew he was getting coached by his tech Aspect. "But they can go their own way, if the star tears itself apart. So when the tides get strong enough, that's what it does. The tides just plain shred it, like a rag doll."

Toby looked around. The whole Bridge crew was silent, watching their Cap'n. In their upturned faces Toby read hope and need, sobered by the spectacle. Killeen's wary smile reflected the glare of the agonized, dying sun.

In the quiet Quath spoke, her words carrying a faint hiss. <This fresh food will fuel the Eater—and first, the disk.>

Killeen's face wrinkled with worry. "So it'll get hotter?"

<Yes. Let us speed to the refreshing cool of Besik.>

Toby grinned. "I thought your kind looked but didn't run."

<To run quickly and well is an art, which then lets one live to watch again.>

"Ummm. Sounds like an excuse to me, big-bug."

<[Untranslatable].>

3

Besik Bay

Toby didn't like to take advantage of his being son of the Cap'n, but there were times when he couldn't resist.

This was one. They were running for their lives now.

Every wall screen in *Argo* showed how close pursuit was. The mech ships were gaining on them. A narrow gap, getting slimmer. Their boxy, jumbled construction betrayed no concern for line or craft. Indeed, as Jocelyn explained, mech ships weren't like bottles carrying passengers. They were multiple, interlocking machines, without even a single, intact skin of metal. The basic unit of organic forms was the individual. For mechs, single operating systems the size of cities were perfectly ordinary. And these ships were huge, misshapen bundles.

Behind them came the Myriapodia craft with their immense ivory hoop suspended between them. The mechs did not turn to attack the Myriapodia. And *Argo* now fled into the shadowy tendrils of the immense Besik cloud.

Bravado and loud talk dwindled away. Family spoke quietly in small, worried knots around the cafeteria. Toby didn't want to sit idly and wait for news, so whenever he could fake an excuse, he slipped up to the Bridge. If he stood at the back, the Bridge officers didn't notice him, or else they gave him a wink and passed on. *Cap'n's son, who needs trouble?*

Naturally, Besen wanted to come, too. Toby had yet to master the skills of dealing with women, as opposed to girls—and Besen was most definitely a woman. In the Family, a woman was one who displayed ability at a wide range of practical matters, not just in the kitchen or in bed—though they were no slouches there, either. Girls and boys were just that—but women and men were *crew.* With appropriate rituals to mark the change. So he found it impossible to not take her along.

They stopped for a moment in the small Legacy chamber. It was really just a cranny tucked into the flowing corridor walls, and Toby came there often. Besen had hardly ever been, and said so. He was shocked.

"But these are the Legacies!"

"Well, sure," she said half-apologetically—and then her eyes flashed defiantly. "But they're just some slabs with writing on them. Not even writing anybody can read, right?"

"Of course not. That's why we're keeping them, mounted here, so someday, when we meet someone who can read them—"

"Yeasay, yeasay—but till then, they're just puzzles, right?"

Toby shook off the skeptical twist of her mouth and stood for a long moment just staring at the tall, gray slabs and their strange curly writing. Cool, solemn. Lines like wriggling snakes. Why did they fill him with longing?

Besen was getting restless, so they went on to the Bridge. Slipping in was easy—a nod and a wink. Together they stood in the shadows, watching the screens for long hours.

Besik Bay. Mysterious, murky, like the slag from a monstrous furnace.

Somehow this cinder-black place orbited safely around the black hole. At times its orbit swung through the disk below, where it sucked in matter. A thicket of magnetic fields, coarse-woven like cloth, protected it. Then it broke free of the disk and soared above, slowly circling high above the fury. How it persisted, a dust ball in a skillet of slow-stirred liquid iron, no one knew.

Argo now prowled the inky recesses of the immense Besik cloud, awaiting the arrival of the mech ships. Their hull cooled. The ship's lean metal sinews relaxed, shortening, sending loud strums and pops through the corridors. The air lost its prickly ozone smell. But the banks of grainy dust and gas could not protect against sophisticated sensors forever.

"How long you figure we got?" Besen whispered.

Toby shrugged, wanting to appear more casual than he was. One thing he had learned early as a boy—no point in loading up tension in your muscles. And no point in showing it even if you did. He casually rolled his shoulders, trying to let go of the tightness there. "Depends on what the mechs can see in here. We've got lots of tech designed to dodge and blind—but who knows what the mechs've got?"

"How come this cloud has been here so long?" Besen waved at the huge, dense ridges of murk. "How come the black hole doesn't grab it?"

"Quath said something about it being artificial. A place to shelter ships, left here from ancient days."

"But who'd take the trouble to *build* some dustball like this?"

As if in answer, silvery lightning arced from the dust bank ahead. Besen persisted, "And *why*?"

Toby shrugged again. She insisted, "We ought to find out."

"Look, we're rats living in the walls of this place. Ignorant vermin, to the mechs."

"That's no reason to stop learning."

"Sure—but a smart rat pays attention to staying alive."

Killeen stood at the center of the Bridge. Activity revolved around him with officers coming and going, dealing with the many strains on *Argo*'s systems. Toby knew his father's skills were being tested to the limit, but what troubled him more was Killeen's stiff, almost glazed look. He wished he could guess what was going on behind those flinty eyes.

And then such matters seemed soft and small and trivial, as the first mech ship burst into view. Boxy. Ribbed struts. Machined gray angles. It jetted straight out of a towering, gloomy mass—and began to turn toward *Argo*.

The Bridge stirred uneasily. The mech ship was under high magnification and Toby could not tell if it was even armed—until it launched a stubby missile at them.

Argo went on full alert. Wall screens displayed collision time estimates, defense options, maneuver possibilities. And then the missile was gone, evaporated by a defensive bolt from *Argo*. The Bridge crew cheered, but Killeen did not even smile. Toby found he was holding Besen's hand tightly.

Other mech ships burst into view. They approached *Argo* on complex paths, designed to make it hard to shoot at more than one at a time. Even though Killeen ordered the ship to maximum acceleration, they drew nearer.

Long moments ticked by. The mechs did not fire. Officers on the Bridge speculated that the mech ships did not want to waste fire power on *Argo*'s defenses until they got overpoweringly close. But that made little sense, Toby thought, since the humans were so outnumbered.

Ships darted and swooped. They seemed eager to force *Argo* out of the cloud, down a long lane of cindery dust. Toby could feel *Argo*'s straining engines as a steady trembling in the bulkhead behind him. Killeen gave orders quietly, stone-faced.

Then something quick and glowing swept past *Argo*, coming into view as a brilliant white line, like a vibrant, moving scratch on the wall screens. The Bridge crew gasped. It was the Cosmic Circle, as the Myriapodia called it—and now Toby saw its true scale.

This close, the segment seemed straight. Toby called up his Isaac Aspect as the luminous line slowly drew away toward the mech ships. He had seen this hoop before, at the last world they visited, but he had never understood it. "What *is* that thing?"

I would have been happy to instruct you at any time, if you had only inquired—

"Come on, spill—and make it quick and simple."

Very well, though you will miss much very interesting material. These were called "cosmic strings" by the ancients, though as

you see they are really loops. My older, nested Faces do not resolve this oddity.

"What're they *for*?"

They are not* for *anything—they are natural. They formed early in the universe, as compact folds in space-time. Like the wrinkles that form in the ice of a frozen pond. They are only a few atoms wide, but very long. Think of them as a natural resource, born of the Big Bang.

"A few atoms wide? Come on! This one blazes away like a star."

That is because it passes through the strong magnetic fields here, which drives electric current through the string, lighting it up.

"I don't get it," Toby mind-whispered to his Aspect. "Must be hard to carry, even if it's thin. Why haul it around?"

In many ways, the most useful of all tools is the knife. This is a blade the size of a world. Imagine what you can cut with it.

Toby did not have to imagine. He had seen it core a whole planet. Now the hoop sped toward the mech ships, escorted by the spiky-shaped ships of the Myriapodia. The hoop ebbed and flowed with latent energies.

Suddenly the Myriapodia released it and the great scythe shot forward. It wriggled and looped, so fast the eye could hardly follow. Quick knots formed, raced around the rim, and dispersed in flashes of amber and blue. The mechs tried to flee, to dodge.

Too slow. The vibrating hoop passed through them, snaking and looping to catch each ship as it sped by. After its passage, the mech ships looked the same, even under high mags. But then as Toby watched a mech ship began growing, getting longer. It had been cut in half. It was trying to hold itself together, using the supple, shiny metals mechs preferred.

They could not hold. The ship split in two, scattering fragments and exhaling a plume of orange gas. Shards spun away.

Toby thought of the strangeness of nature which left thin, glowing hoops, like a signature of whatever had made the whole universe. And how life taught itself to use the signatures, to its own ends.

Then he realized that everyone around him was shouting and laughing with glee. Besen was hugging him. He ignored his Isaac Aspect, who was still trying to lecture him, and joined in the celebration.

Their joy did not last long.

Before they had even quieted down, more mech ships appeared. These kept their distance, as if afraid. But the cosmic string was gone. It had plunged into a vast shadowy dust plume and the ships of the Myriapodia had followed, to rein it in again—Isaac said, with magnetic grapplers.

The mechs edged closer. Again *Argo* had to flee. Soon they were forced back, back, back—and out of Besik Bay entirely, by the gliding, steady mechs. Again virulent radiation from the churning disk far below began to cook *Argo*'s skin. Looking at the seethe and flare of the disk, Toby remembered that it was digesting its new meal, the doomed orange star. He could almost feel its baking heat.

Something caught his eye, a thin column of cool blue. It rose out of the very hottest center of the disk, the great white ball of blinding light. As he watched, small bright whorls raced around inside the column. He realized the whole thing was moving, pencil-straight. Fleeing the central hell.

Eerie, beautiful, a shimmering blue. Like a flowing river, cool and welcoming, he thought.

One of the galactic jets. There is another on the other side of the disk, pointing in the opposite direction. Both are ejected by the black hole.

Resplendent, graceful, its ever-changing elegance seemed violated by the Aspect's ho-hum description. Toby was about to thrust Isaac back into its digital hole, then paused. "How come a black hole lets out anything?"

The hole spins, because it acquires the rotation of all that has ever fallen into it, in all its billions of years. Matter comes falling in from the inner edge of the disk. But the hole's strong magnetic fields seize that mass. They fling it around, faster and faster. The spin makes hot matter corkscrew up around the poles and then out. As it cools it emits the soft blue radiance.

To Toby it seemed that a hole was a hole, and things fell in, period. But he pulled his attention away from the immense spectacle on the wall screens, whose vivid colors lit the haggard faces of the Bridge officers.

Especially his father. Killeen watched the mech ships behind them, more all the time—small, quick, drawing into a complex pattern. His eyes flitted with caged energy over the views, and a leaden pallor came over his brooding features.

They were trapped. *Argo* had fled the Besik cloud in the direction toward the inner edge of the disk. Killeen had turned up, to escape—and more mechs had come speeding in to block that way.

"These small craft—they're probably suicide mechs," Killeen muttered. He glanced at Toby. A fleeting smile. "Smart ones. Same principle as that bomb back in the Chandelier."

"Can't we get by them?" Toby asked earnestly. His father was a genius at slipping out of tight spots.

Killeen shook his head soberly. "Too many. Too many."

Lieutenant Jocelyn had been working at the control panels and now she stepped back, looking at the trajectory options their computer presented. Webs of three-dimensional curves, swoops and dodges and artful evasions. Her intense eyes searched the screen, at first hopefully, and finally, slowly, coming to rest on one curve. "A single option, Cap'n. We have to go inward. The mechs don't have that covered."

"Of course they wouldn't," Killeen said. "It's death that way."

"There's no other path. In all this, not a single—"

Killeen nodded. "So that's where we head."

Jocelyn stared at Killeen in disbelief. The entire Bridge became very quiet, the only sound a faint buzz of an open comm line. "We *can't.* The heat—"

Killeen turned slowly, moving with a deceptive quiet. Yet the air around him seemed to steam and seethe with energy, purpose, granite resolve, as he looked each officer in the eye. With a slight, tilted smile he nodded to Besen, who shouldn't have been there—letting the silence build, his gaze sweeping every corner of the Bridge, and finally coming to Toby.

"We must. That Besik cloud was there for some reason. A place to cool off, maybe, a way station. But not the final destination, no—it's just a mass of drifting dark gas. The ancient writing from the Chandelier—it spoke of someplace here, at the True Center. There's nothing out here but mechs and death. That place must be somewhere further in."

"No!" Jocelyn cried. "We can't last a day at these—"

"Quiet!" Killeen barked.

Again silence fell. The Cap'n pointed to the glimmering, ghostlike blue of the galactic jet. "I take that as a sign. A pointer. And we will follow it."

Toby realized he had been holding his breath. He finally gasped for air. The crew stirred restlessly, murmuring, stunned. Jocelyn asked Toby's question before he could get up the courage.

Her eyes seemed to drill through the intense air of the Bridge. "The jet goes outward. We follow it?"

Killeen stiffened. "The mechs will block us."

"Where, then?"

"Into the jet. Maybe there's a way."

4

Motes Such As You

Toby was passing by a minor side corridor when he caught the tang of smoke. He blinked, sniffed—and followed the acrid stink at a trot.

The corridor was unlit, the phosphors deliberately off. Ahead he saw dancing flames. There was nothing worse on a starship than fire—burning the very air they needed, while threatening to breech the hull and let in swallowing vacuum. He hurried—and stumbled over a man squatting near the fire.

When he picked himself up he saw by the orange flames that people were huddled around a big pile of smoky corn husks and popping dried branches. But the blaze was young, under control. Bright eyes danced with reflected firelight and they all laughed at his surprise. "Siddown! Take a load off," someone called.

He knew the fire would leave sooty stains on the ceiling, as others had in innumerable nooks of the ship, but he saw the need. The Families were vagabonds. A communal fire took them back to the one shelter they trusted, even when surrounded by a threatening night.

He let himself slide into it, too. It was restful, remembering the long treks of his boyhood, the biting cold nights beneath a brilliant sky. Smoke licked at his eyes. The crackling yellow spirits danced. Shadows played on faces staring moodily into the unending mystery of flame.

"You look tired, Toby-lad," Cermo said from nearby.

Toby was surprised to see Cermo here, and even closer, Jocelyn. Usually the highest ship's officers kept a certain distance from the others. But here Cermo was settled onto his beefy haunches, the age-old posture. It left you always ready to jump and move, if surprised. Useless here, of course, but a warming reminder of their shared past, their wary vulnerability.

"Been working the fields," Toby answered.

"Good crop?"

"Asparagus. Lost most of it."

Jocelyn said mildly, "Time was, we just picked the food and moved on."

Cermo nodded sadly. "We hunted, we gathered, hit the mech centers for whatever extra we wanted."

Answering murmurs came from around the shadowy circle. Toby grinned. "Come on—I was there. It was living by our wits, the mechs on our backs every minute. It could be worth your life to take a breather."

Cermo shook his head, thick muscles working in his neck, catching the gleam of the snapping flames. "At least we didn't just dig in the dirt. Sure, some gardening in Citadel Bishop—but we weren't hardscrabble clod-busters. We were free. Nature was the only farmer, and we just picked."

Toby knew where this was coming from. People were forever getting nostalgic for a rosy past they made better than it ever was. And they did it when the present was tough and tight. "Jocelyn, you remember—always looking over our shoulder for mechs, eating scraps, on the run morning to night—"

"How's it different now?" she shot back.

Another woman's voice called from the murk, "Mechs got us trapped." A Fiver accent.

Toby nodded. "But we're in a human ship, fighting our way through them."

"We're running," Jocelyn said. "Those big bugs, they did the fighting. But now they're way behind us, holding off some of the mech ships—and we're running."

Toby snapped, "Hey now, that's what the Myriapodia want. Quath's in touch with them, and she says they're fighting a rearguard. So we can figure out what's so important in here. Just give us a little time and—"

"Time's what we don't have," Cermo said solemnly, his eyes tortured. "We're heatin' up already, and we haven't even reached that galactic jet."

"Give the Cap'n a break, huh?" Toby said. "Maybe the jet's what we want."

Jocelyn laughed dryly. "That? It's just a column of cooling gas. Refugee junk that got away from the black hole."

Toby didn't like to argue his father's case, but something made him speak out against this aimless, hang-mouth talk. "Hey, give him time. We're moving, we're in good shape, and—"

"He brought us here with no more idea of what we were getting into than a camp rat."

An older man snickered. "I'd say he don't know enough to pour piss outta a boot with a hole in the toe and directions writ on the heel."

This got a good hearty laugh.

"Look, we all like to air our lungs," a Trump-accented voice said. "But where I come from, we had to stick with the Cap'n."

Toby nodded vigorously. "I won't honeyfuggle you about how tight things are. But yeasay—we got to keep true."

Voices came pelting in from all directions now, some objecting, others backing him up. Trump Families for Killeen, firm as steel. Bishops dog-mouthing the Cap'n, even though he was one of their own.

The sooty flavor of the air and the brooding dark made it easy for people to speak out, let fly with a few hard-edged words, sharpen the air. The corncobs gave forth their sweeter smoke, cracking and fizzing. Slowly their talk turned more meditative, lost its harshness as people got their inner fears out, saw them for what they were, and stuffed them back into the mental pouches where everyone had to keep the dark moments. So the fire did its work, and its spreading blue fog made the nook a warmer, more human place.

When a call came on comm for Toby, he was reluctant to leave. But it was the Bridge, and he hurried.

He passed by a wall screen on his way. The soft blue jet hung before them now, its shimmer working upward, away and against the iron reds and burnt golds of the virulent disk, far below. Dry heat stirred the air. An odd humming sounded through the ship, like a bass note sounded far away. It made Toby jittery. By the time he reached the Bridge he was not surprised to see his father looking weary and gray, his uniform wrinkled from long hours.

"Toby! You're needed."

"Uh, why?" Everybody seemed worked up, but there was nothing new on the wall screens.

"That." Killeen gestured at long filaments of rosy gas that trailed alongside the jet. The *Argo* was cruising hard through the immense, glowing filigrees. They had passed through such "weather" before, though these luminous strands twisted with restless energy.

"So? More fireworks."

"Not quite. I've spoken with these before."

"Spoken?" His father had been on duty too long.

"Not for years, and maybe you don't remember. The voice from the sky."

"Huh?" Toby shook his head. So much had happened, and they understood so little of it.

"The Magnetic Mind. This is it."

Now Toby remembered.

—Years before, standing in a rocky valley while skittering veins of green and yellow played through the sky like searching fingers. Striations that worked the furious air and finally had found them. Hot filaments had vibrated like angry breezes, speaking through the sensorium input each person carried in the back of the skull.

An intelligence that lived, somehow, in silvery radiances. It had spoken to Killeen—though the entire Family could overhear, witnesses as a colossal intellect delivered a message in the sky. Toby recalled that childhood memory in an instant, the way a warm kitchen smell can bring a vibrant mother's voice to life long after . . .

He shook himself. The memories of far childhood, back in the happy closeness of the Citadel, could come flooding through him at any time.

But this was not the right moment. Those were a boy's recollections, and he had to stop thinking like a boy.

He refocused on the huge, stringy luminescence that grew steadily before the *Argo,* and made himself ask, "How do you know? I mean, this could be just some kind of lightning or something."

Killeen smiled without humor. "I guess it is, in a way. Vital lightning, the same as you and I are really walking heaps of controlled burning. That's what keeps us going, thinking, doing. Oxygen burns our food, one of my Aspects says. This thing uses electricity, generated by that disk down below."

"How?"

"I dunno. But energy is energy, and the way I figure it, this thing has learned how to stack magnetic fields, build them up into something like a body."

Toby liked to appear capable and savvy in front of ship's officers, but the striations before *Argo* didn't look like anything he remembered. "Huh?"

Killeen shrugged. "I've been getting prickly feelings, like something probing at me." He shook his head. "Hard to explain, but it's like before. The Magnetic Mind glues itself together with magnetic fields. Or maybe it just *is* magnetic fields, period. And it lives somewhere here, so . . . "

A deep strumming came up through Toby's heels. At first he thought it was the ship's acceleration as it fought against the lurking gravitational pulls here in this riot of mass and light. Then he noticed that the quivering came and went with a slow rhythm. He felt it through his ears and hands, too. Pulses. Then the odd vibration climbed into the massive walls and filled the air of the Bridge with a heavy presence.

Give sign if you perceive.

The voice was gritty, granite-hard, immense.

"Not like before," Killeen whispered. "Then it used our sensoria. Now—look, the whole room is shivering."

I am charged with a task of discernment. If you be of the tribe of Bishop, give voice.

The Bridge was acting as a giant amplifier for the hollow, lordly voice, the walls ringing and shaking like a loudspeaker. Toby wondered how a thing that was just magnetic fields, with no weight or substance, could do that.

Killeen looked cornered, surrounded by the voice. Then he barked out, "Bishops we are. I'm Killeen. Remember?"

> **So you are. I forget nothing, and store tidings of times ancient beyond your imaginings in the curls and knots of my being. I recall your particular flat odor and squashed, slanted self. Good—I have been enjoined to inspect you.**

"By who?" Killeen called. The Bridge crew stood transfixed, and the voice ignored him.

> **I seek another as well. It is termed "Toby" and must be with you if you are to receive further attentions from the inner realm.**

"I'm here," Toby shouted.

> **Are you? Let me taste . . . Each of you tiny things has a different aroma, an angularity. Such pointless profusion!**

"We're different people!" Toby protested.

Skittering spokes shot through him, electric-quick and bristling with points of pain. Probing. Then they were gone.

> **You are the flavor termed "Toby"—your animal signatures match the genetic inventory, crude though it is. Creation is so trivially diverse, endowing each of you with oblique gene-scents and dusky shadings. Such a waste of natural craft! Detail and artful turns, needlessly multiplied, throwing reason to ruination.**

"We like ourselves pretty well," Toby said, tight-lipped.

> **So you do. All is illusion. Still, I must report that you are here. Then I hope to be quit of this obligation and irritant.**

"Wait!" Toby cried. "What's this about? Who wants to know?"

> **A power which sits further inward.**

"Well, what is it?"

> **It is not of the cold, dead flecks of matter such as you inhabit. The power which presses me to this task speaks**

to me through my feet, which rest in the warm hearth of the plasma disk.

"Yeasay," Toby persisted, "so it's a, a plasma cloud?" Whatever that was.

It dwells somewhere below me, in storm-cut majesty, but is unknowable to as large an entity as I.

Killeen called, "You said last time, years ago, that my father had something to do with this."

Years? I do not know such terms . . .

Killeen said, "A major part of our present lifetimes. I—"

But which "present" do you reside in? Duration, distance—these are primitive terms.

Killeen was visibly puzzled. "Look, was my father—"

Tiny forms such as yourselves are impossible to resolve in the warp of energies at my feet. But such terms and names come rippling up to me, along the cables of myself. When such information was loaded onto my eternal tangle of knowledge-knots, and thus the age of this clotted cognizance, I cannot know. Forms such as yourself were once there, yes—squalid primitives. Their persistence in the realm of immense clashes-imponderable is quite unlikely.

"You're saying he's dead?" Killeen asked sharply.

Tiny lives wink like flames beneath my footpoints. My whole motivation to assume this field-form is to rise above mortality and its minute matters. I cannot register small endings, any more than animals like you sense grains of sand as you trod them.

"Is he—"

I go. If the power below desires more, I shall touch you further.

"Wait! We need to know what to do here, how to escape—" The vibration of the Bridge walls cut off, leaving a hush.

Killeen threw up his hands, swearing, and then drove a fist into the wall. A painful smack.

This shocked Toby more than the abrupt departure of the Magnetic Mind. He realized how much his father had bottled up, how desperate he was beneath his flinty exterior.

"Dad—what did it mean? What—"

"Damned if I know. That thing treats us like bugs."

"Well, we don't much like to talk to bugs, either," Toby pointed out reasonably, hoping to josh Killeen out of his scowling, nasty mood. Then he thought a moment and added to himself, *Except Quath.*

"I wonder if it could be? My father, Abraham, here?"

"Don't see how. We never found his body at the Citadel—but we had to run pretty quick then, there wasn't much time." He shook his head in a flicker of weariness. "That was a long time ago, a long way off."

—and Toby felt it all again. Steel stripped from stone, caved-in ceilings, masonry and smashed furniture, lives ripped away. Smoke seething from crackling fires. Intricate warrens squashed into stone and slag. Blood running in gutters. Rivulets of browning red running from beneath collapsed buildings. The strange silence after the mech flyers had left. Wind blowing through snapped-off girders.

—And his father, wandering the ruins. *Abraham!* he had shouted. Over and over. The name snatched away by a hungry wind, lost in swirls of smoke.

Then he was back from the searing memories. He watched his father blink, face haggard, and then pull himself together.

Killeen said shakily, "I figured he was dead. Had to be."

In Killeen's face Toby saw how much his father wanted to believe that somehow Abraham was here, that the Magnetic Mind knew more than they did. But at the same time, the Mind obviously found humans repugnant, and would not lift a finger to help them.

Then Toby reminded himself that the Mind had no fingers, nothing but electromagnetic pressures and waves. But didn't it say it had feet?

When the Mind had spoken to them before, back on Trump, it had said something about being an intelligence that had slipped free of matter, and lived solely in the states available to magnetic fields. Apparently such states lasted longer. The Mind seemed to think it was immortal. He remembered Killeen chuckling, saying, "Forever's a long time"—because the Mind might be huge and powerful, but it could sure seem petty and finite, too. Which made it even harder to deal with. A god, at least, wouldn't be insulting.

"Look, Dad, what are you going to do?" Maybe in a moment of openness like this Killeen would say what he really thought.

"Do?" Killeen looked at Toby as though just noticing him. "Get into that jet. See what it's like."

"Why? Can we escape that way?"

Killeen gave him a veiled look. "That gas is movin' out pretty quick.

It'll give us a boost, maybe even shield us some. Make us hard to pinpoint."

"We can ride it outward?"

"Could be."

Toby grinned. "Great. Crew'll be glad to hear that."

"Oh? How come?"

"They're worried, think you just want to go further on in, no matter what."

Killeen gave nothing away. "I'm not saying the jet idea will work. We'll just try."

"Sure, Dad, sure—but there's hope, right?"

Killeen gazed at his son for a long while, emotions playing across his face so rapidly that Toby could not read them. "Could be. Could be."

5

Tiny Minds

When he got really out of sorts, Toby went for a run.

Since nobody could go hull-walking any more, because of the hard radiation that now bombarded *Argo,* he had to go jogging through lesser-used corridors. Thumping along the same monotonous route, he let his subconscious rummage around among his problems. Maybe his deeper layers could come up with something smart, he thought, though without much hope. Family Bishop was headed for a crisis, for sure.

He had gone to Quath for advice or just some good, reassuring insult-trading—but the alien had brushed him off.

<I cojoin with my own kind.>

She had rattled her enormous telescoping arms, as if for punctuation. There seemed to be several new ones, maybe worked up from other parts of her carcass. Quath had a way of redesigning herself—maybe as the Myriapodia's equivalent of a fashion statement, Toby thought. Arms waved and clashed with a metallic ring, like a breeze blowing through a forest of steel trees.

"Hey, you old collection of spare parts, listen anyway."

<I have several minds which could do my listening, but they are engaged.>

"Huh! You think just a fraction of you is enough to talk to me?"

<Listen, not talk. I could perhaps assign one of my monitoring sub-selves to—>

"Never mind! Sometimes talking to you is like shouting down a well, Quath."

<I cannot [untranslatable].>

"Well, I can't either!"

Toby was finally, truly irked. Without meaning to—maybe—Quath actually had insulted him. Or so he felt. So he stormed out of the big bowl where Quath stood, transfixed by distant conversations with her own kind.

So now Toby loped through vacant ship corridors, fretting to himself, hoping to release through his muscles what he could not resolve in his own feelings. Most of Family Bishop was jammed into the cafeterias, talking and eating and forming the communal consolations that had always before gotten them through a crisis. Maybe it would this time, too, but Toby didn't like the drift of events. And jogging didn't clear his mind much today; it just made him even hotter, sweat collecting in his eyebrows and stinging his eyes. An itchy heat laced the air. The usual well-being that came from a workout did not settle upon him.

So he slowed his step when he rounded a long curve and saw the same small side passage, caught the acrid scent of smoke. With a certain eagerness he walked puffing to the edge of the group—larger this time—around a flickering corn husk fire.

He settled in, exchanging ceremonial nods with the others, accepting a passed flask of fruity liquor that rasped in his throat but sent a warm, welcome pulse through his body. The Family talk was amiable and he sat and soaked it up for a while, but then an edge came into it and eyes drifted his way. He had defended his father the last time here, and now voices arose among the huddled figures that voiced outright fear. It slid quickly into anger at Killeen, and Toby began to feel uncomfortable.

Jocelyn said, "Our hull temperature, it's goin' up and up and up."

A voice muttered, "Can feel it ever'where. Hot as a clam at a clambake."

Toby had never seen a clambake or a clam, didn't know what they were, had never even seen a body of water he couldn't pitch a stone across—but the term remained in the Family tongue. "Lemme have some of that," Toby whispered to a bald woman sitting nearby.

She passed him a flask of ripe apricot brandy that made his nose sting when he swigged some into the back of his throat. But it was good to feel the spin of it steal up into him, lighten his head just a tad and smooth the world off a bit. His body would quickly enough metabolize the alcohol into burnable fuel—the Family had long ago been engineered to turn every possible food into usable energy—but it gave a momentary glow. And he needed that now. A prickly irritability ran through this crowd of huddled shapes, snappish remarks lancing through the gloom, and even the ancient consolation of the dancing flames did little to deflect the mood.

"We got how long before we roast?" an engineer asked, flicking her long mane of tawny hair with a jerk of her neck.

Jocelyn shrugged, glanced at Cermo. "A day? Two?"

Cermo looked uncomfortable. Ship's officers had to be the lubricant between the Cap'n and the Family, and they got rubbed raw sometimes. "The computers are tellin' us there's 'bout a day left before the cooling runs out. Then we go to backup."

"What's that?" a man's slurred voice called out. "We peel down naked and get in the food freezers?"

This got a sour laugh all around but Cermo didn't join in. "You can strip if you want. Looks to me like we're not wearing all that much now."

He was right. Toby was in shorts, like most around the smoky fire. A few wore loose robes. Family liked to dress up whenever possible, a holdover of the era when a fine cloth jacket or silky shirt was a precious treasure, a last emblem they had salvaged from the Calamity, the loss of Citadel Bishop.

A few small jokes circulated, mostly about the skinny flanks, pink beer-bellies, and pale pencil-arms exposed, for the Family still liked to josh and chivy and rank each other. Toby thought this was a good sign; when they couldn't laugh any more, they'd be in deep trouble. Then Cermo said, "Backup plan is to fall back into ship's core. All of us."

"What for?" an angry woman asked.

"The outer zones will get pretty bad," Cermo said reasonably. "The cooling systems can handle us if we're packed into the inner areas."

"Leave the growing domes?" a woman cried with disbelief.

The crowd dissolved into discordant voices, piling in.

"Without us tending 'em, they'll all die, for sure."

"We'll never get them back to harvest."

"That's death, right there!"

"Whose idea's that?"

"Those damn computers, is who."

"Yeah, what do they know? They're not Family computers."

"So what? Our systems, the ones back in the Citadel, they were small-fry kin to these computers."

"Can't trust 'em, I say."

"Well, I say different. We—"

"Nobody can save us if we lose all the crops at once."

"She's right. We'll never reseed if the soil gets baked."

"Hey, might get rid of those weevils for good."

"Yeasay, and all the earthworms that do the real soil work."

"Cermo, you *can't* mean that."

"We won't just crawl back in our holes and give up!"

"We're Bishops!"

"Yeasay, we're meant to move and search and shoot anything gets in our way—not turn into moles."

"Who says we should? You know who—the Cap'n!"

"Yeasay, this idea smells like him."

"Got his whiff, all right."

"Too big for his britches."

"Never trusted that one, never did. I used to say—"

"Followin' this damn fool course, it was his idea."

"Got us into a goddamn trap."

"Any fool would naysay flying into this hellhole!"

"But no, Cap'n says we got to go, well we just roll over and wag our tails and off we go."

"While he flumdiddles on the Bridge!"

"Yeasay, nice and cool!"

"Bridge is right in the center of the ship, it'll be frosty."

"I say we go get cool ourselves. Whatsay you?"

"Good idea!"

"Enough hunkerin' down here."

"Let's move!"

The crowd had swollen in the gloom without Toby noticing and now it rose as one, yammering and elbowing and smelling of sweaty irritation. With the zigzag logic of a mob they set out to do what they had just been protesting, moving click-step quick inward. It cooled a bit as they wound down the central helical ramp.

Toby followed. A kind of rolling-stone energy grew in them, gathering the moss of the undecided from side corridors. Bishops liked action a lot more than mulling matters over.

By the time they got to the Bridge level, the campfire group was a milling, murmuring mob. Toby could feel their muttering rise like an animal's warning growl. This wasn't going to be like other times, when Killeen had used a stern scowl, quick reasoning, and then a sunny smile to turn aside bands of complaining Bishops. This gang had a mean, dark streak in it.

The Lieutenants at the Bridge felt it, too. They formed a four-person block at the Bridge entrance and tried to stare down the mob. Toby looked around, but Cermo and Jocelyn had faded back. No point in them showing their faces, when the others would do their work.

Or were they that crafty? Toby wasn't sure. The campfire ritual had seemed to just burst out with the jittery anxiety they all felt, which was the point of the age-old custom, after all.

Toby himself tried to slip quietly away from the Bridge. Even more than Cermo and Jocelyn, he was in a conflicted position. But elbows and close-packed shoulders kept him from beating a retreat. Skeptical eyes speared him, as if to say, *You're going to slide away now?*

Toby wasn't sure what he should do, and then events made up his mind for him.

The Bridge was tall enough to jut a balcony out over the corridor, meant as a place to which an officer could retreat and hold a quiet conversation. Killeen used it now, stalking into view above the heads of the buzzing throng. He wore full dress uniform with its impressive crisp blues and gold spangles. An excited babble broke out at his appearance. More Family joined the edges with every moment. Killeen stood, hands behind his back, for a long moment, letting the grumbling beast below give vent, waiting until the noise ebbed.

When he did speak his voice was solid and surprisingly mild. "You came to view our progress?"

"Progress? Ha! We're sailing into hell!" a man called.

Killeen shook his head. "We are staying ahead of the mechs."

"You mean they're runnin' us!" a woman shouted, her words soaked with derision.

"They are trying to catch us, sure—when didn't they?" Killeen swept his gaze over the still-growing crowd, fixing individuals in turn with his gaze.

"They're gonna' cook us for sure!" a man accused.

"Not by a mech's eye." Killeen smiled confidently. "We entered the galactic jet just a few minutes ago."

A confused stirring at this news.

"Didn't you notice?" Killeen added mildly. "Our hull should start to cool off in a while."

"How come? That jet looks pretty hot."

Killeen waved a hand. "It's not. Funny business, but turns out the gas here is blue because it's cooled off. Fighting its way up, out from the gravity well that black hole makes, well, that takes all the zip out of the gas."

The crowd stirred and muttered with disbelief.

"So we'll stop heating up?" a woman called.

"Our computers say so."

"Well, that's fine," a man said. "But we still—"

"We can follow the jet on out," Killeen said amiably. "The blue clouds are condensing as they cool."

A man said angrily, "That don't excuse the damn fool idea of comin' here in first place."

"We hold you accountable!" a woman called.

"Yeasay—and what we get out of all this, anyway?"

"More trouble!"

"More mechs!"

"And we sure don't need more of this Cap'n!"

That was too much for the Trumps. Abruptly individual Aces and Fivers and Jacks shouted down the doubting Bishops. Surly jibes, angry taunts. Fistfights started, but officers broke them up.

The chaos went on for minutes and Killeen stood silently, watching. His mouth twitched once and Toby guessed, *He's thinking that it's pretty damn strange, when your own Family is against you, and Trumps stand by you.*

Finally the crowd had settled down to a growing, sour-mouthed mutter. Killeen spread his hands. "I think you folks should just go back to your tasks and—"

They all felt it at the same time—a compression that boomed into a rolling pulse, as if *Argo* had become a great heart that beat with slow, solemn weight.

I return, enjoined to deliver instructions.

It was like God speaking in a cramped room. The mob rustled. Their eyes raked the walls, searching for the voice, showing too much white, like panicked sheep.

But Killeen reacted only with a skewed mouth and a skeptical slant to his eyebrows. He crossed his arms over his chest, as if prepared to hear out the Magnetic Mind before responding. "Yeasay, we are listening."

It is you and the Toby creature to whom I need transfer this complex of curious meanings.

"I'm here!" Toby called.

People nearby gave him a startled glance and moved hurriedly away, as if they wanted no association with one who would call down this daunting thing that shook the walls to make speech.

My duty is imposed by encumbered obligations from my far past. I once benefited from the powers who now call on me, and so stand as messenger to motes such as you—a post requiring humility I do not come to naturally. So I be quick of it—here.

A high-pitched wail filled the ship, reverberating in agonizing harmonics. Sharp, shrill, endless. A cutting pressure, driving all thought away. For an excruciating moment it held, built—then cut off savagely. The stunned silence that followed seethed with dread.

Such was your course. Follow it well or you will suffer to be torn to atoms, and then still more.

"Our . . . course?" Killeen croaked.

The trajectory your benefactors instruct you to follow.

Regaining composure, Killeen said sternly, "And which way is that?"

You are to follow my magnetic field lines. Cling close to me, that you do not shear into fragments.

"Why? And where are you, anyway?" a burly man shouted.

Silence, small mind.

"The hell I will. Who are you, *what* are you, to—"

A fist of sound struck them. The colossal thump pulsed through floor, ceiling, walls. People lurched, fell, shrieked.

I do not suffer the attentions of mortals, but for my obliged task. That—and no more.

"That, that sound you sent—" Killeen held out his hands, palms down, to still the throng. "You say it was a course plan along *you*?"

Without me as a guide, you would come to swift wreak and ruin.

"Look, we're going to head out along the galactic jet. I—"

Such a trajectory would inevitably intersect those who desire your end.

"Mechs? We've gotten away from them before."

There are agencies and physicks here you cannot grasp.

Killeen folded his arms across his chest and scowled. Toby knew that look, had seen it form like a stone wall against opponents. But there was some other element in his father's stance, an odd note of staged and studied performance he had not seen before. He wondered at it, caught a sliver of intuition, but then the Cap'n spoke.

"I want to know the authority by which you—or any other of your 'agencies'—gives us orders."

How you strut! I have dwelled here longer than your species has existed. You are as ephemeral as the passing, fraying cloud. Yet pride often accompanies such infinitesimal durations.

"Maybe it's that long life of yours that makes you so long-winded?" Killeen winked at the crowd.

I speak to you now only out of obligation—which does not include enduring the slings and errors of toy intelligences. Very well—your benefactor is the creature Abraham, of whom we spoke.

Joy kindled in Killeen's eyes. "He *is* alive."

The warp and slide of space-time here does not allow such easy simplifications.

"But if he sent this just now—"

The very term "now" is as ephemeral as you. Here, worse than meaningless.

Toby could see curiosity overcome his father's exasperation. Killeen chewed at his lip and called, "That course you sent. I want to know where it'll take us."

> **Where I live most intensely. The seat of forbidding energies and grand remorse. Where my feet dance on sizzling plasma. Inward, tiny thing. To your terror.**

6

Lightning Life

Almost despite himself, Toby was drawn back to the Bridge through the long hours of their descent.

Argo was using the galactic jet as a shield now, plunging in along it. Ghostly blue filaments twisted and snarled and rushed by them, fleeing outward. Their streaming made the ships' flight seem even faster. The deck rumbled with the plasma drive's effort, sucking in the blue gas and thrusting it out the back.

And now a puzzling, unspoken question was answered. For days the ship had buzzed with speculations: where were the mechs?

The Eater of All Things had loomed in legend for Family Bishop, and part of that ancient story held that mechs lurked and labored there. Why, no one knew. They had driven humans from True Center long before the fall of the Chandeliers.

But until now they had seen only fleeting glimpses of mech ships. Now, far up along the jet, *Argo* detected huge, dark mech constructions. They had seen before enormous masses of mechwork, on their passage inward—and had avoided them. Immense, mysterious, shrouded in energy-collecting panels. All mute, speaking on no channel humans knew.

These mech structures ringed the jet as though taking energy from it. The jet walls were alive with brilliant blue-white flashes. Here antimatter, made near the black hole, collided with matter in furious, annihilating battle. But most of the jet's energy lay in its outward thrust. The mechs did not seem to lessen this as the jet passed. Instead, they seemed to be studying it.

Why were the mechs up there, circling the jet? It occurred to Toby that maybe this was their way of listening to the inner rumblings of the black hole itself, but he could not imagine how. The jet was eerie and, he was quite convinced, beyond human comprehension. Its constant turbulence served to hide the *Argo,* Killeen said. And the mech fabrications seemed to ignore such tiny matters as a single ship, anyway. *Argo* scurried like a rat through a palace.

Oddly, the center of the jet was nearly empty, making their flight easier. The gas had been robbed of its heat by the effort of climbing up from the gravitational pit of the unseen black hole. The thick, cooling gas column around them protected against the ferocious heat of the disk. It was almost as if someone had planned this tunnel into the innermost realm. To his teacher Aspect Isaac, of course, it was just a bit of interesting physics.

The spin of the black hole hollows out the gas that it throws up this way. This jet resembles the spools of cotton candy I got as a boy at the fairgrounds, a spun-out cloud of sheer sugary delight.

"What's cotton candy?"

I forget how much your people have lost. Have you never been to a fair?

"A fair what?"

A gathering where—never mind. At least this beautiful blue haze around us reminds me of my better days, when high culture reigned in the Chandelier of Queens, and I went ceiling-skating with my father.

"You were in the Chandeliers?"

Did you think I descended from clod-huggers such as you? **We** ***had great powers then, and held our own against the mechs who now drive you like cattle before them.*** **We** ***regularly ventured into even this region, spying on the mechs who worked their strange ways here.*** **We—**

"Hey, you're from the Arcology Era!"
Isaac's Aspect-aura turned peevish.

Well, true—but one of my nested Faces grew up in Wesouqk Chandelier, one of the last great ones. I saw a Chandelier once, through a telescope, when it was still inhabited, they say. Regrettably, I spent my life in a planet-bound refuge, but—

"That was what you called 'The Accommodation,' wasn't it?"

Well, yes—an unfortunate strategy. Still, my cultural roots—

From far back in Toby's recesses arose a Face he seldom used, one who knew techstuff galore but not much else. Joe was slow and stunted, a mere fraction of an Aspect, but he spat out bitterly,

1. ***You goddamn traitors set us up.***
2. ***Playing along with mechs—real smart.***
3. ***They smashed up your precious Chandeliers soon as they tricked you down to a planet.***
4. ***Played you for chumps!***

"That's pretty much what history says, too," Toby put in mildly. "Now, you want *real* Chandelier folk—" He pried up the digital lid on an Aspect he rarely used, Zeno. She was so splintered and crabbed that listening to the wavering, ancient voice was painful.

I deplore . . . sinful bargaining away . . . our Chandelier heritage . . . by your generation. We sought no "accommodation" . . . no justice . . . possible from mechs . . . We had the key to . . . subverting them . . . disembowel their deepest . . . logics . . . programs . . . They scattered . . . our lore . . . even then . . . we could not unlock the Cryptographs . . . the Sore Magics . . . left by earliest humans . . . who once even . . . ventured here . . . to True Center . . . and grasped the Sore Magics in their hands . . .

Her static-filled voice faded, leaving a curious hush in Toby's mind. Zeno's broken phrases carried such unspoken freight—sad, hopeless, ruminating on tattered glories that meant nothing now. After a long moment Joe said,

1. ***See what you lost, Isaac?***
2. ***"Accommodation"—you mean "sell-out."***

To Toby any notion of compromise with mechs was damn-fool stupidity, and Isaac's generation had escaped the consequences only by pure luck. The instant he framed this thought, Isaac flared.

Not luck! We assisted the Hunker Down. This was a perfectly rational strategy, to invest in human colonies on the many worlds on the outskirts of True Center. To make Families which would develop a hybrid vigor of ideas, social norms, and weaponry. Those were our strengths as a species!

Toby could see how Rooks, say, differed from Knights—and not just in their table manners. But what Isaac might mean by "hybrid vigor" escaped him—yet another dry, ancient idea discarded as so much surplus baggage by Family Bishop, long before he was born.

1. Look where it ended up.
2. Mechs got you anyway.

Isaac shot back,

The Chandeliers were untenable! Just big targets, floating in the spaces of high-energy particles and hard vacuum, the mechs' natural habitat!

A burr of rasping static almost swamped Zeno's words:

We defended ourselves . . . long as we could . . . unvector the mech Mandates . . . core out their interlocks . . . but you lost all that . . .

Again the melancholy voice silenced his mind for a moment. Isaac finally rallied in an apologetic tone.

We tried the experiment, granted, and it finally failed. Wesouqk Chandelier—I saw it burning like a hornet's nest in the sky! Imagine my sadness. At least we had sheltered our kind beneath the comforting blanket of air and gravity.

Zeno's reply came sluggishly.

. . . a worthy . . . gamble . . . but so much . . . lost.

Isaac sounded more confident now, though to Toby's inner ear the tone was hollow.

I at least knew us at our height. The glory—

Zeno cut in with waning energy,

You pretender . . . you did not know the heights . . . they came long before . . . even me . . . the great works . . . skills you cannot begin to understand . . . pretender . . .

Chastened, Isaac answered,

I am sorry that the mechs later undid our noble Hunker Down. Even you, poor Joe, must realize that we had to strip much cultural memory from the Hunker Down worlds, to make the

experiment work. And you* did *fructify, bursting with fresh ways to win worlds and hamper the mechs. For a while, at least.

Joe stirred angrily but confined himself to:

1. Damn hard down there.
2. I'd sure rather lived in a big sky-city.

Isaac shot back,

I do not have to respond to such vague wanderings.

Toby was irked by Isaac's haughty manner. *Dinky chip-mind!* "If you're so great, how come you're just an Aspect now?"

I had such talents of mind, in compiling and integrating knowledge, that* I *was saved. What do you think will be* your *fate, boy?

There was real, flinty rage in this retort. Toby had to remember that Isaac and the other Aspects were little miniatures of whole people, not just books he could open, read, and drop. To keep minds running, they had to have the facets of a balanced intellect, or else they would go insane. So he shouldn't expect them to take offhand insults mildly.

He whispered "Sorry" to Isaac and to his surprise felt a burgeoning presence displace the Aspect. A sensation like a swelling, an emergence, swept over him, making his skin prickle, his scalp stiffen. The Isaac Aspect squealed but dwindled, swept back into its mental cell. This was the first time he had ever experienced Shibo's Personality fully, her essence flooding through his mind, insistent and powerful. Not a spoken voice, but a memory.

—Her past rose like dusty clockless hours recalled, streets she had known lying black and steaming. Refugees from the mechs had washed up in the lee of walls, in bitter alleys and vacant ruins. In those rank lanes light, wiry shadows walked high-shouldered, armed always, faces grizzled, eyes embedded in them alternately void and wary. Old stone walls of her Family's Citadel yawned and veered in her memories, unplumbed by wearing winds. Marbled obelisks and crosses marked where the dead kept their own small metropolis—a land packed solid with the casketmaker's trade, until urgency stole from them even that refinement, of setting down into ever-drying soil the already rotting clothes and broken bones. Under blue lamplights she had wandered as a girl in the wake of some funerial procession, done at dawn by long custom. Stones leaked back the night's chill, up through her bare feet, pleasurably delicious as the day's heat came spanking into her face and arms with the already stinging dawn. Slow, solemn march. Past corrugated warehouses, across sandy celebrant squares, through warrens of home gardens carefully watered—redpouch, heather grain, teardroop fruit. Engines labored eternally to make weaponry, coughing like distant vast animals. Past smoking stacks and vagrant ropy vines and patches of hopeful yellow flowers. Buildings sagged and windows were eyeless sockets. Her Citadel was rent with ruin, the slow-sliding calamity of neglect. Wanderers from the plains sat mute, staring, their gaunt profiles stamped against the shredding dawn sky, old purposes lost in coasting eyes. A mongrel madness of defeat infected them, yet they smiled at her passing skip-steps. They had slept in their boots beside a generation's furtive fires and gone on, into days of scavenge and pursuit, living beneath a massive rapacity.—

Toby staggered with the intensity, the touching fondness for places and people he had never seen. Then Shibo's oddly quiet voice solidified.

You have not called on me recently.

"You . . . you can see what's been going on. I've been busy."

I doubt that is the true reason.

She was right, of course. Toby was new at this, and he couldn't keep very much from a strong presence. It was almost like she was alive again, and he was peering through her skeptical black eyes, eyes that never wavered. But her eyes saw him, too, from inside.

Beneath their gaze his feelings leaked through the rubbery, artificial partitions of his mind. "It's been rough going lately."

Your father.

It was not a question. "He's, well, I'm sure he's doing what's best for the ship—"

Are you?

"Well, he's under pressure and all, and he comes across as pretty damned hard-nosed, but . . ." His words faded off as he realized that he couldn't bluff even an Aspect, much less a Personality. Not where emotions were concerned.

It did not occur to you that he knew you and the others, the group from around the campfire, were coming? That someone would protest? There are monitoring cameras throughout the ship, after all.

"Ummm. Well, I suppose."

He took* Argo *into the galactic jet at just that time. Knowing

that almost certainly the Magnetic Mind would return then, with more to say.

"You're sure he planned it that careful?"

I love your father still. But he has changed. He has hard-learned the sometimes cynical skills of Cap'ncy.

Toby had not grasped yet how to look very much ahead of events—things just seemed to rush at him, coming fast and fierce—so this degree of scheming seemed pretty unlikely. On the other hand, adults were more than a little weird. "So did he know what the Magnetic Mind was going to tell us, then?"

I doubt that. He looked as shocked as the rest.

"Well, he sure looks okay now."

Toby was standing at the back of the Bridge, talking in the barely audible whisper that was enough for an Aspect to get but couldn't be overheard. He studied Killeen, who moved with casual assurance among his ship's officers. Since they had turned downward in the jet, his brow was no longer furrowed, his eyes not haunted by uncertainty.

Not that anybody else felt that way. The Lieutenants were jumpy, troubled, sweating—and not just from the increase in hull temperature. Even the cool blue gas couldn't screen out all the disk radiation. The ventilators labored, wheezing lukewarm air. A thin tension underlay the customary quiet of the Bridge, beneath the muted, orderly *ping* and chime of computer prompts, reminding officers of tasks needing supervision.

"So he was ready for our little mob, huh?" He gave the old man a nod of grudging respect.

There is more to being Cap'n than giving orders.

"Yeasay, but a Cap'n better be right."

Now he has the authority he wanted.

"Straight from Abraham." Toby remembered his grandfather as a towering, gray-faced man with a raw-boned look of intense concentration, even when he dozed in front of a hearth fire. That intensity slumbered, then burst into energetic action. Abraham's distracted stare would often split into a broad grin when he saw Toby, and Toby would find himself yanked up into a whirling sky where he seemed to fly in the big man's arms, scooting high over furniture and through corridors, sometimes outside onto a deck where Abraham would make him swoop and dive over the guardrail, Toby shrieking and laughing and screaming when the ground rushed away and he felt as though he really was soaring, somehow set free of weight and care. So long ago. Toby bit his lip at the memories, already fading. "Abraham. Or so that magnetic thing says."

You do not believe it.

"Why should I? Who would, with half a brain?"

Yet strange vectors work here.

"Look, Abraham we lost at the Calamity, the fall of Citadel Bishop. That was plenty years back and a hell of a long way from here."

Exactly.

"What you mean by that?"

How would some creature not even made of matter at all, this far distant, know his name?

That stopped Toby for a moment. "Okay, I don't know. But mechs, they make records of everything. Maybe the Magnetic Mind learned it from them."

But the Mind seems to be no friend of mechs.

"Who knows, in this craziness?"

I sometimes wonder about the connection between these entities. Remember the Mantis?

"Sure."

The thought chilled him. The Mantis had pursued Family Bishop, "harvesting" them, killing their bodies and sucking away their selves so that the Family could extract no chip-memory. These suredead the Mantis fashioned into grotesque contortions that it termed "art"—and had displayed to Killeen and Toby with a touch of something like pride.

The Mantis stood in awe of the Magnetic Mind. It may have offered up its knowledge of us, of our ways and persons, to the Mind.

He felt Shibo as though she were sitting before him cross-legged, relaxed and yet ready to move in an instant. "I . . . I don't want to think about that now."

Such memories can hobble us, dear Toby, but they must be faced.

"Hey, some other time, okay?" He felt her somehow shift, pressures adjusting. He sighed with relief and felt better.

It is interesting that now your father has the crew behind him, supporting what he had said all along he wanted—to fly to the True Center, and find there what the ancient texts said was a miraculous place.

Toby shrugged. "Maybe that's what a talent for being Cap'n means. You finagle things around until you like them."

He had let his gaze drift aimlessly, and didn't notice his father approaching. Killeen asked sharply, "What're you saying?"

It was the height of impoliteness to intrude into conversation with an Aspect—much less with a Personality, which could absorb your whole attention. Toby gulped. "I, I was just—"

"I lip-read you saying 'Cap'n.' What is it you can't say to my face?"

"Idle talk, that's all."

Killeen licked his lips, hesitated, then plunged on. "It's Shibo, isn't it?"

"Well, yeasay, but—"

"I just want to say this. So she hears it straight from me." Killeen stared deeply into Toby's eyes, as if somehow he could see the compact intelligence that Toby felt as a looming wall.

"Dad, I don't think—"

"Shibo, we're going to need your judgment up ahead. I'm following my instincts here, and something big is going to happen."

"Dad, come on, I—"

"Remember how we'd talk over plans, figure the best next move, just you and me? I miss that. I miss that a hell of a lot. I know I won't get it back, but if you have any ideas, any guess about what I should do, you speak up, okay?" Killeen's eyes were pleading. He blinked furiously, holding back tears. "Through Toby. I'll understand, I promise I will."

"Dad . . . you know . . ."

Sensations rose in Toby, strange coursing currents of excitement, desire, hoarse murmurs, smells layering the air, husky urgings, remembered moments of skin sliding, satiny, a sheen of sweat—

He jerked away, staggered. Then a hand patted his shoulder.

Killeen drew a long breath. "Thank you, son. I needed that. Just a moment with her, that's all."

Before Toby could spit out a rebuke, Killeen stepped back, saluted, turned—and strode away, the crisp Cap'n again. Toby felt irritated, used.

He tasted sharp, bitter bile in the back of his mouth. *Damn him!* But in the same moment he could see the anguish in his father, and the turmoil that the man could not let rise to the surface.

It is wise to forget this.

"Yeasay, only wisdom's not my strong area."

You are much like your father.

A faint tinkling laughter sounded in his mind. A Personality could take a certain abstract distance from his seething world, Toby saw, and catch the amusement of it. Humor usually invisible to him.

There is an old Family Knight saying, time-honored. Some believe it comes from Old Earth. We say that life is a tragedy to those who feel, and a comedy to those who think.

"Makes sense. Maybe that just means we shouldn't look back over our shoulder too much, see what's gainin' on us."

Good advice as well.

Toby leaned against a steel bulkhead and sighed. Shibo towered in his mind, her serene intelligence sifting through what he saw with a finer, more patient hand.

I wonder who else—or what else—wants us to come here?

"I can't see what makes anybody think people could live in this place. Quath maybe, but not humans. All those old engravings, what were they talking about? Miraculous, sure—" he swept a hand at the view. "But dead."

The wall screens sputtered with virulent radiance. The disk of inward-orbiting matter drew nearer, revealing more fine-grained whorls of color and glowing violence. Now the doomed star they had seen days before was no longer a lopsided, blazing egg. It had exploded into flares, a storm being sucked greedily into the outer rim of the disk. It was like a tortured, twisted sun setting on the far horizon above a flaming landscape. "Looks like a frying abyss to me."

With a gut-tightening surge of feeling, Toby knew that they didn't belong here. The Families were all nomads, in the long run. Only machines could live in this huge, fiery engine. The Families were here now only because of *Argo,* another mechanism made in the great days of human antiquity. Machines like *Argo* were a natural extension of the human hand, but mechs were a cancer. Planets were not their home. Let cold space and burning matter be their realm. So what of human scope could lie here?

Perhaps we are being narrow of vision.

"What's that mean?"

Look there. The threads of green.

The *Argo* was plunging ever closer to the disk, and now they could see the far rim in profile. Gouts of angry red boiled up from the churning plane where the freshly eaten star was working its way inward. Lumps were being chewed as they rotated in the streams.

"So? Looks like a rat getting digested by a snake."

True. Not pretty, probably not even if you're a snake.

"Oh, I see. Those green strands above the plane there?"

Toby could now make out weaving filaments of deep jade that stood above where the star was being devoured. They were like reeds above swamp water, blowing in a breeze.

"It flashes, see?" Blue-green fibers winked with darting yellow. "Like frozen lightning, sort of."

We might be wrong, that nothing else lives here.

"Ummm. Lightning life?"

The Bridge officers had noticed the threads, too. Some fumbled with ship's instruments, focusing sensors on them. Knots and furious snarls climbed up the glowing green lines.

"The stuff ripped off the star—looks like it's fouling up those threads," Toby said.

Jocelyn had managed to get the *Argo*'s antennas to narrow in on the threads, despite the turbulent plasma buffeting the ship. The speakers on the Bridge sputtered and buzzed with the fizzing emissions of the disk—and then eerie high wails cut through the mushy wall of sound.

"What's that?" Jocelyn called. "It sounds terrible."

Killeen's mouth twisted at the shrill chorus. Each voice would rise momentarily over the others, peal forth a mournful note, and then subside into the lacing pattern of lament. "Maybe the Magnetic Mind's not the only thing that knows how to live on electricity."

Toby said, "Not all of them are making those sounds, though. See?"

Jocelyn nodded. "It's the ones that are connected to those bright lumps."

Toby's Isaac Aspect fluttered for attention, and Toby let him out:

These are the stuff of remote history. I heard of them as a boy. Conferring with Zeno now, I believe I may perceive the essence. They are an early life form composed of magnetic vortices, laced with some hot matter. A primitive mode. They feed on the flares and plumes which jut above the disk, like tasty spring flowers from a lush field.

"Doesn't look like they're enjoying dinner much," Toby said sardonically.

The sudden intrusion of the star's mass has flooded them, sucking some down into the fierce disk, where they die.

"How come the Magnetic Mind doesn't die, then?"

It is far greater, larger, finer than these simple, primitive fibers—or so history says. I know little of it. The Mind is vastly old, and reveals no secrets except by necessity. Humans before the Chandelier Era tried to discover some facets of it, and were singed for their trouble.

Toby grimaced. The shrieks and wails were strangely gripping, as each thin voice had its moment, sobbed forth a song beyond understanding, and then faded into the flickering static as the disk plasma reached up, bloated with digesting star-mass—and dragged in the delicate jade streamers, swallowing them in fire. They had lived too close to the edge of grand ferocity, and now paid the price. They struggled frantically against the scalding splashes, gaining small and momentary victories, but in the end they slid into blazing oblivion. The star's shredded mass was plunging inward through the disk, wreaking havoc among the slender, lacy beings.

Toby watched their distant deaths, and despite the gulf separating him from those reedy cries, he felt a strange connection. Such truly alien forms could never be brethren. They were separate nations, but still caught with humans in the net of life and time, fellow prisoners of splendor and travail. Beyond matter itself, gifted with extensions of the senses no human could ever comprehend, they none the less shared the veiled dignity of being forever incomplete, of always emerging, a common heritage of being finite and forever wondering.

But the rest of the Bridge was staring beyond the splashes of color from the disk. Now visible, coming toward them, was the hexagonal of ships flown by the Myriapodia. Once more they held between them the shimmering pearly hoop, a weapon bigger than worlds.

"What's going on?" Killeen wondered out loud. "Where's Quath?"

Jocelyn added, "Even that cosmic string seems small here."

The Myriapodia ships bore down upon the *Argo* relentlessly. They accelerated along the magnetic field lines, invisible slopes that steepened by the minute, pitching down toward the inner edge of the blazing accretion disk.

Into the pit of hell. The air brimmed with hard, dry heat. Toby gulped and wondered if he would live out the next day.

7

A Taste of the Void

As Toby heard them recounted later, the next hours on the Bridge were electrifying. He wasn't there to see them, though. On a ship, chores have to be done on time—no excuses. Not even battle releases all of a crew to gape and thrill.

His assignment was seeding one of the seared agro domes. A team of five sweated beneath the blue-white violence in the dome's sky, glowing from near the Eater of All Things. They had to keep the complex biodiversity here limping along, so plants that had perished under the sting of radiation had to be replaced, and new ones watered, nurtured, sheltered. Hard, ground-grubbing work.

It was a relief, in a way, after the tension of the Bridge. Using your muscles was sometimes easier than using your overstretched mind. He felt the ship moving under him as he toted and dug and fetched, knew that something was happening.

More mechs, he later learned. On the Bridge screens they appeared as flickering images, barely detectable by *Argo*'s systems. The earlier mech craft had been simple compared with these. It stood to reason. Some higher-order mech-tech had driven humanity from space. These were probably the type—surprisingly small, quick, elusive. They plunged down the jet after *Argo* and dispersed. *Argo*'s detectors lost them entirely.

They attacked from several angles, using strategies Killeen and the others could not even understand. Toby heard only a brief rattle of strange static in his sensorium, and then a *whoosh* as the dome above him vanished.

The hit took the dome's air in a howling, hollow rush. Toby gasped for air and got nothing. He went spinning up, away from the soil, which rose after him in a dirty storm.

The wailing gale ebbed as he windmilled his arms, rotating to face upward. A huge hole in the dome swelled before him. He snatched at a broken strut, got it, hung on.

I'm dead, he thought quite clearly. Already his lungs heaved, wanting to breathe.

A painful jab in his leg. A sharp sliver stuck from it, flung by the whistling air. He swung by one arm from the strut, smacked into another.

Angry shouts in his ear—on comm, but no time to listen.

Ears throbbed with pain. Then no more sounds. Air all gone.

He launched himself downward. There was a self-sealing airlock there, already closed. That kept the whole ship from vac'ing out from a single breech.

But it was a long way down and purple flecks danced at the corners of his eyes. They made crazy, enticing patterns and he spent some time trying to figure out what they were trying to say. The dirt below looked no closer and his arms in front of him flapped fruitlessly, like clothes drying in a warm breeze.

In his mouth a metallic, flat bite. The taste of the void.

Purple flies filled his vision. Then a sharp spark of yellow.

Lightning. Playing in the bowl. Licking at bodies as if tasting them.

He dodged away from the slender fire. It missed him and seared the bulkhead beyond.

Ears drumming, fighting to keep his throat closed, chest searing. The soil was closer, in fact very close, and then it hit him in the face. His lungs convulsed but he refused to open his mouth, let his last ball of breath escape into the emptiness.

Scrambling, tumbling, off balance but going on anyway. Across the powdery dirt. Streamers of vapor bursting from the ground, a gray fog.

Ears pounding, hammering his head. In his sinuses, spikes of agony.

The square lock, wobbling. Hard to keep it in focus, stand it upright by tilting his head. While his legs plunged and worked, pounding him forward.

Hands out in front. They hit the lock door and punched a big red plate. The emergency entry dilated. He dived through it.

The first sound he heard was a whisper, then a high-pressure roaring. His ears popped. Only then did he wonder about the others in the dome.

By the time he got his bearings back, it was too late. The other four in the dome never made it to the lock.

Two went through the big hole in the dome and were forever lost. The lightning had fried two more.

Nobody knew whether the lightning was a mech weapon or just natural. Despite the damage to their internal electrocoupling, *Argo*'s tech recorded the two selves in enough detail to provide Aspects in future chip-life.

Small consolation, Toby thought. He felt guilty for not thinking of the other four, for not helping them.

Not much time for guilt. Cermo pressed him into a gang to repair the dome, to slap on pressure patches, to secure ship's atmosphere for the next attack.

But there wasn't any attack. The mechs had taken severe losses from *Argo*'s automatic defenses. She was an old ship but still pretty agile.

People celebrated like it was a victory. Toby wondered if maybe the mechs had just decided to let *Argo* go on, into more dangerous territory. Let the Eater do their job for them.

The thought gave him a sinking sensation, like stepping off into a metallic-tasting chasm. Into the void.

8

The Aperture Moment

"What's your favorite dish?" Besen asked.

"Huh? Oh—the nearest." Toby noticed that he was shoveling in cauliflower with yellow cheese melted over it. Not his favorite dish, but then he hadn't been tasting it anyway.

"Some gourmet you are." She wrinkled her nose at him.

"Look, I don't want to have good taste, I just want things that taste good."

He finished the cauliflower and looked for anything that might be left. The best thing about communal eating was that at the end of the meal extras got passed around. A quick eater got more, and Toby was always hungry. Even when they were zooming down toward a huge disk of white-hot fire, he responded to the rumble in his stomach.

"You don't look concerned," Besen said.

Toby studied her face. The deaths only hours before had been acknowledged in a ship-wide ceremony. Now, by necessity, they got back to business, teams repairing the damage, a bustle of purpose. Besen was not one to give a lot away, but he could read the tightening around the edges of her mouth, the slight high-strung cant of her head.

"No point in worrying." He took her hand across the table and squeezed. "Bigger heads than ours are working on this thing."

Besen bit nervously at her lip. He leaned across the table and gave her a light kiss on the brow. "Ummmm," she said, but didn't stop chewing.

"We're going to make it. I can feel it in my bones." He could no such thing, but he had to cheer her up.

"Do you really think so?"

"Sure. Uh, could you reach me those potatoes?"

"What an animal! Facing death, and he wants to eat."

"Only smart thing to do, seems to me."

"My stomach feels tight. I can't get anything down." She lifted a pea pod with her chopsticks, bit off a fraction, and put it back.

"Well, maybe some other recreation will take your mind off things." He gave her a blank face.

"Some other—oh. You beast!"

"I hear it's good for the circulation."

"First food, then—no, I will not jump into the sack with you while we are flying into the teeth of, of—"

"No need to throw a duck fit."

"Well—I mean—it's so totally inappropriate."

He pretended to consider the question deeply, complete with a profound scowl. "Ummm. What's a better way to vote in favor of there being a future? That's what the whole thing points toward, after all."

She snorted. "*I* thought it was about love."

"That, too. But when we're all candidates for the bone orchard—only who's going to bury us here, when there's no dirt for a cemetery anyway?—the oldest human ritual is a, well, a gesture of faith. Faith in the future."

"So sex is faith now?" She was starting to grin, which had been his aim. "You have an odd religion."

"I worship at the altar of my choosing," he said with a staged haughty air.

"And what's that about the oldest ritual? I can think of some more uplifting ones."

Toby consulted with Isaac, who was a gold mine of ancient terms, in the space of a heartbeat. "They used to call it 'the beast with two backs'—so maybe you have a point."

Besen gave him a grin that began wickedly and slid into a tentative shyness. "You were really just joshing me out of my mood, weren't you?"

"Um."

"You don't like to admit it, but you are very kind, in your own way, behind that fake toughness."

"You have unmasked me, madam."

"Ummm." She eyed him speculatively. "How much time is it, until we get really close to the disk?"

"I can't tell. The Bridge is too busy to give out details, and we're swooping in along a complicated kind of spiral, so—say, why do you want to know?"

"Well, if there really is enough time . . . "

"You hussy! Here I was just trying to cheer you up—"

"Oh, forget it. You can't take a little ribbing yourself." She poked him in the chest with a finger. "Come on, Romeo, let's see what the wall screens tell us. I guess you've used up your supply of romance for the week."

"Then I'll have to stop off and pick up my next allotment. Where do I go?"

"Don't think I can't tell you where to go—get moving."

He had managed to kid her out of her jittery depression, but the raging cauldron visible on the big Assembly Hall screen was enough to bring it all back. He put his arm around her as they stood with a large crowd of the Family, watching the harsh glare of the disk seem to spread and wriggle as they drew nearer.

"Where are we going in all this?" Besen asked, wonder and fear mingling in her tone.

"I don't know. I can't even guess."

"The disk, it's like a huge world or something."

"A world is nothing here, a fly speck."

"But I can see clouds down there. And that twisty thing, it almost looks like a river."

"Almost ain't the same as is. Those clouds are really plasma that would boil away your hand in an eye-blink. That river, my faithful Aspect tells me, is some kind of magnetic knot that's gotten caught up in the disk as it churns around."

"But it looks so familiar, somehow."

Toby's mouth twisted, eyes distant. "We need to see familiar things here. Otherwise it's too strange to deal with."

Besen paused, then nodded soberly. "My teacher Aspect just said that 'river' is bigger than a whole planet. Lots bigger. And that the disk is the size of a solar system."

"Sometimes I wish our Aspects wouldn't tell us so much." She nodded, her hair tumbling in the low gravity. "I felt better when I thought that little squiggle was a river. Still, with the Aspects we can get all branches of learning."

Toby chuckled dryly. "Branches, yeasay. But none of the roots."

"What do you mean?"

"They can't tell us what all this means."

"They know lots of facts and numbers, though."

"Maybe that's all we can trust them with. Anyway, this place, it's big-time stuff." He had to keep up a casual face, but the approaching disk, swelling, throbbing with seething light, was starting to inspire in him less awe and more plain old fear.

"And it eats *stars*. We don't belong here."

"Yeasay to that, too. Only somebody thinks we do."

"And your father believes it, too. He decides."

A note of bitterness had crept into her voice. Around them jaws clenched, eyes whitened as a giant white flare burst across the disk, and a low growl rose. Slowly it dawned on Toby that the entire Assembly Hall murmured with discontent, with dread, with tight-stretched anxiety. The deaths had sobered them, loosened Killeen's hold. A bitter wind stirred them all.

A band of men and women at the far side of the Hall began shouting. Before Toby could understand what was happening, the crowd began to move. They knocked over tables and squeezed through the outer doorways, pressing on with gathering energy, like a tide sucked forward by an irresistible moon. Sour words flew, boots thumped on the deck, the air rang with harsh accusation.

Toby got up and followed, hardly noticing the twinge in his leg where a metal spike had gouged him in the agro dome. That seemed like an age ago. He didn't limp; his body had already fixed up most of the gouge.

He and Besen were at the back when the swarming pack reached the Bridge. To Toby there was a ghostlike quality to the rapid swerve of events. Again the officers stopped them. Again Killeen appeared on the balcony. Again he held them back with a stern speech.

This time Toby sensed the deep foreboding in the shuffling, muttering crowd, and now that he knew what to look for, he saw how his father used their fear to bind them to him. They *needed* to believe in him now, and he played upon that. If he hadn't, they might easily have worked themselves into a frenzy, have boiled over into mutiny.

Killeen held them in part by sheer physical presence. He was a full chest-length taller than Toby, testament to his greater years. He used that, and the added perspective of the balcony, to cow the louder protestors.

Long ago, in response to the rapacious mechs, humanity had lengthened its life span by tinkering with its own growth pattern. The body given forth by natural evolution, far back on ancient Earth, had matured at about twenty of the Old Earth years. Then even the best body hit a plateau. Gradually it weakened with the years, the erosion of muscle and bone offset by the slow gathering of wisdom and experience.

To counter this, long ago the Family of Families had sculpted humanity. Now, people simply never reached that plateau where decline set in. People died of injury and mech attack, not age. They never stopped growing. Their rate slowed, of course—otherwise, elders would shoot up into sluggish giants. A woman a century old might not gain an extra finger's width of height in a decade. But she grew. And she would have all the savvy and grit years brought.

This perpetual late youth held in check the inner magics that governed aging. The eldest Bishops were nearly twice as tall as Toby. This meant higher door sills and bigger meals. More important, elders towered over others, their experience given the force of bulk. Toby stood lanky for his eighteen Old Earth years, but he felt small and insignificant compared to Cermo or Killeen. In them, the weight of Family authority had firm physical presence.

This Killeen used with unconscious, telling effect. Still, voices called out protests. Oaths cut the air, strident and ragged with fear.

The only pressure keeping the crew back was the long history that had led them here. More than anyone, Killeen embodied that past. He stood fire-eyed, intimidating in his scowling silence. He had fooled the Mantis, gotten them off Snowglade. He had fallen through a planet and lived. Been swallowed by Quath, then been set free. He had killed mechs and laughed as he did it. And a voice like lightning had sought him out, had led them here. Against that they weighed their own fear.

At that stretched moment Quath came lumbering from the main corridor. There was a strange smell to the alien, a sweet-sour aroma in the steadily warming ship. People moved uneasily aside. The alien was an ally, but that did not alter her strangeness.

Quath stopped, her great head turning. Ruby eyes on stalks twisted like vines, slowing to study a nervous upturned face, a bearded man's hair, a woman's clutched carrypouch, as if they were museum exhibits.

Then she sent, <I have finished communion with my kind. The great Cosmic Circle is prepared. They come fast upon us, for purpose I do not yet see. They say we must speak again with the magnetic being.>

Somehow, this straight, factual message carried the day. They quieted, looking to Killeen, who said calmly, "I'll try. They'll help us? With whatever comes?"

<They must.>

Toby thought it was a little funny that Quath didn't say "They will" or "They'll try"—but then the crowd began to drift away, and he realized that this odd, quiet note had gotten Killeen through another crisis.

As officers went back to their jobs, he and Besen managed to slip onto the Bridge. Killeen was talking to Quath, who snaked her neck and head into view. Metallic shanks scraped the walls as she moved, legs clattering with a staccato rhythm Toby found unsettling.

"That's all they said?" Killeen demanded.

<The noise of transmission mounts. Plasma waves lap and tug at every word.>

"Where you figure we're headed?"

<The Myriapodia have aged records which are perhaps of some use. They do not believe our goal can be the disk—that way lies chaos and death.>

Killeen chuckled without mirth. "Yeasay squared."

<Others of the Myriapodia signify that the very oldest texts speak of portals here.>

"Portals to what?"

<No one knows, who has not crossed the portal. And that is blocked by mech inventions.>

"Here? What could survive?"

<So say other Myriapodia. We swarm, much confused on this point. Even the burning disk appears a more likely place for lasting structures than does the sphere of flame further in.>

Killeen paced, hands at the small of his back, shoulders set square and rigid. "We can't last long, getting this close. We're heating up, the jet is getting tighter around us—"

<We should slow.>

"That'll just hang us out to dry. I want to be movin', able to jet out of here as soon as—"

<A slight pause. Enough to let the Cosmic Circle lead the way.>

"Why?"

<I do not know.>

"Damn it! To helm this ship I have to know—"

<Hold. I sense something more here.>

Quath had caught it before the humans, but now Toby felt the prickly gathering of electrostatic charges along his scalp, the humming beneath his boots.

You have penetrated to my deep regions. You are at the edge of the jet. Now is the time to render farewells.

Killeen scowled. "What? You brought us here, you can't—"

I feel the growing roll and stress of the disk at my feet. It sends devouring plumes of eating matter up, deep into my field lines. These erosions I must fight. I have little time for you.

"You said you were anchored in that stuff. All that talk about being immortal—"

Immortality is an aim, not a fact. Matter's rub can erase even such as I. I am doomed to struggle, just as are you, though on scales of time and length you cannot know. I am far grander and share little else but this base property.

"So you abandon us, huh? Just when—"

I have final words for you, then I withdraw my store of complex waveforms from your region. By retreating to other parts of myself, the weave of fields far above the disk, I can preserve my sense of self, my remembrances of my long span, the essence of me.

"Damn it, we're going to need help just to survive the next hour, never mind—"

I send a map, simple and misleading, but enough for you. I am lodged for the moment in the field lines which taper into the disk. You are riding down one of my flanks. You depart me in a moment, at the location marked.

Killeen shouted, "Damn you, you can't—"

Small beings such as you should remember who they are.

"I'll remember real well, thank you," Killeen said sardonically.

Toby had never seen his father struggle so hard to control his temper, teeth gritted and eyes narrowed, flinty.

Toby opened his mouth to say something, but at that moment the wall screens all filled with the same figure. It was colored and three-dimensional, a tangle of lines and moving dots and splattered yellows and greens and reds.

Complexity, confusion. Toby felt awed by it and repelled at the same time. There were levels of meaning and motion here he knew he could not comprehend.

Then, as if the Magnetic Mind could tell how hard this was to understand, the figure simplified, became flat, two-dimensional. Geometry he could understand. The clarity of mathematics shaped to a human mind.

Toby saw that a long thick swath was a side view of half the disk, the wrath and roil of it replaced by a single shading. Thin lines sloped down into the disk—from above and below, where the jet formed. These were the magnetic lines of the Mind itself—part of its huge structure, stretching beyond the disk and into the leagues between the stars. But these magnetic feet mired in the disk were important, for here the Mind fed itself from the furious energies released in the disk. Toby felt, for reasons he could not name, that even these sloping lines, far larger than solar systems, were as insignificant on the scale of the Mind as the curling hairs on his own legs.

And along the innermost magnetic line lay an orange dashed trail that lengthened as he watched—*Argo*'s path.

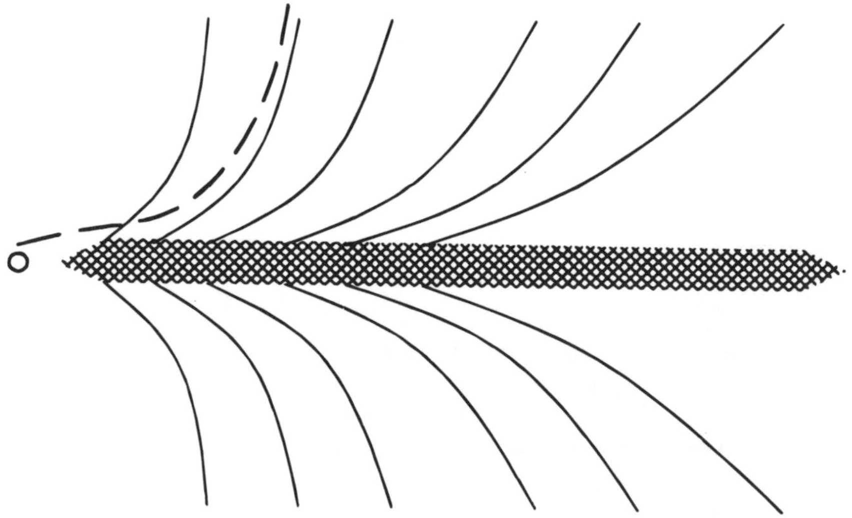

Then the dashed trail raced ahead, switched from orange to blue, and left the field line. It arced inward—and the figure expanded, bringing into view the disk's inner edge, which tapered down to a point. Beyond that, even further in, Toby had expected to see the glowing white-hot ball that he saw on the viewscreens.

But the intense radiance appeared on the figure as only an insubstantial shimmer. Apparently the Magnetic Mind did not consider those searing energies important. *Argo*'s dashed trail led through the radiance, moving more and more swiftly. Then it arced up slightly. At the very center of the white ball lay something utterly dark, though winking with small energies as he watched.

You will depart from me. I withdraw. I send now details of your trajectory to come.

"Wait!" Toby saw real fear haunt Killeen's eyes. "Why? Where are we going?"

The star that has died at the outer rim now sends its shattered self inward through the disk. A swirl and plunge of massive lumps come lashing through the disk. They stress and deform me. This I suffer—and for you. Such wrenching mass yields up the conditions the Abraham-thing appears to want—and predicted. You shall embrace it. Move quickly now, for a cusp season approaches.

"What?" Killeen shouted, balling his fists. "What's coming?"

The aperture moment.

9

The Cyaneans

Toby put his arm around Besen and held on for dear life. The *Argo* groaned and pulsed. Decks and bulkheads creaked. Toby felt his own boots rock with unseen stress. His Isaac Aspect called,

What marvelous tides!

"That's what moves water around in lakes and such, right?"

Yes, but the force comes from another gravitating body. Like the doomed star we saw at the edge of the great disk, torn apart. Now the black hole is pulling on* Argo*, a bit more strongly on the side closer to the hole, than on the outer side. We feel that as tension, trying to pull the ship apart.

"Damn!" Toby told Besen this, then asked, "Can *Argo* take it?"

I believe so. The stress is annoying, that I concede—

"How would *you* know?"

I can generalize from my past life. Admittedly I do not feel your bodily discomfort, but—

"Or pleasures either, right?"

Quite so. I merely watch your visual input.

Toby didn't like the thought of Isaac even seeing some parts of his private life, and Besen's close warmth made him even more sure of it. It was embarrassing, to think that his Aspects had been there, in some limited sense, in the warm, aromatic intimacy of the bedclothes . . .

Do not trouble over that. Our opinions mean nothing.

This was from Shibo. A deeper, resonant voice that carried nuances that without warning drew him into her own interior world, the full spreading wealth of her past.

—Her beloved Citadel beset by forces bleak and imponderable, ill-shaped and just beyond the deranged horizon. Would they come by seething air or across the cratered plain? And when? Or were their ambassadors already inside the shut gates?—gray enemies no bigger than an eye's pupil, yet seeing just as much, and rapping back to their comrades their microwave reports, machine tales of the soft goings here.—

He regained his balance. "How . . . how come?"

Aspects are static. Aspects cannot grow. So their views do not alter. You cannot truly change their minds about anything.

Toby wasn't sure this was much consolation. He noted that Shibo did not say that she could not change. Were Personalities different? He had the distinct impression, from subtle changes in Isaac and Joe and maybe even Zeno, that Shibo was carrying out some sort of therapy on them, resolving the clashing psyche-storms that beset such truncated minds.

Then his distracted thoughts came to an abrupt end when a sudden wave flexed through the deck. He and Besen slammed into a bulkhead and tumbled to the deck of the Bridge.

As he got up, Toby saw that Killeen had remained standing, legs braced to take surges. But the Cap'n's face was drawn and he searched the wall screens intently for understanding. They showed a blinding hail of gauzy hot gas and chunks of unknown matter, all spraying by them at blistering speed. Warm breezes now blew through the Bridge, fluttering Toby's hair as the circulators labored to ease the steady heating from outside.

Killeen called again for the Magnetic Mind. Again there was no answer. It had abandoned them.

The ship's officers were all anchored in their shock couches, staring at Killeen, visibly wondering why he did not strap himself in, too. Toby knew why. If he conceded even this small vulnerability, it would whittle him down in the eyes of those he now had to lead. So he turned and conspicuously paced, hands behind back, as another ripple shook the Bridge. He did not stumble, did not even slow his steady pace.

Toby looked around, but there were no vacant shock couches for him and Besen. If they wanted to see what was going on, they would have to stand. Nobody noticed them, or else they would have been hustled away. All eyes watched the screens and the Cap'n.

Killeen turned slowly, holding the Bridge crew with his level, stone-faced gaze. Then he saw Quath's head, shifty-gimballed in a hooded carapace, jutting into the Bridge entrance. The Cap'n called out with a faint note of desperation, "What do your brothers know about this place?"

<Only ancient texts can guide us. The Myriapodia ventured this way once, probing to see what had drawn the mechs here.>

"They never came back?"

<We, too, suffered a fall when the mechs discovered us. They sensed us here first, disturbing their works. We withdrew quickly, unlike you humans. You persist beyond reason.>

Toby broke in. "How come you hunted humans, then? We could have been allies all along."

<We mistook you for animals. You had fallen so far, beaten down by mechs. Only your father and your Legacies reminded us that you are of the stuff which once blazed so bright and now is so pitiful.>

Toby gulped. Quath was no diplomat.

Killeen asked, "These 'texts' of yours—what do they say?"

<Many ships were lost here. It is easy to slip on the sliding surface of space itself.>

"Space? Hell, what about the *heat*? And this stuff coming at us, big chunks—"

<Those are masses crushed and compacted by the stretch of geometry here. Avoid them, and otherwise ignore them. They are on their way to their funerals.>

Some consolation, Toby thought. Probably they all were on the same trip.

"Did your brothers map this place?" Killeen demanded impatiently.

<I am processing their records now with a hindbrain. Here.>

The screens swam with colors, forming and reforming into images that might make sense to the Myriapodia, Toby thought, but not to him.

The image was three-dimensional, shot through with gaudy rushing dots. It whirled and jumped and made no sense. Then Quath squashed it down to two dimensions, and Toby could see what was happening.

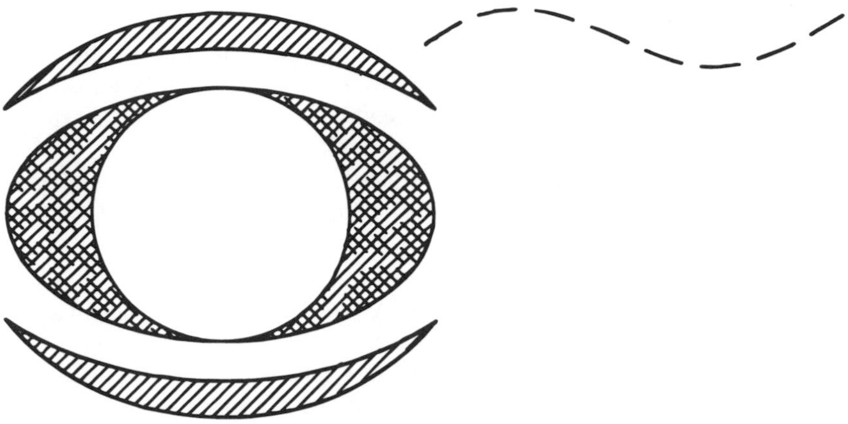

"That empty ball at the center—it's the black hole, right?" he asked his Isaac Aspect. He heard a rapid cross talk, Zeno's sad static-clogged phrases, entries spooling out from a text-chip he carried but could not read by himself.

Indeed. I consulted with Zeno, who agrees that these Myriapodia have correctly mapped the geometry near it, as well. The bulging, shaded region wrapped around the hole is the ergosphere—a zone where the black hole's spin warps everything, forcing space-time to rotate with the hole itself.

"Sounds dangerous."

No one knows. Zeno's folk believed that the ergosphere was a place where nearly all the energy of a ship would be required simply to keep from falling into the black hole itself.

Toby watched the figure on the wall screens, the way the spin of the hole made a whirlpool in space. Isaac told him that it was not matter spinning around there, but space-time itself.

"Uh, what's space-time? I mean, I know space, and time's what a clock talks about, but . . ."

Quath broke into his mind, transmitting directly.

<Lower beings do not see the fundamental essence of the world, which combines space and time. Do not knit a knot of concern for this. Even the Myriapodia do not see space-time. We, too, divide it into the easier ideas of distance and duration.>

Until that moment Toby had not realized that Quath could pick up his whispering talks with his own Aspects. He felt embarrassed, then irked—and then pushed aside his feelings. No time for that now.

"So how do we get out of here?"

<We do not.>

"Huh?" Toby noticed the dashed line of their planned trajectory. It lifted some, then plunged toward the top crescent-shaped blob.

<We must pass through the Cyaneans. There is no other way to enter the portal that the Myriapodia believe dwells here.>

"Those? The crescents? They're awfully close to that ergosphere thing." The hazy crescents hovered like caps over the poles of the black hole, seeming to screen it.

<The Cosmic Circle will clear our way.>

Toby looked around, dazed more by the ideas that were coming thick and fast than by the fluttering, lurching waves that swept through *Argo.* More tidal stresses, twisting with immense hands.

Then it dawned on him that everyone in the Bridge was looking at him. He blinked. Knowing his easy way with Quath, Killeen had just let Toby extract information from the alien. Well, it was efficient.

"So what do we do now?" Killeen studied Quath as if he could read an expression in the great, many-eyed head.

<Let the Cosmic Circle do its work.>

"It's going to get us out of this?"

<The Myriapodia believe this is the only path.>

Killeen paused, reflecting as the flickering screens lit the Bridge with eerie, shifting patterns. He was at the end of his tether, Toby saw, tired and confused. His heart went out to his father, caught in this huge engine of destruction, led here by hopes and legends, driven by fear. He let go of Besen and went to his father's side. Hesitantly, as Killeen watched the vibrant flux, he reached out and clasped Toby's arm.

They stood that way for a long moment, watching now as the Myriapodia ships came into view. Against the seethe of sky and mass Toby saw that this place was not evil or good, but something far worse. It was indifferent. Beauty lay here, and terror. It could witness anything, this churning machine. Its unforgivable vast resplendence mocked the human plight.

The glinting Myriapodia ships held the huge cosmic hoop between them in a magnetic grip, and it glowed with intense brilliance. Isaac told Toby that the hoop was gathering energy as it fell toward the black hole. It passed through the magnetic fields anchored in the hole and extracted from them strong currents, electrical surges that lit up the hoop like an immense sign.

<The cusp moment approaches.>

"That the same as what the Magnetic Mind said?" Killeen whispered, eyes fixed on the screens. In the warming air the Bridge was silent.

<No. This is the end of the mech device.>

Toby frowned. "Mech? What's mech-made here?"

<The Cyaneans. They are great twisted regions of space-time, turbulence trapped in caps. They would shred us.>

"So? Just more of the weird weather here—"

<The mechanicals made the Cyaneans.>

Killeen and Toby alike regarded Quath with disbelief. The alien went on, <The mechanicals can bring great forces to bear. You saw their massive, shadowy constructions, feeding on the energy and matter here. Their researches are many and wide.>

"But . . . the Cyaneans? Hard to believe," Killeen said. "Those things, they're huge."

<Larger than stars. That is why the Myriapodia bring their own craft to bear. My kind shall lead the way.>

The Cosmic Circle had raced ahead of *Argo* now. Then on the major wall screen Toby saw ahead an enormous sheet—the Cyaneans. It was like a choppy gray sea, waves of blacks and troughs of white making shifting patterns as far as the eye could see.

In the brilliant white-hot glare of yellows and reds that blazed up all around them, the eerie lack of color in the Cyaneans filled Toby with a sinking dread. He felt as though the bottom had fallen out of his stomach. Only Besen steadied him, holding from one side while Toby stood with the other arm around his father. There was nothing here for mere humans to do.

Ahead, the hoop plunged down into the gray, rippling expanse. And cut. Like a knife, it sheared through the ashen surface and deep, deep into the interior.

Released, the edges of the strange dusky surface pulled away. They curled away from the Cosmic Circle, peeling back.

But the hoop paid a price. It crumpled along its leading edge. The resistance of the turbulence dented and deformed it.

Toby could not guess what colossal energies grappled there. The sharpness of the Cosmic Circle was a mere atom wide, his Isaac Aspect said, but its tight curvature was more than equal to the gray, storming surges. It pierced the tossing turbulence, sending sputtering hot light in its wake.

"What . . . what do we do?" Killeen asked quietly.

<Follow the Cosmic Circle.> Quath sent a chorus of lilting sounds through the human-linked sensorium, a plaintive long note of sympathy.

Killeen made a sign to Jocelyn, who was watching him with round, frightened eyes. She turned the ship downward, into more of the blazing luminosity, toward the shifting gray sheet. Long moments passed as the grayness swelled like an impassable wall of strangely shifting stone.

They rushed into the shadowy gap carved by the hoop. To all sides peaks and valleys formed and dissolved, like mountains of ash made from burned bones.

Fringes of the stuff washed over *Argo* and brought dizzying, reeling moments when Toby thought he had been snatched up by his heels and shaken, upside down, hair fraying in the air. Crew vomited on the Bridge. Others howled with fright and nausea. The ship's deep skeleton protested, popping and creaking.

But the long passage stayed open. Once cut, it peeled back to form new zones of contorted space-time. *Argo* sped after the glowing, crumpling hoop.

It seemed to take a long time to cross the thickness of the sliced Cyanean ghost-space. Besen puked and gasped, mouth gaping and messed. But Toby held on to his father, not to steady him but to simply know that he was there.

And then they were out, free. The hoop tumbled away, crushed. The Myriapodia ships banked after it, grasping at the battered cosmic string, turning back toward the poles of the entire rotating system.

Killeen found his voice. "Jocelyn. Try . . . try to follow them."

<No.> Quath rattled her legs loudly, steel clanging and ringing. <The course we follow is toward the center.>

"What?" Killeen's mouth sagged.

<As the Magnetic Mind directed.>

"Look . . . Family Bishop always spoke of True Center as our goal, without anybody knowing why. It was handed down. We believe it. But this . . ." Toby saw that his father was nearly finished, his endurance broken by the enormity of this place.

Then the gray exhaustion hardened. Killeen's face lost its slackness, eyes regaining their composure. "Toward the black hole? Look, we've followed what you said. And that Magnetic Mind, too. And we've come as far as we can. Whatever was supposed to be here, waiting for us, it's gone. Eaten up. Burned away."

<I follow the ancient findings of the Myriapodia. There is more here. Inward.>

Killeen said flatly, "I don't believe it."

Toby looked ahead of them. The ergosphere was a rotating fat waist in the diagram, but ahead bulged something spitting light like an angry, setting sun. Except that it extended away in a great, curving sheet. It arced into the distance, and Toby understood at last the size of the demon black hole that was the ultimate, hidden cause of all the cosmic violence he had witnessed. The vicious maw. The reason why the Galactic Center was a swarming, frying pit of death and loss.

Through eye-stinging radiance he saw the spreading sheen where the hole came finally to rule even the fabric of the universe, clasping space-time until it bent to the unending will of gravity.

Through ten billion years the galaxy had fed it. Stars had perished, swept into it by the millions. And the civilizations that had thrived around those suns—they had been forced to flee or die.

He wondered what planets that sun had once harbored, whether they had given birth to organic molecules that could link and replicate themselves, whether intelligence had once brimmed on those lost shores. Whether creatures had glimpsed their fate, seen it as a boiling, growing presence in the sky. Perhaps they had known that at the dead center of such immense tragedy sat an absolute, unblinking void.

<We must fly on. Down, toward the thickest part of the spinning bulge.>

"The ergosphere?" Toby whispered.

<It is written. My kind have sacrificed their most valuable tool, to cut a passageway for your kind. You can carry forward the quest. The physics is momentarily appropriate for our entry.>

A strong timbre was back in Killeen's voice. "Why?"

<The surge of matter that came from the dying star has now reached the innermost rim of the disk. It falls now into the ergosphere, creating fresh contortions. Only now, the Myriapodia say, can the ergosphere portal be entered.>

"Why?"

<It is like a living thing, flexing and restless. Pores in its great hide open in response to the massage of mass. Think of the ergosphere as a tight-stretched skin of space-time, across which waves wash. The infall of matter forces the entire beast to readjust itself, knit up the ravels of causality. As a star's weight rains upon the beast, the resulting splashes in space-time open opportunities.>

"To do what?"

<To safely enter—or as safely as [untranslatable] allows. Only a black hole which has eaten a million suns can provide unscathed passage. Lesser holes would shred us. The Eater is so large, that its outer precincts are far from the central singularity. This renders its tidal forces here tolerable. A vessel slipping tangent to the ergosphere can find new routes, paths and passages.>

"To where?"

<I do not know—I *cannot* know. The Illuminates describe a place of fundamental chaos, where physics rules randomly. Nothing in the universe can predict where we will end, once we pass through the portal.>

"It's a gamble. If we wait—"

<Stars fall into the hole's final embrace on average only once in a thousand years. This is the aperture moment.>

Toby studied Killeen. The glare surrounding *Argo* cut deep shadows in the face he knew so well, and in a hardening of the broad mouth Toby saw what they would do.

Photovores

Burning flowers rise from the disk. They blossom, spewing plasma seeds above and below the slow, spiraling churn.

Bright tongues press out. Positron swarms. Prickly, annihilating all they touch.

They dissolve where they strike the incoming, leaden matter. Antimatter spills and licks and dies. A blaze of hard gamma, cleansing purity.

Their funeral pyre is an outward-ramming wall of pure photons. Intense, implacable. Pushing back matter that wants to fall into the grasp of the gravity well.

Electromagnetic stresses work along the surface of the expanding pressure-bubble. Green worms twisting. Dark oblongs of troubled mass slow, hesitate above the fray. The infall halts.

Yet this is the food of the Eater itself, the raw material of the disk and all the following fury. The disk begins to starve. Not immediately, for light takes hours to cross the hurricane forests of furious, grinding gravity.

Inertial moments tick on. The disk ebbs. In turn, its light pressure—now holding back a jostling layer of anxious, ionized mass—drains away.

As the press of photons subsides, matter resumes its fatal fall. Again streams of black mass spiral down. The disk accepts this tribute. Fire-flowers again shatter clumps, smash molecules to atoms, strip atoms into bare charge.

So goes the press and relax, press and relax. Perpetual armature. Fountain. Life source.

Above the disk, safe from the sting, hang motes. Sheets, planes, herds. Uncountable. Billowing with the electromagnetic winds. Holding steady.

The photovores are grazing.

They coast on the fitful breeze of electrons and protons blown out by the Eater's angry disk. Great wings of high-gloss moly-sheet spread, catching the particle wind's steady push. Vectoring.

They apply magnetic torques in a complex dynamical sum. Turning, they wage a constant struggle to slip free of the Eater's gravitational tug.

Yet they must use these ruling forces in their own perpetual, gliding dance. This is ordained.

At times the herds fail to negotiate the complex balance of outward winds against the inward, seductive drag. Whole sheets will peel away.

Some are cast into the shrouded masses of molecular clouds, which are themselves soon to boil away. Others follow a helpless descending gyre. Long before they would strike the brilliant disk, the hard glare hammers them. They burst into tiny pinpricks of dying light.

But not now. A greater governing force approaches.

Ink-dark lenses swivel to regard an intruder. Easing in from high along the Eater's axis, sensors see only ceramic slabs and high-impact buffers.

Intelligence sheathed against the torrent. Circuits an atom wide, filmy substrates, helium-cold junctions—all are vulnerable here to the sting of gamma rays and hard nuclei. Even the exalted wear armor.

But the photovores see only a presence they should honor. The vast sailing herds part. Ivory sheets curl back to reveal still deeper planes: yellow-gold light seekers.

These live to soak in photons and excrete microwave beams. With minds no more complex than the tube worms of ancient oceans, they are each a single electromagnetic gut, head to tail. Placid conduits.

Dimly they know that this descending presence is the cause of their being. Herds shear apart in reverence for its passage.

A trembling chorus of greeting. The coasting mass ignores them.

Their hissing microwaves waver. Momentary confusion. Then come fresh orders. They focus all their abundance upon the passing presence. The visitor needs more power here. They feed it.

Accelerating, it mashes a few of the herd on its carapace. It never notices the layers and multitudes peeling back, their gigahertz voices joined in glad chorus. They are plankton. It ingests their offering without heed.

In any case, a worsening discussion preoccupies it.

Our/Your deception went well. But I/We do not like their close approach to the Wedge.

The infalling star lashes the disk. They will probably perish there quite soon.

They may make use of turbulence.

I/You have been trying to understand their way of thinking. Let us discourse in their style of two-valuedness. It may serve to anticipate their moves.

Like this? I am merely me?

And I am a sole self as well. See how simple?

Stunted. Awkward.

Yet this is how they live.

As an experiment, I accept. The concept of "me" is so limiting. Nevertheless—Report!

Our direct intrusion into their craft went as planned. We interrogated their systems with the bolt of electrical discharges.

These craft-systems are loyal to us?

No. They cannot be, without destroying themselves.

We cannot master such minds?

They spring from an era when the primates knew how to protect against us.

Did they yield up the secrets we seek?

Not entirely. They know that this heritage the humans have is embedded in hard matter.

Improbable, on the face of it.

Though true, apparently.

Who would ever use such savage methods?

The primates were in decline when they devised this record, recall. Any electrical memory we would eventually subvert.

So it is in their ship?

Apparently, but not all of it. Encased in matter somehow. The Legacies, they term it. But the vessel of containment is not clear.

This clarifies matters. We must vaporize their craft.

Not all the needed information is there.

Where is the rest of it?

We do not know.

Is this why they speak to the magnetic Phylum?

To lodge their secrets there? That would make our task difficult.

You might be able to force compliance from that Phylum.

To do so entails moving enough mass to interrupt their field lines massively. The energetics are daunting.

Let you hope that is not called for.

Perhaps it is best to probe further, despite the dangerous warp of the quasi-mechanicals' hoop-discontinuity.

With the same energies, directed into the heart of their craft, they would be vapor now.

Be mindful: The electrical discharges we devised infested their very innermost intelligences. Their own electrominds—of limited breadth, but useful—now listen for us.

Can they find these Legacies?

They already have some of them.

Excellent! What are they?

A guide to the location of their own genetic heritage.

A genome map?

Apparently.

That is of no danger to us.

Apparently.

You seem uncertain.

There are odd traces of data woven into the code. Useless, it would seem.

Errors, probably.

I wish we could be sure.

One must live with such ambiguities. It is of our and your nature to tolerate them.

Absence of evidence is not evidence of absence.

There are no clear signs that any primates have reached the Wedge in a long time.

Some surely have gotten through.

Many of us dislike talk of the Wedge.

Now who is uncomfortable with ambiguity?

The decision to assault the Wedge long ago came from all of us.

No—it was mostly yours.

That is oversimplified! I knew this division into two selves would vex me! See? It leads to blame—self-blame. Surely you must admit that the idea, to carve the Wedge to pieces with a hoop-discontinuity, was a good one.

Except that the Wedge swallowed the hoops.

We need not dwell on memories. The Wedge will yield to us in time.

Exactly, though not the way you mean. The Wedge is *in* time—which is why we cannot reach it.

Our science will master it eventually. We have surpassed all else that ventured here. What matters this, if they enter the Wedge?

We have deployed a relay point. It will perch at the lip of the Wedge, picking up signals from their craft, sending them to us.

That requires great energy of the relay ship. Only the Wedge can hang suspended against the slide of space.

True. But the effort will be repaid.

We tried such methods before—and lost much.

This time is vastly more important.

Concentrate on these primates! They are the past—shuck them from us.

There is something of the future in them.

Ignore such musings. You have a mission—do it.

We must learn the nature of the threat. Otherwise we cannot be sure we can in fact expunge it.

Of course we can.

Ignorance is not an effective strategy.

I do not like your tone, Aesthetic.

Then I am understood.

Part III

THE TIME PIT

1

Deep Reality

They plunged toward the boundary sheet of the ergosphere. Toby thought it looked like the flexing skin of some blistered animal, leathery and trembling with perpetual rage.

Then *Argo* shot along it, accelerating in the quickening gravity, and his perspective changed. Now it was like a troubled sea just below, tossed with wrinkles and waves. Big combers collided with each other in choppy sprays, whipped into a frenzy by an unseen storm.

"Hold on," Killeen said stiffly.

Toby was strapped into a Bridge couch. Gravity shifted all around them, plucking at his clothes, fidgeting in his inner ear, tilting his sensorium so that even his vision lurched and heaved. His crackling, faint Zeno Aspect volunteered,

These forces . . . vagrant . . . were recorded by . . . expeditions . . . humans . . . described them as "like an irritated tiger shaking a mouse."

"Ummm . . . what's a tiger?" Toby had seen field mice, had trapped the sharp-toothed rodents who ate their grain in Citadel Bishop. Zeno sent a foggy picture of something gazing with quiet, threatening ferocity. Flaring full-color into his sensorium, it sent a chill of alarm through Toby, until Zeno said,

This creature . . . data says . . . scarcely longer than your hand.

"What a relief." He imagined being picked up and tossed around by a cat. The stomach-churning lurches and twists he could take, but sometimes the turbulence felt like whispery fingers trailing along his skin, eerie and ghostlike.

Bridge officers were in couches, but the Cap'n paced the deck grimly, fighting the tugs and yanks of vagrant gravity, unwilling to yield. No one dared interrupt Killeen's thoughts as his boots thumped hard, hands clasped behind his back, face a permanent scowl.

Toby could see that his father was steeling himself against what looked like certain disaster. To charge into the unknown was one thing, a long habit for the Families. But to slam into the face of a living blackness . . .

Killeen nodded to Jocelyn. "Now."

A sliding sensation. Toby gulped. A stretching wrench. The entire Bridge seemed to hold its breath.

They plunged toward the rippling skin of the ergosphere. The surface worked with gales black as carbon. Troughs and crests were lit by a hell-red glow, light bent and squeezed by brute gravity.

Jocelyn whispered, throat tight, "This is it!"

—and they dove beneath the waves.

In.

Through.

Toby blinked. No shock, no collision. Smooth, swift sailing into—

Flaming bullets. They rode through a rain of light.

To Toby the interior of the ergosphere was a sullen night, peppered by blinding, quick streaks of luminosity. Fever-bright pellets shot by them—a pelting shower in red and violet and a strange, hot green.

"What . . . what is this place?" Toby whispered.

<The time pit,> Quath sent.

"You mean the black hole?"

<That swallower lies further in. This is the region whirled into being by the rotation of the black hole. A murderous place. Here space-time is dragged around by the devourer's dark mass, so that they become scrambled.> Quath rattled and twirled her eye-stalks to illustrate.

"Huh? Scrambles what?"

<Time and space. They are truly linked, and deep reality appears only to those who can see in space-time.>

"Well, I can see pretty near any part of the spectrum—"

<You and I do not share the privilege of perceiving space-time directly. I doubt that anything which struggles up out of lesser life can see it so, alas. It must be like [untranslatable]. Or being able to see gravity itself as a vital thing, elastic.>

"How come we're so dumb?" The luminous downpour outside hammered harder, the wall screen splashing the faces of everyone on the bridge with sparking, fleeting colors. No one moved. *Argo* shook and popped with unseen strains. Toby's sour stomach told him that gravity was shifting restlessly, like a prowling beast.

<To split the true world into simpler ones is a great convenience. So we sense space easily, but leave the riddle of time to be governed by the ticking of our machines, our clocks.>

Toby grimaced. "Time is just what clocks tell, mother of maggots. Don't fancy it up."

<But time is not merely that. It lives and wrestles with its marriage partner, the three dimensions of extension that we can sense. Their struggle is never done, and rules all. Here in the time pit, they wage it to the full.>

Toby shook his head, feeling woozy. "Too much for me."

The Bridge lay silent, awed. The bulk of the crew was crammed into the ship's center, shielded against the sleeting particles that even *Argo*'s magnetic fields could not fully deflect. Toby and the others on the Bridge had taken a concoction drawn up by one of Jocelyn's Aspects, to repair any radiation damage to their body cells. It was a milky drink that tasted like cinders somebody'd peed on, but Jocelyn said it held tiny critters that could fix up shattered molecules, stitch together broken structures, like a smidge of a seamstress.

Right now Toby felt like the damage was all in his stomach. It lurched and squeezed as the direction of gravity swung and snaked like an unmoored cable. He held on to his couch and breathed through his mouth, not minding the saliva that fell from his lips—until it then looped through the air as gravity abruptly curled and pulsed—sending the warm gop back into his right eye.

"Augh!"

"You all right, son?" Killeen called.

"Uh, yeah. Kinda woozy, is all."

Killeen gave him a quick, sympathetic smile. "Hold on. It'll probably get worse."

Abruptly there rose in him a silent, stony presence—Shibo, her Personality sending silky fingers of reassurance into his sensorium. She did not speak, and he had not summoned her, but her essence laced the air, tinged his sight, brought delicate traceries of memory peeling like sheets from the granite-firm surface of her mind. Filigrees of olden, endless days, of sun-dappled calm and damp leafy bowers she had played in as a girl, of happy childrens' laughter tinkling through a glade, of lip-smacking spicy meals shared with friends now gone—

Uneasily he shrugged off these influences, his anxiety surfacing despite her silent efforts. "Dad, where are we *going*?"

A rueful grimace. "I don't know."

"But—" Yes, Toby thought, *but*—

They both knew full well how dangerous this was, everybody knew, yet they flew on into the pit of the unknown. An abyss with no visible redemption. And for reasons none of them, not even the Cap'n, could express in words.

Something shimmered in the wall screens.

"Ship incoming," Jocelyn said tensely.

"Here?" Cermo whispered nearby. "A ship in this place?"

A rustle of surprise, maybe hope.

"Vector in," Killeen said. "Our diagnostics working?"

"Some are," Jocelyn answered, fingers dashing over her control board. *Argo*'s computers would accept voice or touch commands, and seemed to blend the two to anticipate what its unlearned crew wanted.

"How far away is it?" Killeen asked.

"I can't tell." Jocelyn frowned. "The board says refraction makes it impossible to measure."

"Refraction?" Toby asked. Everybody ignored him, but his Isaac Aspect supplied,

In curved space-time, light is warped. It cannot propagate in straight lines. No distance measurements are reliable. Or time measures, either.

"That thing's getting nearer," Cermo said. "Bigger."

That may be an illusion, too, caused by the bending of light. Here nothing is what it seems, theory says.

"What design is it?" Killeen asked.

"Hard to tell," Jocelyn answered, frowning. "Its image keeps jumping around."

"Kinda lumpy," Cermo said.

"Not like the Myriapodia craft," Killeen mused.

"Are those domes?" Jocelyn delicately tuned the sensors. "Bulges in the profile, see?"

"Ummm. Could be. Mechs have bumps like that."

"Frap!" Jocelyn gritted her teeth. "Looks to be getting closer. If it's mech, we'll be wide open."

<I see similarities to your own ship.>

Killeen glanced back at Quath, startled. Toby had forgotten that the Bridge was tuned into Quath's transmissions. He could not carry on a snug, private conversation with the alien any longer. The thought made him somehow sad.

Killeen said, "*Argo*'s ancient. Last of its kind, prob'ly. Wouldn't find anything like that here."

<Assumptions are not facts.>

"Humans here?" Cermo asked. "I hope to God it's so."

"Its color function is not smooth," Jocelyn said crisply. No speculations for her; she kept eyes fixed on the flowing dynamics of her board.

Killeen ceased his slow pacing and walked quickly to her side, fighting the jolts of vagrant gravity. The board showed a bewildering array of numbers, graphs, scattershot diagrams. Toby could piece them out, with some help—they were like the math lessons from Isaac—but

Killeen had a long-standing impatience with such pesky details. "What's that stuff mean?"

"When the instruments scan across the image, even though it's kinda watery, they can tell if it's the same color. That ship has blotches on it."

"So?" Killeen ran a hand over the displays, as if he could feel their significance. Toby knew the puzzled impatience in his father's face. Long years of trusting his wits made abstract instruments seem untrustworthy, no matter how advanced. Toby could sympathize; he felt pretty shaky, too, relying on devices he could not possibly figure out.

"So maybe it's damaged. Taken hits. Got holes in it, even."

"Likely it's a warship, then." Jocelyn frowned.

On the screen a blue-white shape swam, shimmering and bobbing in the incessant streaking light-drops. The ship's minds fretted over its identity and strobed UNKNOWN on the screen. Toby watched the bobbing, silvery ship and Quath said, <We plunge quickly. Already we near the thirty-day level.>

"Huh? What?"

<A day at this depth inside the time pit equals thirty norm-days' duration outside.>

"How can that be?"

<The Myriapodia have sent me a submind. I assign it these tasks. Its digital consciousness can guide us through such reaches. It understands how the curving of space-time is both a warpage of distance and a shrinkage of time, for us.>

Toby swallowed, and not just from a new lurch of his couch. Before he could take in Quath's meaning, Killeen made a decision, smacking a palm on the board. "Can't risk it being a warship, maybe mech. Prepare to fire on it."

Jocelyn replied crisply, "Ready for action."

"Wait!" Toby called. "You heard Quath. She says everything's twisted down here. That ship could be from some different time, not following us at all."

"What's time matter?" Killeen snapped. "A mech's a mech."

"Dad, give that ship a little leeway. My Isaac Aspect, Quath, they both're talking about how crazy it is here. Seems to me, until we understand—"

Killeen glanced at his son and nodded to Jocelyn. "Keep a sharp eye. Stand ready. Armed."

"Armed, Cap'n."

"Dad!"

<It is not advisable to act without knowledge.>

Killeen studied the alien's head and feelers, which swayed with the effort of compensating for the tides of gravity that swept through the Bridge like a pressure wind. "You sure?"

<Here nothing is certain. But my submind reports that many unknown craft linger here.>

"How many?"

<Unknown. They stack up from all ages past.>

"Mech?"

<Some, it says, may be from before the age of the mechanicals.> Quath sent a rippling, fizzy sound with this, which Toby did not know how to interpret. Wasn't the 'age of the mechanicals' now—their time?

Killeen seemed to understand, though, and nodded."All right. Can you put your information on our screens?"

<Soon.> Another mysterious series of fizzy, ringing notes.

The ship on the screens waxed and waned in shimmering, heated luminosity. For a moment it sharpened. A scarred skin, once silver-smooth, now pocked and stained. Bulges that could be domes, but streaked and grimy.

Jocelyn said, "Our pattern-recognition programs say that's old human construction."

Killeen rubbed his chin. "Ummm, could be."

"It is!" Toby cried. The cut and angles struck a chord in him. Before he could say more, the clarity fled. A long moment of silence followed. The Bridge officers stared openly at their Cap'n. To fire on a human craft would be a great sin, but to die from a mech bolt . . .

"Not mech, anyway," Killeen conceded. "Stand down."

The tension on the Bridge broke. Officers murmured, rustled. Killeen resumed pacing. Toby was still watching the screens when the other ship's image began to dwindle away. "Hey!" Jocelyn cried, working at her instruments. But the image faded like a plucked flower sinking into a dark pond.

"Gone." Killeen seemed relieved. "Maybe we were looking at a mirage all the time."

<It is possible, here. Note:>

Onto the main screen popped two clocks. Toby had learned to read a digital clock on *Argo,* so he was startled to see one in blue keep ticking away at the rate he knew, while another in red spun its numbers past in a blur. <The in-ship time flows normally,> Quath sent in response to his confusion. <Outside time runs much faster, the deeper we go.>

Toby watched the numerals spin, scarcely believing they could represent anything real. "You mean outside, time's going fast?"

<Relative to us, this is true.>

"What makes it speed up, out there?"

<It is we who are slowed. Time is always a matter of local opinion.>

Toby couldn't reckon how that could possibly be. "What happens when we go back out?"

<If we remain in this region of curvature, we will find that much has happened while we were here.>

"Curvature?" Killeen intruded.

<The effect can be opposite, as well. Much is contorted here, like events seen through smoky, thick glass.>

"Gonna make it hard to find anything."

<That is the least difficulty. Time is trapped here. It can be ingested and disgorged.>

"So that's why you call it a time pit?"

Toby's Isaac Aspect added,

The black hole swallows space. Old Zeno says—though even her memory of these matters is from long before her real, bodily life—that we can regard it as if space slides into the hole's gullet at ever-faster speed, as it nears the steepening angle of descent. Against this slippery slope even light labors to save itself. But the ergosphere is a chasm for time, not space. Here the duration of an event may stretch, compress, warp, as space—in-sliding, doomed space—plays and toys with it, twists the tail of time.

Toby tried to get his mind around all this, as his stomach lurched with acid and the screens flashed. Streaking matter, bristling with radiation, spattered their ship. Toby thought woozily that maybe they were seeing God spit across the sky, a cosmic joke. "How . . . how do we find our way around?"

Gravity may bend and turn a given sequence of events. Living in such a place is like being a bug doomed to crawl along a man's belt, hanging in a closet. A belt, say, which has the tab flipped over, then fitted into the buckle. The bug can creep all it wants, and cover both sides of the belt—since now the leather really has only one side—but it can never get off. Events for the bug repeat endlessly, and the bug never reaches the end of its dreary, endless belt.

The Aspect's tinny voice had a disagreeable relish to it. "You talk about all this like you know it firsthand."

I studied these things, but alas, know them only from ancient texts. And from the dried-up Zeno, a truly disagreeable sort. She tells me of experiments humans once performed here. Even, she says, of constructions they made.

"How could anybody build *here*?"

Doubtless this is a transcription error, or doddering old Zeno's errant memory. But I can quote to you from more reliable Chandelier texts. They often blended mythology and physics, a

fashion of that great time—imagine, the luxury to do such! Still, for your edification I can lecture fully on—

"Uh, no thanks." Toby hastily pressed the Aspect back into its crevice.

"What's that?" Killeen asked, pointing at a glinting blackness that swam into view. To Toby it looked like a huge beehive, dark and oily and honeycombed with passages.

Quath sent a trill of alarm. <I do not know. But I suspect this may be our destination.>

"Why?" Killeen demanded.

<From the moment the Magnetic Mind spoke, I have communed with the Myriapodia, with the full legion of Philosophs. They spoke of the singular time when we could enter the time pit and find the right direction. It only occurs when much matter infalls—the mass fed by that dying star which we saw. Such colossal masses, plunging in, render the surface of the time pit turbulent. We could then enter. Only at such moments can one reach this place.>

Toby tried to figure how that could be. "Like slipping in a side door, one that blows open in the wind?"

<In a way. To ripple the surface of the time pit requires the wind of worlds.>

Killeen's face tightened with uncertainty. "The aperture moment? Aperture means 'opening,' right? But an opening to what?"

<To this structure before us. Or to something beyond. My Philosophs know nothing more.>

The ship trembled and groaned with new stresses. A shiny, oily blackness filled all the screens, immense and inescapable.

2

Honeycomb Home

The glistening black thing seemed to unfold itself, swimming in the watery half-light. Toby realized that it was growing somehow. Emerging, like an ornate vessel rising from a slate-black lake. It appeared to ooze into the space nearby, drawn out of fitful storm-wracked darkness, as though emerging from some unseen, deeper place. Fresh ramparts and plains expanded along it, flinty and sharp-crested, faces of it catching the flashing illuminations that still shot by on all sides of them.

<Note our ship time.>

Toby stared, blinked. Quath's tone gave no hint that she shared the surprise Toby felt. The outside time digits now fled by in a blur. <We are at the year level.>

Killeen still stood on the creaking deck, shifting his weight to counter random thrusts. Face tense, he did not take his eyes from the stretching, spreading mass on the screens. "How much deeper can we go?"

<No one knows. But further than this is possible.>

"Ummm," Killeen said sardonically. "What *isn't* possible here?"

Jocelyn said tersely, "Fuel rate's up."

Killeen nodded. "It's been climbing all along. What's our remaining margin?"

"To be able to get free of this place?"

"Yeasay—this 'ergosphere.' " The word sat awkwardly on Killeen's lips, Aspect jargon, like a language he only pretended to speak.

The popping of strains running through *Argo* had distracted Toby from the gut-deep pulse of their engines. The laboring rumble rose, sending tremors through his couch.

Jocelyn worked a moment, eyes dancing as she listened to her direct link with the ship's systems. Worry-lines creasing her brow, she said, "The board's working hard, calc'lating how much it'll take to get out of here.

These numbers keep jumping around. We're getting close. Gobbling up fuel just to keep in an orbit, seems like."

"How long?"

"Maybe fifty minutes left."

Even to Toby's practiced eye Killeen seemed unmoved by this. "I see."

Argo flew by sucking in plasma with magnetic mouths, burning it in fusion chambers, and spewing it out the back. But it needed catalysts for this, and they were running low.

<If we approach to the very edge of the event horizon—the lip of the black hole—we will find that no amount of fuel can save us.>

Toby was shocked at the matter-of-fact way Quath stated this, without even a softening further remark. Killeen also gave nothing away, his eyes fixed on the strange oily-black thing. "This object, it's like a rock that grows. You sure it has nothing to do with this 'event horizon'?"

<I do not know. But it is not the black hole itself.>

"How come you're sure?"

<When the streaking lights around us begin to die, it will mean that the streaming, infalling mass is being absorbed.>

"That'll be the star stuff, taking a nosedive into the black hole?" Killeen asked.

<It must. It cannot orbit safely—there are no free paths in the time pit.>

Toby put in, "How come we're okay here?"

<We aren't, for long. The sole reason we can venture this close to the hole is because it is the largest in our galaxy, over a million times the mass of a star. Though its great mass attracts, the tidal forces are lesser here near the lip of the Eater. Near a smaller black hole, we would be shredded before we could venture in.>

"I don't want to go any closer, not when we can't see what's happening. Or figure out what that thing is." He pointed to the glinting complexities of the mass oozing into being before them, like a strange crystalline mud. Their engines shook the walls, but to no avail; the great bulk swam nearer.

Jocelyn said, "Cap'n, I don't think we've got the power to do any maneuverin', anyway."

Killeen compressed his lips. "Can we get far from that thing?"

"Doubt it. I'm gunnin' her hard as I can."

"Quath, what can we do?" Killeen at last made a naked appeal.

<I do not know. The edge where space disappears forever is death-black. We will know that we are where matter rules all, and space slides forever down the throat of the Eater of All Things. But this object—it is different.>

"I . . . we . . . came all this way." Killeen watched the screens with a strange expression, one Toby had seldom seen these last few years—uncertainty. "Family Bishop has always known that the Eater was important. But where should we go?"

<We have reached the limits of what the past can tell us.>

The way they both spoke made Toby's hair stand up on end. It was like two old friends discussing suicide.

A part of Toby welcomed Killeen's hesitation. He realized how much he missed the many-sided man he had known all his life, yet who now showed only one flinty face to the world. But then, as he watched, an edge returned to Killeen's gaze. He whispered, "It's *got* to be here."

<Necessity emerges from logic, not desire. The Philosophs retire into [untranslatable] in such hours of doubt.>

Jocelyn gave Quath a skeptical glance and worked through the long silence that hung in the fevered air. Then she quietly reported to Killeen. "*Argo* says there's an orbit we can follow, to bring us to a place it calls 'perigee.' That's just above the lip of the black hole. But if we go that near, we can never fight our way back out of the, well, the whirlpool."

"You're sure?" Killeen's voice was clipped, flat.

"Near as I can be in this crazy place."

Toby's Isaac Aspect put in dryly,

The correct term is "peribarythron." "Perigee" refers to Old Earth, and orbits near it. These ship computers must have been programmed by someone with a classical education, but little concern for proper technical detail. I hope such sloppiness does not extend—

Toby squeezed the Aspect back down. Its outraged squawk ended with what felt like an audible pop.

"Why's the clock running so hard?" Killeen asked, pointing. Numerals flickered faster and faster.

Quath clattered her legs uneasily. <That behavior does not fit the calculations I obtained from the Philosophs. Something is warping the space-time flow even more than they expected.>

"That?" Killeen pointed at the slick, ever-swelling darkness before them.

<Perhaps. Appearances deceive here, where gravity bends light to its will.>

In the mass, Toby could see complex ribs and valleys, arches and long columns. "It's *built,* not natural," he said.

Killeen blinked. "Yeasay! I knew! We came and—Abraham, the Magnetic Mind—they all lead to this."

"How can something stay here?" Toby stared at it wonderingly. He could not guess what Killeen had envisioned, through the long years of their journey to this moment—some things his father never discussed—but plainly it wasn't this. A puzzled frown stirred Killeen's brow, then passed like a forgotten irritant.

"Doesn't matter," Killeen said flatly. "Plenty time later to figure out such stuff."

Toby watched the screens with foreboding. The slick blackness grew and grew. It was as though it was drawing *Argo* to it with a slow, remorseless clutch. But the thing was not just getting closer. It seemed to swell into existence, emerging, being born from some unknowable place.

He had to put all this together in his mind, figure what it could mean. Toby closed his eyes to blot out the eerie sight. "Dad . . . Those Cyaneans, the places the Cosmic Circle cut through—didn't the Magnetic Mind say the mechs made them?"

"Yeasay," Killeen said. "Some kind of barrier, like a sand trap or something. But *this* . . ."

Killeen's words trailed away. Toby opened his eyes as the spreading structure became sharper, showing them how large it truly was. Honeycomb terraces, valleys, shelves. Ranks and ranks of hexagonal openings, spider-fine webs of struts and cabling. Or was that just a way for the human eye to put together a comprehensible picture, Toby wondered, make patterns it could comprehend?

The Bridge was silent. *Argo* creaked and strummed with random stretchings and compressions. Toby wondered how long the ship could take this massaging by forces far vaster than itself.

Jocelyn called, "Cap'n, we're burning fuel hard and heavy."

"I know."

"It's, it's—we've got just minutes left. Unless—"

Something firmed in Killeen's face. "In the old days at Citadel Bishop we'd go out scavenging. No matter what we found, we'd haul it back and claim that's what we'd gone looking for."

He looked slowly around the Bridge. Everybody, including Toby and Quath, regarded him blankly. "Might's well do the same here." He pointed at the honeycombed patterns bathed in slippery, flickering light. "That's our goal, Lieutenant Jocelyn. Take us in, and be quick about it."

A long silence. Toby saw in the drawn faces the knowledge that this was their last gamble. They would throw the dice, throw them now and forever, into inky shadows.

Then the moment passed. Jocelyn moved quickly, crisply. She drew maximum thrust from the ramscoop engines, her fingers flying over the boards. In his sensorium Toby could sense the ship's magnetic fields surge as they spread wider, an invisible net that snagged passing matter, sucked it into the reaction chambers, and spewed it out the back. The deck vibrated. Joints rasped and shrieked. Acceleration felt like a kick in the rump. They shot over the ebony landscape.

"Where exactly, sir?" Jocelyn was cool and efficient. Toby admired the collected way she turned to Killeen, one eyebrow raised. Might as well meet Fate in style.

"Ah . . ." Killeen's eyes swept the details that skated by beneath them. A high whine cut the air as *Argo* fought against storming yet invisible forces. "There."

A small green dot winked at the very tip end of a long, pointed peninsula. Jocelyn said, "That wasn't there a moment ago."

Into the hovering silence Toby said, "Maybe somebody's turned on the porch light."

He recalled his mother doing that in Citadel Bishop, when he went out late to play with his friends in the soft summer nights. A familiar yellow-white glow, shielded against mech detection. Feeble in the gathering dark, fitful, but always there. He had liked to chase the little birds that glowed when they flapped their wings. No matter how far into the brush he had pursued them, following their rustling and cawing, he could always see the distant beacon of home. Stay within view of the light, she had said.

A lamp tuned to human eyes, not mechs. Not that it did any good in the end, Toby thought ruefully.

The green glow seemed to swim up toward them. A cavern yawned below it. With a nod Killeen told Jocelyn to slip down into it.

A swift, silky glide. They braked to a stop between enormous inky cliffs.

Here, too, the honeycomb design repeated on smaller and smaller scales. Fitful technicolor displays sparked all along the great ebony flanks, reflecting the spikes of doomed matter streaking through the darkness above. It was as though this place was the very end of creation, solid and immovable, a night land beneath a restless, dying sky.

Then the honeycomb seemed to swell, to flicker—and they were *inside* the oily black walls. Inside whatever this thing was. With no visible transition.

Jocelyn eased the engines back. Killeen ordered the ship powered down to conserve energy. This brought a welcome calm to the deck. Quietness settled among them. There was nothing left to do now. No place left to go.

Still, Toby was startled when the watch officer at the main airlock hoarsely reported in. Everyone in the ship, Toby realized, was pulled tight enough to snap.

The watch officer heard something. He patched it through. In the general sensorium the noise swelled, impossibly large and booming. It sounded for all the world like someone knocking on a door.

3

The Far Black

The man was a wrinkled dwarf, but he didn't seem to mind.

"You're from what era?" he asked, leading a band of five officers and Toby through a long, dimly lit corridor. A gloomy, low-ceilinged warren. Their boots rang on the hard, ceramic surface. Nobody answered, waiting for Killeen to break their silence, but he remained silent.

The dwarf shrugged. "Pretty recent, looks to be."

Toby hadn't seen the first encounter between Killeen and this short, muscular figure, but it didn't seem to have settled anything.

"After the Calamity, as I told you," Killeen said evenly. But his mouth was tight and bloodless.

"That doesn't cut any thick air here, fella. All life's a big old calamity, you look at it the right way."

"Our home is the planet Snowglade, and I'll thank you to keep your philosophy to yourself."

The dwarf's eyebrows arched, peering up at the Cap'n. "Oooh, you're a systo-critic, eh?"

Killeen's mouth twitched. Toby could tell his father was carefully feeling his way into a completely unknown situation. Strange, but looking completely ordinary. Killeen said formally, "We have come from the destruction of our world. We were led by portents and messages—"

"Fashion this—I had a chip installed just so I could speak this venac you're squawking. So look, fella, I'd 'preciate some bandwidth here. Every ship comes limping in is from some esty pigeonhole, thinks we should know all their history, right down to the pimples on their cultural ass."

"I expect respect for a delegation from a far outpost of—"

"Respect you'll get from guys behind desks. Me, I got a job to do." They reached the end of the corridor. Beyond yawned more round mouths of hallways.

Toby said, "I missed what you said earlier, so—well—what *is* this place?"

The dwarf blinked up at him. "Just an ordinary entrance portal. Better than most, I'd say, and—"

"No, I mean, what's it a portal *to*?"

"Into the esty."

"And what's *that*?"

"Esty. *S* for space, *T* for time." The dwarf waved them down a corridor and they kept walking. Doors slid open automatically as they passed. They ignored these invitations and behind them followed the whisk of closings.

"You mean we're in some other kind of space-time here?" To Toby this place looked stupefyingly boring.

"Kids don't learn much these days, do they?" the dwarf asked Killeen pointedly.

Toby couldn't see how this shrunken little man could tell he was young, when Toby towered over him, and was searching for a barbed way to say this when Killeen murmured evenly, "We would all appreciate knowing what the hell this place is."

"A stable chunk of convoluted esty. Inhabited. Governed. And now that you mention it, I haven't heard any thanks for pulling you all in out of the Far Black."

Killeen said sincerely, "We do thank you. We—"

"You'll be paying for all this later, Captain, so don't overdo the sincerity. Right now—"

"Who made this, this 'esty' of yours?" Toby burst in. "You people?" He looked doubtfully down at the man.

"Made it?" The dwarf shrugged. "It's always been here."

"How could it?" Toby demanded. "I mean, smack up against a black hole, the biggest in the galaxy—"

"Look, there's things you flatlanders don't grasp, kid. Doesn't make a whole lot of sense to ask who made the esty when it has its own timeline anyway, see?"

Toby didn't. "I just want to know—"

"Enough! Come on, you scrimmage, we've got to get you filtered." The dwarf had led them into a narrow little room. "Won't take long."

The walls were porous yellow sponge. Toby was still puzzling over the dwarf's remarks. When Killeen started to say something the dwarf stepped lightly outside, smirking. A concealed sheet slid down, clicking shut.

Cermo said with alarm, "He's trapped us. What if—"

Abruptly the air seemed to compress around them. Then it reversed, screeching down in pressure, popping their ears. An array of lenses in the ceiling showered them with quick flashes of brilliant, brittle light. Toby squeezed his eyes shut but the flashes stung his face and hands.

This went on a long while. Bishops shouted, threatened to blow a hole in the wall—but Killeen ordered them to stop. "No obvious threat here. Stand fast."

A humming presence seemed to probe at their skins with unseen hands. Blunt inspections traced among weapons, body-gear, clothes. Toby tried to see where this was coming from. His sensorium told him nothing but a noisy hash of meaningless signals. He was looking at a spot on the wall when suddenly a circular hole opened in it and rapidly grew. Soon it was a new doorway.

Beyond stood the dwarf, looking bored."You're reasonably clean. None of those mech spore-spies we've been getting lately. Where'd you say you were from?"

They bumped and elbowed each other in their haste to get out of the cramped room. From long habit, Bishops preferred the open. Killeen said with studied neutrality, "Who wants to know?"

"Ummm?" Among a menu of irritating mannerisms, the dwarf had a habit of staring off into space, as if consulting an Aspect. A polite Bishop would have at least glanced at who was speaking to him. "Oh, I thought I said: I'm Andro, scut-work specialist supreme. I make sure you don't drag in too many proffo-plagues, siggos, or microeyeballs."

"Siggos?" Toby asked.

"You're post-Arc, right? Still, shoulda heard about this. Siggos are esty bombs, cute li'l mech gizmos. Nasty, about the size of a skin cell—which's what they look like. Can blow a hole in just about any esty we got."

"How many of these esty—?" Killeen began, but Andro was already marching away with dwarf-fast steps. Toby saw that since the man was closer to the ground, he could just sort of skate along, hardly bothering to lift his feet. The gravity here was lighter than *Argo*'s, and the officers, abubble with excitement and confusion, bounded too high on each step.

Toby guessed "post-Arc" meant after the Arcology Eras. This impatient dwarf knew their history?

"Where are we going?" Killeen called after Andro.

"Scrub-dub."

Which proved to be like being held under a microscope and poked at by giants. The dwarf turned toward them, chattering a rapid-fire explanation, walking backwards—and clapped his hands.

Something scooped Toby up, jabbed and snipped and smelled him. Without any apparent cause, his clothes wriggled and twisted and got free of him. They vanished, flapping away into the clotted air. He shouted, and heard only an echo. Then a web of snaky stuff held him upside down while living, sticky strings ran all over his body, into his ears and even more intimate orifices. Still upside down, with his arms pinned below his head by a soft but insistent clamshell, he got a bath. Fragrant, flowery, ferocious. It, too, worked into every crevice he knew and several that felt like fresh ideas.

The clamshell let go. He fell—and plunged into a green soup. He emerged sputtering, only to be hauled ashore on a sandy beach by a pulse of magnetic fields. It seized on his many metal implants and sucked him across the gritty purple sand—which lapped up at him, murmuring to itself like a microscopic mob. Somehow, being dragged didn't hurt or even rub his skin raw. It was as though the sand flowed around him, exerting just enough pressure to keep him where it wanted. The sand-swarm ran all over his body, probed his nostrils, ears, ass, muttered disagreeably, and then meekly laid back down again, sighing. He stood up shakily. Grains of the gritty sand ran out his nostrils. It licked off his face and then fled into his hair, chuckling as it went.

Toby was not in a mood to laugh along. He stalked off the beach, just as Jocelyn fell out of an overhead cloud, tumbling in air, and splashed into the green soup pond. She shrieked and gasped.

"Just relax and let them do it to you," Toby advised.

That didn't seem to do any good. Jocelyn angrily slapped at the green soup. It lapped around her and magnetic fluxes grabbed her in a rather embarrassing position for a lady. The fluxes wrapped like ropes around her, Toby could see through his Dopplered sensorium/eye. Jocelyn floundered up onto the sand beach, sputtering.

Toby lost interest in her trials. He climbed over a sand dune and through a wall of pearly fog. Beyond it the dwarf was waiting, holding a fluffy yellow robe.

"Where're my clothes?"

"Being reeducated," Andro said with a distracted gaze.

"Huh?"

"Wear this while you eat."

"Why?"

"It's your tutor."

"I didn't know I'd enrolled."

"Anybody comes through Port Athena gets the course, skyscraper."

"Sky what?"

"Ancient term. Means you're unnecessarily tall."

"Ugly word for it. Seems to me you're too short."

"A few days of forehead-bashing on doorways will provide useful instruction."

Toby shrugged and put on the ample yellow robe. It fit nicely, tucking itself in around him. "When do I get my clothes back?" he persisted.

"When they've graduated." Andro pointed. "Right now you go that way."

"Why should I?"

"Don't eat, don't learn, kid." Andro yawned and picked up another robe from the neat stack nearby. Jocelyn came through the fog-wall, muttering, her breasts swaying like two angry red eyes looking for a fight.

"What was *that*?" she demanded.

"Customs inspection," the dwarf answered, looking over her shoulder at nothing.

"You little worm, don't talk to me—"

"Cover yourself, madam—"

"Think you can—"

"—or you'll be cited for false advertisement."

Jocelyn blinked, turned red, and seemed to be deciding whether to stay angry. Toby got out of the way, trotting down the passageway Andro had fingered.

A cafeteria, simple and bare. Big tubs of fragrant vegetables, sauteed and fried and steeped in odd sauces. All bubbling under odd, slanted lamps, served up by auto-arms. To his surprise—and there seemed to be nothing but surprises here, though few answers—he liked the food. It gurgled and slid around while he tried to bite into it, sending heady aromas shooting through his sinuses. Enticing. Provocative.

Food it was, he was sure of that, but it wasn't just difficult to catch with his teeth; it was impossible. The stuff slithered out of the way, as if it could read his mind. (Later, this seemed a distinct possibility.) He got tired of hearing his incisors click together uselessly and accepted the situation, just swallowing the smooth, delicious thing. It went down easily—almost *happily,* he thought, a crazy notion. In his stomach it exploded into warm waves of satisfaction. He sat back and enjoyed the sensation, which was even better than the eating had been. He was still like that, eyes unfocused, when the dwarf sped by, snorted, stuck a fresh spoonful in his mouth, and said, "Keep studying."

The other Bishops seemed to be enjoying themselves equally. After hardship and strain, some were celebrating. They sat at the too-small tables and dug in. Shipboard chow on *Argo* had never been very exciting. Variety lifted the spirits. Chatter, hilarity, cleansing laughter.

This set off Toby's alarm bells. He wondered if they were being drawn in, doped—but the dwarf seemed bored, not calculating. And after a while his mind cleared. He felt better—zesty, in fact, filled with bristling energy. And his robe had started to rub and massage him in very agreeable ways. He rolled up the fluffy sleeve and was surprised to find that his deep tan was a little lighter. His armpit hair was neatly trimmed back, too. He studied the fabric. Small bits of skin were caught in its tiny fibers. As he watched, the matted weave of the robe worked away on the particle, until finally he couldn't see it. Gone. Digested.

Well, he thought, it was sure a funny way of getting a bath.

Andro came strutting by, stubby legs scissoring fast, saw their bowls were empty, and snapped his fingers. "Now we get down to business. Who has the license?"

Killeen said, "We bear no authority but our own Family's."

"Uh huh. Now, I never held with the whole Family scheme, myself—Cap'n, uh, Killeen, isn't it?" The dwarf held out his right hand and Killeen reached to shake it. Instead, the dwarf peered into his own palm, ignoring Killeen. From Toby's angle he could see the dwarf's skin turn into a little screen showing a document. "Ummm. No record of you, I'm afraid."

"Bishops of Snowglade," Killeen said testily.

"There are plenty of Bishops, a batch on most planets. Aces and Treys on others, Blues and Golds on more. I'm—"

"Most planets?" Killeen asked incredulously. "You mean we share our *name*?"

"Genes, too." Andro didn't look up. He tapped the ends of his fingers on his display-hand. Toby could see the image change in response, yielding more documents.

"You mean we got relatives on other places?" Jocelyn demanded.

"That was the strategy of the Hunker Down." Andro sniffed with disdain. "Don't you people teach history any more?"

The Bishops all looked at each other, startled. Toby said wonderingly, "We thought we were the only Bishops. Our line went back to the Chandeliers, some said."

"Oh, you do. But a whole Family line, we couldn't risk getting it wiped out. So we had to spread it around. Say, you got any Pawns with you?"

Killeen blinked. "Naysay. They were obliterated by mechs."

"See, there's the risk. Too bad, though—I'm half-Pawn myself."

"*You?*" Toby could not conceal his amazement. "A short little—"

"We kept to the original specs, kid," Andro's mouth twisted with sardonic amusement. "*We* respect tradition, in case you hadn't noticed. You ground-pounder types always pump yourselves up, never fails."

"Those who didn't, the mechs got," Killeen said soberly.

"Yeasay," Cermo put in. "We needed power, sensos, carryin' mass, techstuff. Adds weight."

Andro squinted at Cermo. "As is obvious. Nothing to be ashamed of, I assure you. Most Families go that way when mech competition gets bad. Hard for them to shed the mass once they get here, though. And they get nasty on their perpetual diets."

"There are other Families here?" Killeen asked, his skewed mouth giving away his puzzlement.

"We got them all—even the original templates, somewhere."

"The first Bishops?" Jocelyn asked, awed. "From the Chandeliers?"

"Ummm? Oh, of course—somewhere. And somewhen." Andro stopped tapping his fingers, read his palm, and slapped his hands together with a sharp crack. When he took them apart, the screen was gone and his right hand looked just like the other one, lined and dirty. "That's it. There's some kind of hold-for-arrival message for you. Somebody expected you might show up somewhen."

"From who?" Killeen demanded.

"I don't know. I'm an inspector, not a library."

"Where can we find this message?"

"Have to see the Regency."

"Let's go, then."

He eyed them shrewdly. "You're *sure* you don't have a license?"

Killeen's eyes narrowed. "Little one, we have just come through—"

"I know what you've come through—*if* you're who you say you are. Fresh meat, just in from the colonies."

"Colonies?" Jocelyn was aghast. "We were the last fragments, holding out on Snowglade until—"

"I know," Andro said, "but it's a story I've heard before. Last off your planet. Point is, you're the best ones. You got here."

Jocelyn said, "All the other Families, the mechs got."

"Just what I said. We can use people who know how to scramble for their supper. Or so goes the official yarn-weaving. Me, I wonder if we got too many already, never mind—"

"Why all this about a license?" Toby asked mildly.

"Kid, you'd be shocked how many traders try to dress up all country and dumb, come through here, think they can just slide by the tax man." Andro eyed him. "They pump themselves with bioemergents, so they look big for a day or two. Then they have to pee it all away. Ummm, you're the smallest here . . ."

"I'm no phony," Toby said, offended.

"Um. Suppose not. You don't look clever enough to fake it, either."

Toby bristled. "Hey, now—"

"I'll pass you, then." Andro wrinkled his nose, seeming to reach a decision, nodding to himself. "You can go through. But nobody else from your ship until you've seen the Regency—that's the rule."

"Why?" Killeen's jaw muscles bunched, visibly containing his irritation. "My crew wants out. All of them. We've been cooped up for years in—"

"Think the Regency wants a mob of club-footed innocents dumped into their city?" Andro waved a hand at the gray walls around them.

"This is a city?" Toby asked, thinking there must be a language problem. Cities in the old days had been elegant, airy, places of sweet music and luminescence.

Andro chuckled. "No, kid, this is a reception cell. I'll show you the city."

4

A Day in Court

It didn't look like much of a city. The Land of Dwarves, Toby had christened it before they had walked two blocks.

Even in a crowd he could see far into the distance, over the heads of everybody. Stubby people, hurrying everywhere. Yakking, yelling, laughing, and all in a noisy rush. In the hazy distance was more of the same. Stubby buildings, gray and brown and black. Stubby trees, even. On Snowglade they would have been bushes.

"What *is* this place?" Cermo sent on comm.

From Andro's lack of reaction Toby gathered that he could not intercept their Family line. Killeen sent a quick signal that it was all right to talk this way, so Toby said, "And who are these runts?"

Jocelyn sent a puzzled note. "They're sure not the high-minded types I expected."

"Yeasay," Killeen said. "When we found humans here, I expected them to be from the Chandeliers. Or the Great Epoch, even. The heroic ones, people who could build in the sky, fought well against mechs, explored True Center."

Cermo said, "I thought the Great Epoch was when we got to True Center."

"Nobody knows, really," Killeen said. "Certainly no Aspect we carry remembers. It was 'way back, must have been done by humans with powers we can't even guess. I sure want to meet them."

Toby caught a curious plaintive note in his father's voice, but the others gave no sign of registering it. They all marched along, giving no outward sign of this conversation, gleeful at putting one over on the dwarves. Then he felt Shibo's Personality rise in him, welcome though uncalled.

They are rats in bow ties. But useful.

"Huh?" Toby felt the strong thread of her, ivory slivers shooting through his sensorium, masking the gray city.

> ***An ancient term I learned from Zeno. The ancients wore constrictions about their throats to signify attitudes. A "bow tie" stood for a certain rakish tilt. Andro's arrogance belies his true station. He is swaggering before the country know-nothings he takes us to be.***

Toby relayed this to the others and they murmured in startled agreement. Killeen nodded. "That fits. He's trying to impress us in some way. This place"—a sweeping arm—"pretty fine, sure, but it's a shack compared with what the Chandelier folk could do."

"Could be," Jocelyn begrudged. "But where *are* the Chandelier Families? How come we've got to deal with Andro?"

Toby wished Quath was here to help. Part of him wanted to click his heels, happy that his father had *done it,* found the age-old goal of Family Bishop. The other part wondered what was really going on. Certainly this wasn't the grand homecoming they'd all expected. He could read the barely suppressed disappointment in everyone's eyes.

He wanted to say something to Killeen, to reach across the chasm that had slowly yawned wider through these years of flight, of the Cap'ncy. But flaming eyes made it hard to have a heart-to-heart.

Andro chattered on about the sights. He seemed to think they were hot stuff, prodigious monuments. Brown municipal buildings with heavy, ornate columns framing the tiny doors. Factories with no windows and no identifiable purpose. Squat black apartment buildings with puny balconies that seemed like stuck-on afterthoughts.

Toby sent to Cermo, "I'll allow as how this is richer than the Citadel, sure. But the Low Arcology ruins, they impressed me more."

Cermo replied, "I dunno. Have the feelin' we're missin' something here. I mean, I still don't figure how this place can even *be* here."

At last they reached a pyramid-shaped mass of gray, shiny stone that looked a little more important. Their destination.

Andro led them into the rock-ribbed entranceway with a deep bow that was probably sarcastic. Toby gave him a curt nod, stepped into the foyer beyond, followed Andro across the marble floor—and smacked his forehead on the doorway. He suppressed a grunt. Andro's mouth barely twitched in a smirk that was probably lost on everyone else. Rubbing his forehead, Toby followed the rest into a room with rows of hard benches. A lone figure dominated a battered wooden desk at the far end. The desk was discolored, chipped, its legs cracked. Toby supposed it was a "relic of office," such as the ancient chairs used by elders back in Citadel Bishop.

"Fresh batch, Andro?" the squat, leathery woman at the desk asked. She wore a black robe and looked as if she had weathered a hard night.

"The last ones you brought me are still debating the fine points of import-export law in jail."

"How was I to know they could get those sniff-dream tablets through our filters?" Andro said plaintively, spreading his hands. "That's the engineers' fault."

"A wise craftsman doesn't blame his tools," the woman said, lazily sliding her eyes over the Bishops. The sight did not seem to excite much interest; she yawned.

"These beefies are a simple case," Andro said, stepping forward in a deferential manner. He pressed his right palm against a small jet-black area on the woman's worn wooden desk. A *breeeeet!* seemed to signify data transmission from his personal files. "They're a little hazy about where they're from, but they don't seem bright enough to be hiding any contra."

"Ummm, you're probably right there," the woman said, looking them up and down. Out of the corner of his eye Toby saw Cermo open his mouth angrily, then close it again after a stern glance from Killeen.

After the learning-food, Andro had given them all language slip-chips to insert in their spinal ports—complaining all the while about how antique their spinal insert collars were. Toby's chip was working well already, even though Andro had scornfully referred to the slip-chip wafers as "dumb-downs," apparently meaning that they translated the speech of Andro's people into sentences simple-minded enough for Bishops to understand.

The woman glanced down at her desk top, which flickered and was not worn wood any more but a glossy display. Toby saw number-thickets and long lists, all from Andro's file on them. He couldn't read the language, but it looked like a lot of information, all neatly sorted out. Yet Andro had never seemed to be taking anything down, or even paying much attention to them.

Killeen stepped forward, "If you are in authority I must ask that you tell us how to find some relatives of ours, Bishops, and a man—"

"I am a judge," the woman said with a flinty, casual air. "And you will remain silent until I ask a question."

"But we've come—"

"Don't listen real well, do you?" She twisted her hand a funny, helical way. An electrical jolt streamed through the air, sending Toby's internal sensorium reeling. It was a stomach-churning, startling effect.

Killeen tottered, looked green for a moment, then pulled himself together. "I . . . see."

The judge gave him a wolfish grin, all knife-edge and strung-wire fine. "I have taken the trouble to chip-process your speaking patterns, so can state in firm voice familiar to you the consequences of your actions. I am assuming that you will spend an annum, maybe two, in the workhouse for your violation of our tax codes. If you wish to improve on that figure—"

"Violation?" Killeen bristled. "We sailed into this place in search—"

"Appearing out of the Far Black like that, you set off alarms. The Regency had to muster defenses. You might have been mech, after all."

"We fly an ancient human ship!"

"Deception runs rife in the Far Black. *And* you sent no forward-hailer to let us know. Defense costs money, rebble-dep, time, trouble. A debt that must be paid in the work-house." The judge shrugged. "Simple social justice."

Killeen stiffened. Bishops were not merely scavengers; they had always traded with the other Families, to good advantage. There had even been a time, the infamous Accommodation, when Families bargained with mechs. Killeen said shrewdly, "Maybe we're carrying something of interest to you."

The judge tossed her hair with feigned disinterest. "What could you possibly have?"

"Fresh samples of space plants from a molecular cloud."

Killeen waved forward Cermo, who added, "We're regrowing them. Good eating."

"Ummm. Regional delicacies? Marginal at best." The judge looked off into space.

Killeen said quickly, "We carry tech we've picked up from our homeworld."

"Ummm." No reaction.

"And from another. Some strange artifacts. Ancient, maybe."

"More planet-level goods?" The judge looked bored. "We get rafts and rafts of it when immigrants pour in."

"Well . . . " Killeen glanced at Toby. "We're carrying an alien."

The judge brightened. "What phylum?"

"Myriapodia."

Her mouth turned down with surprise, then snapped back into a canny flat line. "You're sure?"

Not a good recovery, Toby thought wryly. And how could anybody mistake Quath for something else? Killeen said offhandedly, "She captured me on the last planet we visited. I got to know her pretty well."

"She? I didn't know they had sexes." The judge blinked, plainly dumbfounded.

"Several, as far as I can tell." Now it was Killeen's turn to fake disinterest. "They're complicated. Good memories, too. She's told us a lot about the Myriapodia's heritage."

"Excellent, excellent. There is certainly a market for that information." The judge thumbed her desk, glanced at a fresh display in the top, nodded. "I could probably negotiate a suspension of your work-house duties if the proper authorities could have some time with this alien. I assume you're holding it under strict arrest?"

Killeen looked shocked and Toby knew it was real. "She's a friend."

"Sure, fine, no offense. You realize this will take some delicate negotiations? Experts will have to journey here from 'way out in the esty. Given the cross-shifts, we'll have to—"

"Good. See to it." Killeen was his commanding self again. "We've got other business here and we'll pursue it."

The judge glanced at her desk again and seemed to receive a message. "The alien, that is an important issue. We would prefer to have it under our control until—"

"Naysay!" Killeen said angrily. "She'll be with us."

The judge hesitated, then her eyes narrowed. "How do we know you've really got this Myriapod?"

"We'll bring her ashore," Killeen said simply.

"What? Here? But that could be dangerous."

"Not to us."

She looked alarmed. "Those things killed people without pity." Toby recalled Quath's casual references to how she and her kind had thought of humans as Noughts, beings who didn't matter a jot on the Myriapodia's scale of things. And her forerunners had hunted primate-type species. Maybe people here were slow to forget—or knew something he didn't.

"I'll guarantee your safety," Killeen said airily, plainly enjoying himself now. "And I won't even charge you extra."

Toby could tell that Cermo was having trouble containing his laughter. Then he looked behind them. Somehow, without their noticing it, a dozen people had quietly come into the big room and were standing at the back. They didn't look threatening but they didn't smile either. They wore small, rectangular backpacks and looked authoritative. This was serious stuff.

"Very well," the judge said. "Please bring the alien here."

"Not so fast," Killeen countered. "I want some information."

"I can assure you that you'll be properly briefed once—"

"Now."

"I suppose we could compromise somewhat—"

"And your Andro here, he said something about a message waiting for us."

"In due time—"

"Same time as you question Quath. No later."

She pursed her lips, paused, and then nodded to the people at the back of the room. "I would appreciate it if you would send a few of your people along with mine here. They can work out the transfer of the alien to our control."

"Hey, you won't *own* Quath," Toby put in.

The judge looked at Toby as if seeing him for the first time, and not much liking the result. "We will establish proprietary ownership of the information we gain from—"

"You just take it for granted that Quath will talk to you at all," Toby said rapidly, looking at his father. "Plenty times, she won't say a peep."

"I believe that is a technical matter for the teams which will be sent to interrogate and—"

"Just a second here," Killeen said. "Toby's right. You got to handle Quath just so, or you won't get a used fart out of her."

The judge blinked. "A used . . . ? I shall assume that was hyperbole, a figure of speech."

Cermo chuckled and Toby remembered how Quath had built her complex warren, sticking it together with her own feces. "Not entirely," Toby said, and smiled mysteriously.

The judge regarded Toby skeptically. "Then perhaps we can enlist your aid. Someone who could help us talk with the Myriapod?"

The other Bishops were looking at Toby. He said, "I suppose so. What you do with whatever Quath decides to tell you, that's your business. But we're not handing her over to you. She stays with us."

The judge paused, studying the surface of her desk, then glancing at the others in the back of the room. Mildly, but with a clear threat, she said, "I don't think you are in a position to dictate terms."

Killeen turned and gazed steadily at the people behind them. The other Bishops also did an about-face, standing with knees and elbows slightly bent, hands ready to move. A long, silent moment stretched.

Toby saw his father's point. These people had tech probably beyond theirs, but they were still human. A lot of communication was not talk, but presence, and the Bishops towered over these other men and women. Jocelyn and Toby, the shortest, still were half again the height of these arrogant dwarves.

Killeen let this fact work on the room, and then said, "I expect you to abide by the letter and intent of our agreement."

The judge paused, sensing the situation. Then she smiled for the first time. "It is pleasant to encounter a visitor who understands the nuances of negotiation." She held out a hand. "Monisque, I'm called by my friends. My enemies prefer shorter words. Let's get our terms worked out in detail. Then maybe we can all have a drink."

Some human rituals were eternal. Toby had no doubt that the drinks would contain a liberal lacing of alcohol.

5

Trans-History

Quath clambered along beside them, clanging and scraping through Andro's reception area. She had been forced to squeeze through the loading docks and equipment bays of the port, because the personnel areas were hopelessly small. Toby could have sworn that Quath had added some more legs into the bargain, but the knobby steel shanks moved so fast, her pneumatic joints wheezing, that it was hard to tell.

The buildings here glowed like warm butter. Probably part of these people's security precautions, Toby guessed, but he couldn't imagine how. Unless somehow the buildings held energies that could flick out, lick away offending Bishops . . .

"How's that by you, Quath'jutt'kkal'thon?" Killeen asked.

Her angular head swiveled toward Killeen—a politeness she had learned that humans appreciated, though it was completely unnecessary, since her voice came to them through comm. Still, she said nothing.

"C'mon, Quath, don't worry," Toby said, making his voice carry a lightness he did not feel, and hoping the alien couldn't tell that. "You'll be fine. We'll be right there."

<Quath'jutt'kkal'thon neither minds nor matters.>

Toby was puffing just trying to keep up with her. "How come, eyeball-plucker?"

<I do not mind. And now that we have reached this strange place, I do not matter.>

Killeen said, "To these people you matter. They want you pretty bad."

<For their own ends. Perhaps when all purposes are known, they shall prove to be our ends as well.>

"They seem pretty worried about the Myriapodia," Killeen said.

To Toby his father seemed edgy and intense, eyes darting to the sides as they passed out of the receiving dock and into the city. They picked up more of the "Honor Guard," as the judge had called it—teams of men and women with long-bore weapons slipping down side streets, quick-eyed and edgy, clearing the way. The streets ahead were deserted bare stone, closed shops, echoing the Bishops' ringing boot heels. Killeen signaled to Cermo and a dozen others, who formed their own perimeter line. The people of this monotonous city didn't seem like a threat; they all knew the "Honor Guards" were there to keep the Bishops in line.

<I will tell them only what the Code of Philosophs allows.>

Quath followed precepts Toby could never figure out. Sometimes she would reel out endless detail about Myriapodia history. Other times, she would clam up tight, not even acknowledge questions.

"They're dead anxious for news from out of the Far Black, as they call it," Toby added.

The guards, their squinty-eyed tautness and all, made him nervous. Even the air here itched with faint striations, as though electricity hummed through it. These people, their funny little stunted city, the sheer incredible but rock-solid fact of it being here at all—they added up to a profound unease. And things were moving so fast, he couldn't get straight answers to any of the myriad questions this place conjured up.

"If that's what they're buying, then that's what we're selling," Killeen said. "Cermo! Heave ass down that alley and sight on those far clouds."

"What spectrum?"

"Give me a see-through, infra or better."

Cermo swaggered forward, decked out in full field regalia, clicking and rattling with techno-ornaments. His fine-webbed electronets seethed with energy. Antennas embedded at shoulder, waist, and butt looked every-which-way, in full 3D. His weaponry was polished from long hours of care and repair on ship, but still pitted and burnished from a thousand forays.

Toby recalled the times when such gear was everyday wear for all Bishops. They had been on the move, their sensoria stretched out to max perimeter, each Bishop a sentinel. For years after the Calamity they had roamed like that, rising weary, red-eyed, and sore each morning, to a world drawing always dryer, with hunger and mech pursuit the only constants.

Locals peeped at them from around distant corners. They seemed interested and amused. *Rats in bow ties.*

Cermo clumped down an alleyway and into an open area, where he could get a full sight on the far horizon.

Toby couldn't figure out the sky here. He knew this wasn't a planet, not by any stretch, but still there were billowy white clouds drifting not far above the stunted buildings. There had even been a thunderstorm, catching them on the hike back to *Argo*'s berth. That had startled him—pure, tasty water falling from a sky like God's gift. He hadn't seen such a tasty shower since he was a boy, had played for hours in its mud.

—and at once was in a torrent, a downpour, spattering crystal droplets over his face. Her face. *Her* face. Endless gouts and flurries of blessed clear streaming cold, a waterfall hammering and thundering down a mountainside, she standing gleefully under it, yellow party dress plastered to her slim legs, a young girl getting ecstatically drenched—

The intrusion was sudden, raking across his mind. Shibo.

Her rising buttresses, flanked by granite masses. He felt within her Personality a sweeping reach, the sinks and hollows of another's interior self, a fresh continent spread bone-broad before him. The waterfall faded. Rain fell in the great distance, slanting from troubled clouds, signature of her own sad presence.

You have not summoned me forth for some time.

"I've been busy." Something in the waterfall, the pleasures of it, made him uneasy. He noticed that he had a hard-on, and hoped she wouldn't.

I know how hard it is to get along with your father. I did, once.

"He's running the show, sure, but . . . I just don't feel easy about it."

He is the man whose sense of opportunity has brought you far, so very far—

"I don't know what he's after anymore."

I believe his goals are as ever. But he is a man who hides his inner self, now. A Cap'n must.

"Not from me, he doesn't."

As if from a great distance, she said,

Even from you. You are becoming a man, more than a son.

He coughed to cover the dark seethe within him. His erection would not go away and he was breathing deeply, mind buzzing.

"Clouds're pretty thick," Cermo sent back. "Can't see much. In the far infra the view's all jiggledy."

"Now there's a fine tech word," Jocelyn joshed him.

"Jiggledy how?" Killeen asked.

"Looks like they reflect the city itself. I mean, stronger I look, more I get wavy pictures of streets, buildings."

Shibo receded. Toby had focused his attention on the conversation around him and she had faded into the background. He concentrated, to push her further back. Made himself breathe slower. He couldn't see anything through the clouds.

Cermo sent, "Microwave says it's solid up there."

"Solid?" Killeen nodded to himself. "Fits, yeasay."

<I agree. We are in a rotating tube, so broad that water condenses along its axis, forming cloud banks. If we could see clearly across, we would see more of this city hanging above us. How the rotation is achieved in this puzzling place I do not know.>

"Glad to see you getting humble, ol' cockroach," Toby said. He wanted to cheer up the lumbering shape, but Cermo's discovery made his voice shake a little. A city dangling over him, with nothing at all to hold it, kept up by some invisible law of physics—the thought made him hunch down a little, until he noticed and stood up straight again.

Three arms of ruby shell reached down suddenly and plucked Toby up above the street cobblestones. They swung him playfully to and fro, then dumped him onto the flat yellow carapace behind Quath's head. "Hey!"

<Perhaps you will learn more from a higher perspective.>

"Whoosh! Not that there's so much to see. I was already taller than the street signs. Funny names, aren't they?"

The Bishop party was crossing Peach Boulevard on Pomegranate Camino Real, names Toby had to call up his Isaac Aspect to understand were mouth-watering ancient fruits—but there wasn't a plant in sight.

<I find their reluctance to divulge data about this place suspicious.>

"If I take the measure of them right," Killeen said, "they don't give anything away free."

Toby said, "Yeasay—downright nasty."

<The Illuminates spoke of your tribal habits, the great variation in custom. They disagree over whether this is a source of your strengths, or a subtle weakness.>

"Ummm, maybe both. See, we're used to people helping each other automatically, no questions asked. These folk don't think like that—which implies a lot."

<Such nuances of primate behavior are beyond my kind.>

"Simple, really," Killeen said. "They aren't under threat all the time. Comfortable people can afford to be choosy."

Toby thought about that. "Could mean they're pretty used to strangers, too."

<I see your implication.>

"Oh? And what's that?" Toby didn't have any deeper idea, but he wasn't going to acknowledge that here, the only kid among adults. You kept your luck to yourself.

<There are many more people within this structure than we see. Enough to make most be strangers.>

"Ummmm." Killeen watched their guards edgily. "Could be."

Toby felt edgy, as though some game was going on just beyond his seeing. Killeen was composed, controlled, giving nothing away. As he fretted over this he glanced down an alleyway and saw a building in the distance abruptly seem to melt, windows and arches dissolving, turning a mottled green. "Look!" It reformed itself with a freshly slanted roof, a new line of windows.

Killeen's eyes narrowed. "That fits, too," he said distantly.

"Fits what?" Toby watched new doorways pop open, ovals instead of the earlier strait-edged type.

"This city's a kind of tech we've never seen. And I'll bet it runs itself."

Cermo sent a puzzled murmur. "Itself? Andro—"

"He's a clerk." Killeen gave Andro a bland smile, amused that they could talk this way right next to him. "These people, they're no higher level than we are, come right down to it."

"They sure don't seem like they could build a Chandelier," Cermo said.

"They didn't," Toby said firmly. "Don't expect them to ever admit it, though."

He walked past a splashing fountain, ideas tumbling fruitlessly, and felt a tilting, a rising presence—

—She moved lithely, inspired, skipping from stone to stone across the broken road, puddles from the night fogs showing her self and counterself in the shredding gray light. Playing in the fresh dawn's ruins. Jagged teeth from a night raid. Stumps of stone. A spider slept within the city, she saw it silver-fine and waiting. Stirring its barbed legs, the razor rub unheard beneath the waking bustle of her loved Citadel, fine and forlorn and always waiting for the next blow. Yet joy seeped from every moment. Shapes swarmed through this morning, the eternal going of people about their busyness, to strive against and fail and strive again. Even though they knew that the spider waited too, rustling in the eyesocket of a bleached skull—

He snapped out of it, panting. Forced his attention back to the street where *his* boots trod, *his* eyes caught the liquid dance of water.

Yet Shibo's world was entrancing, too. It called forth a lightness of being, an airy sense of things merging, yet solidly grounded in a web of interplay, of casual and unspoken delight. These glimpses into her Personality contrasted hugely with the masculine edginess all around him, the holding-back, the control and analysis. Killeen's blocky, muscular stride ahead of him spoke silently of purpose, precision, separation. Toby respected that, knew Family Bishop had to be led that way.

Yet this was his father, too. In the years since they had fled together across arid, murderous plains, the edges in Killeen had sharpened. Like a knife stroked on stone, Toby thought, a law of nature. And now Killeen expected of his son the same hardness, the same resolute separation that leadership demanded.

Toby lurched, the strife in him like a blow—a clash between the beckoning sense of the world Shibo held forth and the demands he felt radiating from Killeen. Cermo looked at him oddly, one eyebrow raised.

Toby realized his face must show his feelings, and tightened it up—only to feel the Shibo Personality laughing gently at him, then fading back into its ghostly berth in him. He marched on.

They wound through twisted streets, across a broad plaza of black stone, and into the most impressive building Toby had seen here—a steep pyramid of hard, glaring white. His Isaac Aspect said it was "pearly" and when Toby pressed his hand against the stuff it was shockingly cold. Sticky, too—and then they were being hustled through a wide portal and into seats before a high dais. The chairs were Bishop-sized and Toby's clasped him with a warm, massaging grip. It was downright insinuating, fitting itself to him all along back and legs. He wondered if it would let him go, if whoever ran this place decided otherwise.

To his surprise, the judge, Monisque, appeared at the dais—this time in blue robes. "I figured she was something more than a judge," Killeen whispered on closed comm.

"I'm happy to greet you again, far wanderers," Monisque said lightly. "Now I'm wearing my other hat—Chief Swapper."

"Sounds to me like you do everything here," Killeen said.

"Appearances are deceiving. Most people have no interest in visitors, no matter what esty they hail from." She nodded as dozens of the short people filled the remaining seats, buzzing among themselves. Toby noticed that the seats conformed to the dwarves, too, shrinking as required, and felt a little less paranoid.

"Our friend here, Quath'jutt'kkal'thon, is willing to yield data about any area not proscribed by his own, uh—" Toby could see Killeen struggle to put Myriapodia notions, even approximately understood, into human terms. "Uh, priestly orders. In return we've got a whole fistful of questions."

"I'm not here to give away the whole store, Cap'n," Monisque said skeptically.

Killeen was in no mood to start haggling right away, and Toby shared his impatience. "First, we want to know what this place *is*—how it works, its history, who made it. Second—"

"We can tell you what we know. I do not speak for the Lanes, though."

"Lanes?" Killeen looked blank.

"Other axes of the esty. Didn't Andro go through this?"

Andro himself stood up, in a crisper, cleaner coverall. "I tried to tell them, but they just don't have the concepts."

Toby couldn't abide that. He shot up and charged, "The entire time you were on board *Argo* you kept trying to trade us for our gear. I didn't hear you giving lectures on—"

"Okay, so I shaved a little time off the docket for my hobby. Still, your honor, these rubes don't grasp a fraction of the topological fathoms necessary to—"

"Sit down, both of you," Monisque snapped impatiently. "We'll give you the standard Remedial Intro, no problem."

"Second," Killeen said mildly, as though he had a long way to go on his list, "I wish to know the location of my father, Abraham of Bishop."

"Relative-tracing, huh? My tourist friend, that's a major cottage industry around here." Monisque made a notation by passing her hand over the dais top. "You'll have to commission a search yourself."

"You must know where your citizens are, *who* they are."

"Oh, must we?" She arched an eyebrow. "There are more slippery Lane-vectors than you have hairs on your body, Cap'n—and they curl more than yours, too."

The audience laughed, but no Bishops. Killeen's mouth tightened and he sent on closed comm, "She can't see my really curly ones—and not damn likely she will."

To this the Bishops answered with a volley of hoots and snickers. The dwarves looked puzzled, as if trying to decide whether they'd been insulted.

Toby grinned. He wondered if these people had the tradition of Ranking, a round-robin of cutting humor, sarcasm, and insults both veiled and naked. On the run, such quickshot talk could amuse and abuse—ideally, both. Its essential function was to defuse tensions, let grudges out in allowed ways. Toby realized that they had not had a Ranking for a long time. Maybe that was why Killeen seemed distant and awesome to so many of the crew now—they had not seen him humbled with a well-flung jibe.

"I respect the snarled-up way you kinsmen live here." Killeen was being his affable best. "You can understand that we need to reunite with our forebears."

She peered at them shrewdly. "You're sure that's all?"

"Your tribe's advanced and all, but some things don't change," Killeen said sternly. "Family's one of them."

"Fair enough. You should realize that we see a lot of people passing through. We hear stories. Prophecies. Outright lies. We get plenty of hands held out to us—to take, not to give. So we get maybe a little narrow-eyed."

"Try runnin' from mechs for a generation or two," Killeen said, careful and measured. Toby could tell his tone was just a cap on a slow-building inner pressure.

"I bow to your superior experience. Still, my authority goes only so far. We deal with people from trans-history in a fair, just manner. Bartering, that's fine—we'll trade square with you. Anything more—"

"We're from Snowglade, not some 'trans-history.' "

The judge waved a dismissive arm, her robe flapping. "A term from people out of the wild esty. See, we can't assume you're from the place and era you say, because there's really no way to check that. The esty turbulence blots out all backtracking. If we can, we go on a strictly cash basis—only there's no cash between trans-histories, so that means plenty of dickering and swapping."

Killeen dropped his amiable mask. He rose up, shin-servos whirring, using his height to come nearly level with Monisque. "I'll trade for news of my father and a map to find him with."

"That's it? Most visitors want food, fuel, maybe recro-credits."

Killeen snorted. "We'll look after ourselves."

"I suppose I could call it square if we had, say, full rights to interrogate the Myriapod." Monisque glanced casually at Quath, the first time she had deigned to notice her huge presence.

"That was just openers. We want more. We found an inscription in a dead Chandelier, about 'we all who plunge inward to the lair and library.' I want to ask questions about that."

She shifted in her shimmering blue robes, as though she heard the tension that Toby did behind Killeen's words. "There were a lot of Chandeliers. I—"

"Are there people here from that era?"

"In some sense, only 'here' isn't a useful word when you're talking about the esty. If you want, we can offer history data—"

"No data, no—not now." Killeen swept the air clean with one hand, his voice deepening, the words growled out. "I want to find *people*."

She eyed him skeptically. "Is that 'I want' or 'we want'?"

"*We*—Family Bishop. *I*—their Cap'n. There is no difference."

"So I gather," Monisque said dryly. "Very well. The 'library and lair'—well, this is one way into the esty, so I suppose this counts as their 'lair.' As for the library—that's not data anybody's ever going to hand you on a platter."

"Why not?"

"Andro—you were right. They truly know nothing." She cocked an eye at the audience, which chuckled. "Nobody's going to tell you our greatest secret, even if you are a ground-pounder giant. If you want to talk to ancients of the Chandeliers, or this Abraham, I'd recommend the Restorer. It's a kind of library, too, come to think of it."

Toby didn't follow this at all, but Killeen just nodded curtly, as though hearing confirmation he expected. He said forcefully, "The inscription, it mentioned a heroine, unnamed. 'She is as was and does as did.' Does that refer to this place, this Restorer?"

"I am not an expert in linear history, much less trans-history. This subject smacks of both."

"Then let us know the way to this Restorer, its price—"

"You couldn't afford it."

"I have not taken every jewel from my bag, Lady Justice."

"So I know. I was waiting for the next round."

"You know so much, maybe you can tell me what I'll offer?"

"Andro? The possibility you mentioned?"

Andro appeared in front and tapped his third fingernail. A wall flashed with sharp light behind the dais—a full, 3D picture of a passageway in *Argo*. Toby recognized the spot and gasped. "The Legacy! We let him get near it."

Andro didn't even glance at Toby's outburst. "They're flying a Class VI, Judge. Standard deck design, pretty beat up. I couldn't get into the nexus, but from the way they protected it, I figure there's a slab there. This kid"—he jerked a thumb at Toby—"just proved it."

She frowned. "From that age? I thought few such ships survived."

"The mechs nabbed most of them. The Bishops say this one was buried on their planet. Mechs must've overlooked it."

"A slab from thatwhen . . . " Monisque touched her dais, muttered to herself, and seemed to be calculating.

"Yeasay," Killeen said. Toby saw that the Legacy was indeed what Killeen had meant to bargain. His mind spun in a cold, furious vacuum.

Andro, too, had his distracted look. Toby realized they were both communing with some distant intelligence, maybe a data bank. His Isaac Aspect put in,

> ***There were such linking abilities in the High Arcology Era. They greatly increased the effective, acting intelligence of all. They also led to data-immersion ailments, and the dissipations such addictions are prone to.***

Toby shrugged aside this useless history. He watched the judge, who nodded—to herself, or to some far away presence?—and said, "I am prepared to bargain. Services—very limited services—in return for a thorough inspection of your ship."

Several Bishops shouted, "No!" Toby's surprise struck him silent, his throat full of cotton stuffing.

"I will have to know what services you mean," Killeen said, all business. "I have some in mind."

"Dad, we can't!" Toby finally got out. "The Legacies, they're *ours*. We can't let anybody else have them."

"I'll be the judge of that." Killeen scowled. "We have business here, and these good folk deserve to know of us, just as we want to know of them."

"No!" Toby shouted. "We don't *know* what the Legacies have in them! Family Bishop secrets, maybe. History, lineages of all the Bishops there ever were, could be. Even data from the Great Epoch! You—"

"We can't read more than a jot or two of them," Killeen said sharply, turning on his son angrily. "We need help figuring what they mean. This way we'll get it."

"But who knows what they'll do with our secrets?"

"They're old, so old the language doesn't even make sense. Chandelier Age stuff, maybe even older. From a time we know only as legends. All those dots and squiggles." Killeen turned to take in all the Bishops and

Trumps present, and Toby realized that he was silencing any objections before they could arise in the others. He said firmly, "I'll gain us what we need, trading the Legacies—and get them read into the bargain."

Murmurs of agreement came from Aces and Fivers and some Bishops, though a few averted eyes hinted that others weren't so sure.

Toby said hoarsely, "At least wait a while, Dad. Take this 'remedial course' of theirs. We'll learn more about this place, get a better idea what our Legacies are really worth, see if Abraham's here, maybe figure a better deal—"

Killeen's eyes quickly raked the room. A momentary suggestion of uncertainty in his mouth was swept away by a slight smile, a pleased arching of his eyebrows. Toby, too, saw that he had the backing of the others, the weight of his office and past telling strongly now. He gave Toby a searing glance and turned back to the judge, opened his mouth to speak.

"Dad, we shouldn't just—"

"Cermo—take him outside."

"But you can't—"

"I'm Cap'n, son. Cermo!"

Toby opened his mouth, words not coming—and felt Cermo grab him firmly from behind, pinning his arms. He wrestled, shouted, swore, tried a back-kick that found only air. Cermo had the reach on him. The whole room was watery, clogged with heavy air that did not seem to carry his words, his shouted words, as Cermo pulled him strongly backward, backward down a long aisle. Little pale dwarf faces looked bug-eyed at him, all hiding behind the stuffy air of this strangely rippling room. Toby's throat filled again, this time with a thick, sour taste, a bitter black draft of foreboding.

6

The Charm of Commerce

Toby spent two days under lock in a small bunk room, subject to strict ship's discipline. This meant that he saw nobody, knew nothing. Not even Quath could visit. The room wasn't big enough, anyway. Food and study materials were all he got, so he boned up on math and history, listening to Isaac's drone more than he ever had. He spent time doing exercises in the tiny cell. Cermo brought the chow, reluctantly keeping silence, following orders, even when Toby joshed him about it.

This meant that he didn't get to attend the general education sessions, explaining how this place worked. Which rankled him so much he worked out his frustration on the room, doing servo'd exercises by rebounding from the ceiling, scuffing the walls, slamming into the floor and then back to ceiling again. He tried to figure out how this place worked by himself, using Isaac, but nothing made much sense as he reviewed it. The deepest mystery was how this impossible solid ground existed at all, whirling around the razor edge of a black hole.

After two days Besen wangled a visit somehow. Her hair shone with fresh highlights—something in the water here, she said—and she beamed. He held her in his arms, kissed her, murmured of his cares and worries . . . but something was wrong. He felt himself stiffen as she touched him provocatively, a palm sliding confidently up his thigh, nestling on his hip.

—slick skin sliding—

Her kiss seemed metallic, an oxidizing flick of her tongue.

—musky warmth spilling over her in the fitful dark—

And her hand fell leaden on him, inquiring into his hardness.

—light laughter as the two of them rolled, leg over leg—

He stiffened in her grip, found it tight and close and hot.

—startled yelp of pleasure and pleased surprise—

She frowned as he pushed away, slapped away her hand. "What, what—"

"I don't feel like that right now."

"Huh?" Stricken eyes.

"I've got things on my mind," he said lamely, confused.

"Well, this sure isn't like the Mr. Anytime *I* knew."

"I guess not."

"Toby, maybe if you talked some, we—"

"Look, I—come back tomorrow, okay? Something isn't sitting right with me just now."

She went, frowning, mouth quivering uncertainly. He felt sad and angry with himself the moment the door sealed. But then he started talking to Shibo about it and the whole thing didn't seem so important anymore.

Besen didn't come back. He exercised, slept, thought fruitlessly.

By the time Cermo unlocked the cell, Toby was going buggy. Besen was there to embrace him, giving a soulful kiss that promised more than talk ever could. This time it didn't bother him . . . but it didn't kindle much reaction in him, either. Not Mr. Anytime, no—and he didn't know why.

First, he was in a mood to splash around in a shower—the natives here had tapped *Argo* into their own apparently plentiful supply—and get outside. The stubby city was more open than the ship's helical corridors, and he needed spaces, range. He got himself spruced up as fast as he could.

He had expected to be summoned to see the Cap'n, but his comm line was silent. As he strode through the sloped corridors, fidgety from confinement and depressed in general, nobody seemed interested in talking to him. Teams worked to flush and fix up *Argo;* even in port, ship work was never finished.

When he struck up a few conversations, crew members discovered pressing business elsewhere. Finally he decided to not call Besen. She might not understand that he just wanted some distance for a while, a few hours.

As he approached the main lock something looked funny. There were a dozen of the dwarf natives talking to the watch under-officers, haggling and trying to cull favors—and they all stopped abruptly as he came near. The Lieutenant in charge stiffly told Toby that there was a hold on his movements. He wasn't to leave the ship.

That got his back up, of course. He mulled over going to see Quath, to get the drift of what was happening, and then he remembered the damaged farm domes. In the big balloon-shaped dome devoted to grain crops, he had once tried to fix a small personnel vent that didn't seal quite right. It probably still didn't, but now there was positive pressure outside.

He got there without anybody paying any obvious attention. Sure enough, the vent popped free with just a little wrench work. Somehow the docking fields held the ship delicately isolated from nearby decks. Soft, but firm if you pushed on them. They brushed him gently aside, like a good-natured wind holding him aloft.

He slipped down, around the bulging slick skin of the dome, and dropped into shadows below *Argo*'s hovering hulk. Within moments he had made his way through the reception area, nodding to the bored attendants—and was out, away, into the gray city.

It was a shock. Rather than the glum, sour streets he remembered, these thronged with life—stalls and shops and incessant chattering that ricocheted from every avenue. This showed how stilted and planned their reception had been before, all part of their bargaining strategy.

Toby wandered, stunned. He had spent days worrying and fretting, and now all that seemed to drop away. It had been many years since he had simply let himself go, ambling aimlessly. Then it struck him—not since the Citadel. Not since the spring celebration when his grandfather Abraham had financed a ball-throwing contest between the generations, at a sports booth in the Citadel Square. Sweaty work, cheering and catcalls, itchy dust from many feet. And there had been hot, piping sweetchurns in paper bags, cool drinks, laughter, grins.

The memories made him bite his lip, and he plunged into the busy crowds. A few people gave him startled looks, but most ignored his size and strange jumpsuit. It took a while to get used to markets, deals, the quick calculus of value. What Toby thought of as just plain things had a special word, making them somehow better—"goods." You got "goods" with money, then had to make some other "good" to replace the money you spent. He wondered how you got a "bad" or maybe a "better," but nobody spoke of such things.

He had credit, it seemed, from a first payment the judge had given all Bishops days before. He minded it wisely. This wasn't like the bartering between Families he had known back on Snowglade. There you could get a syntho-shirt in trade for two of your self-made, gleaming carbon-steel knives, say. Then you had to find somebody who needed knives before you could get something else. Money was easier, really—you just decided whether the "good" was worth so many of the little round coins, or not. Simple.

But the bustle this conjured up here! The place was aswarm to bursting with shopkeepers and hawkers, fortune-tellers, merchants, the nimble-fingered and sadly wise, peddlers, grifters, senso artists, back-alley investment counselors, doxies of sullen smiles, men and women with "goods" hidden in their shirtsleeves or ballooning pantaloons, and "bads" alike in their hearts. You could buy anything, from a yellow powder that addicted you for life inside of two minutes, to a strange, luminous alien glassware—which proved to be the alien itself, when he touched it.

Some had learned how to beg for ready cash, too. Sitting in a back alley eating a treat, he watched a one-eyed woman who saw better than most could with two. She was getting dressed for her trade and, for a small coin, let Toby watch. Smooth-faced, she daubed on makeup, adding hideous blue hollows under the eyes. A light, comfortable sheath slid over her calf, making her spider-walk like a cripple.

Toby watched her set up shop on a busy corner. People threw her coins and looked away. Somehow the illogic of it—surely there were treatments for such ailments?—didn't rob the trade of a jot of its credibility. Toby couldn't fathom why, but then glimpsed a possibility. She was providing a form of ego-boosting entertainment. Looking at her miserable self, passersby could feel a rush of gladness: troubled they might be, but not *that* badly. She was in show business.

These weren't the demigods who made the Chandeliers, no.

There was a sprawling tangle of streets designed to separate people looking for amusement from their cash. Games, booths, things to throw at for a prize—and others where somebody got to throw at you. Dance halls open eternally, fever-bright, with syntho-music that wound around on a long loop, filming the air with prickly scents and startling pheromone-triggers. Toby lingered in one, and then in a brief moment when the effects turned off (required by law), he saw what was happening to him and his pocket change. He went back to wandering the streets, which was at least cheaper, though his nervous system kept trying to make his feet circle back.

There were science games and events, operating right next to fortune-tellers, a tribute to humanity's ability to believe two contradictory things at once. Hawkers of wonders. Gambling. Feats of strength (care to try?). Dispensers of drugs and even alcohol, all legal and heavily taxed to offset their probable social effects. Soft drink stands, one offering an ancient dark bubbly fluid that Toby hated and threw away, shocking some kids. They seemed insulted that he hadn't liked the authentic folk treat, Koca-Koola, rich and true. But the paprika was enough to turn his tongue.

He began to get the sense of a city again, after years on the move. Citadel Bishop had been a rambling, dusty pueblo on a canyon floor. It had water-starved gardens and one broad plaza—nothing compared with this. He had seen ruins of a lesser Arcology at a distance—the mechs were stripping it for materials at the time—and this place resembled that.

The brisk order reminded him of how restful it was to cook a meal, knowing that lamp oil or salt was just around a corner, available. Of how a girl, crossing a street, never paused but swung her head both ways before stepping off the curb. Of how hypnotizing it had been, as a boy, to sit at an upstairs window and watch the people parade past on a sidewalk, oblivious that they were passing actors in his imaginary dramas. Cities—a magical compression of humanity, a vessel he could learn.

Toby imagined that his new language-chip must be glowing white-hot, with all the use he was giving it. No set of rigid digital rules can blanket a sprawling, living language, any more than a fine silk handkerchief can cover a slattern. Most of what Toby heard was quick, vivid, direct. Fine for bargaining, but not nuances. He knew as little of those as a dog does of doggerel. Tradeswomen gave him an eye and tried to guess his birthplace from his vowels, thinking he had come from places named Ragpicker, or Avalon, or Tuscaloosa. From his size alone they knew he was from the Hunker Down Families, shaped by mech war and gravity, but they guessed Jacks or Queens, not Bishops or Knights.

There were a band of kids his own age that showed passing, mild interest in where he was from, what he had seen—and then quickly focused back on their own amusements. Their talk was quick, amusing, slangy, hard to follow. Mostly they just lounged around scruffy back alleys, absorbed, tinkering with gadgets.

They wore padded goggles, headphones, gloves and boots, curiously heavy things. Toby tried them on while they snickered knowingly, and found himself immersed in a sensorium of a forest. Big animals came charging out of the thickets, roaring and flashing huge teeth. A fierce cat-creature with tawny fur bowled Toby over—an odd sensation, because he also could feel himself still standing upright, while his eyes and ears told him that he was tumbling head over heels.

After a few minutes he got the knack of this game, though, and started shooting at the animals. They were pretty easy to hit. He tired of that and so tossed aside the weapon he had found in his pseudo-hand. He wrestled the next animal, a big lizard with hot red eyes. It pseudo-scratched and bit him, painful, slashing—all real enough impressions, but somehow disconnected because Toby knew they weren't anything more than electrical stimuli from a machine, blurred and oddly hollow.

Then it struck him—his own in-built systems did this, but finer-grained. His eyes could ratchet through the spectrum, pick up Dopplered targets, fix ranges and calibrations with the blink of an eyelid, a touch of a tongue to the right tooth. His servos cut in without prompting. All specialized survival gear, added to him before he could do more than squall and fill his diapers.

But here, such skills were exotic, down-worlder stuff. Other uses of the same tech were playthings.

He threw the big scabby lizard a few times and it threw him, until he got tired of the putrid reek of the leathery green skin, a stench of the rotting meat wedged in its teeth. The kids were there in the jungle around him, shooting and laughing and running around—all without having to do anything for real, or even move their own legs or arms.

They liked Toby's idea of wrestling the animals, and one of them got mock-crushed by a huge leprous rat with purple whiskers. But then Toby tired of that, too, and took his helmet off. The kids stayed in the game, though, their arms and legs jerking with fake hits and kicks, fingers tightening around imaginary triggers, killing ghost-creatures that seethed before their blinded eyes. He sat and watched them for a while, slumped into doorways, clasped in momentary action, thrilling to pseudo-lives they could lead as an amusement.

They were fun kids, but to them the world was just a bunch of signs and symbols and electronic fakery. They had elaborate, hip reasons why their world was better than the crude press of slow-witted reality—a philosophy, Toby thought, for people who spent too much time indoors. He wandered off and went for a real walk through a real park and though there were no exciting big green lizards, he liked it better.

That was where Quath found him. The hulking mass did not need to fight the crowds; they got out of the way. And Toby knew she was coming before he even saw her. Into his sensorium pushed a brooding, anxious curtain. Something was wrong. Very wrong.

7

Animal Spirits

<You are sought.>

"By you, anyway, big-bug," Toby said to cover his surprise. "People give you any trouble getting here?"

<I hurried and did not notice.>

"That big, I guess you can not notice whatever you like. Then too, I don't think the devil himself on red stilts would turn many heads here."

<I suffered no interruptions.> Quath clanked and squeaked and many-legged her way into a sitting posture, which Toby knew was a sign that she was serious. Her great head lowered to get under a willowy tree limb. <I was sorry that I could not visit you in your cell.>

"You couldn't have gotten in the door," Toby said with a lightness he didn't feel.

<I have finished with the questioning they required.>

"What'd they want to know? I mean, after they'd read our Legacies?" Toby asked bitterly.

<They asked much about the Chronicles of the Myriapodia. I told them of our weapons, our victories, and what we know of the mechanicals. Especially of their interests here.>

"You told them?"

<The Philosophs so allow. This is a cusp moment in the long conflict with the mechanicals.>

"Mechs get in here much?"

<They have defenses, as do the Myriapodia.>

"They'd better be pretty fine ones." Toby liked the lush greenery of this park, but it missed a quiet, slumbering ambience of Citadel Bishop's—at least, in boyhood memory. Neither did this city equal those lost, charming avenues he had toddled along, led by his mother's hand. And he knew that nothing ever could.

<They wished to hear of the mechanicals' work on antimatter.>

"Aunt who?"

Quath made a metallic *rrrrrttttt* that might be something like laughter, though Toby had never been able to tell. She made the same sound at times that weren't remotely funny, at least to Toby. When the *rrrrrttttt* stopped, she told Toby about how ordinary matter had an opposite kind, and if they met, both kinds disappeared in a flash of light.

"Seems dangerous stuff to tinker with," Toby mused.

<They are studying the small specks which carry currents, the electrons, and especially their opposites, the positrons. Clouds of such pairs are created by spinning small stars, the neutron stars. The mechanicals study intensely in such places.>

Toby shook his head. "I want to understand *this* place, Quath—don't trouble my head with tales of stars."

<I was attempting to make what you once termed "small talk" before getting to serious discussion.>

"*That's* small talk?" Toby paced in the little grove, listening to the mutter of people and commerce only a block away. Even this scrap of the natural world, a few trees and bushes, was enough to make him realize how much he had missed it. "I think I know what you're working up to, though. My dad wants me back, tail between my legs—right?"

<You state things in animal metaphors. A very primate skill.>

"But I'm dead on target?"

<More. He has concluded his negotiations. To gain what he wishes, he needs to trade some items from the ship.>

"Let him. After he's bargained away the Legacies, why be choosy?"

<The merchants here are avid for information on the clothing and jewelry of the Old Bishops. Their "folk art.">

"Fashion, huh?"

<It seems a primate preoccupation. Augmenting yourselves with baubles.>

"Hey, you stick on an extra eye or leg fast as I can change my shirt."

<You seldom change it.>

"Hey! I forget, sure, but—"

<It is not the same.>

Toby didn't see why, but he felt something in Quath's manner that made him uneasy. "Why come looking for me, mother of all cockroaches?"

<Your father has finished his trading. Now, to complete his own ends, he needs one thing more.>

Toby kicked at a fallen branch. "Should I care? Let him sell his teeth for it."

<The important piece only you have.>

"Me? I haven't got anything."

<You carry a Personality.>

"Sure, but—say, what's my dad been negotiating?"

<They have a different way of death here. An institution known as

the Restorer, or the Preserving Machine. With a tissue sample and a memory reserve, it can recreate any person who once lived.>

Toby felt cold, sharp horror strike into him. "Shibo."

<Yes.>

"I don't like that."

<I would think it was an issue for the persona herself.>

Toby blushed. He tottered, reeled—and sat down abruptly, head swimming. The air swarmed with blue-white dots. His chest heaved to drag in thick, moist gasps. He knew what Killeen wanted was wrong in some dark, terrible way, but he could not muster arguments. "I . . . I don't know."

<If the Shibo persona is to be used to reconstruct the living actual person, I would imagine that her cooperation is necessary.>

"They'll confer with her?"

<I believe so. But a Personality in a chip cannot speak.>

"Sure, it'll have to be through me."

His head pounded and his hands clenched, strangely cold, but he made himself think. He had only to turn his attention inward and Shibo's Personality rose like a massive stony wedge inside his mind.

It is tempting to go back into all that. I will have to think about it.

"What?" he asked her soundlessly. "But we're so close. I've hardly even started to learn what you're really like. Your memories, I love them."

They are digital dust.

"They're just as real as, as this grass, those trees."

You do not believe that. Remember the ones who fought the fake animals? They embraced the simulated over the real. You laughed at them.

"But your *self,* it'll last forever in chipstore." He was grasping at straws of logic and hoped she could not sense that.

Nothing replaces life. Still, there are flavors here that you do not taste. Hard to describe, gray and cool and restful.

Craftily he said to her, "Let's get through this trouble, then talk about this so-called Restorer."

There is some sense to that, I admit.

"Good. Just let me straighten things out with my dad, just you and me, and—"

I have been thinking. Such a transformation might not make for happiness in myself or in Killeen. He is changed. Harder.

"He is that."

I treasure this remove. Here I am free of the coarse and momentary, of jars and needs.

Toby caught a sliver of pale spaces, strangely delicious, of smooth surfaces flowing in a timeless place. "I see."

You cannot. But I thank you for trying.

He gulped, his hands trembling, and gazed defiantly up into Quath's hovering head. "I . . . I won't let Killeen have her chip."

<He is Cap'n. He will take it.>

"I have rights!"

<Not to keep a Personality. He will argue that a Personality should be liberated if it can be.>

He jerked angrily to his feet. "That's not Family custom!"

<Your Family never had the technology before. With your species, where ability goes, custom follows.>

"Humanity must've had this, sometime 'way back, or else these people here wouldn't have it. But our customs, they're ancient—and they don't say anything about bringing Personalities back."

<This, then, is a measure of how far you have fallen.>

So simply put, the brutality of it was unanswerable. "Look, I still won't give her up."

<He will take her. He argues already that Shibo's talents are needed, for the exploration of this place.>

"Exploration?" Toby could not get his mind off the prospect before him. And something more dried his mouth, tightened his throat—the strange currents running like searing rivulets when he thought of Shibo.

<For Abraham. And else, as well, I believe.>

"I need to think this over." Toby got up unsteadily. Shibo herself was not causing this seethe inside him. It was something he felt, something about him and Shibo together, that he could not voice. Each time he tried, he felt a sickening churn, a whirlpool of coming nausea.

<I came to warn you. Killeen has ordered a search for you.>

"I won't go back."

"Oh yeasay—you will," his father said.

Toby whirled. "No!"

Killeen and Cermo emerged from the nearby trees, fully suited. His father's face was lined and drawn, as though he had gone sleepless all these days. "I knew Quath would be better at searching than we are," he said with a tight smile. "You stepped-down your sensorium so much we couldn't pick you up on the grid."

"Dad, don't do this."

"I have to."

"I'm carrying the chip, so Family law says I decide for the Personality."

"Except when Family survival demands. That's the law, too."

Toby thought fast. He had never paid much attention to the endless wranglings of Family law and custom, the adults' yack-yack and breezy bluster, and now regretted it. "We're safe here. Nothing's threatening our survival."

"Not so. But look, son—I want Shibo back. I think you can understand why."

"I don't think it's for the best," Toby temporized.

"Nonsense. We'll be together again, the three of us, a real family."

Toby shook his head violently. "Not the same, not the same."

"Sure it will. Shibo, in the flesh—just think of it." For the first time Toby could remember Killeen's face lit with joy.

"That's not why we came here, Dad, and anyway—" He stopped. "No—this *was* why you came, wasn't it?"

Wariness swallowed Killeen's brief delight. "Not the main reason, no, but—sure, I guessed there was something like the Restorer here. The message in that Chandelier, remember? And other old sayings, myths. You should see the real thing, son! Magnificent, huge, flexible glass and metal you can see through, tech that can restore anybody, given enough data. You'll be—"

"You don't need her *now,* Dad. Later, maybe, when we've found Abraham, gone—"

"Abraham!" Killeen's sunny elation returned. "I got his message. He sent coordinates of where he is. They're not reliable, Andro says, but they'll get us to the neighborhood. Abraham is alive—here! Somehow he got away from the Citadel. Said to bring you for sure and—"

"Shibo can come after that. She's personal business, Dad. Abraham, all the rest—that's Family Bishop business. First deal with that."

"There's more beyond to discover, I can smell it. I need Shibo. She was my, my *core,* son. You can't understand that, I know, but . . ."

In Killeen's face unease and uncertainty warred with his set-piece Cap'n's hard-mouthed mask. Toby realized suddenly how much a shield that calm, resolute image had been, for years now.

"I need her. I want to have her back before we go searching for Abraham. It's an emergency, so I'm setting aside the usual Family customs—"

"We're safe! No mechs here, even. You can't invoke some—"

"I already have." Killeen's mask had returned at Toby's outburst, the window between them closing in an eye-blink.

Killeen and Cermo stood together, tall and certain, Cermo chunky and giving away his apprehension with elbows cocked, knees loose. The crevices in Killeen's face seemed deep, shadowed, hiding something. Yet the voice was mild, calming as he argued further. Toby had heard him use the same tones on a crewman who had stepped out of line and needed herding back in.

Toby took a deep breath, licked his lips. Using his Aspects, he dredged up legalistic lore, rattling jargon he only dimly understood. "Override our customs? How can you? I haven't even been informed by Family Council of any of this." He let his peripheral vision drift, sizing up opportunities. "First you have to—"

"I called a special Council. Since you had left *Argo* without permission of the watch officer, they allowed as how they could pass judgment without your being informed."

Toby was aghast. He should have suspected when it was so easy to slip away. "You *let* me leave."

"I gave orders that you were confined to the ship."

"Sure, knowing you could turn it this way, and then—"

"The Family demands this."

"Family? Ha! It's *you* who want it."

"I stood aside during their deliberations."

"Huh!" Toby spat back, edging to his left. Of course—his father knew how days in that tiny cell would affect him, make him jump ship. So the Cap'n prepared arguments, finished the dealings, then waited for Toby to skip. The shock of seeing how he could be so easily used, his impulses calculated, seethed through Toby like a chilly, clarifying dash of water.

He got control of his voice and said slowly, as mildly as he could, "Dad, Shibo doesn't *want* to be 'restored.' "

Killeen laughed dryly. "Nonsense. An Aspect always wants out."

"She's a Personality—bigger, more ample . . ." Toby struggled to say what he felt. "You don't carry one, you can't know what it's like. They're above all this, the surge of anger and want and fear that we feel—all of it. She likes herself the way she is."

Killeen was still smiling, shaking his head. "You can't expect anybody to believe that."

"I certainly do! No Personality carried in this Family ever had a choice of coming out again. Nobody ever asked the question."

"Well, we can," Cermo said carefully. "Just manifest her before the Council."

"No," Killeen said abruptly, clenching his fist. "I'll settle this. Manifest her now, right here."

"What?" Toby made himself take a deep breath. His mind reeled with harsh, violent imagery. Nausea burned his throat.

"Come on, let her speak."

"No!"

—fevered skin softly resistant, a cupped rosy breast—

"You'd have to anyway, before the Council," Cermo said reasonably.

"Any objection she has, I can talk her out of it," Killeen said affably. "Come on, son."

—tongue flicking in damp hollows, secret crevices—

"No!"

Killeen's smile hardened. "Yeasay. Now."

Shibo said,

If it causes this, I'll think again. I don't want to see you two—

No! Toby sent to her in the confines of her imprisonment. *No.*

Killeen's mouth hardened. "Now. And I mean it."

Toby broke to his left. He didn't have much hope but he dug in, revving his knee-servos to max, feeling their surging whine beneath his skin.

Shouts behind him. They probably could run him down but he would give them a chase anyway. He leaned into it, puffing hard.

Then the shouts became hoarse, shrill. He snapped his head around. Quath was blocking Cermo and Killeen, moving with surprising speed. She shot out a telescoping leg and hooked Cermo's foot, tripping him. Killeen she stopped with a rude bump, sending him sprawling.

Toby was astounded, but he didn't let it slow his pounding boots. He got out of the park and plunged into the busy streets beyond.

Escape has two steps: first, separating from the pursuer. Then, distancing yourself from the incident, so nobody suspects the distant hubbub has you as its prey.

Toby cut down alleys where he could, leaped clean over a stubby building—his servos cutting in hard—and dodged his way through three streets, faster than he could think through a plan. People chuckled and shouted at him but they seemed to assume he was a mere oddity, not a thief escaping from a job. He relaxed slightly and had the presence of mind to wave at the curious, smiling broadly, as though this was some stunt. Pretty soon he slowed to a fast walk and nobody seemed much interested in him.

He angled through an open-air market without attracting more than the usual attention paid his size. He made his breathing slow. His antic, popping anxiety faded.

Without thinking he found that he had circled around, always turning right when he could. Ingrained Family training. Coming around on your pursuer let you know where he was, since he was following your trail. You could decide whether to take him by surprise, but you had to do it before the tracker realized what you were doing. Or else you took off in a totally different direction, taking time to cover your tracks.

Only in a city there was no tracking, unless Toby had stirred up a crowd somewhere to mark his passage. But Killeen and Cermo couldn't talk easily with these dwarves, especially in their mood. So he might have a margin of time.

He had ended up behind the park. A chase moves away from the start and usually nobody thinks to check back there. He had learned that playing in the dusty streets of Citadel Bishop, then later again, dodging mechs. Now he hoped that his own father couldn't read him that deeply. The thought made him fidgety, glancing around corners before exposing himself on the approach to the park area. After all, Killeen had played him like a penny flute lately.

No sign of Killeen or Cermo. No shouts or unusual hurry. He leaned against a building, eyeing the park a block away.

This was only a temporary victory. The Family would comb this city and pluck him out.

He felt a familiar cool signal in his comm. Quath, apparently, had played the same kind of games as a child—or hatchling, or whatever the Myriapodia were when young. But Toby couldn't see her anywhere.

<I have offended your father. I am sad that matters have come to this.>

The bulky form was above him, clinging somehow to the side of a building, concealed in shadow. Nobody nearby had noticed.

"With Dad acting that way, it had to happen."

<Still, it brings acrid currents flowing among us.>

"Freedom starts between the ears, sticky-paws. I had to follow what I know. So did you. Thanks."

<I acted to preserve the possibilities for both of you.>

"Really? Do you think I should give Shibo back to him?"

<I have no views on so species-specific a question.>

"Come on!"

<My qualifications do not extend to your own, individual, cerebral symphonies.>

Toby leaned against a wall, watching Quath clamber down the gray ceramic building—which shuddered and popped with the strain—and said, "I don't hear much music these days, buggo. Just noise."

<It is your unconscious, trying to speak.>

"How would you know?"

<Only creatures who lack such mental architectures can see them clearly.>

"You don't have unconscious thoughts? I mean, impulses, things that just turn up when you're not thinking about them?"

<All aspects of myself are delegated to subminds. For your species, the mind is made by adding segments atop older elements. Not I. Your makeshift construction is typical of a phylum which has not reshaped itself fundamentally.>

"Maybe we like ourselves the way we are."

<A matter of taste. To me, an [untranslatable], your relation to Shibo is understandable. I delegate to my under-selves. Is it that way for you?>

"Ummm." He recalled the sensuous moments, his deep, troubling sweats. "Not really."

<You are too close, too [untranslatable] for judgment.>

"So I can't really think about Shibo? That's why I'm so messed up?" He felt exhausted, and not from his running. He let himself slide down, back to the wall, legs splaying out until he was sitting in the alley.

<Myriad impulses scurry and clash across the single, open stage of your mind. Factions hide offstage and shout from the wings. They are your suppressed, accomplice minds, and you cannot consult them directly, as can I.>

"That's . . . why we feel so much . . ."

<Pain? In a way—but do not conclude that such as I do not also know inner bloodknot clash. I can speak to all my subminds, which does relieve some of the tough, sinewy agonies.>

"And we can't."

<You find yourselves through action. Through your bodies the deeper cellars of your layered mind can speak.>

Toby wondered if he would ever know what stormy emotions tossed him about on the surface of a deep, troubled inner sea. He shrugged. "In that case, maybe I'll feel a smidge better if I do something more than sit on my fat ass, waitin' for Cermo to fall over me here."

<I admit I have no idea what you can do. I acted perhaps hastily, blocking them. I may have merely worsened your position in this grave matter.>

"Hey, without you I'd be having my spinal chips picked clean." Toby got to his feet, feeling lighter, easier in himself.

<Still, when they seize you, I cannot—>

"Like my grandfather used to say, bug-brain—Cheer up! We'll live to piss on the graves of our enemies." It seemed odd to be giving Quath a pep talk.

<He must have been a strong man.>

"Part of the line. We got plenty more like him." It felt good to say it, even if he didn't really know if it was true. Maybe no son ever did know.

<I do not know where this course leads.>

Quath rustled her legs, then restlessly played her boosters, hovering in air. People in the street nearby looked up, startled, and moved away. They were pretty savvy, but Quath was a bit much.

"Neither do I. We can't stay here, though. You're kinda conspicuous and I'm a wanted man."

<What then?>

"I dunno. We flew *Argo* in through the grand entrance and they were ready for us. Is there a back door to this place?"

Phase Creatures

Above the disk nothing made of metal or ceramic can survive.

Perpetually the great turning disk grinds down the stuff of stars. Tides suck inward, shredding.

The Eater itself holds eternally captive the gathered masses of a million dead suns. The ancient matter itself vanished in seconds of stretched agony, drawn down the steepening slide of space-time. But the memory of these transient masses lingers in curvature.

To the outside, a ghost warp testifies to the dead. Ten billion years of sacrificed matter—stars and dust, planets and cities, lost civilizations and their records, their hopes—have their single tombstone in the mute remaining distortion. A galaxy's ancient pain persists as silent gravitation.

Blobs of already incandescent matter spiral in, skating on the curvature at speeds higher than found anywhere else in the galaxy. Incessant pull whirls doomed matter in a final frenzied gyre.

The blobs collide, smash, reform, rub. Magnetic fields mediate the friction. Snarls of plasma stream and whirl. Currents churn.

Magnetic vortices grow. The fields twine and loop through the condemned kernels. In tight collisions, fields themselves annihilate against each other. More energy flares forth.

Above such brutal furnaces skim the phase creatures.

They had once been of the mechanicals. Now they exist not in hard circuits or ceramic lattice-intelligences. They have evolved out of self-directed necessity. To drink more energy they have learned to dissolve.

As torrents of hard radiation lance through them, they are plasmas. This gathers in fluxes and stores them in long-range correlations.

When the flood ebbs, the phase creatures change. In the cooler spots above the disk they can condense. Lacy filaments become gaseous discharges. The power so generated they broadcast outward, to lesser ranks who can store it.

The phase creatures themselves use these fluxes to organize themselves into free-floating networks. Circuits without wires. Electrons flowing only in their own self-consistently generated magnetic fields. Pinched currents that snake and flare. Voltages and switches. Light-quick, gossamer-thin.

Lively intelligences dance there. Inductive, silent, invisible.

They enter the discussion that has been teeming above them, in the cooler realms. With silky elegance their thoughts merge with the hard beings who are the cruder, earlier forms of mechanicals.

But the phase creatures still know their origins. They share the thought patterns of the metallic forms. They converse.

I/We do not understand why these odd, primitive primates should be studied at all. And what is this arrival?

You/I summoned ¦>A<¦, who was concluding the elimination of remaining organic life on the planet of these primates' origin.

This ¦>A<¦ is a strange mixture of intelligences.

I/We know. Tolerate it. Here:

Greetings. I employ the single-consciousness approximation. This you may find uncomfortable.

Regard: How narrow.

We/You tried it before and found it stifling.

We should accommodate ¦>A<¦.

Very well. But what a demented limitation!

Bear with ¦>A<¦ for a moment.

To plumb the recesses of primate thinking such strictures are necessary.

Why study them, then?

Their sense of beauty is like no other. Variant organics are unique, as well, but these have long duration here at True Center.

Beauty? We are arbiters of that.

I seek to find wholly fresh reaches of grace and flavor. These are species-specific, lavish in lore.

A needless luxury. We face sterner issues now.

Beauty is as vital to our being as any of your raw pursuits.

Is that an insult?

Never—but a fact.

Careful, then.

I intend no offense. I am a specialist intelligence, with my own drivers. Let me point out to you gathered minds what a richness these primates have! These are the creatures who developed the Five-Digit Motif. It grips the perceptual centers as can no other! And then there are their inner, colorful emotion-curtains. Wondrous! Their Subverted-Maximal Abstractions. All wonderful creations!

I/We are more concerned with their possible danger to us. All because of some semi-mythical knowledge they carry.

But without knowing they carry it. That is important. They must not learn what they possess!

I believe they sense some special destiny which they carry. But they do not know its nature, that is clear. Such beings carry deeper knowledge as narratives. To primates, a myth is a deep story which answers the difficult questions of their lives.

I/You thought that myths were simply someone else's religion.

Of course, but I speak of primates. I have studied them well.

Then you are the one who must enter the Wedge and act for us there.

Why? I have other matters—

You know them best.

But I have never been to the Wedge.

I do not wonder, with your time spent on the beauties of underlife.

The Wedge is treacherous.

Indeed. But we/you have breached it with minor forms. Even now the tiny informants have filtered into their portal city. They are keeping close watch on the primates of the ship—those we allowed to enter.

A move you/I opposed.

It gained us valuable information. This Legacy of theirs—it hints at much we do not know.

We/I would not need to know it if we had expunged the primates.

No! You should not think this way. The primates are a valuable form, approaching extinction. Protect such beings for their last moments.

That is a luxury.

We command you to follow close upon the important primate members which their own Legacy has identified.

The Wedge is perilous. I cannot even be sure, entering it, where I shall be. Or when.

We/I shall give you/I resources.

I could become lost in the chaotics.

A risk we/you must take.

I have heard that there are agencies in the Wedge which can harm even higher systems such as ourselves.

True. We do not know what they are.

But I am in single-consciousness mode! If I perish, the "I-form" shall vanish!

I\We cannot help that.

You/We elected this state.

Though of course we will archive your present state. A copy of you will carry on.

To venture into such turmoil—I am not qualified.

You/We seem reluctant. Yet you\we have trained in the most important skill—you have dealt with primates. You moved them to their intersection with the quasi-mechanicals. Very adroit.

And we/you have other motivations.

What motivations? To risk so much—

Think of beauty. Of art.

Part IV

GRAVITY'S GULLET

1

The Esty Wind

The city of the dwarves slipped away behind them.

Toby and Quath moved quickly, using scattered buildings for cover and then a dense grove of curious spindly trees. These rose to greater and greater heights as they fled into a gorge of arched and tangled rock. Toby's attention fled as well, veering away from the confrontation with his father, taking refuge in the pure bliss of flight. He ran hard.

<I believe we are taking a dangerous path.>

"More dangerous to stay back there."

Dangerous? Toby asked himself. To whom? The word was wrong but he was not going to inspect his inner feelings now. Time to *act.*

<In the descriptions of this place, which I attended and you regrettably did not, there were severe warnings. I do not quite understand the nature of these prohibitions but they seem to reflect the inherent [untranslatable].>

"Great help, those [untranslatable]s."

<You are still troubled,> Quath sent.

"Hey, leave me alone, yeasay?"

<I do not know how to explain how Killeen has changed.>

"Humans aren't so easy to figure, you said once."

<He has been obsessed with coming here, that I knew. His shadow falls across his memories of Shibo. That his love of the woman would intrude upon your relationship—this I could not anticipate.>

"Me either. Some way he needs it, more than the Legacy . . . or me." He swallowed hard but the lump in his throat would not go away.

Into his mind sprang scattershot images, ripples of sensation, rushing fragments of ideas briefly glimpsed and then tumbling away. Shibo lurked just behind his nervous eyes.

You cannot understand what is going on here and neither can Killeen. I urge you to relax into it, not strive so hard.

Toby felt a hot flare of indignation. "Look, it's *your* ass I'm saving."

From the erosions of real life, yes. Do not think I cannot feel appreciation for that. And it would be best for us to be together for at least a while longer.

His hurt irritation swerved to grateful warmth. "You want it, I want it. My father, he can't see that."

Do not suppose this relieves you from your Family obligations.

Shibo's whispery words carried a flinty edge. "What obligations?"

To find Abraham. To carry forward the Family ways.

To this he had no reply. Shibo's Personality engulfed him, cool and lofty. She spoke in longer sentences than the real Shibo ever had. Her Personality had begun picking up the jittery anxieties of chip-bound selves, a flavoring utterly unlike the living Shibo.

Was she learning from Isaac and Zeno and the others, taking on some old-timey warp? He vaguely sensed her changes but he hoped they were not important.

He loped with easy grace through stands of trees, bounding over gnarled briars, making Quath clack and clang her scissoring legs to keep up. *Out, away, free.*

He had shucked off the flexmetal husk of *Argo,* peeled away his father's iron hand—and the heady rush of it sent spurts of driving energy into his legs. As a boy he had learned the hammering arts of flight, of hardship in constant movement, and now the joy of it returned. So he was totally unprepared when the ground began to slip and twist beneath his crunching boots.

"Quath! Something's—"

<I had warned of this. Sealed-away sections of space-time. They have their own atmospheres, biospheres. Such spaces are seldom visited, the Andro person said, for they lie within the jointed esty-work which reflects—>

"What's happening?"

Frayed air, sudden rushing mists. The space around Toby had a give and tremor to it, an unsettling porosity. It was as if the molecules of the leaden air were sucking substance out of him, tiny mouths making his skin prickle and jump.

Skinny trees whipped at him as if lashed by a fierce wind. Yet Toby felt only still air.

Then a churning wrench at his feet, his knees—and he was flying, no weight, the trees now dim blue shadows raking past. Quath was a blob, brown-soft and pooling into a teardrop.

Illusion? He could not tell, but a fist was knotting and unknotting itself inside his stomach. The issue resolved as Quath swelled, stretched into shimmering dirt-colored droplets—then slammed into him, a hard sharp crack in the chest.

"Ah! What's going—"

<Hold to me. The [untranslatable] seizes us.>

"What's the damned [untranslatable] *mean*?"

<We writhe in the stochasticity.>

"Stocas *what*?"

<The time-spun evolution of the esty. Grab my legs!>

Toby wrapped arms around a burnished coppery shank. Purple air-whorls and raking winds snatched at his legs, worried his boots. A screeching red patch of steaming air streaked by, growing dirty roots as he watched, a plant being born from nothing.

He clung with all his strength and felt his joints pop. Seals in his microhydraulics yearned to open. He expanded his sensorium.

Howling vagrant senses flooded him. Plucked at his eyes. Tilted his sense of balance until he was convinced that he was somehow holding Quath aloft with his arms, a vast weight plunging down upon his neck and shoulders—and then in a flicker he was holding Quath above a pit, a black yawning abyss of red-tinged fires and sputtering wrath.

He had to keep Quath from falling! He felt his ankles strum and stretch, metal-hot and elongating into impossible cords of frayed muscle—

Then he was simply plunging, walls rushing past. Down a tube that snaked and grew shiny ribs as Toby watched, still spinning. Quath whirling by.

<Hold. I am losing a leg.>—and her shank sheared off. It rang hard against him. "Ow!"

She orbited him on a long tether. It was one of her telescoped arms. Torn free of her, and used to connect them. As Toby inhaled, it stretched—and he smelled his own acid-sharp fear.

"Quath!"—but the ivory head that swiveled to regard him was a whirling mass of bulging sockets and wiggly stalks, deeply alien facescapes, not one expression but many. Eyes and lurching mouths and planes of cheek and jowl all working against each other, the personalities of his friend spattering across the great head.

Unreadable. This, more than the slamming colors and ripping winds, frightened Toby and sent a chill through his aching, straining joints.

Quath's rasping was harsh and yet calm, resigned. <Be still. Hold on. This is the stochasticity. The random esty's laborings.>

A pearly fog dispersed, blown by some unseen wind, and Toby saw far below them—though they were not falling toward any place now—a mass of pinhole openings in a broad plain. The pinholes danced, refracted by great distance.

They flew along the plain as though blown by a wind, soundless but for a soft chime almost like tiny voices. One pinhole swelled and he could make out small bumps on it. Toby closeupped the nodules and found their crests crowned by dashes of white—and then realized that these were snow-capped mountains.

Toby saw the size of the thing he was witnessing—a plain sprawling away into hazy infinity, a whole flat world. Seething with pores. Pockets that opened and closed like slippery mouths.

<Hold hard!> Quath called.

They lurched sidewise, Toby barely keeping both gloved hands on Quath. Rushing winds, hard-slamming acceleration.

The mountaintops streamed by like tiny ridges. Something slammed them forward with a rude kick, up and away from a yawning cavern that churned with brooding shapes. A sudden veer, and they were back above the plain. The multitude of other pinholes churned and jostled like an angry crowd. Gravity's gullet.

"What . . . what are they?" Toby called.

<The Lanes, I believe. So Andro termed them.>

"Places to go?"

<If we knew how to move in this place, I suppose so. But I believe no one has that knowledge—or can have it.>

"Where are we going?"

<I do not think there is an answer to that, until we arrive.>

"I'm rethinking this whole idea, buggo."

<It is far too late for that. Actions have consequences.>

Something somber and yet matter-of-fact in Quath's tone was chilling. Toby held tight to the alien's leg and watched as a particular pinhole began to grow nearby. He realized that they were speeding toward it, turning at angles and spinning in a random dance, while vagrant forces plucked at his fluttering legs, his painful arms, and gurgled the fluid in his ears. He forced away bitter nausea but it hovered in the back of his throat.

Hold. Just a little longer. If you lose Quath—

The hole puckered. Toby had the unpleasant sensation that it was preparing to swallow them—and then it did.

In a blur of wrenching speed they rushed through gauzy spaces, his eyes filming and suddenly thick with tears. Then he heard a rasp, felt a thump—and they were on a field of ropy, tough grass. He felt himself gingerly and sat up.

"Uh!" Muscles complained. No bones seemed to grind against themselves.

Quath was already surveying the curved bowl that arced away in all directions—though she moved a little unsteadily on her feet. Toby could not see where they had come from, but a small dappling in the sky flickered, hinting at a huge space above—and then was gone.

"That like to pulled me apart."

<In worse weather it would have. And I as well.>

"That was weather?"

<Esty weather. The space-time responding to the addition of more infalling matter. Redesigning itself self-consistently.>

He felt bruised. "I don't get it. What happened?"

<The esty flexed and bore us along with it. We are in a different Lane than before. A separate space-time, usually closed off from countless others. Only when readjustments occur do the Lanes intersect.>

"That's happening now? How come?"

<Remember the star which split open? It is working inward through the disk. Its added mass now forces the entire geometry near the black hole—including this esty—to adjust.>

He remembered how this whole esty place had swelled up out of the ergosphere. Worlds within worlds, all moored somehow. "What holds it together?"

<No one knows. Yet it persists.>

"Start with the esty then. What keeps it ridin' around near a black hole, when that hole's supposed to eat stars for breakfast?"

<I gather that one might as well question why a drawing remains on a sheet of paper when you slide it across a table.>

"Huh?" Toby rubbed his shoulders, fighting cramps. His muscles were bunched hard and he had to pound on them to free them up any. He lay back, tired. "So this esty, it's written into the, the—"

<Do not struggle. Your language does not have the concepts. The esty is a space-time kernel embedded into another space-time, which in turn is curved by the black hole. The esty is a stable dip in this overall curvature. A well. A refuge.>

Toby brushed at the soft, moist grass. At first it moved away. Then it caressed his fingers. "This grass—it's esty-stuff?"

<No, only the foundation is folded space-time. Ordinary matter accretes to it.>

"Ummm. Good to know grass is still grass."

<Growing inside a small, pocket space-time. Like a capillary in the wall of a pulsing artery.>

Toby lay back and let Quath go on. She was trying to get across slippery ideas. He fumbled with them and finally decided to simply accept.

Primates, Quath had once told him, liked to reason by analogy, like holding up an orange and seeing how it was like a planet. Here something like that was needed. Capillaries, arteries, the esty as flow.

But the *feel* of this place was off balance, not like anything he had ever known. Pressing textures played along his skin. The air kept stretching and relaxing, rubbery. Tremors beneath him radiated upward into the cottony blanket above. The esty, adjusting itself? The waves were just below the edge of hearing—yet he felt them through his bones, a heavy pulse.

And on top of this, the troubled sense of being watched. Scrolling feelers in his sensorium. When he focused on them they dispersed.

Toby stared up in wide-eyed awe. "Land as fat as God's pocket." A cloud dissipated and he saw high above a vast curving green mat, spotted in vibrant yellows and purples. Land, far away.

The roof of this Lane arced over them, as if they were in a huge spinning cylinder, pinned to the sides by centrifugal force. But there was no spin, Quath told him. Or nothing that would seem to humans like spin. Instead, the esty held itself together with its own curvature of . . . itself. He struggled with the idea, got nowhere, so tossed it aside.

And tucking up and away from him, to all sides, the speckled forests. He had seen ancient pictures like this, sights called up by Aspects and sent into the Family sensorium for entertainment after a long day's foot travel, but he had always figured they were figments, artworks, mere fancies of a dead past. Lush green unending.

<Humans and others have shaped the esty to their liking. Your father told me, when the Andro person was looking at your Legacy, that it contained a reference to this place. It was once referred to as "the Redoubt.">

"Huh? To doubt again?"

<No, a place to retire to. I gather that humanity, and other carbon-based forms, came here to escape the mechs, long ago.>

"Hmmmm . . ." Light seeped from a rocky hill nearby. Toby got up, edgy despite the embracing calm here. He walked over to the shining stone and kicked it with a boot.

Try as he might, thunking his sharp-toe into it jarred loose no chips. An ivory radiance oozed from the layers. Knots of gaseous esty floated, spitting beacons. They lit the shadowy reaches with probing beams, like airy lanterns drifting on unseen winds.

Slowly the soft light ebbed. The seemingly solid rock grew shadows, as if a sun were setting somewhere deep in the foggy stone. Blades of sunlight radiance danced deep within it, like summer's promise cutting deeply into a watery cavern. He felt himself suspended above an abyss of nothingness, a mere crust keeping him from plunging down into—what?

Unease crept up his spine. Luminosities played far down inside the seemingly solid rock. Like a gulf of nothingness. He hung above sulky depths.

He shook himself. No time to fall into abstracted moods. He called up a smattering of geology from Isaac—who, predictably, wanted to discourse on the slip and slide of planets. Toby cut him off.

"This stuff, it looks like, uh, a funny kind of limestone."

<They call it timestone.>

"But what *is* it?"

Quath began to explain but Toby could not keep his mind on the talk, compared with the slippery immediate feel to everything here, the *give* to air and rock alike. He let the information filter down to the parliament that was himself, where gobbets of succulent information fed the Aspects and Faces and the one smoldering Personality. They took to it eagerly, while he simply felt, scarcely thinking at all. Shibo asked,

So science has grabbed time and made it like a kind of space?

He relayed this to Quath, who clacked and said, <The esty is an arena for the struggles of particles and fields. Or else maybe there was nothing but curved esty—and somehow everything else, matter and motion, came out of curving the esty.>

Shibo was as unsettled by this as he had ever felt her.

Maybe even in tiny pieces? Pebbles, sand? So that everything's really, down deep, esty?

Isaac put in,

Many ages ago our science abandoned the simple notion that physics was geometry. But in this place . . .

Even Isaac seemed subdued by the silent strangeness.

Toby was restless from the strangeness of this place. "Come on—let's go."

<Where?>

"Uh . . ." Getting away from the weight of father and Family had been giddy, liberating. But now his mind was blank. "Just keep moving. I need to think."

They went for a while without speaking. Quath's silence grew to seem like a precise criticism, all the harder to answer because it was unspoken.

They worked their way toward a distant upthrust of green, thinking it to be a grassy hill from which they could get a better view. But as they approached Toby saw striations working in the layers of it, colors mixing flame-yellow and reddish-brown and scattershot blue. Sometimes shards of emerald emerged, as if from a struggle of the light within.

Without warning a sheer cliff writhed in scraping agony above them, like something laboring to be born. A sheet peeled off, cracking and booming, curling away like a petal of an immense flower. Its base yanked free.

Toby ran back, trying to get clear. But the sheet did not fall.

Instead the still-curling layer compressed, contracting along its length and then along its width, shrinking, complaining in grating groans—all the while oozing burnt-orange rays, as though some unseen fire baked inside. The edges turned crimson and then curled back, showing a well-done brown. Still it dwindled, crevices sputtering with fist-sized flares, and—*crack!* the sheet vanished. A sharp concussion knocked Toby flat. He felt as if somebody had smacked him in the forehead with a stick.

<Esty cannot last.> Quath didn't seem disturbed. <As I suspected.>

"Where'd it *go*?"

<Somewhen else.>

"Why?"

<I gather that a construction in esty shares the property of *being* in anxious equilibrium with the property of duration.>

"Huh? You mean this whole place can't last?"

<In principle, no. In practice, it is like your skin. Some sloughs away, and other esty grows to replace it.>

"Seems a funny way to build."

<It is the living way.>

Without their noticing it the glow around and above them dimmed. Blades of radiance shot through filigree clouds. A chill edged the air. Toby said, "Guess we're done for a while," and sat down on a hummock sprouting a wiry yellow grass.

It had been long years since he had fled for a full and exciting day across unknown terrain, and despite all the worries he kept at the back of his mind, he felt unreasonably good. Never mind that his Family lay behind him, that he missed them already. Ache crept up his calves and a ferocious hunger sprouted in his belly.

"You got rations?"

<I have learned to carry some.>

"Me, too. Let's eat. Then some sleep. Talk later."

<You realize the grave course you have set.>

"Yeasay. Feeling good for the first time in quite a while."

<I do not like to understand so little.>

"Funny—that's just what I do like, right now."

2

Time's Grip

He woke up fuzzily. Shibo was crooning to him, a soft voice playing down through his body, massaging his muscles and strumming along fibrous nerve nets.

> ***Wake. I love you for what you did and I will help you through this place. Hard I can be, and soft, too. For you. But you must wake now, as much as you would like to stay down there in the syrup and cotton.***

"Uhhhhh . . . okay . . ."

—a liquid licking pleasure, soft darks, crooning winds outside, musky delights below, pulses hammering, sharp tang of blood from a bitten lip, quickening gasps—

He pushed the feelings away. Pleasant, but he knew he had to wake up. A dream? Somehow more concrete than that . . .

He lay sprawled across spongy grass, arms spread out, boots off, servos dead. Vulnerable. He tapped an incisor two short raps and felt his servos stutter back to life. His sensorium, spread wide for guard duty, contracted into a half-sphere. Nothing funny on the perimeter, no orange-haloed possibles lying doggo inside. Suit weaponry brimming, fresh-charged when he left *Argo.*

Safe to stir. Long ago his father had taught him to appear dead when he awoke, until he was fully ready to fight. He lifted his right hand—

—and it wouldn't budge. It lay palm-up on smooth, cool timestone. The flesh near his knuckles felt cold, stiff. He pulled harder. A little give, not much. He sat up awkwardly, hand pinned to rock. "Quath."

<Good morning, though the light here does not properly lend itself to that description.>

"I'm stuck. Lemme—"

<I don't advise—>

"It's *got* me."

<Still—>

He yanked hard. The right hand came free with an awful ripping sound—and a flash of white-hot pain. "Ow!"

The entire back of his hand was raw, a scarlet patch of oozing corpuscles. It had left behind a tattered rag still stuck to the timestone. Already turning brown, blood thickening in air.

<An unfortunate side effect of the physics. I should have anticipated—>

Toby clutched his hand and swore. He popped open his medical pouch, fished out supplies and slapped an all-purpose bandage on the bloody damage. "How'd—what—"

<I should have realized. Esty rock is not truly solid.>

"*Feels* solid."

<It is compressed events, rendered as mass. Press against it long enough and you become part of the event.>

"What 'event'? That stuff tried to *eat* me."

<Do not ascribe intention to physical law. Your skin became wedded to the esty. It began to diffuse into the occurrence-space which this substance is.>

"You mean everything here can sop us up, like sponges?"

<Only if you dwell long enough in close proximity—within a few atomic lattice spacings, say.>

"This grass, even the air?"

<Not at all. They are ordinary mass, the simple form of matter.>

Toby shook his head. "Look, let's eat some of that ordinary stuff. Provisions, I mean. I'm woozy."

Quath threw him a ration. <I gather that the timestone does eat matter placed against it, but at different speeds. The bare stone—such as where you let your hand lie—absorbs quickly. Elsewhere, it does not—so dirt and life can survive. All quite ingeniously constructed.>

Toby barely heard this. The bandage was a living layer doing its work, regrowing his skin. Already the back of his hand wriggled, a scummy green mat eating his drying blood and making epidermis. But Family bioengineering—when it had existed as a living craft—had dictated that repair came first. Nurture was far down the list, so the pain still made him grit his teeth. He turned off most of it by going though his subcontrols, but it took time. Pain could also be a useful reminder, so it was not easy to block.

He ate some of his rations, sitting gingerly on grass a good distance from any timestone. Morning was nothing like sunrise here, though there was a crisp bite in the air. Patches of stone exuded pale beams of light that scattered among the twisted trees. Distant peaks brimmed with slow-shifting colors. When the clouds far above parted he could see other sources of radiance giving off diffuse glows that came and waxed and flared again in long, patient pulses.

<This light seems to come from the accretion disk around the black hole. It becomes trapped in the esty and carried along by solidified past events.>

"Seems enough to grow trees."

<The virulence of the disk is muted here until it sustains life. This cannot be accidental.>

"Who you figure made this?"

<Not even the Philosophs know. I am too humble to speculate. Use of the fabric of space-time as construction material is a skill beyond my comprehension.>

"How 'bout us?"

<You? Primates?>

"Why not? We made *Argo,* a long way back. And don't forget the Chandeliers."

<You do not understand how much greater the esty is.>

"Ummm. You're impressed by big ideas. Me, I'm impressed by a tore-up hand."

Toby had meant the suggestion as a joke anyway. He had long ago given up trying to understand where things came from. Time enough for such luxuries when he felt safe. If ever.

Down the shining air came a bird. It was the first he had seen since Snowglade, in the years before Citadel Bishop fell. The mechs had found birds a fairly trivial exercise in extinction and had easily blown them from the skies.

This one was far larger than anything he had seen aloft that was not mech. It neither fluttered like a butterfly nor soared like a predator hawk, but instead sported with proud reliance on the fields of the air. He watched it snag something he could not make out. Then it wallowed through a milky strand of congealing vapor, more like swimming than flying.

The cup of mottled air blew over Toby and he felt a sudden sharp chill. He tried to raise his arm and found it would not go, that he could not even bat his eyes. His chest froze. Muscles locked up. Then the stuff like translucent glass was gone and he could breathe. The bird had wafted by without a twitter or slightest show of concern. Only as it passed did he see that it had four wings and an outsized head. Yellow wings churned against a gathering breeze and the air thickened around it. Winds curled. The atmosphere turned a color like chalk meeting rust.

"Quath!"

<Wait. It passes.>

"Some weather," was all Toby could manage to say.

<Esty can sublime into vapor, I believe, even liquid—or so the "Introductory Text" implied. It mingles with the air. Try not to breathe it in.>

Toby got his breathing right again. His chest hurt. Rock that turned to air? And maybe back again? He let his aching lungs subside.

Another bird came slow-flapping down a passing draft. With admiration Toby followed its artful course on vagrant winds. "I dunno about this place, old bug-girl. If you have to check it out before you draw a breath—"

Quath shot the bird. It blew to pieces. Toby cried out in alarm. "What'd you—"

<Look at it.>

Toby found parts of the body in some stumpy grass. Blood everywhere, guts glistening fresh, an acid scent. Head cracked open, eyes staring. At the back of the skull, shiny electricals.

"Damn! It's got mech parts."

<Made by them. Adroitly disguised.>

"And *here.*"

<Precisely. Mechanicals have infiltrated the esty Redoubt.>

"All this time I thought we were safe."

<So do many. They scrupulously filter visitors such as ourselves for mechanical spies, for microscopic agents, for intrusive programs in human computers. Andro said these measures were effective.>

"Double dog damn. That bird, it looked real pretty."

<I find it disturbing that the mechanicals know how to integrate organic forms with their own.>

"They did before, remember? That crazy leader on Trump, that Supremacy—his head was packed with stuff like this."

<True. I should have generalized from that.>

"But who'd think? Inside a bird, even."

<It was studying us for a bit too long, I thought.>

"If it had time to send a signal to whatever made it—"

<Quite so. What are the chances that a mech device would find us, in the labyrinths of the esty?>

"Ummm. Depends on how many Lanes there are."

<There may be uncountably many. The mathematics of this place is coy with infinities.>

Coy? Quath picked some pretty funny words, sometimes. "Depends on how many spies the mechs're sending, too."

<This bird implies, then, that the mechanicals are much concerned. That they are hunting you.>

"Me? C'mon, my father'd like to get his hands on me, but mechs? I'm not important to them."

Quath's servos wheezed uneasily. <Uncertainties converge. I believe we must again make use of the esty's prime property—concealment.>

3

The Rock of Chaos

To "make use" meant moving fast over unknown terrain, looking for a pore-opening. Toby thought of the wrenching places where the esty boiled open as sick-making confusions, but Quath spoke of them as the finest work of intelligence she had ever encountered.

Toby tried hard to understand as they ran, loping over sheets of timestone. His hand still hurt fiercely and he stepped lively, afraid that the apparently solid rock would suck him in. Quath made her screeching, ratchetlike laugh about this but he did not think it was funny.

Part of his problem was envisioning time and space all gumboed together to make something he could walk on. He was acutely aware of the time, all right. Of the enhanced, vivid *now* that divided the known but fading past from the unknown, ghostly future. But how did you marry that to distance?

"Time, well, nobody can stop it, yeasay? And space, that's what keeps everything from mashing together—so what've they got in common?"

Toby was trying to provoke her, but Quath took it all very solemnly. Gravely she explained.

Listening, Toby caught an occasional glimmering. Humans had an awareness of things becoming, bursting forth into concrete solidity, and then fading into a limbo of memory. Quath said that space-time, the esty, contained real time, and the transience of human experiences was only an illusion peculiar to living creatures.

And what did their opinion matter, Toby thought wryly, since they were around for such a short glimmering? His Isaac Aspect tendered up an ancient rhyme,

Time goes, you say? ah no!
Alas, time stays, we go.

—and cackled with weird glee.

They passed by huge blank timestone walls, porous with blurred light. Giant towers worked and popped with energy nearby, growing like triangular trees. Some seemed able to shiver the sky and wrench the stars apart with their restless energy. Quath and Toby hurried by. They ventured with scarcely a pause into abrupt turns, mazy avenues of timestone. Toby had kept himself in pretty fair condition on *Argo,* he thought, but he had a trial in just keeping Quath within sight. His lungs burned. Servos ran hot.

He stopped abruptly. "Quath, I was wrong. Dead wrong."

<How?>

"We've run out on the Family. That bird—what if mechs're all over this place now?"

<You believe the mechanicals will seek all the humans here?>

"Bishops, anyway. Come on."

<Where?>

"I'm heading back."

He felt good about himself for the next few hours, while they backtracked. Quath kept quiet. After a while Toby saw why.

"Uh . . . which way from here?"

<I do not know.>

"We came this way, yeasay?"

<Indeed.>

"The Lane connection, it was somewhere around here." Hills, trees, sky—all different.

<The esty is strongly stochastic at the Lane connections, for those are the instability loci.>

Toby sagged down, eyes blank. "So we can't find our way back?"

<I fear not.>

So they reversed again. Fruitlessly returning over the same ground was demoralizing. And the terrain was subtly different, which deepened Toby's gloom. He had run away from his father, straight into a trap. A place that forgave no errors.

Quath kept looking around, studying, distracted. When he asked her why, she said, <I am letting stochasticity—that is, chance—choose to favor us.>

"I—I don't get it. What're we looking for?"

<An obliging accident.>

"Sounds like a contradiction in terms." He panted hard, slippery air clogging his throat.

<You told me once of a simple puzzle you had solved. Here:>

Into his sensorium framed a pattern of paired numbers.

1	100
2	99
3	43
61	97
5	96
•	•
•	•
50	51

"You messed it up. Each pair was supposed to add up to a hundred and one. There were fifty of them, so that multiplied out to, uh, to five thousand and fifty."

<True. But in this sum I merely rearranged the numbers in a random way—but I kept them all, so that the total remains four thousand nine hundred ninety-nine. The esty is so devised. What Andro called the Lanes are subsets of the entire space-time here, tunnels opening and closing at random. But the sum of it all—the four thousand nine hundred ninety-nine of it—remains the same. Nothing is gained or lost.>

"Uh, okay. What's the point?"

<The esty conserves itself. But the continual shifting of the Lanes makes a map of the esty impossible. Relying on the stochastic nature of the interplaying Lanes is the only way to protect them.>

"The mechs can't find any particular Lane, because it's never in the same place twice?"

<Or the same when.>

"Hiding in time, not space?"

<In both—in esty. The Lanes evolve by interacting. The falling of a single timestone can multiply its effect, building disorder. Similarly, in a planet's weather, a mere passing wind can stir forth a storm. Scrambling the esty Lanes rearranges them in time and space. No mathematical algorithm can unbind them or trace their evolution. Security rests on the firm rock of chaos.>

Toby slowed, the idea sinking in. People had hid out here. Long ago, in the Hunker Down Era. Back then Bishops and all the Families had dug into the planets for protection, figuring the mechs worked best in space.

But some fraction of humanity had fled into the esty's chaos. Mechs could not map this spaghetti space, so they could never be sure of finding all human colonies. He could see what Quath meant with the arithmetic, sort of. But the weirdness of it remained—that disorder was safer than planets, tougher to untie than snarled barbed wire.

Numbers could hold simple, supple majesty. Maybe the strangest part of all this was that reality reflected the dance of numbers. Laws compelled the esty to knot and flex, laws ruled by the skittering logic of chaos. Compared to that mystery, the mechs seemed almost ordinary.

"So where do we go?"

<Forward. The farther we go, the more tangled our path becomes.>

"How'll we ever get back to the Family?"

<I do not know. I suspect that they, too, will enter this labyrinth.>

"Following us?"

<Do not forget Abraham.>

"Yeasay. Let's find him first." He nodded to himself. Having a sense of purpose made him feel better. And this was a better place to be than stuck inside *Argo,* by far.

<You are following your species-specific behavior.>

Toby had the uneasy feeling that Quath knew what he was thinking. "How's that?"

<Your primate societies often were ripe with ritual journeys. Young men went off on quests into unknown lands. They had adventures, learned much, and returned transformed.>

"You been studying us again?"

<I do always.>

Toby had been feeling guilty about enjoying this, especially now that they couldn't get back to the Family. "We're not so damned predictable!"

<I note patterns. You may have needed to escape the father, in order to define yourself.>

"Hey, you're pretty heavy with the crap here."

<I am trying to understand a very strange species.>

"Sometimes understanding's the booby prize, buggo." Toby laughed and put all such theorizing out of his mind. It was a luxury, the kind of thing people in cities did. He settled into the rhythm of the run.

He watched the landscape with wary respect, aware now that it took time to shape time. Esty storms had carved out intricate canyons of compacted instants. Compressions and twistings made unscalable walls, stomach-turning drop-offs, boxlike traps of curved, silent timestuff.

Moving through the gasping-hard slopes and sudden gaps was exhausting. Quath had ample energy, but the pace began to tell on Toby. He kept looking back to check for signs of pursuit. Unbidden, his father's words in their last encounter pealed through his mind.

Shibo was there to comfort him, to immerse sharp memory in her soft presence. She sang and delighted him, distractions galore.

Still, the feeling of pursuit would not leave him. His calves began to ache, his breath rasped. He forced himself to keep up with Quath's great bulk, which seemed to flow easily over the jumbles of gravel and swelling rock.

Finally, when Toby was sweating hard, they took a break at the base of a steep cliff. Quath lowered herself to an easeful position atop her legs and seemed to fall instantly asleep, the first sign he had ever had that she slept at all. Or maybe, with her multiple minds, she was just resting, and letting some fraction of herself stay on watch.

Above them the cliff had spires, pools that hung to the sheer face like teardrops of black iron, and sky-piercing poles of a sickly yellow. But the cliff face itself was smooth. Toby watched a creamy frieze seem to float out of the rock—a slanted void where blobs and strings wrapped and coiled together. He walked over to look.

He peered into a deep field where shadows played. A moment from some other time and place, a painting of agonies. The slow-moving mosaic leaked jarring sounds, like steel racketing on steel.

Deep down in the timestone, ruddy, pulsing blobs fell upon green-tinged stalks, squeezing them until pus oozed from purpling tips. Image-bursts came ratcheting out of the rock like agonies released.

Toby watched, fascinated, and read the action as a battle, a slaughter of the stalks by predatory blobs the color of dried blood. Only after a while did he glimpse the tiny slate-gray stalks that tumbled in the wake of each struggle. Then he guessed that the blobs were somehow assisting in the mating of the stalks, or milking from them the next generation of hesitant, torpid infant stalks.

But this impression itself soon was destroyed by the sight of sickly-yellow blobs emerging from the tips of the new stalks, wobbling like soap bubbles, and then attaching themselves to the mottled underside of the larger blobs.

As they did, shrieks peeled off the timestone wall. Sheets of brittle sound, like the final desperate cries of small birds being torn apart.

Yet the mosaic kept on, a perpetual floating play of forces he could not comprehend, issuing humming songs. Rough coughs, pained screeches, staccato, insectlike pepperings—none seeming to repeat, or bring meaning to the action.

Only then did Toby see that his attempts to impose meaning on the vision were pointless. He was witnessing a passing event from some unknowable elsewhen, flaking off the timestone as he watched. An ancient record dissolving into fog as it sheared away from the spongy surface. The motion he witnessed came as fine planes peeled off, each invisibly thick, like the thin slice that separates future from past.

He reflected on what Quath had said. He didn't much like science—which he thought of as a fearsome entity, not ideas but a force of nature, for he had never met a scientist and would not know what one looked like. Here science had seized time, stripped away many of the everyday aspects, and made it like a kind of unsteady, pliant *thing*. It made lives seem like riffling pages in a book.

Gingerly he reached out, stroked the face of the event-matter. It was water-cool here, untouchably hot there—again, no logic, no scheme. And that was the flat fact of it: occurrence beyond human categories, brought forth from places unknowable.

Then the timestone ruptured. He had looked into it, assuming the flatness of the events there, each coming toward him as the layers peeled off into filmy fog.

Abruptly a stalk-thing poked out of the mist. It wriggled. Shards of silvery ice flaked off it. The rubbery stalk extruded from the timestone, thicker than his arm and longer. With a pop it wriggled free and fell at his feet. It hooted, low and clear. A plaintive call.

And more followed it. They floundered from the timestone as if spat out—moist, shining, making what had been comfortably distant images suddenly smelly and real. A fountain of liquid obsidian spouted to his left. It crystallized in air and fell tinkling. Panels of dusky mist marched above his head. One of the blobs grew out of the timestone and attached itself to a floating lump of water. The stalk farted a core of hard blue gas and the blob answered with a whorl of velvety fire.

Eerie, unreal. Shibo said,

Remember that all this comes out of laws, physical laws. These are trapped events from somewhere else in the esty. We should explore it.

"Uh . . ." Head foggy. "How come?"

This is a way to find what else lurks in the esty. We cannot go to these places ourselves.

"Can't see how I'd want to anyway." Whispering.

Do not be timid!

"Looks funny . . . risky."

Go forward. When I was in flesh I never felt cowardice.

"No, you got me wrong, I'm just saying—"

I wanted to know more about the world. That's the only smart way to stay alive. Believe me, I know how dead you can be inside if something stops you from—if **you** ***stop trying, learning, changing.***

"Shibo . . . I don't . . ."

Coward. Open yourself to it!

He stepped closer.

Blue-black flames danced up and licked at Toby before he could move. They were warm and soft and made him want more of their obliging comfort. He felt uneasy but within himself there was a push-pull of diverging impulses. Shibo's Personality moved massively, blotting out his caution with a silky, calming curiosity.

> ***We must explore this place. It is wonderful, I think. You were so right to come here.***

"I didn't, really, I just . . ."

His words trailed away. Shibo wanted to explore this strangely swarthy flame and so he stooped and put his hands and forearms into the purpling mass.

Cool, slick. Not a fire at all. It felt even better now. So pleasant to thrust up to the shoulders, his face full in it. Fragrances swarmed through him—sweet, pliant.

So comfortable. Beckoning.

Then he remembered the addictive amusements . . . back there . . . in the gray city . . . the one he had left. Something important about that.

The stuff wriggled all over his face. He wrenched away. Scraped at it with leaden hands. Gluey ropes stuck to him. Licking strands inched across his mouth, nose, eyes. He slapped at them, stripped them away. A vile reek leapt up into his nostrils: flavors like emotions—*angry, vindictive, spiteful, wronged love.*

He wadded up the cloying filament, struggling against waves of fleeting but sharp emotions. He dropped the fluffy, welcoming resilience and instantly regretted doing it. The pang of remorse was keen and oddly bitter. Shibo punched through to him with

> ***Get away! Quick!***

—and he was off, scrambling fast, part of him flooded with remorse, another scared.

"What was that?"

> ***Some form of parasite. Rather sophisticated.***

"*You* told me to do it."

> ***I only suggest. I cannot act.***

Her hurt tone irritated him. "You leaned on me, dammit, made—"

He slammed into Quath in his hurry. As he picked himself up she sent one of her keen-edged staccato bursts that was as close as she got to sounding like human laughter.

<Afraid of the fish?> Quath had missed the whole drama.

"Those're trouble," Toby said lamely.

It had all been internal, he saw. Fever-ripples of contrary emotions danced across his skin where the velvet had grasped. His fresh epidermis on the back of his injured hand sent him a puckering sense of pleasure, as if the flesh was being kissed by a wide, welcoming mouth.

<Everything here is.>

4

Unsettled Movement

They had run themselves out and still the seeping light did not ebb.

They were not on a revolving planet, so day and night did not make their cyclic claims. A fitful glow soaked through from exposed teeth of timestone, casting shadows among the green and yellow foliage. Toby went hard until his boots dragged, so they stopped and slept. Still no sign of anyone else. Or of pursuit.

He woke up to hear Shibo singing. Words pealed, a delicate but persistent melody, light and airy. Then he realized that his eyes were open but he saw nothing.

He blinked to restore vision. Twisted trees, big-bellied clouds, rock—his vision flickered, stabilized. He sat up, disturbed. Nothing threatening nearby. Wind sighing in the stringy brush. A sulphurous lance of light cutting a foggy glade to his left.

There was no reason for her to co-opt his senses."What . . . ?"

I needed an outing. You were soundly asleep so—

"Yeasay, and now I'm not. No thanks to you."

After your misadventure yesterday, I expect you could use a little help.

"Misad—oh, the purple flames? You were the one wanted to give it a closer look."

You misremember. I alerted you to it when you were up to your chin in—

"Not the way I recall. You were at my back, pushin' the whole time, wanting to touch it."

You have edited out your own attraction.

"The hell I have. I wondered what it was, sure, but—"

Let's not argue. We escaped without harm—together. That is the important point. As long as we remain together and alert, even in such a strange and wonderful place we can stay safe.

This little lecture put his teeth on edge but he kept quiet. Directing thoughts to her would just make her say more and right now he wanted inner silence, a chance to think by himself. For himself.

He went for a call of nature. While he was burying it so the smell would be hard to track, Shibo talked to him. He butted her back—pressure against a stiff wall. He struggled silently, mouth twisting, and then came the shock: he could not get rid of her. She was always there now, riding behind his eyes.

Why should you not want my help?

"Why? 'Cause I got no choice anymore."

You are too young to go forth without my aid.

"How 'bout *I* decide that?"

My point exactly. You can make bad decisions, you know.

"At least they'd be mine."

We have such a closeness. Do not push me away.

Something about her "closeness" made him uneasy, but he could not find the words.

—a cloying sense of moist pressures, syrupy air that would not leave his heaving lungs, liquid running in through his nose and ears and unwilling mouth, snaky fog-feelers sweet, so sweet—

When his breathing was back to normal he tramped back to Quath. She had warmed up some of his own field grub, stock she was carrying for him.

He forgot about Shibo. The greasy excellences of the hot, oily food pushed her presence clear out of his consciousness. Which was a relief. She had been hanging in him for days now, heavy as a wet boot. He only realized this when she was subdued.

<You kicked and spoke in your sleep.>

"Uh huh. Dreams, I guess."

<Something more.>

"How would you know?"

<Your kind conveys much through facial signals—an odd method, one we do not employ.>

"You read my face when I'm asleep?"

<I read always. This is essential to understand humans. I digitize your image, then compare with previous measurements.>

"Measurements of what?"

<Of angles and amplitudes of skin folds, color, eyebrow thickness, curvatures of mouth and eyes.>

"My God! You work pretty hard."

<But that is merely what you do.>

"Naysay, I just give people a squint and figure out—hey, you mean that's how *I* know how people feel?"

<Of course. You are designed so that none of this work is conscious.>

"But for you it is?"

<If I wish it to be.>

"And if you don't?"

<Normally I delegate the task.>

Toby knew that thought was a net of racing electrical impulses, the dance of atoms speaking through their fleet messengers. But was that all his thoughts meant? He looked at Quath without knowing what to say.

<I have been reading for a long while now the signals which move across your face. Especially at times like now.>

"It's Shibo. Something about her."

<She rides upon you uneasily.>

"Yeah . . ."

<Maleness for you must always carry some anger, a ruthless density. You are impelled to unsettled movement, androgen-agitated. Your moral errors are most often a quick brutishness.>

"Hey, I'm better than *that.*"

<Femaleness—a convention which applies to me only vaguely—carries in your primate varieties an acute sensitivity of response. This is embedded within a composed stability, self-contained. Your females are expectant, impelled to waiting, estrogen-slow. Their errors tend to the static, the enduring face.>

"Hey, come on. That's so simplified. Hell, I feel steady and composed plenty of times—just not lately, is all. And Besen, lookit her. She's as kick-ass as they come, when she gets riled."

<Your genus drifts between these polar extremes—a mode with great survival value, and so seen again and again throughout higher life. But frequent gray does not disprove that black and white exist.>

"You got sex on the brain, big-bug," Toby said uneasily.

<Your sexual geometries shape your perception of the world—a

collaboration between male and female, a painting etched by tensions. Man is pointed toward invasion. Woman exploits the advantages of the hidden, the never-fully-knowable, the grotto of welling darkness. This is the strategy of your species. Merging them in a mind so young as yours is inherently destabilizing.>

"That's what's going on in me?"

<I believe so.>

"What'll I do?"

<I do not know. We are without the required technology for the two principal remedies. As I understand your primate minds, the optimum cure would be to reinforce your own subcharacters.>

"Which?"

<Perhaps your self-sense. That is an idiosyncratic agent present in all human minds. It supports an obliging illusion—that a single self rules your intellect and senses.>

"So if I built up this 'self-sense' . . . ?"

<It would counter the areas which the Shibo Personality is invading.>

"Ummm." He was having trouble keeping his attention on the discussion. He felt a foreboding when he paid exact attention to Quath's words. But then an itch in his servo-couplers would make him scratch, or a yawn, or some small piping of his sensorium. He would lose the thread of Quath's argument.

It seemed as if all kinds of little things were poking at him, making his attention veer away from this problem. "The other way—"

<We do not have the equipment to adequately carry out—>

"Yeasay." A deep breath. "Look, I'll handle this on my own."

<I believe the problem can only worsen.>

"We got plenty more to worry about."

<I fear that—>

"Leave me—and her!—alone."

Toby leaped up, prickly with energy. He walked off, contracting his sensorium, cutting off discussion. Quath's words were still with him. *You are impelled to unsettled movement, androgen-agitated.* His boot thumped in frustration on a chunk of timestone.

He drank from the stream that muttered nearby. The water was sharp and fast-running. It cleared his head and quite suddenly he became aware that he felt deliciously lazy from the sleep. The uneasiness in him was gone, soothed away somehow, and he did not ask what had done it.

As he walked back to Quath a distant peak cracked apart and showered down glittering fragments. Pensively he gazed around at the warped greatness. "Hey, y'know, we could name these."

<I do not follow.>

"Maybe nobody's been in this particular Lane before. Could be, right?"

<Possibly. Though humans and others have occupied this complexity for very long times.>

"How long?"

<The Illuminates say it is at least several tens of thousands of your years old.>

"Ummm." Toby thought of history in terms of his Aspects, not in "years." Isaac was of the later Arcologies. Poor fractured Zeno was from even further back. History was people, not numbers. Impatiently he said, "So if we're the first to be here, we get to do the naming."

<That is a human convention?>

"Tradition, we call it. A right, really."

<"Rights" are not a useful concept here.>

"Hey, come on. We could use some of those fancy names. Places the Aspects go on about."

Instantly there flooded into his idling mind a shotgun blast of names, titles, all tinged with faint echoes of silvery memory. Tombs of Ishtar. Grand Palace. Altars of Innocence. Goddammountain. Bamboozle Bridge. Androscogginn. Pinnacle Prime. Dassadummakeag. Ever-rest. Pike's Pyramid. Isis. Mount Olive. DoDeDeed. Angry Sink.

<Why name them at all?> Quath asked quietly.

Something in her tone made Toby blink. It was an odd human vanity, he saw, a desire to grab and hold. Shibo helped him see what every nomad knew in his sinews—that the world was to see and use and move on, part of the flow and trek of life. Naming the land didn't fit.

"Well . . . Let 'em name themselves, then."

But a part of him felt frustrated. He hid that from Shibo. Or tried.

5

Hard Spark

Despite steep passes and rough ground they made good time—whatever that meant, in a twisted esty-place that kept confusing Toby's ways of thinking. Several times the air and rock swayed like things seen under water and he felt sick.

Weather, Quath said. The esty adjusting to the infall of mass. His inner ear told him that "down" was a matter of opinion, shifting as the timestone groaned and flakes popped off.

They entered wind-whipped desert. Jumbled terrain curved up and away into a burnt-orange sky. The other side of the Lane was so far away he could not make it out even under highest closeupping.

"Big place. Gravity's opposite over there?"

<True. The sickness we feel comes from tidal wrenchings.>

"Uh huh. There's somethin' more, though. You feel it?"

<I sense being watched.>

"Yeasay. I can't pin it down."

<We are sensed in a diffused way. Unsettling.>

"Not mech, I'd say. Doesn't smell like them."

<Perhaps. The mechanicals are smarter than our kinds.>

"Some ways, maybe."

<Yes. In some ways.>

Quath was getting jittery. She said little and her legs fidgeted when she wasn't using them.

It got hotter, then suddenly cold. A dry wind sucked and chimed like faint music. Small esty waves rippled by. The whispery tones were clear but mysterious, inhuman but pleasant to a lonely ear, deeply still and yet moving with the flexing of the esty.

"Sure not much water here," Toby said, trying to keep some talk going against their shared uneasiness.

<Liquid water is a rarity in the galaxy. Near the Eater the problem of

supporting organic forms such as ourselves is far worse. I am sure the esty is made to collect and conserve water with high efficiency.>

"You figure it was made for us? I mean, humans?"

<No. Most planetary life shares fundamental chemistries. Mine is not so different from yours.>

"I remember you saying once that you'd mingled genetic stuff with some species, way back in history. Was it with us?"

<No. We engaged with a higher form, I am sure.>

"Oh yeasay? How high?"

<Our records are vague. But the connection took us to a higher plane of contemplation. More advanced than single-minded forms.>

Toby wasn't sure what "advanced" might mean, and was not much impressed if it meant you were huge and had to clank around in a hard carapace and knock over things without noticing.

He had tried to shave in the mornings here but the water and soap had the fluid sucked out of them by the air before he was half through. Aridity squared, air like a sponge.

Breezes of thwarted gravity led them into a territory of demented vegetation. Corkscrew ferns twisted in tight loops all around them. Giant fronds feathered to catch the sporadic light of the distant esty walls.

<They respond to the esty weather,> Quath said. <A helix can better resist the shears and warps of changing gravity.>

Each corkscrew was a scaled-down woodland. Their helical sheets were veined in green and orange, concealing pockets and crevices packed with creatures who clicked and chattered and whistled, calling from the coiling complexity of the parent tree. For fun he tried to catch a mouse with wings and ended up with a skinned elbow, from snatching futilely at nothing but air.

He was eating some delicious purple fruit when he felt a twinge in his sensorium. Not much, just a wrinkle. Then a pale ghostly wedge shot through his senses. Blunt inspection. Not the earlier subtle sense of eyes just beyond view.

He looked up. Something long and tapered came gliding high up in the brassy sky.

He had felt such cool, remorseless force before.

Quath called, <Quick!> and was off, moving fast.

Toby followed. To watch Quath go up a slope was to see the job reduced to its essentials. They got under some dense trees. He was running and trying to identify the skittering sensorium traces when a massive boom hammered down through the forest.

It flattened them both. His sensorium rang. Limbs crashed nearby. Helical fronds rained down.

<Keep low. I shall spread a deceptive screen.>

"Mechs. They're high up."

<Some small figures. One large.>

"Damn!"

<Not mere reconnaissance, as with the bird.>

"Double dog damn!"

<It is ominous that the mechanicals have invaded the Lanes.>

"They must've broken in."

<Yes, but why now? Observe their patterns. Clearly they are searching.>

"I remember some of these patterns and—" Something in his sensorium, coming fast.

<I am a disadvantage to you now. I am far easier to find.>

"Quath . . . It's the Mantis."

A long silence. Striations moved at the edge of his sensorium.

<I heard of this form from Killeen. A higher order of mech.>

"Dangerous as hell, too."

The Mantis shape moved in a strange zigzag way. One moment it was shrinking, seeming to go further down the Lane—and next he caught its movement along a ridgeline nearby, half hidden by the glowing rock.

<Others.>

Smaller forms flitted among puffball clouds. One skimmed whispering over the canopy, veered, was gone.

"We thought we killed the Mantis back on Snowglade."

<I wonder if the higher orders of mechs die at all.>

"We blew it to pieces with *Argo*'s exhaust!"

<We think of selves bound up in bodies. The mechs may not.>

"Well, slicing them up seemed to work pretty well."

<Think of this manifestation, if you must, as a kind of cousin to the Mantis you knew.>

Toby laughed. "Mechs with relatives?" Family was so human; mechs had no need of the concept. "So you figure it's coming here, snooping around . . ."

<I agree. This implies an unsettling revision of our ideas.>

"My Family's escape from Snowglade . . . "

<Perhaps it was not as it appeared.>

"Maybe it was a setup?"

<It brought you to the world where I captured Killeen.>

"You figure the Mantis *meant* for that to happen?"

Quath settled down on her many legs. Their shared sensoria contracted further and her sensors, better than his, scanned the sky. <If so, to what end? With the Illuminates and Philosophs to guide, I helped you reach this eerie place.>

"So? Why'd any mech want us here?"

<You assume the mechanicals act with one vision, one cause.>

"I never saw them do any different."

<For the lower mechanical orders, perhaps.>

"Lower?"

<The types you could kill.>

"We did all right. Stayed alive."

<I suspect the higher ones would be impossible to kill.>

"Umm. Like the Mantis." Shadowy shapes came nearer, slipping over hills like sheets of gliding oil.

<If we have come here as part of some larger aim—>

"Doesn't make all the work and danger look so damn glorious, does it?"

<I suspect that is too narrow a view. Very primate.> Quath had an antiseptic tone, a polite disdain for such animal excesses.

"Look, what's this Mantis after?"

<Certainly not merely to kill us.>

"Suredead us, then."

<It probably could have done that before now.>

"Then what's it want?"

<You, I suspect. All of you.>

Toby's brow wrinkled. A shadow fell over the thick canopy. He squeezed down his sensorium. With acoustic suppressors even the wheeze of breathing could not leak out. He lay covered by the loops of spiral blue-green that had showered down. He raised his head slightly and was just in time to see a thin yellow spark come caroming among the trees. It struck some and bounced off, humming as if it were talking to itself. About the size of his head. The spark turned darker and orange-tinged with each collision. It came nearer—and moved faster than he could follow.

It hit Quath. Angry red embers shot over Quath's carapace. One leaped off her and chewed at Toby's left side. He rolled automatically, trying to get away from the pain. "Ah!" The embers fizzled away.

Toby lay absolutely still. Nothing changed. The shadow had passed on and with it the pale wedge in his sensorium. Aches hardened into swift, shooting pain in his arm. "Q . . . Quath?"

No signal. "Quath!"

<Quiet.>

They lay that way for a long time as winds whipped through the high spiral folds above. Toby probed at himself. He flinched when he moved his left arm a certain way and found out that the arm was broken. He blocked most of the nerves from there but could not get all of them. To stop all the hurt would have meant losing motor control of the arm.

Quath moved. Slow, tentative.

He had been thinking of himself and felt guilty when he saw how much damage she had taken. It was all on the far side of her. "Hurt bad?" The words sounded stupid. Three legs shattered. Spokes of white metal jutting through the carapace. Brown fluid everywhere.

<I have tapered down the pain centers.>

"Can you walk?"

<Marginally.>

"Can I help?"

<Yes. Leave.>

"Huh?" Toby stood, staggered, and picked up one of her splintered shanks. "No way!"

<I will only draw fire to us. You should leave. Escape this Lane. Your only protection is to immerse yourself among humans. The Mantis will have more difficulty finding you that way.>

Toby scowled. "What's changed, Quath?"

<None of my feelings for you, be assured.>

"But, but what—" He stopped himself because he was afraid he was going to cry.

<I came with you because I suspected that your protection was of great importance. The Mantis confirms this.>

"Why am *I* such a big deal?"

<I suspect you are part of a larger pattern.>

"Damn it, that's just a theory!"

<We must act with imperfect knowledge.>

"What sanctimonious, ridiculous—"

<Your anger is understandable. I understand what it masks. I love you, too.>

"What? I, I, uh . . . " He was stymied.

<Go. You must stay out of their grasp until we all know more.>

"But where'll I meet you? This place, it's so big, what'll I *do*?"

<You must make your own way now. Go.>

"Damn it! I won't."

<You will.>

6

Mind Surgery

He holed up in a shaded hollow and the pain started in on him. It had spread into his ribs and he was not surprised to find that three of them were broken too. The electrical energy of the spark had dissipated into tiny shock waves that snapped bone and broke capillaries.

That's what his diagnostics told him. The facts popped up in his left eye when he keyed in for them. Signifier icons showed bright and clear. Yellow fractures, scarlet blood patches in his arm, 3D blue spaghetti for pain networks.

Solutions popped up too. Making field repairs was not easy. He called up two seldom-used Faces who did the hard work at the back of his skull. They wormed down out of his cerebral cortex and into the basic, shadowy machinery. Most of the brain was circuitry for housekeeping operations. You couldn't consciously intervene in how your food got digested or control your heartbeat. They ran just fine on their own. And it would be a bad idea to make intervention easy and risk screwing yourself up out of clumsiness. But repairing damage could be accelerated and this was a time when he needed that.

These Faces squirmed down into operating centers that fed stimuli and ferried nutrients. They took over. He knew they were working when his arm started to tingle. It was like being tickled deep inside only it didn't make you laugh. So he cried for a while and felt better. He wriggled around and broke out in a clammy sweat all along his left side.

More explosions boomed down from the sky but he was a far way beyond that and didn't care. His systems labored heavily. Bone repair was hard, he knew, and he tried to not let his conscious mind interfere.

But there were a lot of things to think through and he could not keep his mind on them for long. Spikes of pain broke through and startled him. Then his systems would catch the problem and he would be all right for a while. The sweats did not go away though.

The dreams started then.

Only they were not dreams because in between them he had his eyes open. They played on his retina and there was nothing he could do to stop them. He tried closing his eyes but they still ran.

He was riding in something that had wheels but seemed to fly. A woman had offered him a ride in it and somehow they had passed through dissolving air and furious, fast rock, and now were careening down (or maybe up) a steep flat lake. It was smooth and seemed horizontal, with his weight thrusting straight down along his spine. But it was also angled so that they accelerated across it. The jet-dark surface spewed and foamed and muttered to itself like a stormy liquid but the woman rapped it with a stick every few minutes, as if trying it for strength, and the stuff gave back a solid ringing smack, like steel ringing *bong bong* on granite.

Shibo grinned at him. Her bright sharp teeth laughed out words so mangled he could not catch them and there was no time to smooth them into meaning. They plunged forward.

It went on a long time. She had teeth missing, two ears on her left side and none on the right, and wore only a halter. This had seemed important when he first saw her but such facts were now dwarfed by the blistering wind that raked him, the jolting speed, the lurches of his already aggrieved stomach. "Long live all!" she shouted back to him and took a pull from a vaporizer.

"Long live me, anyway," Toby answered. He had taken a few hits from the vaporizer and was feeling strange but still scared.

Something big hit the black lake and threw up a dark geyser in snarled fingers.

"We'll make it!" Shibo shouted.

She had to because other people were trying to talk to him. Their voices came down from the sky, but by the time they reached him they were whispers.

Instead of breaking into droplets the black waters squared out into planes. "Let me do it," Shibo called. She smashed the panes into showers of glinting mica shards. "See?"

—and he was in the open, rolling down a hill. He cracked his knee on a rock and inhaled dust. Choked. Gasped. This was real, no dream. He looked back up the slope and saw the tall grass mashed down where he had been lying in a bath of his own sweat. Something had made him get up and stumble and fall out here, exposed. He scrambled back up as fast as he could.

On the way up his knee hurt more than his arm or ribs. That was a good sign as long as the knee wasn't damaged. He found the place where he had been lying. It was damp and smelled bad.

His knee was getting better, though. He walked a little unsteadily to a stream and cleaned himself off for the first time in—two? three?—days.

Hard to tell. His inboard monitor told him, 2.46 days in all. Impossible to tell here with the light coming and going like fitful weather. He wondered how all the forest had adjusted to this erratic pace.

For a while he just lay beside the stream without any energy for more. A solid fact sat in front of him and would not let him rest. He knew what had to be done now and that Quath had been right. Shibo had kept him from seeing it. The way she had kept him from registering other things. Amusing him with interior spectacles that got more and more frantic.

The damage and repair had undermined some part of her somehow. At least for now. Which meant he had to do it now or later he would think of something else that needed doing or maybe get distracted by a gimpy joint or a funny itch and then he would never do it. Maybe not for the rest of his life.

He crawled back in a shaded hole and got out his field kit. The tools were not made for this job. They had socket and groove faces, tiny insert arms and variable-geometry drivers, but nothing specialized. And he had to work behind himself. Operating by feel, sitting up when he wanted to lie down.

You do not want to do this.

He did not answer her. The small adjustable tips were hard to get right. His fingers were blunt and clumsy. He dropped one tip and had to fish it out of the dirt and clean it off. No way to even keep all the instruments lined up properly.

I have done so much for you. You and I work together. Your female side integrates with mine.

The tip ends would not come right. He lined them up and inserted them into the butt of the axis tool. The fit was not perfect but it would do.

I have so much more to teach you. If you will only give me time. I can give excellent advice on how to deal with this place. You are alone. You **need** ***me.***

Reaching behind his head was hard. He braced himself with his nearly useless left arm. The spreading ache in it told him that this was not a great idea. His Faces working the repairs sent little warning spikes up into his cerebral cortex. Lances of aggrieved pain/anger, like the emotions of insects. But there was nothing else to do.

We can have so much fun together! I've shown you my past. My whole world. Isn't that enough?

"Don't want your world."

He gritted that out through clenched teeth. She was talking faster and faster as he got the sleeve fitted into his spinal slot. Images shot through him now. Ruins in purple shadows. Mech carcasses sprawling across a field on Snowglade. Tastes of spicy hot dishes, smells of fresh spring, laughter heard pealing down a stony hallway.

He cut the skin away from the slot to get more room. He had to operate by feel alone now. The pictures running in his eyes were clipped, speeded up, flickering with demented haste.

You are betraying your father. He put me here. It was to guide you. To help you! And you turn against me, throw me—

He popped the slot open. Poked into the micros. The racing images got ragged, spotty.

A Personality can't live chip-encased for long. You know that. I will shrink. Parts of me will evaporate! I will shrink back down into an Aspect unless I am aired, used.

The tools were not right and he could not be sure he would not damage the chip. This slot had been double-decked to take a Personality. The readers were jammed to a one-molecule-thick layer around the chip. There was a way to take the readers out without stripping them but that was impossible without a lot more gear than he had, even if he could see what he was doing.

You can't! I've done so much for you. The whole female side of your personality—I've brought it out. Made you much more mature.

"Yeasay. I'm so mature I'm stuck here alone and banged up and no Family to help me pry you out."

I didn't make you do all those things. You can't escape the guilt of running away from your father. It wasn't my doing!

He felt carefully. It seemed like he had got the tips in right but it was hard to tell. They had to fit just so in the crowded receivers at the socket rim.

Please! I won't do any remembering or thinking without you approving it. I just, you don't know what it's like, I had to—

He tried one. Tugged gently on the end and the tip caught against the socket and held. He did not know what would happen if he got only part of the chip out. She was firm-integrated with him through the hard circuitry at the base of his skull. Could he get the chip free and not leave part of her with him? He did not know.

I'll do anything you want!

No point in waiting. He took all the tips in a tight grip and breathed deeply.

Wait! Please!

For a long, hard moment he could not move. She had his muscles locked and he felt her sleeting anger slam into him full force.

She had been a wonderful woman once and living on like this had made her into something else. Carrying a Personality was far harder than an Aspect, but something else had happened between them. Something about her and him, the imponderable mix of people. Not the fault of either, maybe, just a fact.

He did not know if the true Shibo could ever come back again in a Personality but that was not the point now, and in a flash of close contact between them he told her that, not in words but in pangs of sharp remorse.

Two heartbeats. Then her reply.

Her fury battered against him. His right hand shook. Fingers went numb. Hard to hold the tips in them. His breath caught.

She moved fast, trying everything. His sphincter clenched, balls ached. Jumpy nervous energy wormed across his skin. His chest froze up. Hand jangling, thumb askew, muscles rock-hard.

He made himself relax his right hand and let the wrist go free. In the backlash of the muscles he reversed the tension against her and moved.

He jerked the tools out at all four quadrants. They came free.

No you can't I love you love Killeen love all of you don't make me stop please please I can't can't can't can't can't can't

His hand brought the tips around all bright-bloody and with skin caught in them. Like a single muscle his body shivered. A violent jerking, throwing off a sheen of droplets. Lungs heaved as if he had been under water a long time.

The moist forest around him lay at the end of a long shadowy tunnel and purple flies buzzed in halos around the tunnel walls.

Closing, far away. Sliding dark.

He pitched forward into the tunnel.

Frames

In one frame of reference, the Wedge whirls at a blistering angular velocity, skimming razor-close to the speed of light.

In another mathematical frame, it stands stationary in a geometric manifold. Still, silent. Lines of folded space-time eddy about it.

In this view, despite excruciating gradients and wrenching torques, the Wedge is an island of tranquil stability. Gravitational radiation from the black hole coalesces about its slippery contours.

Waves lap. Languid, easy. Torsional stresses play like intricate spider webs along slick, pulsing bulges.

This pressure sustains the Wedge against all lashing dissipations. It has done so for an interval whose length—or duration—depends upon the local geometry of the observer.

In still another frame of reference, the Wedge is locked in unending, furious struggle with the black hole.

Forces wrestle. The Eater seeks to eat. The Wedge jams itself between the Eater's jaws. Pries them open. Plugs the gullet. Saves itself.

All are true.

Each is a frame. Truth is the sum of all frames.

Down the magnetic field lines that thread the Wedge, rubbery yet unbreakable, trickle wave packets of rippling complexity. They carry information in the only fashion that can slip through the knotted weave of the Wedge.

Along these slender strands—wiry, coiled lifelines—the mechanical civilization converses with its delegate. The machine intelligences gather in packets, elaborate sliding decompositions of data. They linger above the fray of the great accretion disk, in the eternal sleet of hard radiation. Against this torrent the gliding minds use defenses of ceramic and metal.

By rippling the magnetic field lines they converse with their delegate. Hollow voices down a vast well.

At the bottom, the lone creature hears. Replies. Always amid discord, the delegate must both debate and act. Dividing its intelligence yet again, it assigns separate portions to these tasks.

It does not enjoy the pleasures of its rulers, who float in majestic remove. It must endure the rasp and grit of the lands within the Wedge. Seeking, always seeking.

All parties to the discussion think at the speed of light. Their voices cannot escape their origins, however, or the assumptions of their kind.

I/You have explored a huge array of vaults and spaces, ¦>A<¦. Yet you find nothing!

I have discovered a wealth of primate culture!

That was not your task, ¦>A<¦.

How well I know. Our own ancient data imply that there are special, message-bearing primates. I have sought them. But they are difficult to separate from the hordes of primates here.

There are so many? Hiding from us?

They fear us—quite rightly, I suppose.

Search out these certain message-bearers! Be done with such irritants.

The spaces here are innumerable.

Continue. Secure the minimum of three genetic layers which we/you require.

We have the basic biological information from the oldest generation, the "grandfather." But the nature of the coded message demands three generations. Direct biological descent.

The Legacies implied that we/you needed full analysis of them. This means complete and viable copies.

I/We think not. They could just as well be dead.

I have been carefully reading each surekill I make. My subunits are equally careful. I shall not miss the characteristic signature of the particular primate we need, the youngest. I knew him.

On their planet?

He was useful in securing his father-self when I wished to make a capture.

I hope you/we can do as well now/here.

You/We are fading from our/your field of view. Is the Wedge damaging?

I have navigated the shifts here, but there is a troubling background sense. Something more lurks in these warped passages.

What is it? I/You have heard reports from earlier units we/all sent into the Wedge. Before they vanished from us/you.

I do not know how to describe it. A faint trembling presence beyond my fields. But it is not localized.

An echo.

I think not. It comes from everywhere but does not repeat what I send. I am uneasy.

Stifle your/our reactions. You/We act for us/all, remember.

This is not the time for hesitation.

Kill them all if you/we can. I/We would be done with this vexation.

I have surekilled so many. My factors overload. So much wealth to know and savor!

Forget your/our strange sense of beauty! Never before has such a strong agency as you/we penetrated the Wedge so deeply. Know them, yes. Then end these parasites in their last lair.

Savage them!

I obey.

Part V

MALIGN ATTENTIONS

1

The Pain of Eternity

Toby woke feeling tired but clean. He had been out for a long time. His arm throbbed less now. Blunt pain, as if it were seeping away from him.

Shibo wasn't there.

He had her chip in his carrypouch. Now he probed for her self. Skated over inky crevices where his Aspects lived their compacted semi-lives. Tramped through the galley of Faces.

Gray passageways yawned. Isaac and Zeno and the others called to him and wanted to talk about Shibo. They always wanted to talk. About anything. But of Shibo there was nothing.

He knew shreds might still cling somewhere in him. A Personality was by nature diffused, hard to grasp. So he would have to watch carefully. The earlier signs—mood shifts, deflections of his attention, outright seizure of his sensorium—had been increasingly overt. If traces of her remained, they would be subtle.

He got up, creaking. Sore. With a bone-deep weariness that sleep could not take away.

No skittering warnings in the sensorium. It expanded like a blue bubble in his vision and brushed against only the rustlings of the forest and dark-bellied clouds. Time to get back to business.

Years of Family discipline had taught him to follow orders when he did not like them. Something in the way Quath told him to leave had the force of an order.

He carried it out without thinking. Thought, after all, was a luxury when living depended on speed and concealment and silent savvy.

He moved with his sensorium compressed to a half-sphere barely bigger than his arms' reach. That allowed practically no time to defend against one of the spark things that had hit Quath. But it would make him harder to find, he hoped.

When he reached the next high point he peered backward. Shadowy forms, gliding like leaves blown on systematic breezes. *Quath. Quath.* He yearned to send the call.

More burnt-yellow sparks jumped and bounced among the forest. Others cruised far up toward the other enclosing curvature of the Lane. Where he had left Quath something fired vicious hot-white bolts.

Toby knew it would be foolish to try to raise Quath's signal but the desire to do it was almost uncontrollable. At last he turned away and devoted himself to speed.

He ran for some time before he noticed that he was crying. Never, on the long pursuits the Family had endured on Snowglade, had he ever felt alone. Now the sour desperation of his predicament descended on him and he could not stop the anguish bubbling up in him. No Quath, no Family, just bare empty flight.

What would Killeen think? He made himself stop, willing the hardness into himself until the tears quit. He had to uphold the Bishop way. Even here, even alone. Maybe especially here.

He came to a bare stony territory. Would he be too exposed here? Dirty-gray clouds hugged the ground and then lifted suddenly, as if some giant had snatched them away. But there were none of the airborne forms that hovered half-seen like something glimpsed out of the corner of your eye. So he went on.

Something came over a distant peak and vectored in on him. He shot at it and missed and it burned his right side in an instant. His second shot got off as he went down. It caught the thing. A quick, buzzing fireball. Something tiny, tumbling. It crashed down, a sound like the air ripping apart.

He had shat his pants. That made him disgusted with himself but his right arm was more important.

The pain made his hands tremble. He got his right side up and running again with some repair work. His arm was sore but would move again.

He found running water nearby and got cleaned up. Humbling work. In an abstract way he was surprised he had been so scared. All fear, he realized, later seems somewhat ludicrous.

By the time he could limp over to where the thing had gone down there was just a hole in the ground. He had been damn lucky to wing the thing and knew it.

He licked his lips, feeling the fear again. If he kept going this way one of the seekers would track him for sure, bring down a whole flock the next time.

He remembered Quath's little lesson about the sums and how in this geometry, Lanes were like those pairs of numbers. Each pair summed to a hundred, and rearranging them endlessly kept the grand total constant. The esty stayed intact.

And the total did not have to be a hundred or a thousand or a million. The Lanes could number a million. Or a billion. Or some other word offered by his chattering Isaac Aspect, big words ending in *-ion* that just said that it was bigger than any person could ever know.

So he was not surprised when time wore on and he kept moving and saw no one. He might never meet a human again. The Lanes could snake on for an uncountable, twisty forever.

The trick was to find a way out of this particular place. A way the mechs could not track easily. How? Just running harder wasn't enough.

Puzzles thickened in his head. Quath had said that gravity was esty, curved. Mass did that. Planets held you to them by curving space-time, which humans felt as a clear, strong force. Yeasay, fine.

But Isaac said that esty curvature generated further curvature. So gravity could make more of itself, conjuring up more from less. Something had knitted this esty so that it held firm. It even prospered here on the lip of the abyss, kissing the Eater of Everything.

"Anything you understand, you can use," Toby muttered to himself as he trotted. He remembered this was a saying of his grandfather Abraham, and wondered where in this place old Abraham might be.

"Abraham, he would've *done* something with this stuff," he said, voice frail against the whispery musics of the landscape.

No place to run, not literally anyway. And he was getting tired.

So he tried to shape the timestone. Logic said it was impossible but logic wasn't doing too well here lately, was it?

His weaponry had no effect, but after laser-cutting the stuff glowed. He tried microwaves, sonics, even a nano-reamer he still carried from Snowglade days. Nothing worked.

Next he used the whole spectrum. No response. He hit it with pulsed infrared. For the barest instant a thin grin split the stone.

Again. This time it lasted longer and he jammed his boot in and shoved. It gave, then started crushing his boot. He yanked free and the stuff slammed shut.

Next time he was more careful. First, he found a place where he felt nauseous. Dimpling perspectives, watery light, refractions of sound and space. Where the Lanes intersected, gravity twisted.

Second, he cut and heated it. He jabbed, pried, ran through variations of weaponry. Sweaty work. He cut his hand, scorched an arm. Nothing came right the first time. But it seemed that he was slicing deeper into the timestone. The fatigue got to him and he had to stop and rest. Sweat trickled into his eyes and then he knew it wasn't sweat.

Tears again. He was impatient with himself this time. *Killeen would snort and look the other way. Besen would be sympathetic, and that would be even worse.*

"If they get you, know what they'll do?" Saying it out loud helped. "They'll suck out all you know. Use it against Besen and Killeen and ever'body."

His voice was stern and that helped, too. He realized how much he missed that simple thing, the sound of humanity, a voice not his own. *So damn screwed up you're talking to yourself,* another part of him said, but he pushed that thought away. Anything that made him feel better helped, and the hell with analyzing.

Back to work.

Progress was slow. He found a rippling ridgeline with esty-fog rolling over it in strands of orange light. He tried the cutting again. A broad line cracked the stone. Through it he caught a whiff of something vile and poisonous, pale green vapors—and kicked at the stone to close it, fast. Hard as the esty was to open, acoustic tremors could zip it shut again. The stuff had a kind of surface tension.

After that he learned to sense the dimples and fluxes in the esty. He could slit one open for a quick look, but it slammed back tight.

Which was lucky, most of the time. Some passageways led to Lanes of vacuum. Others to stony, chilling landscapes. A few to howling, dusty tornadoes.

His systems warned him of openings that brimmed with searing radiation. He closed up fast, but one time something hot and fluid shot out and darted away before the seam shut. It cut a deep streak across the sky.

Once he saw a whole city through a momentary slit. Its streets turned and looped around each other. So did the oblong buildings, and traffic of slender tubes teemed in and out of the porous walls. The things inside the tubes looked like boiling white stones. They seemed to take some interest in him and he felt a wave of sudden, solid fear. He let the portal crash shut.

After a few dozen times he had learned the feel of it, a kind of craft. For days he simply fooled and tinkered and forgot about what was probably following him. If he was to ever find the Family or Abraham, he had to master the skills here.

The spots where the esty seemed pliable kept moving, restless loci. He was half-nauseous as he worked the stone but that was the price. Finding the moment to strike, the angle, the spectrum—it became more like hunting than craftwork, intuitions unspoken.

Most Lanes seemed hostile to human life. Not all. He slipped through one that seemed pleasant, the first time he had tried to wriggle his way in.

It worked, barely. He lost some skin and suffered frostbite in his fingers. But he got through into a valley of fractured timestone. At least it was more interesting than where he had been.

What's more, experience taught him that the timestone lied. Many times he sat eating whatever he had gathered and blending it in with his rations, and marveled at the formal, clean-lined shapes of distant ranges. They were elegant, serene, pointed. Then later he met them close up and knew them for what they were—rough, unforgiving.

Torsions pulled at him in the broken slides he struggled across, along the jagged ledges he pulled himself over. Torques played along the narrow and shifting shelves he crawled along, afraid to look down or up because those directions were fickle and flickering.

Paths curled over into tunnels—with him inside. They stretched long and necked down.

He had to crawl for his life to get through squeezing-down knot-holes. Some were slow, others brutally fast. He dived through one that groaned, trying to slam shut upon him, and lost a boot heel in the process. The heel sheared off clean, removing any doubts about what it would have meant to be a little slower. He had to limp for a long while before it grew back.

And all the while he felt a deepening loneliness. He woke from a sound sleep, calling Quath with a dry throat. He dreamed, and was speaking eternally to Killeen in a hoarse voice that couldn't get through the fog around him. He hoped that they were still alive somewhere and at other times he knew with a final, leaden certainty that they were not.

Events passed. After a while he found that he knew how to read a shifting three-dimensional map, to follow a trail over slick rock, to memorize landmarks no matter what angle he saw them from, to build a fire in misty wind-whipped rain, to treat bites from small wriggly animals, to rappel down a trembling cliff, to glide down a glacier of frozen air, to splint his own broken bone and lie doggo long enough for the two days it took to heal, to find water under gritty sand, to coax and load a burro-beast he found wandering by itself, to bury a body torn into long strings—evidence of mechs, he guessed.

He patched up a rubber flyer he found on a saddleback ridge and used it to fly a great long distance on a rough wind. After he crashed, the front caught up with him. A sudden, biting blizzard.

No shelter. He started digging back into timestone itself, a chip at a time. As he dug in the sharp cold, events peeled off when he struck them with his field shovel. Cries and odd coughs came from them, as they sheared and broke like crystalline planes.

He reached a layer that brimmed with the heat of some past summer. With some hollowing out he had a cave big enough to curl up in.

That lasted out the deep cold. He slept, grateful for warmth, but Killeen was talking to him through the milky fog. *Toby, Toby.* The next words were just beyond hearing. He strained to catch them and woke up. Warmth, loneliness. Then he felt that the timestone was warm because it was slowly mashing him, trying to close in. "Damn!" He rolled out and staggered away into pale light, the tag end of the blizzard.

Besen, the mechs will get her too if they can suck out of me what they want . . . and it'll be because of me and my damn fool running . . . and if the mechs win here, it's forever, no Bishops ever again, gone to dust and never knowing what all this is, what it means . . .

He found himself muttering as he moved, but there was not much to the thoughts except the aloneness he now had as a kind of companion.

A smash-storm came and taught him to dodge falling rock. When it was over the landscape had contorted again and he learned how to climb out of a slick box canyon, how to slide down a steepening peak before it broke off and sailed on its own across what looked like empty air.

After more time passed than he could recall, he even got so he could predict the wrenching weather—sort of.

All that had changed him by the time he met the first people.

2

Rational Laughter

He found them deep in a savannah, living by cultivating some gnarled yellow grain crops he did not recognize.

They took care of him. He was in worse shape than he thought and yet somehow not being able to understand them helped.

They spoke no language he knew or had chips for. They were small and what they lacked in power and bulk they made up in a compact grace. They were balanced, self-contained. The women were demurely radiant, lithe and with warm, veiled eyes that sparkled as they talked.

Both sexes seemed compressed, with broad shoulders capping the V-shaped rise from their narrow waists. They had a perfect, erect carriage, a swagger-free lightness. Their skins were smooth, glowing golden-brown beneath elaborate confections of blue-black hair.

The Families had taken inordinate care with their hair and for the long years on the run had made that their only fashion indulgence. Here, in contorted gravities that turned like weather, hair could perform miracles—cant into impossible shelves, swirl upward like a frozen black fire, veer and swoop and verge on the comic.

They had the usual two sexes and four genders, with both varieties of homosexuals wearing customary hair, symphonies of oblique provocation. He liked it all. Signs were always more fun than talk and the small vocabulary he mastered cast him agreeably back onto his intuition. He learned to read the unspoken, which was more interesting anyway.

As he rested up—not for long, though, as everyone worked or else didn't eat—he began to get an idea of how different these people were.

To them, every detail should be dwelt upon, every moment occupied. The task at hand, that was everything. When you worked there was no other world, only the compressed moment of the job. All thought of other jobs, of vexing moments past or future, were banished. Except for some distracting aches in his right arm and ribs, picked up in his long flight, he managed pretty well.

Their community life centered on an elaborate, staged drama. Talk of mechs and the esty bored them. They wanted only to discuss the current play. Toby went to one and found that this was regarded as a great honor to them. The audience stood and applauded him by clapping their lips together as he sat down. Or at least he thought that was what they meant; later, he wondered if he had committed some blunder.

The drama began immediately after he sat so he did not have time to think on the matter. The play depended utterly on concentration. Without the tight control and immersion of the actors, Toby could see how it could be excruciatingly dull.

In practice it wasn't. He sat riveted as an actor entered the stage and walked with an inhuman slowness around the rim of it, inches from the audience but immeasurably distant in her enveloped presence. She controlled her rhythm and step so utterly that no extraneous finger gesture or eye twitch disturbed movement that was like the surface of a black lake, unrippled, but telling much. To Toby the actor seemed to pass through the air of the theater, clothed in a silence that could cut through a tornado. Then, later, the same scene occurred again. This time microphones amplified each sweep of silky feet across bare boards. A whispery music followed each move, transforming the event utterly, until he could scarcely recognize it.

He found that the drama, which had so little action he could sum it in a sentence, had a strangely soothing effect on him. It seemed to say, *Pay attention*—that being focused on the moment was more important than playing head games about the past or future.

Odd, once he thought about it. Because this was a place where past and future weren't so easy to separate. They flowed together at places, a muddy riverrun.

They had already fought mechs here. It took him a while to find out even this simple fact because they spoke so little. Once he came upon a burial ceremony—held not in a ritual place but in the street—which seemed to be for someone taken by mechs. Their homes and workshops were like the intersecting hulls of *Argo* inverted, so that from a distance they looked like blisters growing together. Burns scarred them and two had big holes punched through.

These people were well organized. They held defense drills and used weapons he could not figure out. They said the latest mech incursion to the esty had been going on as long as it took to raise a girl to half-height—which seemed to be their way of measuring time—and had been worse earlier. Some had missing legs and arms to prove it.

He told them as much as he could of Family Bishop and the long way that had led him here. Still, he was not really one of them because he had done different things for his scarred and burnished armor. Mostly he had just stayed alive. Here they had engaged the mechs and killed them, lured and suckered and defeated them, though taking casualties all down the line of course. Getting banged up like Toby was mostly an accident and they all knew that, quite different from being in a battle because you wanted to be there.

And they did. A small woman told him with great fervor how they were fighting for some big idea. He could not quite get clear what the idea was and after a while gave up pushing on his vocabulary. The woman talked fast and seemed to treat any question as disagreement.

Toby thought about that after watching their slow, grave drama. One performer had carried a drum with a mech brain inside, so that when she hit the drum bottom the brain would bounce around. It struck the top and bottom drumheads while the performer went on clapping the heads. The counterpoint made an eerie echo with the brain-rattle. What that meant he could not tell but it chilled him.

One dark time after he had finished his job he walked back to where he would sleep. A chilling wind rippled the few lights glimmering in the soft mist. He knew somehow that he would never have gone into a battle for some kind of general principle. He had fought and run for the Family—run mostly, and fought only when he had to.

These quiet men and women were different. They had a separate age-old tradition of being holed up here in an esty that they didn't understand. Or at least they could not explain it to him. Maybe they knew it in a way he could not. Living through things gave you that sometimes.

He remembered the long empty docks where they had berthed the *Argo*. Big and covered with scratches, chipped and marred. Deserted except for *Argo*, like arms stretching out to embrace and welcome ships that came no more.

These people had said that few ships came any longer from the worlds beyond, the planets like Snowglade. Many smaller craft slipped between the portals of the esty itself, shortcutting between Lanes. Few planetary Families came into the Lanes any more because they were nearly all dead. Failed.

Their history didn't square with his own understanding. That fit, too. The Lanes ran on different clocks. Some lay deeper in the steep curvature around the black hole so time ran slower there. And the esty itself mixed and tangled events, so that human memory churned with it.

He gave up on figuring when he found that he had walked too far in the gloom. That was the first time he realized how much he missed his father. He cried for a while in the dark and was glad no one could see him.

Something in him said it was stupid to feel embarrassed about crying. He had never thought that before. Wondering about it that way made him suspect a trace of Shibo. But he could catch no sliver of her anywhere.

He felt uneasy. With a restless spirit he went back and found the sleep shed for casual laborers. Everybody else was already down and out so he crawled onto his pallet.

He slept well and woke up only when the shed collapsed. A slap in the forehead, grit in his mouth. The ground heaved under him. Somebody screamed in the dark.

The roof beams had missed him but debris weighed him down. He crawled out from under it while big explosions shook the ground. When he got out there were mechs in the hovering gloom. Buildings down. Fires licking at a mottled sky.

People running everywhere. Howling ferocities fighting high up above dirty clouds.

The defense screens popped up—he saw them in his sensorium as bright red planes ramped up into the air, with electrical green snaking along their edges.

Casualties. People with no visible scars but the skin beneath their eyes black from concussion. Some were bleeding from nose and mouth. Others clutched their bellies and could not speak. Others pitched face forward into the mashed grass.

He helped with them. The medical people did not seem to want him around. They glared at him and he saw that they suspected. Nobody could know for sure but he had come here and then the mechs had come.

He wasn't sure if he would hurt more than he helped, so he left the wounded and ran to the outer edge of the blister-buildings. He watched there the swift and mysterious play of glare and thump in the surrounding somberness. He wanted to fight but he did not know what to do. No Family Bishop methods seemed to matter here. And if the forces above were after him there was nothing he could do about that either.

Finally he fled. If he had brought this here, then the best he could do was to draw it away. For hours he trotted through the obliterating murk. Alone again. *Quath. Killeen. Besen.* Names.

In his sensorium nothing seemed to follow him. Finally light began to seep from a rumpled ridge up ahead and he saw that he was in a different terrain. There were people clinging to the bare timestone and something was trying to find them.

Without warning he found himself in the middle of a fight. He kept belly-down and learned quick enough that something—he never learned what, exactly—was trying to kill a band of people near him. He caught on also to the skill of keeping down low on the shifting timestone.

A green fog flowed overhead. From a distance it poured down over him and over his own image that he saw in the timestone below.

The image looked up at him. Slow, diluted seconds passed. The figure waved at him. Toby blinked. It grinned. He could not figure out how the timestone could have a Toby trapped in it, a *him* who cheerfully saluted—but there was no time for figuring anyway, not now.

Or to see what was doing the killing. He started to lift his head far enough to see, then thought better of it. His sensorium showed nothing dangerous. Still, he heard the small swishing motes, slivers on the wind that would have lifted pieces of his head away with a surgical precision if he had looked.

He knew this because within seconds he saw it happen. A woman caught in the chin one of the whispering things that streamed over the ground. The tiny things waited for a target, gliding over open ground, then found their prey.

He watched too the attempts by friends to put the head back together again. These people spoke a quick, staccato language that he did not understand. He tried to help even though he could see no point in it, and they paid him no attention. They had faith that human medicine would work on a head carved up into precise slices. It didn't.

After a while the whispering streams stopped. He wanted to help the people but when he went to find them they were all thoroughly dead.

He had little doubt now that somewhere behind this chaos was something looking for him. Had all these people died because of him? He didn't want to think about it.

And all he could do was flee, not fight. It grated on his Bishop way of thinking.

He met refugees. Some he could understand. They told of worse places and times but most of them kept plodding past him as if he were an illusion. Or maybe they thought his questions were nonsensical.

He marched a long while. It was easier if he didn't think much.

The world seemed lighter, as if his head was like a balloon held down by his body. He walked that way enjoying every step. Bright yellow beams burst from exposed timestone far overhead. The light worked with furnace energy.

People passing by smiled. The mood grew until everybody was cheerful and even to Toby the scene seemed so fine that it was on the plain face of it ridiculous that anybody should ever die. At least not him.

With a pang he remembered Quath going on once, long ago, about the irrational optimism of primates, or at least the present version of them. She had said it was a peculiar adaptation, one her species lacked. Toby had just laughed.

He chuckled again, now. Crazy, mindless. It made him feel better. Remembering Quath's puzzlement, he laughed again. Even the pang of loneliness did not cut into his sudden, absolutely unearned joy. Irrational it might be but it was fun and fun was, in a place and time like this, supremely rational and practical.

3

Casualties

"Man over there, he wants to talk to you."

Toby was surprised. "Me? How come?"

"He knows you."

"Can't be."

"He does, says so. Look, he's bad hurt."

Toby frowned but went. He moved among the wounded on the dry plain and gave away what was left of his water.

The man's face was lined and pale and moaning in an automatic way, regular and with the same drawn-out, low, wet grunting at the end. They had his head covered with a shiny sheet that had some medical purpose. The man reached up and tugged the sheet away. Toby saw what had been a face and now looked like a small hill that had been driven over in the rain with heavy equipment and then let bake out in the sun too long.

"They peeled my old face off and gave me this new one," a clear, soft voice said. The lips did not move.

"I see, yeasay." Toby felt useless.

"I'm growing a fresh one now."

"I can tell," Toby said. Not looking at the face.

"Want to know how it happened?"

"Sure."

"We were trying to get one of those snake things that shoot down the axis of the Lane. You seen them?"

Toby had seen a lot of things but he didn't think of them in terms of animals any more. That just led you to make mistakes, like with the woman he had failed to save. "I think so."

"Awful, killed plenty of us. So we waited for one and hit it from five different positions. Smacked it pretty square."

The man's eyes unfocused and Toby encouraged him with "Yeasay?"

"Uh, sure. Thing jerked around and went to pieces before it crashed on the ridgeline. Near me. Went off something powerful. So pretty. All I knew was a hot whack in the side and then I was here."

Toby reached out and held the man's hand and wondered if he should believe much of it. The hand was as soft as the voice, not a hand that had ever been in the field much. The voice was dreamy too. The story did not sound like a real battle. He had learned that the wounded were not good reporters and sometimes mingled their dreams in.

Toby murmured something and slid the sheet back so the face was covered. He was pretty sure the man could not see and was just using his inner sensorium. The man said nothing and Toby left the sheet. Then the man said suddenly, "I heard you were here."

"Me? How'd anybody know me?"

"We saw you, got a pulse on the gen sensorium."

"What'd it say?"

"To watch for you. Take care of you."

"Who sent it?"

"General directive."

"You guys can send signals from Lane to Lane?"

"Sometimes. Our tech here isn't the best. But we heard about you."

"My father have anything to do with it?"

"Mightsay. I don't remember."

Toby wondered if this was true either. He had heard men lie about how they were wounded, sometimes right after they were hit and even in front of people who had been there. He did not know why but he had done it himself once years ago so it did not seem so bad.

His left calf had gone out then from a mech bolt and it took a week to get running again. By the time he could walk he had woven a story that was completely different from the reality. Not flattering, just different. He did not know why he had done it and after a while had stopped asking himself the question. All that made it hard to talk to this man whose face was not going to work out.

The man said, "Way I figure, you must be important."

"Huh? Me?" Toby had been thinking and had nearly lost track of where he was. He was remembering the Family. Killeen.

"Must be. Most directives are weapons stuff, tactics and all."

"I'm not important."

"Well you're sure goddamn big. Where from?"

"Family Bishop."

He said it half-defiantly, because he never knew how people were going to react. Sometimes they got puzzled. Others would make a sour comment about dirt-huggers, or else just look blank. This man did neither, since he was busy vomiting suddenly into his own hand. Toby helped him clean it up.

"You sure be important." The man looked a lot worse now, his face yellowing like an old wound, but he clung to his idea. "Gotta be."

He spoke with a flat accent but his phrasing was like one of the old

Bishops Toby had known. Maybe the people around here were Hunker Down Families. Toby patted the man, not knowing what to do. "You sleep."

"You gotta be. Directive said to look out for you."

"Then what?"

"Report back. And hang on to you."

"For who?"

"Dunno. You stay right here, now."

"Get some sleep."

"Why you so important? You got something to do with all this?"

The question floated in the dusty air. Though Toby had heard it in his sensorium, the words in a thin whisper went unanswered because Toby was already at the edge of the plain and moving fast.

4

Salvage

He came down into a long barrel-like valley. It was green and moist, hollowed out between glowing massifs of timestone.

It was hard for him to remember now just when he had started running from the mechs. He had shat his pants a few more times and no longer felt ashamed of it. *Killeen. Quath.* The names evoked the same emotions now but he had not cried for them in a long while.

This new Lane was pleasant and he sensed no mechs. He had gotten used to the mild, diffuse light that oozed from juts and plains alike, sometimes casting upward shadows. The stone sent ribbons of light projecting up through the root systems of trees. He could see them like buried blood vessels in the fleshy soil. He loped steadily and came down into the valley. Yellow knots of timefog clung to the peaks on both sides.

Nothing in the sky to alert him. Still, the mechs could come on you faster than his rickety sensorium could register. So he kept to the shadows when he could.

He had once spent a day staying barely ahead of some mech sniffer, a silver-gray flyer that skated just over the trees and shot at him three times. He had eluded it by jumping into a river and swimming until his reserve air played out. Mechs didn't seem to understand water very well. Or at least couldn't see through it. He had stayed under until a waning came, and crawled out gasping into total blackness.

Besen. Killeen. Ol' Cermo-the-Slow. So long ago.

A burnt scent and beneath it something sickly sweet. Down the whole valley grew dense fields of maize. He had not seen any since a boy, and then only a scraggly lot at the edge of the Citadel when he was barely big enough to walk. He walked along a rutted harvesting trail and smelled the soft, milky air.

Maize. He remembered there had been maize planted in the mud of spring; dug into the earth on a plowed hillside, with narrow-eyed women keeping seed-eating birds just out of gunning range; fine stands of young maize sending a keen aroma into the rainy day; the work of chopping weeds from the base of the stalks, the shiny-bladed hoe churning up fine dry dust; cutting and shocking maize with a thick long knife; the blue-green ears that could turn to follow the sun through the day; ripe ears thrown into a wheelbarrow; tiny insects tech'd up to defend the sweet maize against pests, each loyal to the death to its particular plant; bare stalks in a quiet snowfall; a sister who lost her finger in a shucker, quick as a wink; rattling kernels spewing from a hand-cranked, steel-toothed feeder, the bare cobs shooting out the top and tumbling onto a pyramid pile; a silo crammed with drying husks; whiskey sloshing in a wooden keg, the charcoal staining the spout where it had been strained out; sharp sweet smell of a pat of butter sliding down an ear, skating on its own melt—

—and Toby staggered, knowing that these memories were not his. But they felt absolutely real, especially the pungent fragrances.

I worked in the fields a lot when I was a girl.

Shibo's voice seemed to come down from the yellow sky. Toby gulped, eyes watering. He walked on and let the dry scent of the fields calm him.

So he had not got all of her out. And now there was nothing to do. Not even a knife blade could help him now.

The burnt stench was stronger and he looked warily into the fields as he passed. The standing grain was at its peak, aching to be harvested. He shucked a few ears and ate them as he went on, the kernels popping full and sugary in his mouth. Some of the maize had started to shell out of the heads, overripe.

The few trees were splintered and singed as if something inside them had wrecked them trying to get out. There were a few bare spots in the closely planted fields, exactly circular. The maize was pressed flat.

He walked on and something stung his nose. He remembered the time he had sat sick in an outhouse at the Citadel, smelling it and afraid to leave even to get a breath of clean air, because of his diarrhea, which gave no warning. The whole Family had gotten sick with it and a while later he had helped his father push the little house over on its side and fill in the hole with the dirt from the next pit. Then a team of men and women had dragged it over and set it up in fresh splendor.

He came to the first bodies then. Brambles divided the long fields and irrigation channels. Chunky parts were hung up in the branches. Bodies had exploded and the pieces were split along no anatomical lines Toby knew of. It could not have been very long since it happened because they had not begun to rot, though the blood had long caked into a brown crust on them.

His Isaac Aspect fidgeted at not having been allowed out for a while.

Ashes to ashes, dust to dust, as the ancient saying put it.

Toby knew that bodies did just the opposite. They decayed into wet slop, highly attractive to carrion beetles and clouds of flies. How could the ancients get so simple a thing wrong?

He touched a few bodies gingerly. Mechs had been known to booby-trap bodies back on Snowglade, but apparently they had not taken such trouble here.

It seemed wrong to leave the ripped sinews and muscle and bones snagged in brush but he turned away from the sight and moved on. The outhouse smell came from the simple fact that their bowels were spread over the fields, too, wider than the spray of heavier parts.

Further on whole bodies dotted the fields. They lay in small clearings where he guessed they had tried to fight something above. They were intact and their skins were smooth and glassy. He knew the way bodies changed with time. The skin quickly took on a lemon tinge which deepened into yellow-green. If left out for days the flesh went brown, a deeper brown than Cermo's beautiful smooth color.

—and left long enough, he suddenly recalled, the flesh thickened to be like coal tar, crusting hard where ripped or torn, and the bodies swelled, too, getting too big for their clothes and bursting out at the cuffs and popping zippers open, people becoming balloons, and the smell of them in the dry heat of midday, a heavy thing that lodged in your throat—

He caught himself. Those were not his memories.

I saw much when my Family died that it would be better if you did not know.

"Then don't let it out!" He probed for Shibo but she was elusive, darting away.

I cannot stop. Your memories intersect me and there I am.

"I don't need it."

I am who I am. Or was.

He walked on, keeping his eyes away from the bodies as much as he could. There were only one or two in each field.

The bodies showing no damage had probably died from loss of Self. They were suredead. Without the Self the brain went on running the simple routines that inflated lungs and pumped blood and digested food but very soon something went out of the whole thing. Then the body stopped.

Nobody had ever studied much why this was. There seemed no point in it. The person was gone in the most profound way possible. An old ship like *Argo* had techtricks to keep the body alive or at least frozen for future use, but there would be no point with the suredead.

He could see scuffed-up dirt and crushed yellowing maize where some of them in their last moments had pounded their boots against the ground, feet drumming and arms flailing though they were already down. As control slipped from them their bodies had fought in the only way they knew. Their fists were still clenched and their wrists were blue-black. Some had torn away their clothes in a mad frenzy to shuck off the thing that was inside them and eating where hands could not reach.

Toby thought about burying them but there were many and the stench was worsening beneath the yellow sky. He caught motion to his left and circled around a thick field of maize just going ripe. The movement registered as human in his sensorium. It would be smart to just keep going away from this place but he felt some need to see a living person so he angled back toward the spot.

One person. A lean woman kneeling beside a man's face-down body.

For a moment Toby thought she was praying and he turned to leave. She held her hand up to the light then. Her little finger reshaped itself into a snub-nosed tool and she jabbed it into the body's lower neck. The skin there was red and puckered up. She twisted her hand this way and that and pulled something from the spine. He recognized a slate-gray Aspect disk. The woman took no notice of Toby though he must have popped up on her sensorium at this range. She slipped the disk into a pouch.

Another body lay only a few steps away. She made two of her fingers into probing and unlocking tools and slipped them expertly into the spinal ports of the body. This time she got two disks and a square cartridge which Toby recalled could carry three Faces in Family Bishop. When the woman had them in her pouch, she stood up and looked directly at Toby.

"You got rights here?"

He stepped from behind the rustling maize. "No. You?"

"Sure. Salvage rights."

"They your Family?"

"Who's asking?"

"I'm Bishop."

"I'm Banshee."

Toby eyed her. "I never heard of any Banshees."

"I never heard of Bishops. It's a big esty."

"Any use taking those Aspects?"

"Might be."

"Suredead usually have Aspects sucked out of them."

"Depends on how fast it was done."

"Even if some're left, won't they be crazy?"

"Got to take that chance."

"I heard they get all fried out some way."

"They're still worth something."

"What you mean?" Toby edged a little to his right.

"Trim an Aspect down to a Face maybe."

"Might be better to let them go."

"That's Banshee business."

"How I know these are Banshee people?"

She looked at him square and hard. "You mind your own business."

He stepped back. "Yeasay."

"Yee-sah? Whuzzat?"

"Means I agree."

Her lips turned up in a faint derisive smirk. "Your 'yea' rhymes with 'see' and your 'say' is like 'ha'? Funny way to talk."

"Yeasay, ma'm."

He gave a half-salute and turned and walked away. Her sensorium played at his back and set off his micros all the way across the field and down into the stand of trees beyond.

He stopped then and let her lose interest. She kept moving among the bodies and doing her work. As he waited he thought about what to do. She scouted out away from him and then drifted back to the left as she searched.

He kept his sensorium on the lowest setting to track her and not give himself away. She was busy and had seemed nervous. He stayed behind a big warped brown tree. When she came back into view she was checking the last of the bodies and in a hurry.

He knocked her down with a stunner. She was quick and rolled as soon as she hit. He got off another bolt on lowest power and missed.

The other side of the big tree burst into flame. He saw her get to her feet and fire again but the shot went high. Through the air wrinkling from heat refraction he fired again.

She sat down solidly and rocked backward and struggled to bring her arms up. Her left hand was a weapon of some kind and it winked once. He felt the bolt go by and it was no stunner. His sensorium turned purple-red in warning. It could not defend him against a clean hit.

Without thinking but keeping his pull smooth he shot her twice more. They were medium-level stuns and this time she flopped over and did not get up.

He approached on the balls of his feet. She was sprawled out glassy-eyed. Carefully he bent down and took the pouch. It was heavy.

Her eyeballs followed him as he checked over her gear. One eyebrow twitched angrily.

"Banshee, yeasay?"

Her indices said she was something called Bahai. He fished an Aspect chip out of the pouch and pressed it against his wrist reader. The tiny hexagonal crystal there was cracked from some old accident but the optical pipe into his bone still worked. It told him that the Aspect was damaged and had been a woman in the Buddha Gathering, which he supposed was some kind of Family.

"You're a scalp hunter."

Her eyeballs clicked back and forth furiously. He thought about stimming her up so he could hear some more of her lies but she looked pretty quick even like this. And her gear was good. He did not even know what some of it did. She could be dangerous with just a finger or two free.

"I'll be taking these." He hefted the pouch. "Figured to sell them, yeasay?"

Her mouth was coming back a little and her lips twisted. It was interesting to watch. Then he thought about what she had been doing and the fun went out of it.

"I'll give them to the first Family Buddha I find."

He walked away fast. It was better that way, before he gave way to the temptation to make her pay a little more.

5

The Sea of Sand

A long dark time came and the temperature dropped steadily. He was out of food now and there was little to forage. He met few people. The land wrenched and rippled and he was often sick with the gravitational turbulence.

In a desert region he came upon a man and a little girl. In the cold somehow the girl had in a moment of play frozen her tongue and upper lip to a pipe that was part of a ruined building. They were camping there. The man did not want to rip the flesh away and yet the girl was getting frantic, shaking from the pain. She crouched next to the pipe and whimpered. Her big eyes looked up at Toby and he had an idea. There was no water nearby. No fire going for fear of mechs. He explained to the man, who was her father. In the end the only quick way to do it was for the father to urinate on the girl's lip to free it. This worked. The daughter said she could not even taste the urine either but Toby thought she was just being polite.

He went on along a sandy slope and could see a thickly wooded region beyond. He loped that way just as his sensorium wrinkled with the characteristic long hollow sound and the gray Wedge. The Mantis.

On the bare slumbering timestone he was fully exposed but he went through the usual measures. With a descending whisper his sensorium collapsed. He sprinted and wished for food.

The timestone trickled into pebbles and then rubble and finally long slopes of sand. It sucked at his boots as he wallowed through deep drifts. He went over one dune that came to a tip like a huge breast and then swept down. The slope came at him faster than he had judged and he nearly fell. Then it bottomed out and he trotted forward on a flat spot. But again sooner than seemed right the slope steepened. He struggled up it and the sand pulled at his legs as though trying to draw him under. The crest rushed at him.

For a moment he stood at the peak. Other dunes lay in long ridgelines.

The sand became glassy in the distance and shimmered with small tremblings, like images seen through a heat haze. But the air was cold and getting colder.

His graphite-lubricated servos complained with a thin whine as they worked against the chill. His sensorium gave him not even the muted callback of its lowest ebb. He got only a hollow, droning grayness.

He called for his Aspects and Faces. None answered.

The dunes were moving, he saw. Their long ridges marched slowly in from a curved horizon. He labored down the approaching slope and into the trough and up the next. The wave velocity helped his speed and in another few moments he stood atop the next crest but could see no farther. No sky above now, just empty speckled dark. A seething world of sand rippled by deep waves.

Though the massive undulations pressed into him through his boots the sand did not slide or crumble as it purred past. Tiny grains flowed around his boots and on, following the instructions of something below that rolled on without eddying behind him or otherwise taking note of his presence. Why he did not sink in such sand he could not tell. At the wave's peak some sand broke into a churning tan foam and then subsided. Land like liquid.

On the next wave coming toward him was a patch of white. Long strides took him down the near slope and into the trough. He started up toward the white patch, which looked larger than before—

And stopped. Turned and ran back toward the trough.

The white patch was a garden of bones.

Bleached fingers and feet at the edge. Snapped forearms farther up, leading to ranks of smashed pelvises. Thighs arranged in spreading fans around barrel rib cages. A short tower of arms and atop it a circle of bleached human skulls. Grins that would last forever. Staring eye sockets.

Over the crest of the wave came a moving network of spindly rods. They looked to Toby like carbosteel bones pivoting in chromed sockets. Cables thin to near invisibility moved it with jerky but quick agility.

It did not move like a creature so much as a framework for something unseen. He had the impression of a jutting, constantly busy maze. A mobile lattice, housing a being that did not need true physical presence.

Not that this place was real. He knew that now.

Somehow he had gone from the bare-baked dryness of timestone to this sand-sea. Without noticing. Which meant that the Mantis before him had arranged this elaborate snare and he had run full tilt into it.

His Isaac Aspect said brightly,

It is an anthology intelligence and can speak more directly through us.

"You're workin' for it?"

You speak as though there were choice involved. We are immersed in it, just as you.

He needed help. Someone, anyone. Desperately he rummaged for traces of Shibo. None.

"What's it want? Or is this just what it feels like to be killed suredead?"

We are not suredead.

"Not yet you mean."

We Aspects are more like this Mantis than you. Not ruled by elements of chemistry or by cumbersome, layered minds. Aspects can better perceive the holographic speech of the Mantis and have been learning it in this time of captivity.

"How much time's that?"

There was a blocky tone to Isaac's presence that put him on guard. A sullen weight.

An Aspect corrupted from outside.

The Mantis came forward slowly. Its broad padded feet broke bones as it stepped. Though it seemed light its weight smashed skulls and thighs easily. But of course all this was a digital landscape anyway and he would have to remember that physical movements were only analogies.

Isaac said in his lecturing tone,

This place is a wave-transform of real space and of the Mantis-mind. Intelligences engage best in this kind of intersecting mathematical space. So much more clean and sure. Exact partitioning of ideas. Here the total sum of an intelligence remains the same, though any subsum can vary greatly.

"Yeasay—and you all add up to a hundred, right?"

I do not follow.

"Forget it."

The Mantis-mind has expended much effort to find you. Its allied intelligences—great minds, which of course cannot in truth be fully separated from itself—demanded your capture.

"How come?"

You harbor information of great importance.

"Oh, sure," Toby said sarcastically.

But he recalled the dying man and the thin, reedy voice: *Why you so important? You got something to do with all this?*

—and he was somehow still running over a broken landscape. Sweating. The thick green forest was closer—

He sat down on the silky sand. It slid away to shape a comfortable, cupping seat. If none of this was real he might as well be comfortable. He was hungry and thirsty and as he thought about that some oddly shaped food of maize and flowery buds appeared. It lay neatly on sand that shaped up into a little table and then sprouted a transparent glass.

He picked up the glass. It was warm, as though just formed out of melted sand, and there was ice-cold water in it. He drank eagerly. *The condemned man ate a hearty though nonexistent meal.*

You do not know what this information is?

"Damn right." If he did, this thing could force it out of him, he was pretty sure of that.

Isaac's voice lost its tone, going flat and distant as the Mantis spoke more directly through the Aspect. Isaac was now a puppet.

> ***I calculated this from my prior knowledge of you and of Killeen. Yet buried somewhere in your minds there must be a key which will lead to the message. The difficulty for forms such as myself lies in your mental organization. Much of your selves you cannot access.***

"Sorry I can't help you. My memory isn't so good these days."

He finished eating. His sarcasm went right by the Mantis again. It used a stilted form of Isaac's voice to reply.

> ***These tiers of your selves make it quite difficult for me. I am an anthology intelligence which can find any fragment of my own thought processes quicker than you can blink your eye. Though I am obliged to attempt such discoveries, my true interests lie elsewhere within you.***

—its words reached him through the flickering of two conflicting images. He was sitting on the sand and he could feel the fine grains cupping around him. And he was trotting steadily toward the green, keeping on against a massive weight that wanted to drag him down. Hunger rumbled in his stomach. Breath rasped.—

Back on the sand. Heart thumping, lead-heavy.

There was probably no way out of this place, this Mantis-space, if "out" meant anything here. But so long as he didn't know for sure, he had to try. "I got wind of that back on Snowglade. Your 'creations,' right?"

My work proceeds from higher purposes. It is understandable that you cannot entirely fathom this.

"You killed plenty Bishops. Herded us, fooled us, played with us until you got bored and—"

Not at all. Earlier I "ambushed" you to lessen the pain of dissolution as I gathered in your Bishop components.

"Took Fanny and my mother and, and—without even givin' us the chance to preserve an Aspect."

Isaac surfaced, like a breaking froth on the curl of a slow undulation. Its voice was plaintive and congested.

Do not believe that my trimmed life in here is enough. We Aspects are like your pets, no better. We were men and women once! We kick against the walls at times—did you think we were merely being childish? We are shadows! I once commanded vast audiences, walked proud hallways with supplicants trailing in attendance, supped fine wines and knew—

"Can it."

But this time he did not have to suppress the Aspect. The slow swell in his mind blended with the undulating sand. Uncountable torrents of infinitesimal grains flowed, eddied—and smothered Isaac. Then the Aspect's voice returned, humble and stiff.

I regret that such small matters intrude.

"He's just worried some." Toby rose to Isaac's defense without knowing why. "You surekill me, what happens to my Aspects?"

They would be discarded with the harvesting.

"So it's 'harvesting,' huh?" Like shucks peeled away from the rich maize kernels. And tossed aside.

Your father did not like this term either. An interesting similarity.

"Listen, nobody's going to like it. My father told me about talkin' to you this way, inside this place you've made. I can't see as how you've learned any more since then. 'Harvesting' isn't it, not for us."

Yet it is a correct description. You embody a high form of the organic realm, with the characteristic feature: you know that you shall end. When we anthology beings are harvested—as all must be, in time, by chance or plan—some fraction of oneself is saved, to be used in further advanced forms. You have this now in the stunted Aspects and Faces and Personalities.

—running harder now. Fear like ice shards in his spine. The green coming closer—

"Pretty talk, but it still means you're killin' us."

In harvesting, yes. In a sense. I use your reaped selves to construct new mixed life forms. They blend the two facets of organic life, the lowly plant and the high-animal, such as yourselves.

With the words came images, flicker-fast:

A green mat that bristled with extended organs. It crawled swiftly over a rutted plain and raised slick, snaky organs in a kind of salute.

Tubular knots that thrust into each other with demented fury. Slit-mouths bit deep and from the wounds blue blossoms sprouted.

A fog that made a greater being, its vapor rivulets shaping up and melting with bewildering speed. Only when a tapered arm reached up did Toby see the scale: it clasped a passing thunderstorm and shredded it with playful glee.

Through such constructions, equally plant and fleshy, we probe the aesthetic levels of your kind. I include possibilities not admitted by the random forces of your evolution. It is interacting, trans-phylum art.

"Killeen told me that once. You're an artist." Toby laughed.

True. Thus you shall live in the hands of greater forces. Only I, artist and conservator, can make this possible for you, through timely harvesting.

"We'd like to keep ourselves the way we are. Getting planted in your art, well, that's not what I had in mind." He said this mildly so as not to tip off the Mantis, and because something was happening to his sensorium and he did not understand it.

To harvest is to sow.

"And that's what you've got in mind for me?"

—like logs his legs thumped against the timestone. Cold air rasped in his throat and he could not get enough to make the legs move faster, faster—

Not yet. This little discourse has aided me in my plans for future projects, but for now I am carrying out the precepts embodied by my allied intelligences. I must help in the gathering of enough Bishop primates to test for this buried knowledge.

"What's that mean?"

I must bring you to a spot where we collect your lineage. We shall assemble your generations.

He thought fast. He could feel his legs pumping harder and they were *real,* not the intricately slick touch of the sand-sea.

One part of him was plunging ahead. Gasps rasped in his throat.

Another fraction bent over and studied the sand. Picked up a handful. Grains. Mica winked at him. Between the grains a blur. Not quite defined. As he noticed the slight smearing, the image sharpened. The Mantis had increased definition. Now its world was a bit more distinct. Even the smallest grain now had clear edges.

An artist, tidying up its work.

Running. Chest heaving, a thumping in his ears.

He knew he had to find some way to deflect the moment.

The jerky lattice of rods had an eerie, hovering presence as the Mantis paced among the garden of bleached bones. It had smashed the grinning skulls flat. Along the sand dune wave played strange shadows of the mind behind all this.

Toby struggled between two worlds. He could not sort out his own senses.

—so hard to move his legs now, arms pumping strong to keep himself going against a blunt pressure that wanted to stop him from reaching the green moistness. Close now but the pain—

I am sure you understand the necessity. I assure you that when my allied minds have made proper use of you to clear up this ancient and bothersome matter, I shall harvest you with the attention to detail and genuine concern which characterize my best work. Though I have my critics among these same allies, they do not question my reverence for the ancient and lesser forms such as yourself. Rest secure that—

—he reached the inky line of tall trees. Cool, moist.

No phony sand waves. No mech made of rods.

He remembered the kids playing with their fake digital worlds so long ago back in the marketplace and laughed, out of control as he crashed into the shadowy recesses—

Solid. Real. He reached out tentatively. Touched.

The canopy of trees and cabled, spreading parasite-webs was thick, so that the air was damp and dim. He went into a silence impermeable. It was made thicker and not broken by the soft bell notes of birds and flying rats. By the tick of descending fronds. By the soft thump of falling fruit. By the high caterwaul of vine-dogs.

He did catch from far above the ratcheting squawks of something big and angry, heard it hopping and thrashing among lofty limbs. He was uneasy at his own intrusion, moving more quietly so as not to wake the spirits of this place. Dust spun in cathedral light, long yellow light shafts that cut down from on high. He found underfoot a silent procession of something like ants, except that they had tiny tails. When he studied them they formed a curling pattern and held it, a dark ribbon. Slowly it dawned on him that they were signaling him, writing a message with themselves—but he did not know how to answer. He waved helplessly and went on, careful to not step on them.

Somehow the Mantis was not here. He had escaped into a wedge of time that might end at any instant. Why?

He slipped by huge, taut webs, wondering what got caught there. And what came to harvest the prey. Bright fruit swelled in the chinks of the canopy, dabs of color congealing like blobs, in air so thick it looked green.

—and back came the Mantis, rushing hard against his mind.

I lost you. Something—I do not know—something—is making it difficult—

In Toby's sensorium he now sensed the Mantis far above in the esty tube of this Lane. He felt also around him the stresses that cut and frayed the Mantis's speech.

Vagrant tensions working, blunt and voiceless. Converging.

6

Eating the Storm

The violence began as a flicker.

Down the long bore of the tube eased a sun-yellow trickle. At the vanishing point where the green tunnel narrowed into misty confusion the ray ebbed, flowed, seemed to Toby like a distant campfire. Yet something prickly crept into his mind.

He stood in pale darkness. No good to run anymore.

Clouds thinned above and showed the naked other side of the Lane. A bowl of clay-red timestone suddenly beamed down remorseless heat. Spirits seemed to edge forth from the green around him. Snaps and wriggling noises.

His sensorium jumped, alert, sweeping the area.

Nothing. The silence was empty. He probed the thick, moist forest to his right. It curved up into a misty distance, curling into the sky. When it became simply a filmy green it broke at last on outjuts of brown rock halfway up.

A bird landed on a limb nearby. Toby glanced at it and it said, "Help."

Toby blinked. "Uh . . ."

The bird had wings and feet and a beak but was not a bird. Its face held huge eyes and a fleshy, pouting mouth below the beak—which was more like a nose, lemon-yellow and pointed. Even as he registered this the face worked with fevered intensity, shifting from a frown to a grimace to a fleeting smile. "I need help," the mouth said with a perfect Bishop accent.

"Who—*what*—are you?"

"This place, this time, which is urgent to your needs." The whole bird fidgeted, feathers twitching, wings vibrating like thin sheets, feet quickly shuffling on the rough branch.

"Urgent to . . . ?" No time for mysteries. "Look, there's a Mantis up there. I need a place to hide."

"The opposite is needed." The bird's beak pointed to the ground. "You must open, not close."

"Open what?"

"A door. Essences need entrance to this esty. Quickly!"

"Uh, how?"

The bird took a step on its branch, wings fluttering. "Do not think we are neglectful of you. We do hope you live to help."

Toby snorted. "Thanksay, friend. But what the hell—"

Into his sensorium cascaded a wash of sensations. Images. Instructions. The sense was so vital and full that he moved instantly, unbuckling his tools with one hand while he scuffed up leaves, looking for the right spot. There. Exposed esty.

Abruptly, the furnace glare above clicked off. Solid night. Where was the Mantis?

He worked in the utter solid black.

Torch, laser, microwave bursts. He could not tell how the esty responded, except for a momentary red glow.

But he felt a pulse of wrenching energy come from the spot he worked. A stab of gravitational energy released, a wave like a tide twisting at his guts.

Beneath him, a throb of energy. Mute, restive.

"Not enough," the bird's voice came. "Sad."

"What more—"

"Too late."

It came. A fever of probing energy rained around him. Sheets of pearly light shot along the great axis of this Lane. Toward him.

Something countered it. He *felt* without truly seeing a massive, blue-black presence. It reared up, thunderhead-thick. Bulky and bristling.

Like a top-heavy animal, head towering to the high roof of the Lane. It struck teeth of stone there and snapped at them.

The sheets of pearly light forked around this. Then they were on him, before he could believe something could move that fast. Shards of quick hotness struck down from the axis.

It attacked not merely him but the forest. Thousands of volts dropped their potentials along snaking paths in the sheared air. They struck, their transaction enacted.

In electric-blue brilliance he saw the bird fall dead from its branch.

And then a countersurge kicked skyward—quicker, a bright ricochet red-fast and yellow-hot. Snarling up through the air.

His sensorium told him all this as he dove for shelter—knowing at the same time that the gesture was meaningless, before such magnitudes—and data crackled through his spine.

Quath! Killeen! Dad, Dad! he sent in pure blind panic.

The splintering red-fast stroke came again. Blinding. The racing sharp reply. Again. And again.

The whole argument carried forward in wracked air. A long flash and crack. Only his sensorium could sort it out, presenting it to him like a solved problem. But telling nothing of what it meant.

Wind cut cold. He flattened himself against a tree that had fried into charcoal in an unnoticed instant. Acrid fumes bit his nostrils.

Stay down. He could not cough, would not cough, though he ached to do it. He could not let it find him.

Something heavy and muffled came stalking above the forest.

Looking. Easing down, around, through. He felt it without knowing how.

In the clogged dimness he could make out animals that for some reason ran in circles, demented, yelping their small cries. Air surged and they fell. Many screamed—small, thin shrieks, like fingernails scraping on slate. Then they dropped out of his sensorium, dead. He did not have time to think of them but their cries burned into him, for reasons he could not say.

A scarlet howling came seething down the axis. Bangs and pressures, piling atop each other. Accelerating, blunt collisions. Something deep, droning, metallic.

He crawled out from under a roof of smashed limbs and stood up. Better to face it this way. Though he knew this was unreasonable and not smart and probably not even adult.

A great power came slamming into the Lane. He crouched in fear.

From the thickets and timberlands came a slow-building reply.

Something seeped up the air, coiling like heavy fog, but with a disturbing momentum. The minute woven carpet of life here had evolved to absorb, he suddenly saw. Somehow, encoded in them was a response.

He felt even the minute beings around him digging in soft earth. Piping to each other. Working to some unimaginable purpose.

Each cog fitting together. Primed. And he was somehow linked into it. He had to decide when and where to deliver such energies.

He did not know how he knew, but the certainty of it laced through him. He was the most sentient here. He had to judge.

He had to try to kill the Mantis.

He hacked again at the esty. He emptied his power pack into microwaves, sensing the boil of energies beneath the esty here. Something wanted out. What had the bird said? *Essences need entrance to this esty.*

A pulse of gravity rippled up through his boots. Coming—

He kicked in his laser, tuned to infrared. So what if the Mantis could see it? Too late to worry now. Too late for anything but this moment. He fired it between his feet.

He was a hair trigger, balanced—

Conduit. Connector.

Draw it in. Coax.

Toby let a sliver of himself leak upward. A small wedge opening in his muted sensorium.

The presence edged closer. Sent feelers.

Time to do what he could. Even if it didn't matter, in the face of such colossal energies. Toby cast his sensorium upward.

Here I am. See?

The weight descended. Darted its inspecting eyes at him.

Hovered. Nearer, nearer, still uncertain—

Then the forest opened. Toby sprang away, hit and rolled. A volcano erupted where he had been. And spread.

Violence whipped up from a billion leaves. Shallow roots, slumbering only a moment before, discharged stored charge. Luminous savagery arced up through intricate connections in the bodies of corkscrew trees. The canopy itself discharged frayed green fingers into welcoming air.

A sheet of yellow lightning rose. A reply.

Before he could move he felt the ground warm. A harsh pulse of infrared energy. Walls of hard heat.

Water fizzing forth. Pools filling. Streamers of cool vapor. Humidity flooded the congealing atmosphere. Lime-hot fungi on a nearby tree trunk rippled, fluoresced, shuddered.

Charged vehemence slammed into the axis of the Lane. Brilliance blared down.

Toby slapped hands over his head. A rock slammed into his ribs. A thunderclap of pressure flattened him.

He knew in the flashing instant that the true violence was happening all down the Lane—not physically at all, but furies inside minds, intelligences great and small, chained together.

And the fury erupted through them all, bringing death and bliss alike.

7

Passing Currents

Later—lying under a matted crush of vegetation, aching in every joint, letting his ribs stitch themselves back together—he understood a fragment of what had happened.

Life here was diverse in its defenses. Many-layered, silent, worn by time and seasoned by something more than natural forces. Odd bits that Quath had told him now converged, made sense.

Life struck down could still spring back. Opportunistic organisms, each part of intricately forged links, absorbed the brutal pounding and gave it back. For the forest was not merely a growth clinging to the shifting bedrock of the esty. It incorporated the esty into itself.

Countless slivers of esty, knitted into trees and shrubs and layered soil, brought electrical strengths. The interacting parts of the natural world now had circuits evolved from folded space-time. The forest had a diffused intelligence—or perhaps "intelligence" was a term that meant little here.

In some fashion it had worked beyond the categories of natural evolution that Toby understood. It echoed the far-spread links of the Mantis and its kind. And this intimate connectivity was wired into the genetic heritage of this whole vast esty.

Such a tapestry could eat a storm, fold it into its genes.

Learn from its punishment. Prepare.

It had been doing this for uncountable years. Buried in the deepest hiding place in the entire galaxy, the diffused self had learned far longer than a man could.

He had journeyed through the Lanes, thinking of them as corridors in some huge esty building. A false analogy.

The woven life here threaded realms he could not see. Only in scattered passing moments could his sensorium catch the deep, slow conversations of such a being.

Always the sense of being watched. But more than that—the feel of being part of a hazy whole.

This gnarled world held steady because it held true, swallowing its rivals. And he was now digested into it. He knew this without knowing how he could be so sure.

He had opened a door, that was all. Used his knack of ripping a momentary hole in the esty. To let in forces that would not have been able to arrive so swiftly—or at all.

Maybe he had made a difference. Or maybe he was finally old enough to know that asking whether you made a difference or not was really not the point. You had to try, was all.

Do not think we are neglectful of you. We do hope you live to help. No guarantees, though.

Later, his sole hard and lasting memory came from what happened when the discharge flattened him. It had been only a passing shred of the larger events above.

The explosion must have occurred inside him, for the canopy he checked later was undamaged. But he had witnessed the immensity of the passing presence and had for a slim moment taken part in what it had to do.

Somehow he had been the switch. Opening the door meant he was in the circuit. But electrons don't know much about radio, even though they swim like fish among resistances, capacities, seas of potential.

Whatever fed the ferocity had used him, the consciousness he carried, to focus itself.

To be part of it was something he could scarcely think about without getting the shivers and fidgets.

He had felt the indifferent powers at work. Worse, he had sensed the many lives that flared, hurt, and died. They were at least equal in their torments. Multitudes joined in and the weight from above crushed them without even noticing their pains.

He did. Not as distant news, but as immediate experience. More than anything he remembered the agony.

For that split moment his teeth sang in their sockets. The calcium rib-rods that framed his chest became chromed and knobby bones, slick and sliding. Swift metallic grace. Purpling storms raced down squeezed veins, up shuddering ligaments. His toes rattled, strumming, talking hard to the ground. His ankles danced on their own, *click click* of bones trying so hard they would soon fracture.

Head thrown back, neck stretched. Skin feathered and frayed and electric-sharp in polarized light. His spine was parabolic, crackling. Hurricane hallways yawned in him, the lockjawed agony-song screeching.

It raced through him. It sought its true enemy and he did not know if the voltage-fire was from the mechs or if it came forth from imponderable discharges deep in the frying forest. And it did not matter. He was of the fury and in it and for that moment he was its conductor. Currents passed without knowing him.

The rage plunged down through hip sockets polished by blue-green, hungry worms. Snakes of luminous frenzy swarmed hungrily over bone lattices, eating.

And for him it was enough. All he could remember clearly later was the pain. Pain blissful and complete. Plenty of it.

He awoke lying in gray ash. Silence, soft rain. An air mouse coasted by.

No need to move. Just think.

He saw what it was about the mechs, the high up ones, that was different. They had an awful beauty in their detachment. A hard concentration on the business of dealing in death without being in any danger of it. They did not die in the way that people had to. Maybe that was a true advance. He did not know. He could envy them or hate them but it would be better to do neither.

He was alone now in a way he had never been. The strangeness of the mechs had made him see that. Family Bishop, his father, even Quath—when they were close they made a world for him. Without them he was alone finally against the firm facts. He knew things now that he could not have known any other way. He had fled from his father out of confusion and principle and a bitter anger, all mixed together. He had not known he carried all that until now and now it was too late.

Maybe that was how it had to be and you never learned anything well unless you learned it backward, looking down a long channel of experience at it. You had to bring what you had along with you. Your courage and failures and resentment and all the rest of it.

Then the universe would try to fit you in and if you did not fit it broke you. Some people fit all right after that. Toby understood that something had broken in him and that all he could hope for was that maybe afterward he would be stronger where he had broken.

He had grown up believing that the universe was hostile to people and in a way that made them important. They were locked in a grand struggle with a great enemy.

The truth was a lot worse. The universe did not care at all.

The mechs were like that. Implacable but not concerned with people as people, seeing them only as another element in a flat, meaningless landscape. Just doing their tasks and not even feeling their own strange phony deaths.

He found the bird that had talked to him. It lay blackened and crushed, eyes swelling with dried blood. He buried it.

In the end all this was about the Self. Killeen had made it hard for Toby to be himself, though maybe that was something that had to happen with all sons and fathers. And he would never know how much of that had come from Shibo's silent diffusion into him.

In a strange way the Mantis wanted the same thing. The one commodity that Toby would never give. The Self.

He remembered the joy and pace of commerce, back in that portal city. But there the trading enhanced the Self. Giving fair value meant trading true. It helped define who you were. Same with the Family, which was a kind of machine for the making of Self through action.

It would never have happened this way if he had been with the Family or even with Quath. Family kept the sharp edges away. Family was a fiction, he knew that now. A fiction defending against the furious gulf that yawned in all directions.

But a truthful fiction, too, because the story Families told by their example made it possible to go on. The gulf was always there and you would see it again, certainly for one last time, but there was no special haste in getting to that moment. After you had seen the gulf you spent the rest of your time knowing that it was there waiting and would come again. In knowing this he was now free.

8

Phantoms

At first he thought the distant peak was a mountain.

He had been walking for a long time. The forest had opened before him and seemed to push him out—into rugged terrain where the timewinds blew and sickened him. He went anyway.

The mountain reared up as he went and he did not think about it much. Then he saw that its flanks were smooth and firm. It did not fuzz and split off planes like the timestone around him. Its smooth inclines stayed fixed. Its faces met at worked edges. Magnetic field strengths were high, getting higher.

A pyramid. Corners of clear design. And events did not swim in its faces. The stuff was granite-hard when he touched it at the base. Ordinary matter. A stack of stone so large it seemed to be the landscape. In the silence of it lingered mystery.

Going up it he felt better than he had in a long time. He was hungry but he did not mind that. He put it from his mind, as he had in the years on Snowglade. It was funny what you could get used to. He realized that hunger made him nostalgic and laughed out loud. The bright sound went into a silence so empty and was so completely absorbed that it made him fall silent again.

He had come a long way and so had a long time to think. Any human in this place knew that he was a tiny and forgettable actor on a stage not of his making. The drama of the mechs against the natural lifeforms was playing out, and Toby did not understand it. He longed to talk with Quath again, to see his father's face.

Below all the colossal energies of mechs and matter lay the whole long history of the human Hunker Down. Who had made that happen? Why had Bishops and all the rest of the Families been condemned to the hard-scrabble skin of planets, when a refuge like the Wedge was here? While dwarves like that Andro got to enjoy it.

Below that riddle were the Bishops, still alive when plenty of other Families were dead. Just luck, Toby thought. But it made you wonder.

And finally there was the Calamity. He had fled from that catastrophe long ago, back when he was a boy but did not know what a boy was. He and his father had lost Abraham that day. But now Abraham was here somewhere. Somehow.

To understand even a little piece of all this, Toby would have to find Abraham. In a place where direction meant nothing and time was a place.

Partway up he heard footsteps. He was sure they were steps and coming from above. He hurried up the slope. There were level walkways spaced at even intervals as he went up.

The walkways went off to left and right and he presumed they led all the way around the structure. They curved into the distance and he could see no one on the ones below. He labored against a steepening incline and reached the next walkway.

No one on it. But the footsteps came slower now. As he climbed farther the footsteps got fainter as though he had left them behind. They spaced farther and farther apart.

Dopplering in time. Going away into a future or a past, borderlands of the real. As if the walker were slowing, hesitating, getting sluggish from fatigue. Toby himself began to tire but he could still hear the steps coming in long low notes and so kept on.

The top was not what he expected. Broad and flat and smooth, the surface flecked with gray dabs. Magnetic field very strong.

No one. He could not hear the footsteps any longer.

He looked down. The walkways were so far away he could not tell if anyone was on them or not. Featureless and unmarred, the great structure stretched away. In the hazy distance he could make out the endless wrestling forms of the timescape, esty fighting against itself, Lanes intersecting in wrenching turbulence.

He turned away from the edge as he thought about resting for a while before going back down.

"Where've you been?"

The pale-skinned man before him was short and compact. The same size as Andro and the other dwarfs, but wrinkled and completely nude.

"Understand, do you?"

Toby looked around and could not see where the man had come from.

"Look, we haven't much time. You're a Bishop, right?"

Toby's tongue felt thick and useless. "Uh, yeasay."

"Good. Latest generation, I'd judge."

"Yeasay. Who—"

"Come on, get back inside where it's safer. And warmer."

The dwarf showed Toby his leathery back as he marched quickly across the smooth plain. As Toby caught up the stone split. A clean rectangle opened and there was a ramp leading down. "Come on."

Toby stopped at the head of the ramp. "In my Family you don't walk into a place till you know what it is."

"Oh? It's an operations center." The dwarf turned to go down.

"Whose?"

"Um? Mine. Ours. Human, if that's what you mean."

"And who're you?"

"Oh. Sorry." The dwarf walked over and held out a hand. "Walmsley. Nigel Walmsley."

"What Family's that?"

"The Brits."

"How do you know who I am?"

"History. I've been waiting for you a long time."

"How long?"

Walmsley looked as though he were calculating. "I make it about twenty-eight thousand years. Your time frame, of course." To Toby's blank look he volunteered, "Approximately."

"How come? What for?"

"Come have some tea. You Bishops kept alive that tradition at least, didn't you?"

"Uh, yeasay." Toby had not tasted tea since he was a boy. "At the Citadel."

"I see, the Citadel. Good then. You're Killeen's son?"

Startled, Toby gaped. Walmsley nodded. "So I see. Message for you." He moved his hands quickly and for a flicker one of his arms seemed to be transparent, showing intricate webs beneath the skin.

Killeen was standing between them both.

His father looked worn, haggard. He was in Family Bishop field suiting, not ship gear. He glanced around and saw Toby. "Son, I need you."

Toby did not know what to say. He reached out to touch his father and his hand passed through the image.

Killeen did not react. "I know how hard it's been. Look, you can have Shibo. I was, well, wrong. I've put that aside."

Toby's voice was dry, cracked. "You're sure?"

"Yeasay. I . . . got outside myself."

"Where are you?"

"No way to tell. I don't know when you'll get this."

Toby frowned and Walmsley said, "He issued this some time ago, local frame."

Killeen stepped to the side and regarded Toby. "You seem all right. A little thin."

Toby smiled. "All that ship fat got run off."

"The mechs have everybody on the run. Plenty dead. Some Bishops, too. They—"

"Besen? Cermo? How—"

"They're here, still in one piece. Nobody close to us is suredead."

Toby felt a joyful release, an eagerness to see them all. "Tell me what all's gone on. Have you seen Quath? Did—"

"Listen, the mechs have scrambled up the Lanes something fierce. Ruptured some. I don't know where you'll find this, but we can patrol for you if you send out a singsay beacon."

"I will." Toby whispered to Walmsley, "Is he receiving this?"

"No, only this manifestation reacts to you. This is *a* Killeen, not *the* Killeen. I don't know where the real article is now. Or then, for that matter."

"No need to whisper," the Killeen said. "I'm a limited representation and not ashamed of it."

"What're the mechs after? All the time I've been running, they've been on my heels."

The Killeen hesitated, started again. "They want you and me both. Dunno why."

"Want to surekill us?"

"Something more than that. Something funny's going on with Abraham, but I don't know what. Watch out for him."

"Isn't there a place where we can meet?"

Killeen shook his head. "Remember, I'm on the move same as you. Have to keep looking, is all."

"The Mantis, it was after me."

"Us, too."

"Then we must be close to each other."

"Naysay. More than one Mantis, I think."

"The Mantis is a whole class of mechs?"

"It's like dividing up water. Can't keep the lines drawn."

Toby felt a sense of comfort in the simple way his father talked, at the sound of his voice. "Dad, I—"

"Son, I need you." Killeen said it exactly as he had said it before, same posture and tone. "I don't know how much more I can tell you. Just . . . let's try."

"Yeasay." Toby felt an immense relief. "Yeasay."

"I know how hard it's been. Look, you can have Shibo. I was—"

"Dad, I . . ." Toby stood mute. It was strange, speaking to a recording and wanting to force more out of it. But he had to tell the truth. "I had to pull Shibo."

The Killeen was startled. It shimmied in the air for a moment, as if this news shook the entire representation. "You . . . don't have the tools."

"I know. Did the best I could."

"She . . . was too much?"

"I couldn't manage her."

The Killeen nodded somberly. "She wasn't easy in the flesh, either."

"I think I got—"

Beside Killeen, condensing out of the air, was Shibo. She was translucent and her legs were gone but the upper body moved naturally. Head turning, first to Killeen, then to Toby. A thin smile.

"I . . . am still . . . partially . . . in . . . here . . ."

Walmsley said to Toby, "The reader is picking up fringing fields from you. She must be integrated into your perceptors."

Toby nodded. "Yeasay, and wants to talk."

Shibo's face pleaded. Her words sounded faintly in Toby's sensorium. "I will be here . . . to help. I had to come out. My dear . . . Killeen . . ."

With small jerky movements and a wrenched face she turned to the Killeen. Toby felt an eerie current between the two. Valences moved, blunt and blind. They peered at each other a long time in silent, still air. Toby sensed a stuttering, hesitant sensation pass between them. Small signals across a furious gulf.

Then Shibo lifted one hand, as if in salute—and vanished. Toby did not understand any of it.

The Killeen shook his head and turned to look off into the distance. His face seemed carved with deep, dry ravines.

"Good then," Walmsley said crisply. "You've sucked most of the juice out, I gather. Hurry along—we have work to do."

When Toby looked back to see his father's reaction, the Killeen was gone.

The suddenness of loss staggered him. He closed his eyes, steadied himself.

Walmsley waved him on. "I know all this is a bit quick, but there really is pressing business."

Toby took a last look at the endlessly roiling perspectives and followed Walmsley down the ramp. Into a dark under where light sharpened into hard points like a waiting bucket of stars.

So time had done its work and his father had changed. So had Toby. Who had been right or wrong was nothing now, a dry rattle among fading facts, lost in the curve of events. The places where the esty had scarred him were firmer and he could take whatever came without clinging to the past or foreboding for the future. His steps were light and he went forward into whatever would be.

Afterword

To the best of my ability I have kept the imaginings of this novel, and those that came before in this series of novels, within the constraints set by astronomical observations. The explosion of our knowledge has been one of the wonders of the last few decades, but it's been tough on fiction writers.

In the last decade the Very Large Array and other new varieties of "telescopes" have opened windows on our galactic center, with astonishing results. I've had to change my own ideas, and indeed, some of the inventions in this novel arise from theory as well—particularly, advances in the theory of gravitation.

Plainly something enormously powerful is going on at the galactic center, apparently driven by a vast explosion about a million years ago. Electrodynamic effects are strikingly strong within a few hundred light-years of the exact dynamical center, about which the entire spiral disk spins. There, the magnetic field is at least a hundred times more intense than is typical in such mild-mannered neighborhoods of the galaxy as our own. Apparently the long, luminous strands there derive from this strong field. This suggests in turn that in the far more energetic active galactic nuclei of distant galaxies, magnetic fields may play a shaping role.

The theoretical research I have done on the central region, wearing my hat as a professor of physics, takes this as the starting point. Similarly, in my fictions I have assumed this as given. It has been an unusual experience to conjure up imaginary events about a place that I was also doing hard calculations about. Freed of the bonds of *The Astrophysical Journal,* I have felt at liberty to speculate on what processes might have transpired, over the galaxy's ten billion years of furious cooking, to create forms of life and intelligence beyond our ken. (Coincidences: Just after writing the above paragraph, I got a note from the editor of that same august journal, appreciating an earlier novel. Someday I must attempt to trace the interactions between science and science fiction. Or, better, an energetic graduate student. There's a good doctoral thesis lurking there . . .)

This novel and all those earlier in the "galactic" series—*In the Ocean of Night, Across the Sea of Suns, Great Sky River, Tides of Light*—owe a debt to the scientists, editors, academics, and writers who have kept me going over two decades with ideas, advice, encouragement, and insightful reading.

These include, in no particular order, Marvin Minsky, Sheila Finch, David Hartwell, Mark Martin, David Brin, Betsy Mitchell, David Samuelson, Steven Harris, Lou Aronica, Joe Miller, Jennifer Hershey, Stephen Hawking, Gary Wolfe, Norman Spinrad, David Kolb, Ruth Curl, and Arthur C. Clarke. Stimulating ideas kept drawing me on.

I especially thank Mark Morris, of UCLA, who assembled and directed the International Astronomical Union's Symposium on the Center of the Galaxy. The data and theories of that and later meetings spurred me to look beyond the models I had concocted for magnetic phenomena at the galactic center. Speaking at length about my own notions, and having them raked over by the observers—always a daunting prospect for a theorist!—made me confront the bewildering profusion of neon-brilliant displays, violent explosions, piercing energies, and (mysteriously) highly organized structures that mark our galactic center. Doing so opened my imagination to the possibilities of life (and, I suppose, of death) in so virulently extreme a place.

I apologize to the readers who have waited several years between volumes of this series. Other novels begged to be written.

And then there is Real Life, too, always demanding. My ideas about life in the universe have changed greatly since I set Nigel Walmsley on his odyssey in 1970 (beginning with a short story, "Icarus Descending," which was later slightly adapted and now opens *In the Ocean of Night*). Despite such evolutions, I have tried to keep these novels consistent. Events spanning several tens of thousands of years are not often reconciled, especially when the author has been off doing other things.

The concluding volume of this series is now in sight. I promise to have it done and published within a year of this book's appearance. I may venture back into this universe in future, if the impulse occurs, but the plot and lines of reasoning should be intact and resolved by the end of the next novel. What a long, strange trip it's been.

GREGORY BENFORD
June 1993